Harry's heart beat faster, and he could hear Lucy's soft breathing. He didn't think. He just kissed her soft lips gently.

Her eyes remained closed for a moment. When she opened them, he knew one chaste kiss would not suffice. "Wrap your arms around my neck."

When she complied, he kissed her with a fierce hunger. He touched his tongue to her mouth, and when her lips parted, he tasted her. She clung to him as he deepened the kiss. He loved the way she felt in his arms, all soft curves and sweet surrender. His blood ran hot, and the temptation to touch her gripped him hard, but he mustn't drive her away by moving too quickly. There was all the time in the world, and he wanted to savor every moment.

He lifted his mouth. "I am undone."

"I did not . . . know what it would be like."

Something inside him melted. It was her first kiss.

She bent her head. "I should not have let you."

"I'm glad you did...."

GLOWING PRAISE FOR
VICKY DREILING'S NOVELS

WHAT A RECKLESS ROGUE NEEDS

"Top Pick! 4½ stars! Dreiling brings the Regency to life in a wonderfully evocative fashion...believable, intelligent characters...[This] moving tale, fraught with sexual tension, hits just the right notes."
—*RT Book Reviews*

"A deliciously slow-burning plot makes this story worth savoring."
—*Publishers Weekly*

"It was wonderful to see the love between these two enemies seep into every interaction...a delightful read!"
—**HeroesandHeartbreakers.com**

"Sassy and fun...Her heroines are always fun and a bit daring, and her heroes are always the dashing rakes we want to swoon for...Can't wait for the next scoundrel."
—**UndertheCoversBookBlog.com**

"Engaging and romantic...a solid read for fans of regency romances."
—**NightOwlReviews.com**

WHAT A WICKED EARL WANTS

"Top pick! Four-and-a-half stars…Wonderful! Rife with the Regency's penchant for gossip, scandal, and matchmaking, *What a Wicked Earl Wants* is a delightful romance featuring a rakish hero, an innocent widow, corrupt villains, and a secondary cast of characters who add dimension, wit, and tenderness to the plot… Readers will find this a real pleasure to savor."
—RT Book Reviews

"With amazing characters and a story line that kept me turning the pages, *What a Wicked Earl Wants* is another winner from Ms. Dreiling."
—UndertheCoversBookblog.com

"I fell in love with [this] book. Who wouldn't with the romance, society, reputations, and extremely dreamy high-society men?"
—ReadingwithStyle.blogspot.com

A SEASON FOR SIN

"A master of the genre."
—Library Journal

HOW TO RAVISH A RAKE

"Dreiling secures her reputation as a writer of charming, matchmaking romances with engaging characters...her cast of quirky, unconventional characters sets her stories apart. Fans of marriage-of-convenience love stories have a treat."
—RT Book Reviews

"A guaranteed delectable indulgence!...Vicky Dreiling is fast becoming an absolute must-buy for Regency fans."
—Affaire de Coeur

"Five stars! Packed with a delectable plot, charming characters, clever banter, humor, scandal, and lots of love, this story is a winner."
—RomanceJunkiesReviews.com

HOW TO SEDUCE A SCOUNDREL

"Regency matchmaking, rakes, rogues, innocence, and scandal: oh what fun! Dreiling knows how to combine these ingredients into a delightfully delicious, wickedly witty slice of reading pleasure."
—RT Book Reviews

"5 stars! This was an enchanting tale that had me grinning from ear to ear. The chemistry between Marc and Julianne was flammable and only needed a spark to set it off."
—SeducedbyaBook.com

HOW TO MARRY A DUKE

"Sexy, fresh, and witty...A delicious read! Better than chocolate! Vicky Dreiling is an author to watch!"
—Sophie Jordan, *New York Times* bestselling author

"A terrific romp of a read!...Vicky is a bright new voice in romance."
—Sarah MacLean, *New York Times* bestselling author

"Delightful...the inherent charm of the characters (especially the dowager duchess) keeps the pages flying until the surprising conclusion. Dreiling is definitely a newcomer to watch."
—*RT Book Reviews*

"A witty, nourishing romp of a romance...impossible to put down...Dreiling mesmerizes as she brings an era to life. She fills the pages with laughter, sensuality, and charm. *How to Marry a Duke* is an irresistible ride readers will return to again and again."
—Examiner.com

Also by Vicky Dreiling

What a Devilish Duke Desires

Book 3—The Sinful Scoundrels Series

VICKY DREILING

FOREVER

NEW YORK   BOSTON

Copyright © 2015 by Vicky Dreiling
Excerpt from *What a Wicked Earl Wants* © 2013 by Vicky Dreiling
All rights reserved. In accordance with the U.S. Copyright Act of 1976, the scanning, uploading, and electronic sharing of any part of this book without the permission of the publisher constitute unlawful piracy and theft of the author's intellectual property. If you would like to use material from the book (other than for review purposes), prior written permission must be obtained by contacting the publisher at permissions@hbgusa.com. Thank you for your support of the author's rights.

Forever
Hachette Book Group
1290 Avenue of the Americas
New York, NY 10104

www.HachetteBookGroup.com

Printed in the United States of America

First Edition: February 2015
10 9 8 7 6 5 4 3 2 1

OPM

Forever is an imprint of Grand Central Publishing.
The Forever name and logo are trademarks of Hachette Book Group, Inc.

The Hachette Speakers Bureau provides a wide range of authors for speaking events. To find out more, go to www.hachettespeakersbureau.com or call (866) 376-6591.

The publisher is not responsible for websites (or their content) that are not owned by the publisher.

ATTENTION CORPORATIONS AND ORGANIZATIONS:

Most Hachette Book Group books are available at quantity discounts with bulk purchase for educational, business, or sales promotional use. For information, please call or write:

Special Markets Department, Hachette Book Group
1290 Avenue of the Americas, New York, NY 10104
Telephone: 1-800-222-6747 Fax: 1-800-477-5925

*To all of the wonderful readers for
your kind words about my books. You
mean the world to me.*

Acknowledgments

To the two most important partners in my career: Lucienne Diver and Michele Bidelspach. You have both made an incredible difference in my writing life. Thank you for everything.

If once to Almack's you belong,
Like Monarchs you can do no wrong;
But banished thence on Wednesday night,
By Jove, you can do nothing right.

Henry Luttrell (1765–1851),
English writer of society verse

What a
Devilish Duke
Desires

Chapter One

London 1822

Harry Norcliffe, the Duke of Granfield, descended the hackney and shivered a bit from the cold breeze. A glowing gas lamp lit the pavement and made a fine display of the bow window at White's.

He could hardly believe three months had passed since Uncle Hugh's unexpected death. Nothing would ever be the same again. The loss of Hugh often hit him when he least expected it. It still seemed like a bad dream, but it was all too real.

The world he'd known would never be the same, but tonight he was meeting his closest friends and hoped to find comfort in the life he'd left behind three months ago.

A servant appeared at the door and bowed. The scent of beeswax candles was an instant familiarity.

"Welcome back, Your Grace."

Your Grace. The words pummeled him like a fist. By now, he ought to be accustomed to his new address, but he still felt as if he were an imposter.

The servant shifted his weight. "Your Grace, may I take your greatcoat?"

The awkward moment eased. "Thank you."

As he divested himself of his hat, greatcoat, and gloves, he remembered thinking there would be changes, but he'd not been prepared for so many.

The sight of the betting book drew him. Here was a part of his old life. He'd always made it a ritual to read the latest wagers. For the first time in what seemed an age, he smiled as he read a wager written this evening. Apparently Aubery had bet Rollins ten guineas that it would rain on Thursday. Harry turned back the pages to read the bets he'd missed while he'd been gone. When he saw his name mentioned three months ago, he paused.

Mr. Brockton bet Mr. Norcliffe two shillings that he would eat no bacon when he visits his uncle's pig farm.

His chest felt as if a shard of glass had pierced his heart. He gritted his teeth, determined to overcome these unguarded moments. He must go forward and reclaim his old life. But blast it all, he missed Hugh.

"I'll be damned. It's the devil come to London again."

His spirits rose at the familiar voice. Harry swiveled his gaze toward his friend, and relief poured over him at the sight of Andrew Carrington, the Earl of Bellingham. "I suppose you've been stoking the fires of hell," Harry said.

Bell clapped him on the shoulder. "My former rakehell days are long over."

Harry laughed. "You are the last person I'd ever expect to reform."

"No one is more surprised than me."

There was a subtle difference in Bellingham's demeanor. When they'd first met, Bell had been restless and prone to pacing. Now he seemed relaxed and at peace.

"Enough about me," Bell said. "My friend, you look a bit careworn."

"Yes, but I'm glad to see you."

"I hope you're ready for a good beefsteak and a bottle or two," Bell said.

"I am." It was the first step to returning to his old life, though there would always be an empty place inside now that his uncle was gone.

Bell grinned. "How does it feel to be the last bachelor among us?"

"I thought for certain you would be a bachelor for life," Harry said, "but you fooled us all."

"Laura made an honest man out of me. Come, our old table is waiting, and there is someone you must see."

They had almost reached the stairs when Lord Fitzhugh and Mr. Castelle intercepted them. "Congratulations on the dukedom," Fitzhugh said, clapping his back.

"You're a lucky man," Castelle added.

Harry felt as if hot coals were burning a path to his temples. His fingers curled into his palms, but he tamped down the misplaced anger that sometimes struck out of nowhere, even when he knew the person meant well. "Thank you." What else could he say?

When Bell mentioned their party was waiting, Harry was grateful.

As they continued on, Bell glanced at him thoughtfully. "After my family perished, I grew cross when others made thoughtless comments. While I knew they meant well, I treated them coldly. My refusal to deal with my grief made matters far worse. Castelle and Fitzhugh know that an inheritance can never replace your loss, but like most people, they're uncomfortable speaking of death."

Harry nodded. It helped to have a friend who understood. Over the past three months, he'd learned that grief came in many forms. Tonight, however, all he wanted was to relax with his trusted friends.

As they climbed the stairs, the clink of glasses and silverware echoed from the dining room. The rumble of masculine voices grew louder as they reached the second floor. The distinctive aroma of beefsteak teased his senses.

When they reached the table, Colin Brockhurst, Earl of Ravenshire, his oldest friend from boyhood, stood and pounded him on the back. "Harry, it's good to see you."

"And you. How is married life?"

"Well, Angeline hasn't thrown me out on my arse yet," Colin said.

"Oh, ho!" Harry said, laughing.

Bell motioned to a young man. "Do you remember this fellow?"

Harry frowned. When recognition dawned, he was stunned. "Is that Justin?"

Justin Davenport, the Earl of Chesfield and Bell's stepson, grinned as he extended his hand. "Pleased to see you, Harry."

"Good Lord." Harry turned his attention to Bell. "He was a skinny cub the last time I saw him."

"He's twenty-one now," Bell said, "and six feet, three inches tall."

"What are you feeding him?" Harry said. "He's as big as an oak."

Bell laughed. "A great deal of beef. He's gained a few muscles fencing as well."

Harry signaled the waiter to bring a bottle of brandy.

When it arrived, he poured and looked at Bell. "I can't believe you're letting the sprig drink spirits."

"He's of age and knows his limits. I wouldn't have met his mother if not for that flask of brandy Justin hid very poorly," Bell said.

Justin laughed. "It wasn't my brightest idea, Father."

"Fortunately, you're past sowing wild oats." Bell narrowed his eyes. "Correct?"

Justin's smile slanted to one side. "Am I supposed to answer that?"

Colin guffawed, and Harry nearly spewed brandy.

Three years ago, Colin and Harry had met Bellingham. Bell had fallen hard for Laura Davenport and her son. All of them had been fond of the recalcitrant lad, but he was a grown man now. How had time flown by so quickly?

Colin proposed a toast. "To Bell, for saving our sorry hides that night in the Thames."

Justin frowned. "What?"

"It's where we met Bell," Colin said.

"In the Thames?" Justin said with an astounded expression.

Harry's shoulders shook with laughter. "Lord, what a caper. I was so foxed I managed to lose the fare for the waterman and somehow fell in the stinking river."

"Hah," Colin said. "A trollop robbed you blind."

"Of two shillings—my total worth at the time," Harry said.

"Yes, and we had to pull you out before you drowned," Bell said. "When you came to, you looked at me and said, 'Lord, it's my savior.'"

They all laughed.

"My clothes smelled so bad my valet actually gagged," Bell said. "I had to throw them in the rubbish."

"Those were the good old days," Harry said.

Justin pulled a face. "I really hope you're jesting."

Bell mussed his son's hair. "It's much better viewed from afar."

Harry set his brandy aside and regarded Colin. "I was glad to receive your letter. Congratulations on your impending fatherhood."

"Harry, Bellingham has already agreed to be one of the male godparents. Would you consider being the other godparent?"

"I would be honored." Then, because he wasn't comfortable with the unexpected emotion for his friend and himself, he said, "I promise not to drop the babe."

Everyone laughed.

Colin shrugged. "I'm more worried that one of my twin sisters will drop the babe if it's a girl. My wife insists the twins have matured and should be the female godparents, but I've got my doubts."

"Maybe you'll have twins," Harry said.

"God forbid," Colin said. "We'll never get a moment's peace."

Listening to his friends, Harry had a moment of clarity. There was a greater purpose in his life, one that would see Havenwood, his uncle's legacy, continue in a direct descent long after he was gone from this world.

Harry figured his friends would likely be astounded if they knew his thoughts. A year ago, he would have never thought about marriage, but Uncle Hugh's death had changed everything.

"My wife insists the babe is a boy," Colin said. "To be honest, I'm hoping for a girl."

"Take my advice," Bell said. "Just agree with whatever your wife says, even if she contradicts it five minutes later."

Colin shook his head. "I have no say in the matter. Her mother and my stepmother declare it's a boy because she's carrying the babe high. It's all nonsense to me, but I'm not about to naysay them."

"Harry, do you still keep rooms at the Albany?" Colin asked.

"Yes," he said. He'd found his old rooms rather comforting. "I even kept the shabby furnishings."

"Lord, I've never forgotten that lumpy sofa," Colin said, "and the dog fur everywhere."

"What have I missed while I was gone?" Harry asked.

"Pembroke lost more hair," Bell said. "Old Lord Leighton is in love with the widowed Lady Atherton, but she swears she prefers her sherry to him." He paused. "I almost forgot. Justin's former friend George wrecked the second curricle his father unwisely purchased for him."

"Some things never change, I suppose." He paused and said, "Thank you for the letter, Bell. It was good to hear your news about the birth of your daughter, Sarah. I imagine Stephen is growing."

"Oh yes. He turned two last week and celebrated by manfully using the water closet. I must say his aim needs improvement."

Harry laughed. "Well, I suppose you can't blame the little fellow for trying." He poured two fingers of brandy for everyone. Of all of them, Bell had changed the most. When they had first met, he'd been rather guarded. Over the course of one season, he'd become an indispensable friend to both Harry and Colin. Bellingham was the sort of fellow a man could count on.

The food arrived. Now that he was relaxing with friends, Harry wolfed down the beef, potatoes, and cheesecake. "I'm stuffed."

"Me too," Colin said.

After the waiter brought the port, Justin rose. "Please, excuse me. Paul just arrived, and I'm planning to trounce him at the billiards table."

"Go on, then," Bell said. "Hail a hackney and don't make a lot of racket when you come home. You do not want to face your mother's wrath."

When Justin retreated, Harry said, "You've certainly tamed his rebelliousness. Well done."

"He only needed guidance. I suppose we'll keep him after all."

Harry laughed. It felt like old times again.

"What about your family, Harry?" Bell asked.

"My girl cousins haven't changed much."

Bell's brows rose. "I'm surprised your family isn't pressing you to marry now that you've inherited."

He shrugged, unsure if he was ready to confess his intentions.

Bell frowned. "You're aware that I was prepared to let my property go back to the Crown—or so I thought. Then Laura asked why I hadn't sold it."

"I took Havenwood for granted over the years, but I owe much to my late uncle."

"He was a good man," Colin said. "The best."

"After Uncle Hugh passed, I realized how much the property means to me," Harry said. "There are so many memories. I know he would want me to ensure his legacy thrived for many generations in a direct line of descent." One day, God willing, it would pass to his own son.

"Does this mean you will join the old married men's club?" Colin said.

He was a little embarrassed, so he resorted to a joke. "Not tonight."

His friends chortled.

"Harry, that reminds me," Bell said. "Laura invited you to dinner in a sennight."

"Let me guess. I will be seated next to a single lady that your countess has chosen especially for me."

Bell's shoulders shook with laughter. "Laura will be heartbroken if you do not attend, but don't feel the least bit obligated."

Harry smiled. "Maybe another time." He'd never thought much about having a family before. His own father had died when he was eight. It had been hard on him at school until Colin had befriended him. They had been like brothers ever since.

"Your uncle was an exceptional man," Colin said. "I have fond memories of spending summers with you at his farm."

Harry's spirits rose. "Remember the time Uncle Hugh caught us having a pissing contest out the window?"

Colin grinned. "Oh, Lord, you pissed on the gardener."

"Uncle Hugh made us muck pig shit out of the pen. There are reasons I don't eat bacon."

Harry's smile faded. He would have to return to the farm in late summer. He didn't know how he would bear his uncle's absence. After the funeral, he'd kept expecting his uncle to walk into the room. But he knew his duty, and he loved Havenwood for all it represented for his uncle and now him.

"Harry, I assume you are confident in your uncle's advisors and solicitors," Bell said.

"Yes, they're capable men." He'd never admit it, but he was woefully ignorant about many of his uncle's affairs. In hindsight, he ought to have insisted upon helping with the estate business while his uncle was alive, but regrets were useless.

Bell picked up his glass and swirled his port. "When I returned from the Continent all those years ago, I made the steward, solicitors, and bankers explain everything in detail."

Harry nodded, knowing it was Bell's way of making a suggestion.

Bell retrieved his watch. "Ah, damn, it's getting late."

"I must be going, too," Colin said. "My wife and I have an early appointment with an architect. Pity me. Angeline is determined to tear down half the town house I just bought."

Harry laughed, but truthfully, he was a bit disappointed. In the old days, they would smoke cheroots and drink well past midnight, but his friends had responsibilities to their families.

Bell rose. "Gentlemen, same time next week?"

"Absolutely," Colin said. "Harry, are you in?"

His spirits rose. "Definitely."

Harry followed them downstairs. They donned their outerwear and walked out of the club. His breath frosted and the cold air chafed his face as he shook hands with his friends.

"Can I give you a lift?" Bell said.

"No, it's only a few blocks." Harry wrapped the woolen scarf around his neck. "The streetlamps are lighted and a walk will clear my head of the brandy."

Lucy Longmore finished sweeping the scraps of material and thread from the floor of the dress shop. She'd been searching for a new second job that paid better, but without a letter of character, she faced difficult odds. After she stacked bolts of fabric on a shelf, she glanced at her friends. Evelyn and Mary were still sorting their sewing notions.

"Evelyn, did you have many customers this morning?" Lucy asked.

"Yes, a number of lofty ladies and their daughters came. Most of 'em too particular."

"Or couldn't make up their minds." Mary mimicked them: "Mama, I simply cannot wear primrose, for it makes me look sallow."

"My favorite story is the mama and the biscuit jar," Lucy said.

Evelyn grinned and mimicked the girl's fretful voice. "Mama, why is the seamstress having trouble with the hooks?"

All three of them said in unison, "Because you cannot keep your hand out of the biscuit jar."

They all laughed.

Evelyn sighed. "There's nothing more irritating than a spoiled aristo."

"I sort of felt sorry for Biscuit Jar Girl," Lucy said.

"That's because you have a soft heart," Evelyn said, "but you misplace your sympathy with the spoiled rich girls."

"Well, if I were rich," Lucy said, "I would have no trouble at all making a decision on a gown."

Mary closed her sewing box. "If you had lots of choices, you might."

"No," Lucy said, grinning. "I would choose them all."

Evelyn eyed Mary with a smile. "Leave it to Lucy."

Lucy wished she had dozens of choices, but one day, she intended to make her dreams of owning a dance studio come true. She might not have much more than her dreams, but she would do everything possible to make them come true.

Ida, the new girl, sidled past them. She'd started working for Madame Delanger two days ago and didn't look a day over fourteen. Lucy and her friends had tried to befriend her, but Ida had regarded them with suspicion and rebuffed their attempts to include her. The only thing they knew about the girl was that Madame allowed her to sleep on the floor in the sewing room at night. Lucy felt sorry for Ida, as she obviously had no home.

At the sound of footsteps, Mary cleared her throat, a signal to mind one's words. Moments later, the temperamental shop owner, Madame Delanger, entered the main floor. "Ida, do not forget to check behind the dressing screens for missing items. I check the inventory every day."

"Yes, Madame," Ida mumbled as she walked behind one of the screens.

"Je suis fatigué." Madame Delanger groaned as she leaned against the arm of a red chaise longue where the illustrious customers often rested while waiting to be fitted for a gown. "The beginning of the season is always hectic, but I commissioned four new gowns and sold ten pairs of stockings and six pairs of gloves today." Then she frowned and crossed over to Mary. "Are you checking for dust? If there is even a speck on the fabric, I will deduct the cost from your wages."

Mary adopted a blank mien. "Yes, Madame, I will check once more."

Lucy glanced out the shop window and sighed inwardly. If she could hurry Madame along a bit, she and her friends could avoid walking the entire way in the dark. Regardless, she mustn't allow her impatience to show. They all treaded lightly around Madame, for her moods were unpredictable. Lucy needed the work and must be respectful.

"Ida," Madame Delanger said, raising her voice. "You will finish the lace on that gown tonight. I had better not find you asleep while the gown is unfinished."

"Yes, Madame," Ida mumbled.

Lucy shared a speaking look with her friends. Madame was taking advantage of Ida's youth. Yet none of them dared to defend the girl, because it could cost them their jobs. It made Lucy feel wretched, but she had to think of her grandmother and herself first.

"Tomorrow, you must all arrive at six in the morning and be prepared to sew for the next twelve hours," Madame said. "This is the busiest time of the year, and everything must be ready when the ladies come to shop."

Lucy's heart beat faster. Madame had never insisted upon such long hours before. When she'd hired Lucy three months ago, she'd been perfectly willing to let her leave to assist the dance instructor for two hours, but that had been before the height of the season.

Lucy drew in her breath. "Madame, I will gladly arrive at six o'clock tomorrow morning, but I have a dancing lesson in the afternoon. As before, I will return in two hours as I've done previously."

Madame sighed. "Come with me."

The back of Lucy's neck prickled as she followed Madame to the tiny sewing room. With every step, she told herself that Madame would not sack her. She needed both of her jobs and hoped Madame would understand.

"Be seated," Madame said.

After Lucy took a chair, she said, "Madame, when you hired me, you said I could take time off to teach my dance lessons. I have always returned promptly."

"Matters have changed," Madame said. "I need seamstresses who are able to work the required twelve hours."

Fear gripped her hard. She didn't want to give up her dance instruction, because she wanted to develop her own clients. How else would she open her own dance studio?

"Madame, with all due respect, I could sew during the weekends to make up for the time I'm out teaching dance."

"I cannot afford to employ four seamstresses."

She stared at Madame. "But...you just hired Ida two days ago."

"Ida does not ask for special privileges."

The realization slammed into Lucy like a fist to her belly. Madame had hired Ida to replace her—no doubt for much lower wages.

Desperation gripped her. She took a deep breath, prepared to agree to lower wages and longer hours—anything to avoid being out of work, but it wasn't really a choice. She couldn't leave her grandmother alone for up to twelve hours.

"Times are difficult," Madame Delanger said. "Wait a moment, and I will settle up with you."

Numbness set in. Everything seemed a little hazy, as if she were awakening from a bad dream. The denial didn't last long. Her eyes welled, but she blinked back the tears. She might have little more than her pride, but she would hold her head high.

When Madame Delanger returned, she handed over her wages and a folded paper.

Lucy couldn't be certain, but she thought she saw a twinge of guilt in Madame Delanger's expression. When Lucy unfolded the paper, she inhaled. It was a letter of character. Dear God, it was the one thing she'd lacked that had held her back in her search for better employment. "Thank you," she said. Then it occurred to her how absurd it was for her to thank Madame when she knew the woman had treated her unfairly.

"I wish I could do more, but you will prevail," Madame said.

A spurt of anger rose up in her, and Lucy gritted her teeth. It was an insincere platitude that would never make up for Madame's underhanded dismissal.

Lucy rose and walked out of the sewing room, holding

her head high like a queen. She vowed to do everything in her power to find work, and she would let nothing stop her. Somehow, someway, she would open her own dance studio one day. She would be master of her own destiny.

Lucy put the precious coins in her small purse and tucked the letter of character in her apron pocket. She donned her cloak and gloves. Then she picked up her basket and waited for Evelyn and Mary to put on their wraps. She had never wanted to leave a place as badly as she did now.

As they walked out into the night, the jingle of the shop door sounded altogether too cheerful, given her bad news. Lucy pulled the hood of her cape over her head, because the night air was damp and chilly. The misty fog swirled all around them. It had become their habit to walk together until their paths divided. It had made her feel safer, for at least part of the walk.

"Lucy, I know something is wrong," Evelyn said. "Your face was very pale after Madame took you to the sewing room."

"She sacked me, but I expected it. Madame cannot afford four seamstresses and needs someone who can work twelve hours—and for less pay in all likelihood."

Mary exchanged a long look with Evelyn. "That explains why she hired Ida. No doubt the girl accepted a pittance for wages."

"I suspect Ida is working in exchange for sleeping on the shop floor," Evelyn said.

Lucy winced. "That is awful."

Mary halted. "Lucy, I can loan you a bit of coin."

"So can I," Evelyn said.

"Oh no, I cannot allow it. I'll earn wages tomorrow after my dance lesson. I'll find a second position soon." She must find it quickly. Her earnings as an assistant to Mr. Buckley, the dancing master, were barely sufficient, and more than once he'd shorted her based on some trumped up mistake she'd supposedly made.

Lucy held her basket closer as they approached a street vendor. She bought two meat pasties and a quarter loaf of bread for dinner. Then they resumed their walk.

"We will all persevere so that we can look forward to bright futures," Lucy said. Her words were at odds with the fear gripping her, but she mustn't give in to despair. She'd managed to pay for lodgings and food for herself and her grandmother these past six months, and she would manage again. A bit of pluck and a prayer would see her through this latest setback.

She hoped.

"I'm done up tonight," Evelyn said.

Mary sighed. "I shall dream about the future tonight. Billy says we'll marry when he saves up enough money."

Lucy shared an inscrutable look with Evelyn. Billy made promises to Mary, but according to Evelyn, he spent most of his wages in the tavern. Privately, she'd told Lucy that Mary wasn't the only woman in Billy's life. Lucy had never met him, but she feared Billy would break Mary's heart. Perhaps it would be best if he did. Mary deserved better treatment.

"We'll miss you at the shop," Mary said.

Lucy's breath frosted. "We could meet at Green Park on Sunday afternoon if the weather is nice."

Evelyn sighed. "Madame needs us to sew this Sunday, too."

Lucy feared Madame would pressure them to work seven days a week.

The three stopped at the corner of Piccadilly and Regent, where their paths would split.

"Lucy, I know this is hard for you now," Evelyn said, "but

if you continued to work for Madame, you would not be able to teach dance."

Mary nodded. "Do whatever you must to earn wages, but don't give up your dream of having your own dance studio."

She hugged her friends quickly. "Thank you for believing in me. Now I must go."

"Be safe," Evelyn said. "Remember the story we told you about the girl who disappeared forever after she let a man take her up in his carriage."

Lucy shuddered. "I remember."

"If a man offers to escort you, run," Evelyn said.

"Remember, speak to no one, and make sure no one follows you," Mary said.

She nodded, remembering her friends' many warnings. Their tales of girls snatched off the street and sold into prostitution had made her skin crawl.

"I'll not forget," Lucy said. "Godspeed."

Lucy shivered more from the frigid wind than the threat of danger. She stood beneath the lighted gas lamp, watching her friends walk away until they were no longer visible. Her chest tightened. It would be harder to meet them now that she'd lost her sewing job, but Lucy swore she would make it happen.

In that one unguarded moment, a filthy man grabbed hold of her basket and tugged hard.

The misty fog swirled around Harry as he strode along Piccadilly, but it wasn't too dense tonight. Soon he must buy a carriage. He'd need one for inclement weather, and now that he was a bloody duke, he supposed he ought to have a decent vehicle for traveling. God knew he'd inherited an enormous fortune and could afford whatever caught his fancy. He'd always thought money would bring him happiness, but it hadn't. Perhaps in time he would feel differently.

He was only a block away from his rooms at the Albany when he saw a thief tugging on a woman's basket. When she screamed, Harry ran as fast as he could and shouted, "Stop, thief!" The ragged man took one look at him and ducked down an alley.

"Are you hurt?" Harry said as he reached the woman. Lord, his heart was hammering in his chest.

"No, but I thank you, kind sir," she said, picking up the small loaf of bread and dusting it off.

He couldn't help noticing her shabby glove as she set the bread beneath a cloth in her basket. Yet she spoke in a crisp, educated manner. The hood of her red, threadbare cloak fell back as she straightened her small frame. The lighted oil lamp nearby revealed her thick, red curls. She had the kind of hair that made a man want to take it down, but that only reminded him of her peril. "You ought not to be on the streets alone at night," he said. "It's dangerous for a woman."

She pulled her hood up and scoffed. "Sir, I assure you, I would not set foot on these mean streets if I had any other choice."

The woman's plump lips and bright emerald eyes drew him. She was a rare beauty. "If you will allow it, I will escort you for your safety," he said, smiling. "Surely you will not object to protection."

Her eyes narrowed. "You've done your good deed for the evening, Sir Galahad." She reached in her basket and brandished a wicked-looking knife. "My trusty blade is protection enough."

Holy hell. It was a large blade, but she held it too low. He also noticed her arm trembled. She clearly had no idea how to use the blade. One sharp blow to her arm would incapacitate her, and the knife would fall to the ground.

She looked him over and shook her head. "Perhaps I should escort you for your safety."

He laughed. "That's rich."

"Evidently, so are you."

She'd obviously taken stock of his clothing and deduced he was wealthy. "Come now, I'm a man and far stronger than you. I can defend myself."

She angled her head. "Have a care, sir. I quickly deduced you have a full purse inside your inner breast pocket. And if I can surmise that this quickly, you can be sure ruffians will, too."

"You heard the coins jingling while I ran."

She looked him over. "I wager those boots were made at Hoby's. They're worth a fortune. So is all of your clothing. At the very least, you ought to carry one of those canes with a hidden blade. Not everyone is as merciful as I am."

"You believe *I* am in danger?" How the devil had this conversation taken such a bizarre turn?

She regarded him with a world of knowledge in her eyes. "Tonight, Sir Galahad, you are far more vulnerable than I am."

Stunned into silence, he watched her disappear into the wispy fog. Then he reached inside another inner pocket and took out his penknife. A second, longer blade, far more wicked, folded out at the opposite end. He'd kept it hidden because he didn't want to frighten her. So much for gallantry, he thought wryly. He wrapped the wool scarf around his neck to ward off the chill and continued on his way home, her impertinent green eyes haunting him the entire walk. And damned if they didn't coax a smile out of him.

* * *

When Lucy arrived at the door to her lodgings, her heart still raced and her legs quivered like jelly. Although her breath frosted and her nose was cold, she must calm herself first. The last thing she wanted was to worry her grandmother.

She'd been furious with the thief and determined to make a scene to scare him off. Then the handsome stranger had come to her rescue. The moment the man she'd dubbed Sir Galahad had offered to escort her, she'd recalled her friends' warnings about strange men and brandished her weapon. She'd expected him to express fear, but his brows had merely risen a little. In truth, he'd seemed amused as a smile spread across his face as if he were mocking her. In retrospect, his cavalier demeanor infuriated her. Apparently he thought himself invincible. The entire incident struck her as bizarre, but it was over. She would never see him again. In an effort to appear unruffled when she greeted her grandmother, Lucy inhaled and exhaled slowly. Then she rapped the door.

"Lucy? Is that you?"

"Yes, Grandmama."

Her grandmother's stick tapped on the wooden floor. Lucy heard the sound of the latch, and then the door opened.

"Oh, dear, hurry for the wind is cold," Grandmama said. "And I know it must be very late."

Lucy stepped inside and bolted the door. "Oh, I feel better already."

She set the basket on the floor, hung her cape on one of the pegs, and removed her worn gloves. Then she took out the bread and meat pasties and covered the basket again.

"Sorry it took so long. Madame Delanger delayed me."

"Oh, what happened?" Grandmama said.

She told her grandmother the abbreviated version of her dismissal.

"That is unfair of her to sack you in favor of the new girl."

It no longer mattered. "Madame Delanger needed someone who would sew for up to twelve hours." Of course, Lucy could not leave her grandmother alone that long, but she kept that to herself.

Grandmama tapped her stick as she walked to the table. "I know you're worried, and I know we'll have to scrimp, but I have faith you'll find another job soon. To be honest, I'm glad you are no longer working nights for Madame Delanger. I worried about you walking in the dark. It isn't safe."

No, she'd discovered that firsthand tonight. "I walked with my friends." She deliberately omitted that they accompanied her only part of the way. She certainly had no intention of revealing her encounter with Sir Galahad.

"I'll make tea." She filled the kettle from the pump and set it on the hob. When she retrieved the cups, her hands trembled and the cups rattled on the saucers. She was far more unnerved than she'd realized.

"Dearest, are you overset?" Grandmama said. "There is something different in your voice. You sound a little breathless."

"It's just from the cold," she said. "A hot cup of tea will warm me." She must calm herself. Grandmama had lost her sight many years ago, but she'd honed her other senses and could easily discern when something was awry. The last thing she wanted was for Grandmama to fret about her, but she was more than a little concerned about money. She needed to find work as quickly as possible.

Lucy kissed her grandmother's cheek. "Have a seat at the table while I pour the tea."

"That would be lovely, dear, but I fear you work too hard."

"You know I love to dance more than anything in the world," she said. "I'm fortunate to have found a position assisting Mr. Buckley with lessons." She didn't tell her grandmother that she loathed Buckley because he sometimes shorted her wages for trumped up reasons. What was the point? It would only add to Grandmama's worries. On the morrow, Lucy would have to endure his unfair treatment, but she didn't want to waste what was left of her evening thinking about him.

After the kettle whistled, Lucy carefully measured out the tea leaves into the pot, poured the hot water, and let it grow dark. The caddy had belonged to her late mother, who had hoarded the leaves. They never could have afforded the expensive tea otherwise. "Buckley sent a messenger boy round to Madame Delanger's shop earlier today. I have a dancing lesson tomorrow."

"I'm glad you enjoy teaching dance," Grandmama said, "but I wish you did not have to work."

If wishes were horses, beggars would ride. "I'm fortunate, compared to many other women." It was true. Even though she found Buckley unpleasant, she enjoyed teaching dance.

Lucy set the pasties on the plates and poured the tea. The cup warmed her hands and the food was savory.

After they finished their late supper, Lucy sighed. "Shall I read to you?"

"Not tonight, dear. I hear the weariness in your voice. You must rest."

The lingering fear had left her spent, but if she went to bed now, she knew she would toss and turn with worry over finding a new job. "I doubt I can rest yet, Grandmama, and

I want to spend time with you. Let me read another chapter of *Pride and Prejudice*." She'd splurged on a subscription at the library, but she refused to regret it. In the days ahead, she must pursue every possible avenue for another job, but tonight, she needed to be with her grandmother and immerse herself in a good book.

She had no idea how long she'd been reading when she heard her grandmother's slow, steady breathing. Lucy had little money and few possessions, but she was fortunate to have such a sweet and wise grandmother. Grandmama had enriched her life immensely and had always encouraged her to reach for her dreams. Lucy kissed her forehead and awakened her.

"Oh, dear, I fell asleep. I'm so sorry."

"Do not be sorry," Lucy said, putting a ribbon in the book to mark her place. "I'll read to you tomorrow evening. Now come and let me tuck you in."

"Oh, that isn't necessary. My trusty stick will see me to my room. Good night, dear."

"Good night, Grandmama."

Lucy banked the fire and sat on the sofa, contemplating her dream of owning a dance studio. The lessons would not make her rich, but she meant to make a comfortable and safe life for herself and her grandmother.

As much as she wanted to pursue her dream, she must think of the immediate concerns. She had to find another job to supplement their income. Her stomach clenched as she contemplated the consequences of failure. Dear God, what would happen to them if she didn't find another position quickly?

Chapter Two

The next afternoon

Lucy found the address of Lady Blenborough in an elegant house situated near Green Park. She felt relatively safe in this neighborhood. Well, from everyone except her disgusting employer, Mr. Buckley. As much as she despised him, she needed the employment. While she was his assistant, she often did all of the teaching while Buckley tried to charm the lady clients. At least she had found a job using her dancing skills. It provided her with an income, though she sometimes struggled to make ends meet.

She went round to the servant's entrance, and the kindly cook gave her a cup of tea and a roll. Lucy ate half the roll and stored the rest in her apron pocket for later. When Buckley peered inside the kitchen, he scowled. "I'll dock your pay for fraternizing with the servants."

She had learned the art of making her expression as blank as possible. It was her only defense against her horrid employer. When she followed Buckley to the drawing room, Lucy saw a plump girl who looked to be about twelve. A lady wearing a fine morning gown sat in a chair with a bored expression.

"Lucy, show Prudence the steps," Buckley said. "Lady Blenborough, do not despair. Soon Lady Prudence will be performing the dance steps with elegance and lightness."

Lady Blenborough rolled her eyes and unfurled her fan. "Please get on with the lesson," she said in a curt tone.

"Lucy," Buckley said, clapping his hands. "Do not dally."

She turned her attention to Prudence. "Is this your first dance lesson?"

"Hardly," Lady Blenborough said. "My daughter is graceless."

Lucy was horrified at Lady Blenborough's harsh words in front of everyone.

When Prudence's lower lip trembled, Lucy's heart went out to her. "Prudence," Lucy said gently. "Do not worry if you make a mistake."

Mrs. Blenborough rolled her eyes. "She needs no encouragement to fail."

Lucy drew in a deep breath, knowing she could not contradict Lady Blenborough, but the lady's cruel words must be crushing Prudence. Why would her mother treat her daughter with such indignity?

Lucy knew how important it was for Prudence to learn the steps. One simply could not get on well in society without learning to dance gracefully. Years ago, her mother had taught all the young people in their village to dance and Lucy had assisted her as she'd grown older.

Lucy leaned closer to Prudence, hoping it would help her.

"I know you can learn if you concentrate. "Will you do that, Prudence?"

She nodded.

"Now, watch me the first time," Lucy said. "This is the chassé step. Right foot forward takes the weight; the following foot closes behind." Lucy regarded the girl. "Watch me once more. Now you step with me slowly. Right foot forward."

Prudence used the left foot.

"Oh, for heaven's sake, Prudence," Lady Blenborough said, "use your *right* foot."

"Prudence," Lucy said, "let us try again. Right foot forward taking your weight and close the back foot behind."

Prudence put her weight on her right foot, and then she glanced at her mother and froze.

Lady Blenborough spoke sharply. "Prudence, attend."

The sharp command startled Prudence. She closed her back foot, but Lucy had to catch Prudence's arm to keep her upright.

"Prudence, let us step together slowly," Lucy said. "Right foot forward taking the weight, very good, and close your back foot behind." Lucy smiled at her. "You did very well. Now let's try it up tempo. Watch me first."

After the demonstration, Lucy said, "Let us try it together. Right foot forward taking the weight…"

Prudence lost her balance and fell on her bottom. Lucy immediately helped the girl to her feet. "It's all right," she said under her breath, even though she knew it wasn't.

"Prudence, you are hopelessly clumsy," Lady Blenborough said. "I've seen enough. The lesson is over."

Lucy couldn't help comparing Lady Blenborough's cruelty with her own mother's gentle patience. She remembered how much her mother's approval had meant to her and knew poor Prudence would never gain confidence with such a horrible mother.

"Lady Blenborough," Buckley said, his voice oily in his attempts to soothe, "allow me to demonstrate with my assistant. Perhaps that will help Prudence. Lucy." He snapped his fingers.

Lucy knew what was coming and braced herself. He stood behind her and his foul breath on her neck made her want to shiver. When he attempted to move closer, she knew he would try to touch her, because he'd done it before. She pretended to misunderstand and performed the steps on her own. *Chassé close, chassé close, chassé close.* Lucy ended with a graceful plié.

"Prudence," Lady Blenborough said, "try again."

The girl had wandered over to the sideboard and stiffened upon hearing her mother's voice. Guilt was written all over Prudence's face as she held her hands behind her back.

Lady Blenborough rose. Her eyes narrowed as she yanked her daughter's hand forward. Sweetmeats scattered all over the floor.

"If you wish to make a pig of yourself, Prudence, then do so. I wash my hands of you," Lady Blenborough said.

Lucy winced as tears spilled down Prudence's face. She wanted to comfort the girl, but it was not her place.

"My lady," Buckley said. "Do not despair. I am sure we will make a dancer of Prudence yet."

"She is nothing but an embarrassment to me, " Lady Blenborough said.

Lucy bit her lip. How could Lady Blenborough treat her daughter so callously? With patience, the girl could learn to execute the steps, but her mother obviously had taken a disgust of her own daughter. Lucy found it painful to witness.

"Lady Blenborough," Mr. Buckley said, "I shall return next week to help Prudence in her dance lessons."

"There will be no more lessons," Lady Blenborough said. "My daughter is hopeless. I have no more need of your services. You are dismissed." She waved her hand.

Buckley glared at Lucy as if she'd done something wrong and took her by the upper arm as they quit the drawing room. "I'm reducing your pay," he said. "See that you do not consort with the servants again." Then he handed over half the coins that were due her. Lucy held in the anger threatening to boil over until they exited the servant's entrance. It wasn't the first time he'd found an excuse to reduce her pay, but it still infuriated her.

Once they reached the pavement, Lucy turned on Buckley. "I did nothing wrong. The cook offered me a roll, because I arrived early. You owe me the rest of my wages."

"How dare you question me. You are lucky I hired you. If it weren't for me, you would have no job. I'll not tolerate your insolence." He took a step closer and the smell of strong drink was on his breath as usual. "See that you remember it."

She clenched her fists as she strode off. If it weren't for her, he would have to exert himself and actually teach the dance lessons. As much as she despised him, she needed the job, but he would continue to cheat her. She must find other employment. There was much she didn't have, but she was smart and educated. All she needed was one person to give her a chance.

Lucy walked to Oxford Street and popped inside a milliner's shop. A pudgy woman greeted her. "I'm Mrs. Jamison, proprietor. How may I help you?"

"I'm looking for work," Lucy said. "I'm experienced with sewing and trimming bonnets."

"I am sorry, but my daughters assist me. Good luck to you, miss."

"Thank you," Lucy said. She quit the shop and made her way to Piccadilly. She walked inside the Burlington Arcade. There were multiple shops and she meant to inquire about a position at as many as she could today.

Four hours later, she'd made little progress. No one seemed to need the services of a seamstress or milliner today.

She stopped at a costermonger's stand to buy meat pasties for dinner and hoped that she would find a job quickly. The rent was due in two days, and she had only one option left.

Lucy managed only a few bites of the pie that evening. It was hard to concentrate on anything because of her fears. She got up to stir the coals, because it was something to do other than sit and fret over what she must do.

When it grew dark, Lucy bid her grandmother good night and went to her room. She set the candle on the night table and opened the drawer. When she drew out a velvet pouch, her hands shook a little. She rubbed her thumb on the fuzzy velvet surface and opened the drawstring. Her heart ached as she took out her mother's pearls. She fingered the clasp where a short chain with a tiny gold heart dangled. Lucy remembered her mother used to let her touch the pearls when she was a little girl. Now she would give anything to hug her mother just once more.

Her stomach clenched. It was so hard to give up her one remaining link to her mother, but she had barely slept the past two nights wondering how she would manage to keep a roof over their heads.

She kissed the pearls and put them back in the pouch. Then she closed the drawer and brushed away the tears. There was no other choice. She had to pay the rent.

Tomorrow, she would pawn the pearls...

* * *

The next morning, Lucy bargained hard with the pawnbroker. Even so, she knew the pearls were worth more than she'd gotten for them. After she left, she swiped at the tears tracking down her face. The important thing was that she had enough money to pay the rent for another month. She lifted her chin, but she felt a little empty as she strode away.

She inquired about work again at several shops she'd missed at the Burlington Arcade yesterday, but the proprietors of the other dress shops did not have a vacancy. None of the eight milliners, hosiers, or glovers had open positions, either.

Lucy walked along Piccadilly, turned on St. James, and found herself on King Street. A boy stood outside of a large building and called out to those passing by. "Servers needed for Almack's. Wednesday nights," the boy called out. "Must be clean and polite."

An older, white-haired gentleman dressed in elegant clothing opened the doors. Lucy did not hesitate. She ran to him and bobbed a curtsy. "Sir, I understand servers are needed. I'd be obliged if you would consider me."

"I'm Mr. Wilson, master of ceremonies," he said. "Come inside."

Lucy followed him. Once past the foyer, her eyes widened upon seeing the enormous mirrors that reflected the stately columns. A half-circular balcony was suspended high above the floor.

"You have a refined accent, young lady," Mr. Wilson said.

"I'm educated, sir, but my family has fallen on hard times." She swallowed. "If it pleases you, Mr. Wilson, I would like to apply for the position."

"The pay isn't much for serving once a week—only a shilling."

"I'd be grateful for the work, sir."

His white bushy brows furrowed. "Do you have other employment, miss?"

"I assist a dance master during the day, sir," she said. "I'm more than willing to do other work." She bit her lip, fearing he would reject her.

"Very well. Come to the back door on Wednesday in a sennight at seven sharp in the evening," Mr. Wilson said. "You mustn't be late. The lady patronesses are unforgiving."

"I won't be late. Thank you, sir." Elated at the opportunity, she started to turn away when Mr. Wilson cleared his throat. "Miss, what is your name?"

"Lucy Longmore, sir."

Mr. Wilson considered her for a moment. He took her hand and set coins in her palm. Then he closed her fingers over them.

Temptation gripped her, but in the end, pride won. "Sir, I cannot take the money. I've not earned it."

He clasped his hands behind his back. "When I was a young man and desperate for employment, a kind soul helped me. I swore that one day I would do the same for someone else. Will you allow me to do so now?"

She suspected he'd concocted the story, but she could hardly refuse without insulting him. "Very well," she said, putting the coins in a small purse she hid in her apron. "Thank you, sir."

"Godspeed, dear. We will see you at Almack's next week."

Her spirits rose as she walked out and crossed the street, dodging the mud and horse droppings. She realized she was near the place where she'd threatened the handsome stranger with her knife last night. In retrospect, she thought she'd misjudged him, but she shook off her guilt. A rich man like him hardly needed her sympathy. Her survival and that of her grandmama depended on keeping her wits about her.

She slowed her step as she neared a large building. A well-dressed gentleman handed over his horse's reins to a groom. Lucy had heard of the Albany, the famous gentleman's quarters. It occurred to her that she might inquire about employment there. Surely a place designated for bachelors would require the services of maids. Now that she had a letter of character, she had a far better chance of finding decent employment. She told herself not to get her hopes up, but she had nothing to lose, so she rapped the knocker.

Two hours later, Lucy had passed muster with Mrs. Finkle, the head housekeeper. The rules were simple enough. All she had to do was clean until the rooms were spotless, and of course, she mustn't fraternize with the gentlemen residents. Lucy had no intention of jeopardizing her new position. She was thrilled that her pay would be twice what she made assisting Buckley. For the first time in six months, she dared to hope that she and Grandmama might improve their circumstances.

Mrs. Norcliffe's drawing room, that same afternoon

"I am exceedingly concerned about attendance at Almack's," Mrs. Norcliffe, the newest patroness, said. "The gentlemen have been abandoning our fair temple of respectability in droves these last few years. Something must be done."

Lady Jersey sniffed. "One would think that the quadrille would entice the gentlemen."

Mrs. Norcliffe thought no such thing, but as the newest

patroness, she kept silent. Everybody knew that Lady Jersey had introduced the quadrille to Almack's. "I will be honest, ladies. I have a personal concern in seeing Almack's returned to its former popularity with all of the beau monde."

Lady Cowper, whom everyone knew was having an affaire de coeur with Lord Palmerstone, sighed. "I believe we must resort to stronger measures, but, Mrs. Norcliffe, you speak of your own concerns. Does this perchance relate to Granfield?"

Mrs. Norcliffe set her dish of tea aside. "My son refuses to leave his rooms at the Albany, even though he is now a duke. I fear he will take after his bachelor uncle, God rest his soul. The dukedom is in jeopardy. I must find my son a bride, for he surely will not pursue it."

Lady Castlereagh sniffed. "Well, if there is no heir, he has no choice."

Mrs. Norcliffe sighed. "I've tried for years to put suitable young ladies of good breeding and fortune in my son's way. Naturally he wants nothing to do with any of them, but I must find him a bride soon. He desperately needs an heir and a spare."

"I've yet to meet a bachelor who did not resist marriage," Lady Cowper said. "My advice is to trap him."

"Oh, dear," Mrs. Norcliffe said. "I could not lower myself to such tactics." *Not yet, at any rate.*

Mrs. Drummond-Burrell, known as one of the highest sticklers, drew her quizzing glass to her eye. "You must find a way to entice Granfield. He will want someone young and pretty with at least ten thousand for her marriage portion."

Princess Esterhazy's eyes twinkled. "A few years ago, that rakehell Mr. Darcett lured Miss Amy Hardwick into a cellar overnight. They were forced to wed."

"Oh, dear," Mrs. Norcliffe said, fanning her face.

"Let us not forget that His Grace has already inherited a fortune," Lady Jersey said. "You need stronger inducement, Mrs. Norcliffe. I recommend an introduction to a beautiful young woman. If all goes well, he will conceive a grand passion for her."

"He's likely to run the other way," Mrs. Drummond-Burrell said. "The author of *Pride and Prejudice* got it wrong in my opinion. Everybody knows a single man in possession of a fortune must be in want of his *freedom*."

Lady Castlereagh cleared her throat. "The only thing that entices gentlemen is their clubs. They gamble, they drink, and they take snuff. How many lose and win fortunes every night? It is scandalous."

Mrs. Norcliffe smoothed her skirts. "I had hoped that he would accept Lady Bellingham's invitation to dine. She had meant to invite Miss Lingley and her parents, but apparently my son begged off due to other commitments."

"Well, we all know what that means," Lady Sefton said.

Mrs. Norcliffe sighed. "Indeed, the clubs."

"I think they would live in them if possible," Lady Cowper said.

"Perish the thought," Countess Lieven said.

Lady Sefton pursed her lips. "I heard Lord Percival was found snoring beneath a gaming table at White's—the next morning."

Mrs. Norcliffe clutched the arms of her chair. "God save Lady Percival."

"No need to worry," Countess Lieven said. "They have an arrangement whereby he only comes home for the occasional dinner party in town. In autumn, he's much taken with his hunting and dogs. Lady Percival is quite satisfied with her circumstances."

Lady Cowper snorted. "And with her young Italian lover who plays the harp."

Mrs. Norcliffe fanned her face. "How risqué."

Lady Cowper lifted her brows. "One hears he plays his instrument well."

"Oh, dear," Mrs. Drummond-Burrell said. "We must take care not to venture into indecent topics."

Mrs. Norcliffe would never admit it, but she wished to hear more about the illicit Italian lover.

"I pity you, Mrs. Norcliffe, but something must be done about Granfield," Mrs. Drummond-Burrell said. "A dukedom is too important. However, I have a suggestion. Mrs. Osterham's daughter Hortense is quite accomplished, and at eighteen, she is biddable. You could take her in hand and mold her into the perfect bride for your son."

Mrs. Norcliffe clasped her hands to her heart. "Thank you, Mrs. Drummond-Burrell. I'm much obliged."

"Perhaps you could introduce your son at the opening of Almack's," Countess Lieven said.

Mrs. Norcliffe knew her son wouldn't go near Almack's unless there was an inducement. If something didn't change soon, she feared Harry would end up a lifelong bachelor like his freewheeling pigheaded uncle before him, God rest his soul.

"Do not fret, Mrs. Norcliffe," Mrs. Drummond-Burrell said. "Dancing is the mode of courtship, is it not? Do we not encourage our fair offspring to find their perfectly suitable partners for life at a ball?"

"Yes, of course," Lady Sefton said, "but, Mrs. Norcliffe, I suspect you wish to make a point, do you not?"

"Yes, indeed," Mrs. Norcliffe said. "The problem is how to lure the gentlemen away from their dice, liquor, and clubs? We need to make the experience exciting for them."

"No spirits," Mrs. Drummond-Burrell said. "The gentlemen will huddle around the sideboard all evening and become foxed."

"Mrs. Norcliffe, how do you propose to create excitement?" Lady Cowper said.

"It is rather daring," Mrs. Norcliffe said. Anxiety gripped her as she struggled to invent a plan. When it popped into her head, she knew the patronesses would proclaim it either brilliant or utter rubbish. She'd managed to become one of the patronesses, and she meant to secure her place. Sometimes one had to be bold.

"One thing we know about gentlemen is that they are fond of competition," Mrs. Norcliffe said.

All of the ladies leaned the slightest bit forward.

"I propose a dancing competition, one that would stir up passions not only for the dancers, but for the observers as well."

When there was no immediate reply, Mrs. Norcliffe resisted the urge to squirm.

"Your point, Mrs. Norcliffe?" Lady Jersey said.

"I hope to find my dear son a wife during the competition."

Princess Esterhazy applied her fan. "How can you be sure the dancing competition will work?"

"Indeed," Lady Castlereagh said. "Suppose the gentlemen refuse to participate. What then?"

"We need an incentive to entice them," Mrs. Norcliffe said. "Otherwise, they will return to their clubs."

"An incentive implies commerce." Lady Cowper fanned her face as if money were akin to devilment.

"In this case, it implies competition, and that is something no gentleman can resist," Mrs. Norcliffe said. "Imagine how many will be envious of those who are able to participate or observe at close hand. Almack's will once again rise as the temple of exclusivity."

"How are we to spread the word?" Princess Esterhazy said.

"It is easy enough to tip off the scandal sheets," Mrs. Norcliffe said. "Imagine all of London anticipating the competition each week. News will circulate far and wide. Everyone who is anyone will not want to miss the weekly winners."

"Winners?" Lady Sefton said in a faint tone.

Mrs. Norcliffe's stomach tightened, but she'd learned long ago to feign her way through almost any situation. "Each week the couples will dance and compete to stay in the competition another week," Mrs. Norcliffe said. "Some will be eliminated and others will remain until the very last."

"We are to judge them?" Lady Jersey asked.

"Of course," Mrs. Norcliffe said. "Who better than the patronesses to make the decisions?"

"It is rather bold," Lady Jersey said, "but we are the patronesses. Who will dare criticize if we sanction the competition?"

"Indeed, it could result in the loss of one's voucher," Mrs. Norcliffe said.

"What will the prize be?" Lady Jersey asked. "It must be sufficient to draw the gentlemen away from their liquor, cards, and dice."

"Ladies, what do you say to five hundred pounds as the prize for the most elegant dancing couple? Are we prepared to contribute seventy-two pounds each?" Mrs. Norcliffe said.

"That leaves four pounds unaccounted for," Lady Sefton said.

"We will buy extra lemonade and buttered sandwiches," Mrs. Norcliffe said.

"I must admit this is all rather exciting," Princess Esterhazy said.

"Indeed," Lady Jersey said. "Everyone will be anxious to get a voucher on Wednesday nights."

"Of course, only the most elite will have their vouchers approved," Mrs. Drummond-Burrell said. "We must maintain our high standards."

"Well, ladies, I believe we are all prepared for the first annual Almack's dancing competition," Mrs. Norcliffe said.

Lady Jersey observed Mrs. Norcliffe with a sly expression. "Pray tell, how do you propose to tempt *your* son into participating?"

Mrs. Norcliffe smiled. "What every mother resorts to when faced with an obstinate son. I will make him feel guilty."

Chapter Three

The next day

*L*ucy donned her bonnet and set out for the Mayfair address. She dreaded the scene that would arise when she confronted Buckley after the dance lesson today, but once it ended, she would never have to see him again. She made her way to the elegant town house in Grosvenor Square and knocked at the servant's door. A squat housekeeper admitted her and took her cloak. "Follow me upstairs," the housekeeper said. "They're waitin' in the first-floor drawing room."

When Lucy entered, Buckley narrowed his bloodshot eyes. He'd probably drunk himself into a stupor the previous night. It reminded her too much of her late father's nasty temper when he'd started drinking heavily after her mother's death.

"You are late, Lucy," he said. "It is disrespectful to Mrs. Vernon."

She ground her teeth. Oh, how she despised him for his unfair criticism, but she must control her reactions in front of Mrs. Vernon.

The clock struck the hour, proving she had actually arrived a bit early.

The two young misses covered their mouths and giggled.

"Girls, mind your manners," Mrs. Vernon said.

"Yes, Mama," they said in unison.

Lucy stood still, waiting for Buckley's instruction.

He cleared his throat. "Mrs. Vernon, with your permission, my assistant will show the fleuret steps to Miss Marie Vernon and Miss Anne Vernon."

Mrs. Vernon took a seat and sipped her tea. "Very well. My daughters are not acquainted with the steps. They need basic instruction."

Buckley snapped his fingers. "Lucy, will you demonstrate?"

She inclined her head. "Of course."

Naturally he ignored the young ladies and hovered near Mrs. Vernon, no doubt trying to curry favor with the lady, who paid him scarce attention. Lucy wasn't surprised. Buckley seldom exerted himself. After today, he would have no choice, unless he found a new assistant.

Lucy faced the young ladies. "The steps of the fleuret are in three/four time." She demonstrated slowly, saying, "Step, step, step, plié." She paused and said, "Now perform the steps with me."

Both girls made the mistake of taking a fourth step.

Lucy leaned down and smiled. "One thing you must remember is that it takes everyone a bit of time to learn a new dance. When I was a girl, I practiced a great deal. So please do not become discouraged. The more you practice, the easier it will become," she said.

The relief on the girls' faces told her that she'd succeeded

WHAT A DEVILISH DUKE DESIRES   41

in making them feel that there was no shame in making mistakes.

"Let us try it very slowly," Lucy said. "Watch and perform with me."

The girls practiced three times slowly, though they had a bit of trouble with the plié.

"Very good," Lucy said. "Now we will dance the steps at the correct tempo."

The girls floundered at the quicker pace the first time, but they improved quickly.

She worked with the young ladies for another half hour and praised them for their efforts. She leaned down to be closer to their level. "Continued practice will serve you well," Lucy said. "Again, the most important thing is not to become discouraged. I have confidence in both of you."

"Thank you, Miss Longmore," the girls said in unison.

Lucy glanced over at Buckley for further instruction.

When he leaned closer to Mrs. Vernon, Lucy winced because she'd smelled the spirits on his breath earlier. Mrs. Vernon's expression registered repugnance, and she stood abruptly. Naturally, Buckley rose as well. "Is anything amiss, Mrs. Vernon?" he asked.

"Pardon me." She marched over to her daughters. "Anne, Marie, please return to your rooms immediately," Mrs. Vernon said, her voice shaking.

"Yes, Mama," they said, and quit the room.

Lucy's heart thudded. She was certain Mrs. Vernon would dismiss them both without pay.

Mrs. Vernon returned her attention to Buckley. "Sir, you are dismissed."

His fleshy lips parted. "Mrs. Vernon, clearly you are distressed that my assistant was unable to teach the girls properly. I assure you it will never happen again."

"I have no quarrel with your assistant, but I smelled the liquor on your breath. I do not tolerate drunkards," Mrs. Vernon said.

He mopped his forehead with a dingy handkerchief. "Madame, this has all been a terrible misunderstanding. It is the tonic for my sore throat you smelled."

"I understand drunkards perfectly," Mrs. Vernon said. "You smell like a brew house. I will not allow you in my home ever again. You are dismissed without pay."

Lucy sighed inwardly. The moment Buckley had accused her of being tardy, she'd known he wouldn't pay her full wages, but now she would receive nothing.

"Madam, please reconsider," Buckley said.

"You are dismissed," Mrs. Vernon said tersely. "I suggest you leave immediately."

Lucy started to follow him, but Mrs. Vernon spoke. "Miss Longmore, may I have a word with you?"

Buckley glared at Lucy as if she were responsible for his inebriated state. She kept her expression as neutral as possible as he walked unsteadily out of the drawing room.

Mrs. Vernon closed the drawing room doors and faced Lucy. "You acquitted yourself in a patient and excellent manner while teaching the dance steps to my girls, but I wonder why you work for a man of Mr. Buckley's ilk."

"I have only been in London for six months," Lucy said. "I did not know his character well when I accepted the position." Truthfully, she would have taken it regardless, because she'd needed the money.

"Will you return next week at the same time to teach my daughters?" Mrs. Vernon asked. "I will pay you two shillings per lesson, the same as Mr. Buckley."

She schooled her expression, but inside she rejoiced, because Buckley had paid her only a sixpence, when he

•

didn't short her. "Thank you, madame. I'm pleased to accept."

"Very good." Mrs. Vernon's brows furrowed. "One moment please." She opened the doors and signaled a footman. Mrs. Vernon spoke quietly to him there. Lucy turned to the view of the green lawn and the trees so that it wouldn't appear she was eavesdropping. She wondered why Mrs. Vernon had continued to detain her.

"Miss Longmore?"

Lucy faced Mrs. Vernon and bobbed a curtsy.

Mrs. Vernon handed her a small purse. "Please do not share any part of your wages with that horrid man. He deserves none of it. Are you able to return next week at the same time?"

"Yes, thank you, madame." Lucy curtsied and hurried down the back stairs to the servant's entrance. She was thrilled because Mrs. Vernon would retain her for dancing lessons next week. Perhaps her luck had changed at long last.

Buckley had waited on the step outside the servant's entrance. "If you're looking for wages, you will be sorely disappointed. See that you remember yourself next time."

"There will not be a next time," she said. "I will no longer work for you."

"What?" he shouted.

"You heard me. From the beginning, you have cheated me out of my wages when I did nothing wrong. I'll not work for you ever again."

He took two steps and grabbed her by the arm. "Ungrateful wench. You intentionally sullied my reputation with Mrs. Vernon."

When Buckley lurched, she realized he was drunker than she'd first thought, and that gave her an advantage. "No, you did that to yourself." She pushed him away and hurried up the steps. When she heard his footfalls behind her, she ran faster.

"Damn you," he shouted.

She kept running, determined to escape him.

A thud sounded. Buckley howled. "My ankle."

Lucy glanced back.

"Help me, you bitch!"

She ignored him and scurried up to the street and strode off. His bellowing would alert the servants, who would get rid of him. Lucy kept walking quickly and looked over her shoulder, but there was no sign of him.

When she was well away from Buckley, she slowed her pace until she could breathe normally again. The tension in her arms and legs eased. Relief filled her. She was free of him forever. Moreover, Mrs. Vernon had retained her to teach her daughters. If all went well, the lady might recommend Lucy to her friends.

Her heart lightened. In a mere six months since coming to London, she'd taken charge of her life. Today, Mrs. Vernon had given her an opportunity to teach her girls. In addition, she held a steady job as a maid at the Albany. And once a week on Wednesday night, she would serve lemonade at Almack's where she would be able to listen to the orchestra and perhaps peek at the aristocratic ladies in their beautiful gowns.

As she strode along Bond Street, the acrid scent of chimney smoke filled the air. Numerous wagons, carriages, and smart phaetons crowded the street. A crossing sweeper darted past a hackney driver, who shouted at him. Costermongers hawked their wares on the street corners in barely recognizable English.

All the best shops were located on Bond Street, including

Madame Delanger's establishment. Lucy liked looking in the windows as she passed. While she was tempted to pop in to see Evelyn and Mary, she didn't want to interrupt their work. As Lucy drew nearer, a carriage stopped in front of the shop. Three elegantly dressed young ladies and an older one who must be their mother stepped out. Their white day gowns featured rows of fine lace on the flounces. The silk flowers and lovely ribbons in their jaunty bonnets proclaimed them as part of the quality.

How would it feel to have no cares at all in the world, save for shopping and attending balls?

The older lady noticed her watching and regarded her with a haughty expression.

Heat suffused Lucy's face and ears as she stepped back into a shop doorway. When the bell to Madame Delanger's shop jingled, Lucy judged that it was safe to continue on. She hurried past the shop where she'd swept the floors only three nights ago. Of course, it was foolish of her to care about the haughty lady. After all, that lady had likely forgotten all about her the instant she'd pranced inside Madame Delanger's shop.

Lucy crossed the street, dodging horse droppings and numerous vehicles rumbling along. When she reached the other side, she stopped to catch her breath. She shook off her wounded pride and decided *she* should forget that haughty lady. After all, she would never cross paths with the woman again.

She turned on to Piccadilly and checked her watch again. She was early, but since this was her first day working as a maid, she figured an early arrival would put her in Mrs. Finkle's good book.

The servant's entrance was on Vigo Street and discreetly hidden from public view. She walked past it at first and had to double back. Mindful of doing nothing to attract attention, Lucy hurried to the servant's entrance and rapped on the door.

"Come in."

Mrs. Finkle handed over a sack of laundry to a boy. "Don't dawdle. I'm timin' you."

The boy tugged his cap and escaped out the door.

Mrs. Finkle released a sigh. "I see you're prompt on your first day. Let that be your habit. Here, you must wear a mobcap. It will protect your hair."

"Yes, ma'am," Lucy said, tucking her hair into the cap.

"Let's go over the rules. The gentlemen's rooms are called *sets*. Always knock first. If no one answers, use the keys I'll give you. Return 'em to me when you're finished cleaning. Once inside, call out 'maid service.' If you hear nothin', start workin'. Tidy up all items, but leave them where they are, unless it's somethin' what fell to the floor. Dust all surfaces and polish the furniture. Everything should be tip-top."

Mrs. Finkle placed the sheets in Lucy's arms. "There's beeswax for polishing, plus rags and brooms in the closet. Never speak to the gentleman or his servant, unless one or the other has a question. Maids should be seen and not heard. Strip the sheets last and bring them downstairs. Those will go to the laundry woman. Any questions? Ask now 'cause I ain't repeating it tomorrow."

"I have no questions," Lucy said.

"One more thing. If I catch you dallying with one of the gents, I'll sack you without a character. You'll never get another job in service."

"I assure you that will never happen," Lucy said.

"Proof is in the puddin'. Go on, then."

Three hours later, Lucy had cleaned all but one of her

assigned *sets*. She crossed over to the last set assigned to her on the other side of the hall. Upon reaching set G1, she knocked and called out, "Maid service." She counted to twenty before using the spare key to unlock the door. Once again, she called out, "Maid service." When there was no response, she walked inside and set out to clean. After polishing the furnishings, she noticed pet hair on an old sofa and managed to clean it off, though it took ages. Since she'd heard no barking, she assumed there was a cat hiding somewhere.

She opened the double doors and walked into the bedchamber. The covers were thrown back, and a book stood tented on the sheets. Lucy carefully picked the book up by the spine, turned it over, and gasped. The couple in the engraving was doing something with their mouths she was certain mouths weren't meant to do.

Disgusted, she set it on the table next to the bed and tried not to look at it while she stripped the sheets and made up the bed with clean ones. She glared at the horrid book and made a decision. She stood the book in the middle of the bed exactly how he'd left it. "I hope this shames you," she said under her breath.

Later that same afternoon

Harry's carriage rolled to a halt on Vigo Street. When he climbed out, he saw Barlow, his manservant, walking Bandit, Harry's new puppy. His old companion Brutus had died last year. His rooms had been a little too quiet for his taste, so he'd decided to get another collie.

Harry held out his hand for the leash. "I'll take him for his walk, Barlow."

Barlow lifted his brows as if a gentleman walking his dog

was some breach of etiquette. "I just returned from walking him, Your Grace."

Bandit pawed at Harry's trousers. Clearly the puppy hadn't gotten sufficient exercise. "I've been cooped up indoors with solicitors all day," Harry said. "I'll take him to the park."

Just then, a woman wearing an apron came out of one of the offices and walked away. Red tendrils had escaped her cap. Shock reverberated along Harry's spine. Was she the knife-wielding redhead he'd met on the street?

"Barlow, who is that woman?"

"I'm unsure, Your Grace," Barlow said. "A new maid, I believe."

Harry watched as she strode away.

"Do you wish me to make inquiries about her?" Barlow said. "I can speak to the housekeeper."

Distracted by the sway of her hips, he didn't reply immediately.

"Your Grace?" Barlow repeated. "I would be happy to inquire."

"No," Harry said. "That won't be necessary."

"Is there anything else, Your Grace?" Barlow said.

"No, thank you. That will be all."

By now, she'd disappeared from his sight. Something about her did not add up. She'd spoken in a cultured accent that misty night, but he remembered her worn glove. That reminded him of the words she'd spoken.

Sir, I assure you, I would not set foot on these mean streets if I had any other choice.

He'd thought to rescue a damsel in distress, but she'd lectured him about parading along the dark streets advertising his expensive clothing and jingling purse. At the time, he'd been rather bemused by her cautionary advice.

Clearly she'd fallen on hard times, but perhaps he was mistaken. It had been dark and from a distance he couldn't swear it was the same woman.

Bandit strained on his leash and barked at a passing groom. Harry dismissed the memory of the redhead and strode off with his impatient dog.

Lucy strolled along Piccadilly, where she stopped to buy an orange from a costermonger and put it in her pocket. Then she headed to Green Park, where she found a bench. A red squirrel darted up one of the oaks, scattering a flock of birds. There weren't many peaceful places in London where one could enjoy a breeze and relative solitude. On sunny days like this, she missed her former home in Wiltshire.

Her earliest memories involved helping her mother in the garden and chopping the vegetables for the savory stew her mama had made from mutton or hare. She missed helping her mother in the warm kitchen most of all. Lucy wanted to hold on to the happy memories of her mother, but the ache in her chest never quite went away.

Sometimes her mama had taken her to the village to look at the pretty bonnets, ribbons, and buttons at Mrs. White's shop. Once on her birthday, her mother had taken her there and bought her a pretty straw bonnet with a green ribbon. Mrs. White had been kind to her mother. Others in the village had treated her mother with suspicion, because her refined accent marked her as different—not one of the local villagers.

A barking dog interrupted her thoughts.

She shaded her hand over her bonnet brim and saw an exceptionally tall man running after a dog.

The puppy bounded over to her, sat, and panted. The attached leash meant he'd escaped. Lucy smiled. "What a cute puppy, you are."

As the man neared, she thought she might swallow her tongue. It was Sir Galahad. Her heart beat faster as she recalled threatening him with the knife. The fine hairs on her neck stiffened. He was the last person she wanted to encounter, but it was too late to escape unnoticed now.

He was breathing fast as he halted and put his hands on his thighs. "I beg your pardon, miss..." His words died. Then he arched his brows. He'd obviously recognized her.

For a moment, she was struck dumb by his brilliant blue eyes. That night, she'd not been able to see him clearly, but his eyes were rather deep set, and his brows were thick. While his nose was a trifle wide, it fit him. She'd seen plenty of foppish dandies strolling along Bond Street. He was not one of them. There was no padding in the shoulders of his green wool coat. In the light of day, she couldn't miss his big, muscular frame.

He doffed his hat and bowed, revealing a shock of dark hair. Then he regarded her with a slow smile. "So we meet again."

Her face grew as hot as a live coal. "I do beg your pardon."

His brows furrowed. "You mean for threatening me with a knife?"

Oh, this was mortifying. She'd been so sure she would never see him again. "The blade was for protection."

"So you said that night we met." His expression turned fierce. "A bit of advice. One strong chop on your arm from a tall man, and your blade would be on the ground, making you defenseless. If you mean to carry a knife, crouch and swipe. Like this."

He demonstrated the stance for her. "Don't try to stab

your assailant; you could get hurt. Your goal is to put enough distance between you and the attacker, and at the first opportunity run for your life."

She released her pent-up breath. "Yes, that makes a great deal of sense. Thank you for the advice."

He opened his mouth as if meaning to speak again, but the puppy wagged his tail and pawed her skirt.

"Bandit, no," he said in a sharp command.

The puppy ran to him. Sir Galahad squatted. "Bandit, you bad dog."

When the puppy licked his face, he grimaced. "Ugh, dog breath."

Lucy laughed. She couldn't help liking him and his funny puppy.

He grasped the dog's leash, rose, and regarded her with an amused expression. "I did try to teach him manners, but clearly he is a heathen." As if to prove his master correct, Bandit promptly urinated on a tree.

Sir Galahad shrugged. "There is your proof. I've had many dogs over the years, and all of them loved to water trees and roll in things best not mentioned in a lady's presence."

She ought to remain aloof, but he was rather charming. "What breed is he?"

"A collie. I had one for many years, but he died a few months ago."

Was she imagining a hint of melancholy in his expression?

"I missed having a companion, so I got another and now I regret it."

"Why?" she asked.

"Thus far, he has chewed a pair of leather slippers, wet the carpet, which of course I had to replace, and put more than a few tooth marks on the sofa legs."

"Oh dear," she said, laughing.

He sat next to her on the bench without so much as a by-your-leave. "I hope you don't mind if I join you." His blue eyes were full of mischief. "Did I forget to ask?"

"You are brazen, sir." But she couldn't help smiling.

He sniffed. "I smell an orange."

"Oh, it's in my apron pocket," she said, taking it out.

"Do you plan to eat it?"

For a moment she was mesmerized by his startlingly blue eyes, and something else. It was a familiar soap scent, but she couldn't place it. The moment suspended, and then her face heated. She'd been so taken with him she'd forgotten to answer. "Would you like to share with me?"

He regarded her from the corner of his eye. "I thought you'd never ask."

Oh dear. He was charm personified.

When he stripped off his gloves, she found herself examining his big hands. She should *not* be thinking about his hands.

He reached inside his coat and pulled out a penknife. Then he cut the bottom off and continued peeling with the knife in ever-widening circles. Afterward, he handed her the orange and rolled the peel tightly. "Hold out your palm."

She hesitated. "What are you about?"

"You'll see. Your palm, please."

Her heart beat a little faster as he gently set the peel in her hand. The sensitive skin of her palm tingled a little at the slight brush of his fingers. When she looked at him, his stunned expression mirrored her own reaction. She averted her eyes, but something had happened between them. She couldn't name it and had never experienced it before. All she knew was that there was tension surrounding them.

Still a bit off balance, she looked at the peel in wonder.

"You made a rose of it." Her words came out with a breathy quality. She was aware of something invisible between them—something she couldn't quite describe, but she was highly aware of how near he was to her.

When she met his gaze again, his lips parted just a little. The breeze stirred her skirts, and for some reason, she felt a little breathless. "Very clever of you." She set the rose in her apron and offered the orange to him. He plucked a slice and ate it. She took a slice as well. The tangy scent of orange enveloped them.

"Your fingers will be sticky," he said, handing her his handkerchief.

"Thank you." She marked the initials embroidered on it: HJN. Curiosity gripped her. There was something about him that was impossible to resist. She wanted to know more about him, but he was a stranger. She knew she shouldn't be here with him.

He looked directly into her eyes, as if he meant to pull her under his spell. "You positively light up when you smile."

"I imagine many women fall quickly for your charm, but let me assure you I am no easy conquest."

"Neither am I."

He startled a laugh out of her. Of course she recognized he was adept at disarming others with his wit and amiable manners. He was the sort of man who could easily beguile a woman. He was also a stranger, and she shouldn't trust him.

Lucy rose. "You will excuse me. I must go now."

He stood as well. "Don't leave. Bandit is a fine dog, but his conversation is rather limited." She was tempted to stay, but she'd already taken a risk with a man she knew nothing about.

"Do you have some objection to me?" he asked.

"I can neither object nor approve. I don't know you."

He looked around him. "It appears there is no one to perform the introductions. Shall we exchange the honors with one another?"

She mustn't let him turn her head, but of course he'd already managed it—all too easily. "I can't," she said.

"Come now, I don't bite and neither does Bandit."

Charm must flow in his veins.

Lucy realized it would be all too easy to fall under his charismatic spell, but she mustn't let that happen. She had to focus on earning wages and put aside what she could for a rainy day. There was no room for a beau in her life, especially one she knew nothing about.

"We could arrange to meet here another day," he said.

She wondered how many women he'd managed to captivate. "Sir, I'm not in the habit of forming acquaintances with strangers."

"Well, we're here. You can tell me a bit about yourself."

"I don't think that is wise."

"Why? You can't think I mean you harm after I rescued you—or rather your basket." His grin made him look a bit boyish, but his height and wide shoulders suggested he was thirty or perhaps a bit older.

"Any acquaintance between us is impossible," she said.

"There's no ring on your finger. You're not married, so there's no impediment."

"You are impertinent, sir," she said, her voice rising.

His smile could light up all of Vauxhall. "I don't mean to be. I just avoid flirting with other men's wives. Saves the trouble of pistols at dawn. I'm fond of my sleep, you see."

"Are you always so glib?"

"You must answer my question first."

She lifted her chin. "On the contrary, Sir Galahad. I don't have to answer you at all."

He closed the distance between them. He was so much taller that she imagined the top of her head barely reached his chin. When she met his gaze, she was momentarily spellbound by his blue eyes. Then, remembering herself, she stepped back.

"I was only jesting," he said, his voice rumbling.

"You are outrageous," she said, standing her ground.

"You're not the first to say so." His smile was hard to resist, but resist him she must.

"Truly, there is nothing to prevent us from becoming acquainted," he said.

"I'm certain we do not inhabit the same social sphere."

"Come now. Your manner of speaking tells me you are a gentleman's daughter."

She had no intention of enlightening him. "There are certain realities, sir. I must work, whereas you appear to lead a carefree life."

His smile faded. "My life is far from carefree. I have numerous responsibilities to my family and all those under my employ."

"So you are a successful man of business?"

"I have a number of ventures."

"Such as?"

"I don't wish to bore you. Shall we walk?"

She curtsied. "Good day, sir."

"Don't leave. Bandit will be disappointed."

The collie tilted his head upon hearing his name.

Temptation beckoned. Lucy hesitated. She'd liked matching wits with him, but no respectable lady met a gentleman alone. In this case, she'd been bantering with a stranger. While Sir Galahad did not seem dangerous in the least, she thought of her friends' warnings. It wasn't wise to take chances. If anything were to happen to her, Grandmama would suffer. But she had no intention of allowing the handsome stranger into her life. "Excuse me. I really must leave."

He wanted to know who she was and why she'd chosen to work as a maid when she was clearly educated. Then he remembered her worn glove and figured it wasn't a choice. After she turned her back, his frustration climbed, but he meant to challenge her. "I didn't take you for a coward," he said, raising his voice.

She whipped around with an indignant expression in her green eyes. "I beg your pardon?"

He wagered she would not ignore his next comment. "It's quite obvious you are intimidated."

She drew in a sharp breath and marched up to him. "I'm not intimidated, but I could never be a part your world any more than you could be a part of mine. For all I know you're a criminal."

He laughed. "That's rich."

"Your clothing and demeanor are a clear indication that you are a wealthy gentleman. My apron shows I am clearly a servant. We cannot associate with one another. It just isn't done."

He fisted his hands on his hips. "So we are not permitted to exchange pleasantries in the park because of my clothing?"

"Do not be absurd. It is a matter of class, as you well know."

"Are we so different?" he said.

She let out a long sigh. "Do not be obtuse. No one would ever accept me in your social circle. Furthermore, I'm not in the habit of meeting strange men alone—not purposely at any rate."

"I beg your pardon. Of course you cannot meet me here

alone. Bring a family member with you as a chaperone. You can't argue with that, now, can you?"

"As a matter of fact, I can."

"Oh, come now. I didn't mean to frighten you."

She drew in a sharp breath. "Do I look frightened?"

His brows arched. "You're not?"

"Of course not."

"Very well, bring your chaperone and meet me here at three o'clock on Sunday afternoon. It will all be done up properly."

Her green eyes narrowed. "You did that on purpose, but I am not falling for your ruse."

"Rats," he said.

He was too clever. "Why do you not choose a girl from amongst your own class?"

"You intrigued me from the moment we met."

She scoffed. "I fear you are in for disappointment, but I will discuss it with my grandmother," she said. "If I'm not here by three sharp, you will know she counseled against it."

He closed the slight distance between them.

She squared her shoulders and lifted her chin.

Her plump lips tempted him. She was breathing a bit fast. But if he rushed his fences, she would likely bolt. For now, he would tease and charm her. "Be honest," he said. "You're not planning to meet me, are you?"

"Why do you persist?" she asked.

Because you intrigue me in a way no other woman has ever done. "Why did you dodge my question?"

"You just evaded my question," she said.

He chuckled. "I asked first, but the reason is because there is mystery surrounding you."

She spread her arms in a graceful manner. "I am who I appear to be. There is nothing to be gained by meeting here again."

He knew differently. "You also happen to be very pretty."

She scoffed. "I wager you say that to any passably attractive girl you meet. Sorry, Sir Galahad, I'm not falling for that old trick."

"I'll see you here on Sunday at three sharp," he said.

"*If* my grandmother approves."

"What is your name?" he asked.

"I'll tell you on Sunday, provided my grandmother agrees."

When she turned her back and marched off, he smiled. She would show on Sunday, because she wanted to prove she wasn't intimidated.

Chapter Four

She strode off, muttering under her breath. Frivolous man. The part that irritated her was that he'd managed to charm her. She wagered he had a pocketful of compliments that he used to entice unwary women. He probably hooked a new female every day with his winning smile and witty repartee.

She'd let him lure her with his orange trick. Worst of all, she'd been so impressed she'd kept the peeled rose. Lucy released a disgusted sigh. She'd thought she was insusceptible to flirtation, and she had tried to resist, but he'd managed to beguile her. It aggrieved her that she'd let him.

Why should she even care? She meant to put him out of her thoughts permanently. That proved more difficult than she'd expected. She kept remembering his witticisms and the way her palm had tingled when he'd set the orange peel rose in her hand.

Once again, she attempted to shove thoughts of him out of her head as she bought a mutton pie from Mrs. Hoffman, her favorite pie seller. As she walked home, she knew Sir Galahad had purposely goaded her so she would turn up at the park on Sunday.

Oh, she really must forget him, but she couldn't. He'd expressed curiosity about her, but he wasn't the only one. There was no doubt in her mind that he'd purposely omitted details about his business and his interest in her. That alone should check her. Evelyn and Mary had told her more than a few cautionary tales about men bent on seduction. She couldn't afford to get involved with a man she knew nothing about.

Yet, he'd been the one to suggest she bring a chaperone to the park. A man bent on seduction would hardly suggest such a thing. If she were honest with herself, she would admit she'd liked him...more than a little. But even if Grandmama approved of meeting him, Lucy intended to keep her feet firmly on the ground.

When she arrived home, she kissed her grandmother's cheek and set the pie on the table. "How was your day?"

Grandmama smiled. "Well, I finished knitting a woolen scarf for you."

She gasped. "Oh, it is beautiful. The white wool is so soft." Lucy pressed it to her cheek. "Thank you so much. You are talented, Grandmama."

"I hope it turned out well and that it will keep you warm when you must walk to your dancing lessons."

"I'm sure it will." She wished there was some miracle that could restore Grandmama's sight, but there was no use in wishing for the impossible.

Grandmama sniffed. "I smell oranges."

"I ate one at the park." She took the orange peel rose out of her apron. It was only part of the truth, but she would tell her grandmother the rest after supper.

"Did the juice drip on you?"

"No." Why was she hesitating to tell Grandmama? Because she knew her grandmother would not approve of her speaking to a strange man.

"Lucy, I know something is in the wind. I can always hear it in your voice."

She should have known she could not—and probably should not—conceal things from her grandmother. "I met a gentleman at the park today."

Her grandmother's long pause seemed to go on for ages. "I see. Have you met him before?"

Heaven above, she could not make herself tell her grandmother she'd threatened him with a knife. "His puppy ran over to me today. We struck up a conversation. I know I shouldn't have spoken to a stranger, but it just happened. He conducted himself as a gentleman."

"How marvelous," Grandmama said, clasping her hands. "What a lucky happenstance. You must invite him to call."

"Grandmama," she said, shocked at her grandmother's response.

"What is his name?" Grandmama asked.

Oh dear. She'd better concoct a story quickly. "Obviously there was no one he could apply to for an introduction to me," Lucy said. "I jested that his name must be Sir Galahad." She was stretching the truth, but what else could she do?

"Oh, that will be a lovely story to share with your children," Grandmama said.

Lucy burst out laughing. "Grandmama, I do not even know his name, and you already have wedding bells and babies ringing in your ears."

"Did you make plans to meet him again?"

Lucy was tempted to take the easy way out and pretend Sir Galahad had not requested that she bring a chaperone to meet him at the park. But her temper ignited as she recalled his words. *I never took you for a coward.* How dare he judge her? She was no coward. After her father's death, she'd hired men to pack every possession they owned into a wagon and traveled from Wiltshire to London on her own with very little money. What would a wealthy gentleman know about bravery? Precious little, she'd wager.

"Lucy, what are you thinking?"

"At the moment, I'm thinking you are entirely too wily." She sighed. "Very well, I know you will hound me until I tell you. He wanted to meet at the park on Sunday and suggested I bring along a chaperone. I said I would have to consult you. Of course, we won't go."

"We most certainly will," Grandmama said. "How very gentlemanly of him to suggest you must be chaperoned. I should very much like to meet your young man."

"He is not my young man," she said. She decided to change the subject. "I'll pump water into the kettle for our tea."

After supper, Lucy settled on the sofa with Grandmama and opened *Pride and Prejudice.* "I'm going to miss the story after I return it to the circulating library tomorrow."

"Ah, but a good book will stay with you always," Grandmama said, pulling the woolen blanket she'd knitted over them both for extra warmth. "Now read the last chapter to me."

When Lucy reached the end of the last page, she sighed.

"Oh, what a wonderful love story," Grandmama said. "So full of trials and troubles. Those are the best ones."

Lucy laughed. "In real life it would not be much fun, but Mr. Darcy and Elizabeth certainly kept me on edge. Well, I didn't like Darcy at first, especially when he slighted Lizzy."

"Ah, but he secretly admired her," Grandmama said. "In the end, he proved himself a wonderful hero."

Lucy ran her finger down the page. She didn't want to close the book yet, because she wanted to hold on to the lovely ending. "I wish I could read a book like this one every single night."

Grandmama smiled. "Ah, stories entertain us, but we must also live our real lives."

"Tell me the story of how you met Grandpapa."

"I've told you that story many times."

"I never tire of hearing it," Lucy said.

"Very well," she said. "My mother sent me to the hen-house to gather eggs. I was afraid of the chickens. I didn't want them to peck me. It was a silly fear, but nonetheless I was terrified when I tried to get the eggs."

Lucy grinned. "Go on."

"Well, I managed to grab some eggs and put them in my apron, but I heard footsteps and nearly landed on a chicken's foot. I stepped sideways, crushed an egg, and slipped. Your Grandpapa literally caught me."

"I love that story," Lucy said. "I miss Grandpapa."

"So do I, dear, but we have wonderful memories of him, and we have each other, but you've grown quiet again. I suspect you're indecisive about going to the park on Sunday."

Lucy sighed. "I don't think we should meet Sir Galahad."

"Why not?" Grandmama said. "He suggested you bring a chaperone. Clearly his intentions are proper and good."

"You don't understand. His clothing and manners proclaim him a wealthy man, something he did not deny. From what little he told me, he is a well-off businessman."

"You would condemn him for being successful?" Grandmama said in an astounded tone.

"No, but we cannot be true friends. The strict social distinctions prevent it."

"Well, if he were an aristocrat, I would agree with you," Grandmama said. "Their society is a closed one, meant for those who have titles, great properties, and ancient bloodlines. "But I see no barrier to an acquaintance."

Her father had not owned land and had never been considered a gentleman. Even if he had been a gentleman, he would not have deserved the term, but she would not voice the words for fear of oversetting her grandmother. Grandmama knew the truth. Her father had taken to drinking strong spirits after Lucy's mother had died. All he'd cared about was his own woes and his daily bottle.

"I suspect he realizes you are no ordinary working girl," Grandmama continued. "He must have noticed your manner of speaking and your demeanor."

Lucy sighed. "I think he is a frivolous flirt."

Grandmama smiled. "Ah, now I begin to understand."

"Understand what?" Lucy said.

"He obviously likes you, does he not?"

"I think he is the sort of man who likes to trifle with ladies. Why else would he bother with a girl like me?"

"Well, I may not be able to see, but I know you're a pretty young woman. I imagine that was the initial reason for his interest."

"He wanted some diversion. That is all."

"How do you know?"

Lucy released a loud sigh. "He is exceptionally handsome, and he probably never wants for feminine admiration."

Grandmama laughed. "Describe him to me."

"He's very tall and appears to be quite fit. His blue eyes are his most distinctive feature. Well, that and his smile."

"Ah, he has a nice smile," Grandmama said.

"Yes, he grins a lot as if he knows a good joke," Lucy

said. "I think he's a flippant sort of fellow, to be honest. No doubt the ladies probably flirt with him."

"But not you?" Grandmama said with a smile.

"I'm sure he could entice the birds off trees if he wished."

"Ah, so he is a charmer, like your grandfather, God rest his soul. I tried to resist him, but in the end he won me over."

"Well, I can safely say this gentleman will never woo or win me."

"Do not be too hasty," Grandmama said in a teasing voice. "I think you should pretend that you are not interested."

"No pretense is needed because I'm not interested in him at all."

Grandmama laughed. "I think you admire him more than you wish to admit."

"I do not," she said. "He's too persistent...and...too handsome."

Grandmama chortled. "Oh, so now you prefer plain gentlemen?"

"I prefer no man," Lucy said, laughing. "He may have a fair countenance, but I'm convinced he is the most flirtatious man I've ever met."

"So you prefer a gentleman who is very serious and sober," Grandmama said.

"Aargh," Lucy said, throwing up her hands. "I surrender."

"Excellent," Grandmama said. "That will make my matchmaking efforts easier."

"You would not dare," Lucy said. "Swear to me you will not try your hand at matchmaking."

Grandmama laughed. "On one condition."

"Dare I ask what condition?"

"You will allow yourself to enjoy your gentleman's company on Sunday."

"I will try, but I cannot promise."

"That is all I ask," Grandmama said.

Lucy snorted. "I know you too well to believe that is *all* you will ask."

"Tell me the truth," Grandmama said. "Do you disapprove of him?"

"I cannot approve or disapprove because I don't know him. Why am I even worrying about this? No doubt he will forget all about meeting us."

"I have the opposite opinion," Grandmama said, "but there is only one way to find out. "Let us meet him at the park on Sunday. I will take his measure and give you my honest opinion. Besides, I would dearly love to visit the park now that the weather is warmer."

Grandmama's wistful tone tugged at Lucy's heart. It had been a fortnight since she'd taken her grandmother on an outing. "If the weather is fine, we will take advantage of the sunshine at the park."

That night

Harry had been restless and knew the reason for it. Much as he liked his dog, Bandit wasn't the companion he needed.

While he still met his friends at the club periodically, it wasn't the same. The days where the three of them drank brandy and smoked cheroots until the wee hours of the morning were over. Granted, he had a number of acquaintances at White's. He decided to join Castelle and Fitzhugh for a brandy. The three sat smoking cheroots.

"You're looking rather glum," Castelle said.

Fitzhugh poured himself another brandy, splashing more than a little on the table. He squinted in the glass. "I think I should visit my mistress."

"Not a good idea. You're three sheets to the wind, old boy," Castelle said.

Fitzhugh hiccupped. "Found her at Mrs. Fleur's salon. Pretty piece." He tried to stand and stumbled.

"Bloody hell," Harry said. "He's completely foxed."

"I'll make sure he gets to his rooms," Castelle said.

After they left, it occurred to Harry that he might set up a mistress. Erotic engravings and self-pleasure weren't nearly as satisfying as bedding a woman. In the past, he'd never had the wherewithal to keep a mistress, but he would certainly enjoy regular bedsport—with the right woman. All he had to do was find a mistress who would suit him. Several gentlemen, including Fitzhugh, had mentioned Mrs. Fleur's salon. Apparently, she was known for attracting the most elegant and beautiful women of the demimonde to her salon. He decided to call at Mrs. Fleur's establishment in hopes of finding a beautiful, witty mistress who had a passionate nature.

Half an hour later, he entered the ornate salon. Everywhere he looked he saw women perched on gentlemen's laps. A footman topped up brandy glasses as he circulated the room. One woman with short curls plucked the strings of a harp while half a dozen men gazed at her rouged nipples showing through her diaphanous bodice. Any moment, Harry expected their tongues to fall out of their mouths.

Mrs. Fleur rose to greet him with excessive enthusiasm. She had painted brows and wore gold serpent bracelets on her upper arms. When she smiled, her face powder accentuated the lines bracketing her mouth. "Your Grace, I am delighted you called. London has not been the same during your long absence. I declare I pined for your presence."

A year ago, when he had pockets to let, Mrs. Fleur had not been so effusive in her welcome, and he'd struck out.

Apparently his recently acquired wealth and title made him far more desirable. Well, his money at any rate.

"I am so honored you have chosen to attend my humble salon this evening," she said.

The gilded chandelier, marble side tables, and Ionic columns hardly counted as humble, but he kept that opinion to himself. Evidently Mrs. Fleur's salon was flourishing.

The proprietress took his arm and strolled through the room. "Ah, here are my favorite girls. Your Grace, may I introduce you to Mrs. Roseberg and Mrs. Larkspur?"

Harry bowed. "I'm pleased to meet you." He'd forgotten Mrs. Fleur insisted that all of her *girls* use flowery names, a departure from the usual habit of using a former protector's surname. He supposed it was for the best. His mother would be horrified if she ever learned a trollop was using "Mrs. Norcliffe" as a nom de guerre.

Mrs. Fleur clasped her hands. "Mrs. Roseberg and Mrs. Larkspur will be happy to entertain you this evening. I hope they are pleasing to the eye?"

"Absolutely," he said. The two lightskirts had evidently dispensed with their shifts and petticoats. He needed no imagination to see every plump curve of breast, thigh, and buttock through their sheer gowns. His blood definitely heated.

"I wish to ready a private room for you," Mrs. Fleur said.

"A private room would suite me." He envisioned hours of sweaty bedsport, and he'd brought along a French letter for protection.

"Only the best for Your Grace," Mrs. Fleur said. "A footman will direct you shortly."

Having never been invited to use the private room before, Harry wondered exactly how much the entertainment would cost for the evening. Granted, he had deep pockets, but his objective was to find a mistress. He had no intention of setting up two of them. He figured after sampling both he could discreetly discuss terms with Mrs. Fleur. If he was satisfied, he would direct his attorney to draw up a contract.

Bedding two strumpets held a certain appeal. Harry had no doubt he would be up for both occasions. Of course, he'd have to return another night to make the proposition. First, he had to ascertain whether either one of them met his expectations.

"I'd heard you were tall and handsome," Mrs. Larkspur said, taking his arm and brushing her breast against him. "You have surpassed all that I imagined."

"On a five-minute acquaintance?" he said.

"Your reputation precedes you," Mrs. Larkspur amended.

Mrs. Roseberg clutched his other arm. She regarded him with a coquettish expression and squeezed his biceps. "Your Grace is the embodiment of elegance and athleticism."

"No other gentleman here is as handsome as Your Grace," Mrs. Larkspur added.

They were pouring the compliments on rather thick. He imagined they would be pleased by any man—for the right price.

Mrs. Larkspur tittered. "I do hope you're feeling frisky."

The word made him think of Bandit—and not in a complimentary manner. A dull ache started in his temples. He wasn't altogether enraptured by the two trollops, but he would give them a chance to prove their talents.

A footman approached and bade them to follow him to the private chamber that featured a red sofa and a large bed with red velvet drapes. A covered table held two bottles of Madeira, lobster patties, pickled eels, and sweetmeats.

Mrs. Larkspur led him to the sofa while Mrs. Roseberg made up a plate of the delicacies and tried to feed them to him.

Harry held up his hand. "No thank you. A glass of wine is sufficient, but please partake of the food."

The footman poured the wine and handed round glasses. "Will there be anything else, Your Grace?"

"No, thank you." He gave the footman a sixpence.

Meanwhile, Mrs. Larkspur and Mrs. Roseberg piled food on the small plates and ate with the gusto of farmhands. Harry was accustomed to ladies eating like birds, so he was rather astonished.

Mrs. Larkspur swallowed a bite and smiled at him. "Mrs. Fleur encourages our appetites. She says the gentlemen like a bit of flesh on our bones."

"I see." They did appear well fed, but thus far, he'd felt no stirrings of desire for either one of them.

Mrs. Roseberg rummaged in her reticule, brought out a bottle, and liberally dabbed her neck.

When Mrs. Larkspur walked over to the bed, she patted it. "Will you join me?"

"Of course," he said, wondering what exactly Mrs. Larkspur had in mind. She slid her hand over his thigh. "My, my, I can feel those muscles beneath your trousers."

When she reached for a button on his falls, he caught her hand. "I prefer a leisurely seduction—an appetizer, so to speak."

"Oh, I think there are a few pickled eels left."

He pulled a face. "It was a figure of speech."

Mrs. Larkspur looked confused. "You wish to make a speech, Your Grace?"

He shook his head. "Never mind." Her simplemindedness did not appeal to him at all.

Mrs. Roseberg sat on the other side of him and walked her fingers up his waistcoat. He managed a smile, but her cheap perfume made his eyes water. Ye gods, had she bathed in it?

Mrs. Roseberg leaned closer. A cloud of perfume assaulted him. His nose itched like the devil. When she attempted to kiss his mouth, Harry hastily grabbed his handkerchief and sneezed...repeatedly.

"I beg your pardon," he said in a nasally voice.

"I'm sure you will recover quickly," Mrs. Larkspur said, breathing into his ear.

Harry sneezed three times. "S-sorry," he said.

At that moment, Mrs. Fleur entered. Her determined smile faded quickly. "Your Grace, are you unwell?"

He wanted nothing to do with this pair and seized the excuse. "I fear so," he managed, sneezing again. "Perhaps... a-another...achoo!"

"Girls, you may entertain other gentlemen," Mrs. Fleur said. "His Grace is unwell."

When the two women left, Mrs. Fleur regarded him regretfully. "I am sorry for your sudden affliction."

Harry blew his nose. He wasn't sorry at all.

Mrs. Fleur sighed. "This is most indelicate, but there is the matter of the bill. You do understand, I hope."

He put away his handkerchief. When he examined the bill, his jaw dropped. "A guinea?" he said.

"I must keep up my high standards. One does not serve substandard refreshments," Mrs. Fleur said. "You know how difficult it is to find and retain a talented chef."

Her talented chef probably did double duty as a groom and escorted gents who got belligerent after one too many bottles. Harry had no intention of arguing over the matter. He rummaged in his purse and produced the guinea.

"I do hope Your Grace will return when you're recovered," Mrs. Fleur said. "I'm sure one of my other girls could take care of your needs. Here is a list of services," she said.

Out of curiosity, he perused the offerings and barely managed to keep a straight face. The "services" included Mama's boy, the Thrashing, and the Bath.

"We've recently added the Vicar," Mrs. Fleur said.

His mouth twitched. "The Vicar?"

"Some gentlemen prefer a sermon…afterward."

The devil! "How…interesting."

"You are always welcome, Your Grace. If none of these meet your needs, I'm sure we can accommodate your preferences…"

"I'll keep that in mind," he said. *Good Lord.*

Harry barely made it out of Mrs. Fleur's salon before guffawing.

After his carriage rolled into the yard at the Albany, Harry stepped out. The cold breeze lifted the capes on his greatcoat. He climbed the stairs and rummaged in his inner coat pocket for his key since he didn't wish to wake Barlow, who served as butler, valet, and dog walker.

Harry unlocked the door, and naturally Bandit started barking. Fortunately, Barlow had left a candle branch burning so he could see to hang his hat and greatcoat. Then he squatted to pet the puppy. "Hush now. The neighbors will complain if you keep up this racket." Then he carried the candle branch to his desk. Bandit followed, his nails clicking on the floor until he reached the carpet. Harry frowned at the stacks of papers. Someone had straightened the piles, but that wasn't part of Barlow's duties. Then Harry remembered that he'd added maid services to his bill, which was probably for the best, considering the amount of dog hair everywhere.

Bandit followed him to his bedchamber. He set the candle branch aside, took off his coat, and sniffed it. It smelled of cheap perfume and cheroots. Harry wasn't altogether certain Barlow could get the stench out. No doubt Barlow would take a disgust of Harry's stinky coat.

He stripped off his clothes, turned to the bed, and blinked. The book of erotic engravings stood like the letter *A* in the middle of the turned down bed. Obviously, the maid had put the book exactly where he'd left it. "Good Lord," he muttered, and laughed at the thought of what the maid must have seen.

Harry picked it up and saw the engraving of a couple engaged in *soixante-neuf*. Last night, he'd pleasured himself while looking at the engravings. Tonight, he set the book aside as a different image floated in his mind. He imagined a petite and saucy young woman sweeping her long red locks over his naked body. He definitely did not need the book to pleasure himself tonight.

The next morning

Buckley collected a purse from Old Bess on Grub Street after delivering a fresh-faced farm girl named Nelly to the well-known bawd. Bess promised Nelly a job in service.

Buckley chortled, thinking of her horror when she found out what kind of service she'd be providing—on her back.

He limped along the pavement, cursing his aching ankle. It still hadn't healed, and he blamed that backstabbing bitch Lucy Longmore. He hated her more than ever, but he'd yet to catch her off guard. It was just a matter of time before he nabbed her.

Buckley broke out in a cold sweat. He needed laudanum badly. Now that he was in funds again, he could buy a bottle from the apothecary. He scratched his itchy face and licked his lips. His mouth was bone dry, and he was feeling anxious.

He limped to the apothecary's shop. The bell rang as he entered, and the apothecary scowled at him. "Your credit's no good here."

Buckley pushed his coins across the counter. "I assume my money is."

When the apothecary set the bottle on the counter, Buckley took a swig right away.

The apothecary rubbed his chin. "What pocket did you pick?"

"Not a one. I sold a girl to Old Bess."

The apothecary licked his fat lips. "Why let the bawd take her cut when you did the work? I'll put a mattress in the back room," he said, indicating with his thumb. "Mayhap we can do business."

"What's in it for me?" Buckley said.

"Two bottles of laudanum each night and a quarter of the takings."

"Half," Buckley said.

"Deal, but you have to bring the girls," the apothecary said.

Buckley departed and limped along the street. His head felt a little light. He got confused and couldn't remember where he was. Three times he got lost. Finally, he met up with a man selling gin and fortified himself. He felt better now that his mouth wasn't so dry.

The gin seller gave him directions to Grosvenor Square. Buckley saw all the carriages on the pavement and pulled out the filthy piece of paper with the address. He limped slowly along. He'd no idea of the time when he finally dragged himself up on the step. Then he mopped his forehead and rang the bell. The butler scowled at him and took his card. "Wait here," the butler said, and walked upstairs.

Buckley looked around the foyer for valuables to purloin and put a silver candlesnuffer inside his coat. He reckoned he could pawn it after he finished the dance lesson.

Mrs. Norcliffe's drawing room

There was not a single empty seat in Mrs. Norcliffe's drawing room, but that was not at all unusual.

"Dear friends," Mrs. Norcliffe said, clasping her hands, "I am so happy to see everyone's interest in the dancing instruction. We will begin shortly. Meanwhile, please make yourselves comfortable."

Mrs. Norcliffe had decided to hire a dance master in order to ensure that her niece Mina and Lord Everleigh were as prepared as possible for the dancing competition. She would not trust in fate when it came to the competition at Almack's. Mrs. Norcliffe had great plans for Mina and Everleigh, as she was determined that they would win the dance competition. What could be more romantic for the happy couple? Surely a wedding would follow.

Mrs. Norcliffe glanced at the mantel clock and pursed her lips. The dance master Lady Blenborough had recommended should have arrived fifteen minutes ago. She did not appreciate his tardiness and meant to rebuke him after the dancing practice.

"Aunt, did Harry reply to your missive?" Mina asked.

Mrs. Norcliffe scowled. "He claimed he had important business in parliament."

"Oh, Aunt," Mina said, smiling. "Let us give Harry the benefit of the doubt."

"Humph," Mrs. Norcliffe said. Her son was not as dutiful as she wished. In truth, Harry had a stubborn streak that she found vastly irritating. Nevertheless, she would deal with him later. For now, she pasted on her society smile and made the rounds of the drawing room.

When Mrs. Norcliffe noticed Lady Greystoke and Lady Blenborough whispering to each other, she knew it was time to intervene. Those two cats were known for raking others over the coals, and in this case, Mrs. Norcliffe feared she was the one getting burned. "Ladies, I do apologize for the slight delay. I hope you are both well and excited about the opening of Almack's next week."

"Indeed," Lady Greystoke said, fanning her face. "One hears fantastical rumors. The scandal sheets report all manner of stories."

"Oh? I've been so busy I didn't notice," Mrs. Norcliffe said, which of course was a complete fabrication. In truth, ever since the patronesses had agreed to her plan for a dancing competition at Almack's, she had sent anonymous messages to the tawdry scandal sheets, hinting at a spectacular event occurring at Almack's in a sennight.

Mrs. Norcliffe had her own ambitions. Viscount Everleigh had formed an attachment to dear Mina. Best of all, Mrs. Norcliffe, who knew all the best gossip, had learned that Viscount Everleigh had twenty thousand a year. As far as Mrs. Norcliffe was concerned, that *almost* sealed the deal. The only event that would make it perfect was if Mina and Everleigh won the Almack's dancing competition. Mrs. Norcliffe meant to do everything in her power to make it happen. But first she must ensure Mina and Everleigh practiced until they knew every step of all the most popular dances.

Of course, she wished to see Harry dancing in the competition, but Mrs. Norcliffe had no illusions where her son was concerned. She would likely have to trick him into dancing—that is, if he didn't take refuge in the gaming rooms before she could present Miss Hortense Osterham to him.

When the clock chimed the half hour, Lady Blenborough frowned. "Where is Mr. Buckley? It is not like him to be so tardy."

"Do you suppose something has happened to him?" Lady Greystoke said.

"I've no idea," Lady Blenborough said. "Unfortunately, I must beg your leave, Mrs. Norcliffe. I have an appointment with the modiste."

"I understand," Mrs. Norcliffe said, and continued circulating among her guests. She was growing increasingly vexed at the delay. If the dance master did not arrive soon, her guests would leave in droves. Dear heaven, she prided herself on having the most illustrious drawing room in London. Now because of a tardy dance master she stood to lose face among the other patronesses. *Quelle horreur!*

At long last, Gibson returned to the drawing room to report Mr. Buckley had arrived.

"Please show him up," Mrs. Norcliffe said.

"Yes, madame." Gibson hesitated. "Madame, you might wish to keep the guests at some distance from Mr. Buckley."

Mrs. Norcliffe frowned. "Why ever for?"

"To be honest, madame, there is a strong odor about his person."

Mrs. Norcliffe released an exasperated sigh. Now she had a dilemma. Either she lied and said the dance master failed to show or she took a chance that Mr. Buckley would remain at a sufficient distance. Since her guests had waited for some time, Mrs. Norcliffe decided to allow Mr. Buckley to teach. "Gibson, do instruct Mr. Buckley to keep his distance from the dancers."

"Yes, madame."

When Gibson returned, he said, "Madame, Mr. Buckley."

Buckley bowed. "Madame, I am at your service."

Mrs. Norcliffe was aghast. Dear Lord, the dance master was dressed in a slovenly manner, his eyes were bloodshot, and he was limping. "Sir, you are very late," Mrs. Norcliffe said.

Mr. Buckley bowed again and mopped his forehead with a dingy handkerchief. "My apologies, madame. I took a wrong turn," he said, licking his lips.

"Sir, it appears you are injured," Mrs. Norcliffe said. "How can you dance?"

"Do not concern yourself, madame. It is only the rheumatism. I have a tonic for it."

Mrs. Norcliffe was horrorstruck at his appearance, and he smelled strongly of perspiration. Since others were watching, she thought it best to proceed. "I wish for you to instruct the quadrille," she said to Mr. Buckley.

"Yes, madame, I will gladly instruct the dancers."

"Very well," she said. The man's pasty complexion, greasy hair, and copious sweating did not bode well at all.

"If the gentlemen will lead in the ladies, we will start," Buckley said, mopping his forehead again. "Everyone bow to your partners."

"Mr. Buckley, you must give them time to select partners," Mrs. Norcliffe said.

"Yes, of course, how remiss of me. I was just overly eager."

While Mina urged her sisters and the few gentlemen present to participate, Mrs. Norcliffe watched Buckley with narrowed eyes.

Mina joined Mrs. Norcliffe. "He drank from an apothecary bottle."

"He said it was a tonic for his rheumatism," Mrs.

Norcliffe said, "but I cannot fathom how he can instruct dance when he is limping."

"Perhaps he will demonstrate the steps slowly," Mina said.

Mrs. Norcliffe scoffed. "Perhaps he will grow wings on his feet, too. Go join the dancers, Mina."

Castelle, Everleigh, and Justin Davenport agreed to partner with Mina, Helena, and Amelia.

"Now," Mr. Buckley said. "Please bow to your partners. We will dance the quadrille."

The dancers took their places and watched him with puzzlement as he wiped his forehead again.

"The first couple should proceed up the middle," Buckley said.

Mina frowned. "I beg your pardon, Mr. Buckley. Did you mean down the middle?"

"Oh yes, of course," he said, licking his lips.

Mina and Everleigh led down the middle and turned forward.

"The first couple will cast off on the sidclines," Buckley said.

Everleigh frowned. "Mr. Buckley, my partner and I have already done so."

"Oh, how remiss of me. I meant second place. Now the opposite couple will lead up the middle and cast off."

Mrs. Norcliffe covered her mouth in horror. The dancers were instructing the dance master. Now she was suspicious that Lady Blenborough had purposely recommended this buffoon to embarrass her. They were old rivals from years ago during their debuts. Mrs. Norcliffe ought to have known better than to trust Lady Blenborough.

"Next, the gentlemen clasp hands," Mr. Buckley said, "while the ladies dance on the outer circle."

Mrs. Norcliffe was astounded. "Sir, I believe the ladies dance in the inner circle. Perhaps you might demonstrate the steps first."

"Oh yes, just a moment," he said, stumbling sideways. "Forgive me. I just need my tonic—for the rheumatism."

By now everyone was whispering. Clearly, the dance master was incompetent. "Mr. Buckley," Mrs. Norcliffe said, "you are sweating profusely even though you have not exerted yourself. Are you ill, sir?"

"Not at all, madame."

"Everyone, please take your ease," Mrs. Norcliffe said. "I will return directly. Mr. Buckley, please come with me."

When she led him out of the drawing room, she shut the door, only to find Buckley lurching sideways. Mrs. Norcliffe caught his arm to keep him from falling. The smell of strong spirits assaulted her. "Sir, you are foxed," she said in shocked tones. No wonder he'd made an ass out of himself.

"Oh no, it is only the tonic for my rheumatism," Mr. Buckley said.

"You will leave immediately, sir."

"What about my wages?" he said in a belligerent tone.

Mrs. Norcliffe did not like his disrespectful tone or the ugly expression on his face. "Sir, if you wish to be paid, you must be competent, and you are not. You arrived late and you were unable to instruct in a professional manner. You will receive no compensation because you did nothing to earn it," Mrs. Norcliffe said. "Now, please leave."

Fortunately, Gibson noticed something was awry and summoned two burly footmen to evict Mr. Buckley. The horrid man started protesting. "I have been robbed. I demand wages for my work," he squawked.

Mrs. Norcliffe's nostrils flared. "Sir, you will cease shouting immediately."

"I have been swindled," he yelled. "Let me go, you cretins!"

Meanwhile, several maids, the housekeeper, and the cook were watching the spectacle unfold. Gibson had to remind the servants to return to their duties.

The footmen managed to drag Buckley out of the great hall. Mrs. Norcliffe winced as Buckley's shouts echoed from the foyer. No doubt the guests in the drawing room heard every word as the footmen threw him out of the house. What a catastrophe.

Mina exited the drawing room. "Aunt, I heard shouting. Is he gone?"

"Yes. I cannot believe Lady Blenborough recommended him. I smelled spirits on his breath. This is a disaster," Mrs. Norcliffe said.

After all of the guests departed, Gibson approached Mrs. Norcliffe. "Madame, I regret to report that a silver candle snuffer is missing from the foyer table. "I'm very sorry, my lady. Evidently Mr. Buckley stole it when I went to the drawing room to report his arrival."

"Thank you, Gibson. We are well rid of Mr. Buckley," Mrs. Norcliffe said.

Chapter Five

Sunday afternoon

$\mathcal{L}$ucy was glad the sun was shining as she led her grandmother outside. It was a rather long walk from her lodgings, but once they reached Regents Street, she stopped. "Now we wait here," she said.

Grandmama frowned as the clatter of hooves approached. "For what?"

"I'm hailing a hackney."

Her grandmother gasped. "But it will cost a fortune."

"I saved enough coin for our outing." She'd not spent any of the money that Mr. Wilson had given her, because she'd wanted to use it for a special occasion. She really didn't think Sir Galahad would show today, but she knew the outing would please Grandmama.

When the hackney slowed, Lucy inquired about the fare and helped her grandmother inside. After it rolled away,

Grandmama murmured, "This is too extravagant. And I hear shouts and voices everywhere."

"Even on Sunday London is always teeming with people, horses, and carriages," Lucy said. "Ah, there's the park now."

Lucy paid the driver and led her grandmother along the grassy path. "There is a pool of water farther down the path," she said.

Grandmama lifted her face. "I'm glad you insisted. The breeze is invigorating."

"There's a stone bench," Lucy said. "Let us sit there."

"When your young man arrives, you must not coddle me. I'm quite content to sit and enjoy the sun," Grandmama said.

"I'm glad we came," Lucy said. Only a few people were walking about. Notably, Sir Galahad was not among them. She ought to be glad, but for some reason she felt a little disappointed, which was ridiculous.

The sun speared through the branches of an oak tree. Birds chirped in the nearby trees. "Starlings," Grandmama said with a smile.

"How can you tell?"

"Their calls are distinctive, almost like a whistle. I've always loved springtime."

"Tell me more about my grandfather," Lucy said.

"I told you the story about the chickens recently," Grandmama said.

"Yes, but I wish to hear the story about the country assembly."

"Very well. Your grandfather was a handsome young man and quite debonair. I thought him rather conceited when I first saw him at an assembly. He asked me to dance, and that first night, he told me that he meant to marry me. He was entirely too sure of himself, so I told him that he was the last man on earth I would wed. From that moment on, he was determined to win me over, but I was not about to capitulate so easily. One night after I'd danced with two other gentlemen, I saw your grandfather watching me. He did not dance with any other ladies. Instead he paced back and forth. When the assembly ended, he watched me with the most miserable expression.

"The next afternoon, he called and said he could not live without me. He got down on his knee and begged me to put him out of his misery. Well, I was always practical like you, and I told him I wasn't going to shoot him."

Lucy laughed.

"At first he was startled, and then he guffawed. We had many happy years together, and I always managed to make him laugh."

"You were happy," Lucy said.

"We had our share of disagreements, but they never lasted long. We were very much in love." Grandmama found her hand and squeezed it. "You will find love, Lucy."

She couldn't even let herself think about love and marriage. Her focus was far more practical. She wanted security, a safe place to live, and a nest egg to see her through difficult times. Today, however, was for her grandmother, and Lucy meant to see that she enjoyed the afternoon.

Lucy vowed to bring her grandmother to the park more often. Now that she had two steady jobs, she should be able to save enough coin to return again soon. "Sunday is my favorite day, because I get to spend it with you," she said.

"I confess I am enjoying the warm sun," Grandmama said. "I can smell the scent of grass. Describe the park to me."

"It's appropriately named," Lucy said. "The grass is very green. Red squirrels are scampering up the oak and beech trees, but the park isn't overly crowded today." She shaded her eyes above the brim of her bonnet. "There is a young couple walking."

Grandmama turned her face up. "I do love spring. It reminds me of when your grandfather and I used to hold your hands and walk along the grounds. I can still see you in my mind with your red braids. In the autumn, you liked to dive into the piles of leaves."

Lucy sighed. "I remember." Those were happier times before her mother's health declined.

"Thank you for bringing me," Grandmama said. "I'm enjoying the outing very much."

"I hope next time, you will meet my friends." *If Madame Delanger will allow them a day off.*

A man's shout startled Lucy. She turned to see Sir Galahad, reining in Bandit with the leash. "He has a puppy, Grandmama."

"Oh, I hear barking."

When Sir Galahad neared, Lucy gave him a warning look, for her grandmother's affliction must be obvious to him.

He seemed unruffled. "Bandit, your manners are atrocious. Shake hands with the lady."

Lucy held out her hand, and Bandit put his paw in it. "Oh, how clever he is."

"What sort of dog is he?" Grandmama asked.

"A collie. He's only a puppy, but I'm attempting to train him." He paused and bowed. "I do beg your pardon," he said, his eyes dancing with merriment. "Will you introduce me to your grandmother?"

Lucy rose and helped her grandmother. "Sir, may I introduce my grandmother, Mrs. Longmore?"

He doffed his hat and swept a dark lock off his forehead. "I'm pleased to make your acquaintance. Granfield at your service." When he straightened his tall frame and replaced his hat, he grinned at Lucy, as if they were sharing a secret joke.

"Sir, it is a pleasure to meet you," Grandmama said. "I understand you met my granddaughter at the park recently."

"Indeed I did meet her here, all thanks to my puppy Bandit. I hope you will excuse him, I'm trying to train him with mixed results."

"Certainly, we will make allowances for young Bandit, will we not, Lucy?"

Her face heated. Now he knew her Christian name. "Of course, Grandmama."

"Bandit may need lessons in manners, but you are certainly courteous and gentlemanly," Grandmama said.

"Thank you, Mrs. Longmore." He winked at Lucy. "May I say your granddaughter is exceptionally pretty?"

"Of course you may," Mrs. Longmore said.

Lucy's face grew warm.

"I told her when we first met," he said, "but we engaged in a debate about intimidation."

Lucy gave him a speaking look. "He jests, Grandmama."

Naturally his shoulders shook with laughter.

"Well, that's a rather odd topic," Grandmama said, frowning.

When Lucy shot him another warning look, the rogue winked at her. "I think it was a draw. What say you, Miss Longmore?"

"I say I won."

Mrs. Longmore smiled. "That sounds promising—for Lucy."

He met Lucy's gaze. "There is something I must tell you after we take a turn in the park," he whispered; then, in a normal tone of voice, he said, "Now, have you and your grandmother been to the queen's basin?"

"No, we have not," Lucy said.

"Mrs. Longmore, may I be permitted to escort you and your granddaughter?" he asked.

"I'm sure Lucy would be delighted," Grandmama said. "I will wait here so I won't be in the way."

"Please take my arm, Mrs. Longmore," he said. "Bandit and I would be delighted to escort both of you."

"You are very gentlemanly, sir," Grandmama said.

"My mother will be glad to hear it."

Lucy drew in her breath. If he had only focused on her, she could have resisted him, but his consideration for her grandmother won her over completely. She'd judged him to be little more than a flirt when they'd met at the park, but now she saw a very different side of him. He was everything a gentleman ought to be.

"I'm glad for the company and the fair weather," he said, slowing his steps to match Grandmama's slower pace. Then he stole a heated look at Lucy. He was mischievous and a charmer, but Lucy could not deny he was amiable and chivalrous, too. He likely had his faults, but he'd impressed her today.

Bandit kept straining on the leash. "He thinks he can escape," Mr. Granfield said.

"Puppies have a great deal of energy," Grandmama said.

"Bandit plays hard and then flops over to sleep immediately. Last night I made the mistake of letting him lie at the foot of the bed. He woke me this morning by licking my cheek. I'm afraid my yelp frightened him. It took a while to calm him."

Lucy smiled at him. "How did you calm him?"

"I held the little fellow and then petted him. Bandit likes to sit near my desk and chew his bone."

Bandit barked.

"He heard his name," Lucy said. "He's very smart."

"What are you trying to tell us, Bandit?" Mr. Granfield said. He gazed at Lucy. "Bandit is probably hoping to find a pretty lady dog in the park—that or a red squirrel to chase."

Lucy laughed. "Which does he prefer?"

"Both if he can manage it," he said.

"You are very amusing, sir," Grandmama said.

"Ah, we're nearing the water," he said.

"I hear it," Grandmama said with wonder in her voice.

Lucy swore she would bring her grandmother again as soon as possible.

"Do you know the history of the Queen's Walk?" he asked her grandmother.

"No," Grandmama said.

"It is an interesting one. Charles the Second wanted to walk all the way from Hyde Park to St. James without leaving his royal property. He commissioned a brick wall to be built around the area and called it upper St. James Park. He also built an ice house, and his illustrious guests were served cold drinks."

"Oh, how lavish," Grandmama said. "What do you suppose they drank?"

"I've no idea," he said. "Perhaps lemonade."

Lucy glanced at him sideways. "Or something stronger," she said.

"Perhaps he served champagne. Have you ever drunk champagne, Miss Longmore?"

"No, I have not," she said. When her mother still lived, they would drink homemade elderberry wine at Christmas dinner.

"Ah, here we are," he said. "Now, your granddaughter has no doubt observed there are no flowers."

Lucy looked around. "Oh my goodness. I didn't notice."

Probably because he'd managed to charm her, but today she didn't mind. He'd been amiable and considerate of her grandmother. She could find no fault with him today. In truth, she felt ebullient and lighthearted in his presence.

"No flowers at all?" Grandmama said.

"That's correct," he said. When he winked at Lucy, she blushed again.

"According to legend," he said, "Charles's queen learned that he had picked flowers for another lady. The queen must have been livid, because she ordered all the flowers removed, and no flowers have been planted since then."

"I approve of the queen's decision," Grandmama said with a sniff.

He laughed. "I can't be one hundred percent certain the story is true, but I've never seen flowers here."

"What about the basin?" Grandmama said. "Is there a story about it?"

"Yes, there is," he said. "In the previous century, Queen Caroline had the reservoir built to provide water to St. James's Palace."

"A very practical decision," Grandmama said. "It was truly gallant of you to take us on this tour."

"I enjoyed your company," he said, smiling at Lucy as Bandit sniffed the grass.

"Thank you," Lucy said. Whatever doubts she'd held about him had vanished today.

He was witty, attentive, and his manners were pleasing. She'd misjudged him the first time they had met. Now she secretly hoped that something might blossom between them. Could it be possible that he might be the one? Oh, she knew it was entirely too early to even think of a future with him, but she hoped very much that he would wish to see her again.

"Mrs. Longmore, will you allow me to escort you and your granddaughter in my carriage?"

"That's very kind of you, thank you," Grandmama said.

"Excellent. Miss Longmore, I take it you have no objection?"

She could not object when her grandmother had accepted. "No, of course not." But she was uneasy.

He looked at Lucy. "What is the address?"

She lifted her chin. "Soho, south of Tottenham Road."

His expression froze for the briefest moment. Then, just as quickly, he recovered.

Clearly he knew their lodgings were not far from the notorious Seven Dials, an impoverished and dangerous area near Covent Gardens. "Actually, we will take a hackney, as our lodgings are out of your way."

"A gentleman always honors his promise," he said, "and it is no trouble."

Yes, but you undoubtedly regret your hasty invitation to such a rough locale.

After he helped them up the carriage steps, he picked up his dog. "Miss Longmore, would you mind watching Bandit for me?"

"Not at all," she said, setting the puppy on her lap.

"Where did he go?" Grandmama said.

"I imagine he went to give his driver directions." He'd been so kind today, but when she'd given him her address, she'd seen the momentary look of shock on his face. Gentleman that he was he'd tried to hide it.

"I like him very much," Grandmama said. "He is a charmer like your late grandfather."

"We know very little about him. Why would he persist in making our acquaintance when we could never be part of his social set?"

"Mr. Granfield is likely part of the landed gentry. So he is not so elevated to prevent an acquaintance...or perhaps more," Grandmama said with a smile.

"He is wealthy," Lucy said.

"Why in heaven's name would you complain?" Grandmama said. "You ought to snap him up before someone else does."

"Grandmama!" she said, shocked.

Her grandmother laughed. "I was teasing. In all seriousness, you should judge him by his character, not by his wealth or lack thereof."

"No one is without faults," Lucy said.

"I wonder why you are so determined to dislike him," Grandmama said.

"I don't dislike him—quite the opposite. It's just that our circumstances are miles apart."

"Why not give him a chance?" Grandmama said. "I truly believe he cares for you. Why else would he spend the entire afternoon with us?"

Because I fear he will wound me. "I keep asking myself why he isn't courting proper ladies who have large marriage portions."

"Perhaps he wants love, not riches, in a wife," Grandmama said.

Part of her wanted to believe that he was the gentleman of her dreams. She wanted to experience the exhilarating feelings again when he teased her and smiled at her. But if she allowed hope to blossom, she could find herself heartbroken. "I'm sure he was only being courteous today."

"Keep this in mind. No gentleman spends that much time with a lady if he's not interested," Grandmama said. "If it were me, I wouldn't let him get away."

"Shhh," Lucy said. "I hear footsteps on the pavement."

When she looked out the window, the light was just beginning to fade a bit.

When Granfield returned, he sat with his back to the horses. He took Bandit from Lucy and set him on the seat beside him. Then he knocked his cane on the roof. When the carriage rolled into motion, he stroked the puppy's fur with his gloved hand, drawing Lucy's attention. She couldn't help noticing the muscles in his tight trousers. Her face grew warm. What was wrong with her? She didn't want him to catch her ogling him.

"Are you comfortable, Mrs. Longmore?" he asked.

"Indeed I am," Grandmama said. "You have a well-sprung carriage."

He set his hat aside. "I enjoyed your excellent company today."

"You've been very kind, sir," Lucy said.

"It was a fine day," he said. "One of the best I've had in quite some time. Thank you for meeting me at the park."

"Do you live with your family?" Grandmama asked.

"No, ma'am. My three cousins, all girls, live with my mother."

Lucy returned her attention to him but kept silent.

"You made no mention of your father," Grandmama said.

"He died a long time ago."

"I'm sorry to hear it. Why do you not live with your mother?" Grandmama said.

"Grandmama, we should not pry."

"It's not a deep, dark secret," he said. "My mother is strong-willed, and I find we get along better when we are not in each other's pockets."

"Ah," Grandmama said. "Then you must be equally as strong-willed as your mother."

He laughed. "Only when warranted, I assure you."

"Are your cousins very young?" Grandmama asked.

"No, they range in age from nineteen to twenty-one."

"None have married?" Grandmama asked.

"Not yet," he said. "My mother is determined to find them all suitable husbands, but there's no rush."

Lucy figured his mother was equally anxious to pair him with a genteel young lady with a generous marriage portion. Then, remembering Grandmama's rebuke about cynicism, she vowed to work on her attitude. There was nothing to be gained by viewing life with a negative perspective.

"Your mother must care very much for them," Grandmama said.

"Yes, she took my cousins in when their parents died in a carriage accident."

"Oh, I'm sorry," Grandmama said.

"It happened long ago," he said. "My mother is fond of the girls and so am I."

"I don't doubt it," Grandmama said. "Have you always lived in London?"

"Only part of the year—during the spring season."

"Grandmama," Lucy said. "We should not press him."

"I take no offense," he said.

"Do you have business in London?" Grandmama asked.

"Yes, I do," he said.

"What sort of business is it?" Grandmama said.

Lucy's cheeks grew hot. "Really, we should not inquire about his business."

He laughed. "Mrs. Longmore, have you and your granddaughter always lived in London?"

"Oh no. We hail from Westbury in the county of Wiltshire."

"Ah, you must have visited Stonehenge."

"No, we have not had the privilege," Lucy said. "To be

honest, the only journey we have ever undertaken was the one that led us to London. This is our home now."

"I particularly thank you for the history of the park. It was quite diverting," Grandmama said. "From all appearances, you're a prosperous gentleman."

"Many consider me lucky."

"You needn't be modest," Lucy said. "Doubtless you have worked hard for your success."

There was no hint of amusement in his expression when he met her gaze. "Three months ago, my uncle passed, and I inherited the property. His untimely death was completely unexpected. He was like a father to me."

Lucy's heart sank. "I'm sorry for your loss."

"Thank you," he said. "Far too many people offer congratulations on the inheritance."

He took a deep breath as if steeling himself.

Earlier, he'd said he had something to tell her. "Is something wrong?" Lucy said.

"No, but I inherited more than property," he said. "I inherited my uncle's ducal title."

The fine hairs at the nape of Lucy's neck stiffened. She covered her mouth.

His eyes registered disappointment.

Surely he'd known his words would stun them. She set her hand in her lap. "Why did you not tell us sooner?" The moment the words popped out, she realized her tone held an accusation, but he ought to have told them when he'd requested an introduction to her grandmother.

His expression turned cold. "I made it clear I had something to tell you after we toured the park."

Lucy curled her nails into her palms. "You concealed an important fact about yourself." How dare he make himself agreeable and then announce he held one of the highest titles in the land as if it were an afterthought. "You misled us."

"I did not," he said. "My title is Granfield. Everything I have said to you is the absolute truth."

"Surely you knew your words would shock us," she said. "You deliberately waited to reveal your identity until now."

"I alerted you from the beginning. Now you know."

Lucy was no stranger to disappointment, but something hot rushed up to her temples, making them ache. "You ought to have revealed it much sooner."

"Be fair, Miss Longmore. Does it really matter that I waited to tell you after our walk in the park?"

"While I appreciate your attentiveness today, our circumstances are so different we might as well live on different sides of the Atlantic. You knew that when you met us at the park today. You made sure you had all the advantage, and then you gave insufficient reason for hiding an essential fact about yourself."

Grandmama squeezed Lucy's hand, a warning signal. "Your Grace, why did you wait?"

"I had no intention of concealing my identity. That is the reason I alerted your granddaughter that there was something I must tell her. Then we conversed, and I wanted to give you a tour of Green Park and its history. From the beginning, I intended to tell you and I have. That is the end of it."

"Your Grace, you had a responsibility to introduce yourself using your title when we first met today," Grandmama said. "I am willing to make a onetime exception, but you know that if you expect honesty from others, you must also be forthcoming."

Lucy was not so forgiving. He'd seemed to be everything in a man she'd ever wanted, but she ought to have known he would prove to be too good to be true.

"Since you are sharing your honest feelings, I will share mine," Lucy said. "I thought you were a gentleman in the truest sense of the word, but it seems you are a deceiver. You are the sort of man who trifles with women for your own amusement. Let me be clear. I am not amused."

He narrowed his eyes. "This is your entire opinion of me based upon a short acquaintance?"

She lifted her chin. "Yes, it is." She despised deception. Her father had lied multiple times about selling their valuables so that he could buy spirits. She'd loathed him for it, and she would have nothing to do with a deceiver.

It would not hurt nearly as much if he had not been so attentive to her grandmother and her. She'd known he was a flirt, but he apparently was like a chameleon, able to make himself amiable and charming for his own purposes.

While the carriage rocked along, Lucy turned her face to the window, because she did not want to look at him. There were long shadows from the buildings and numerous conveyances cluttering the streets. The ride seemed to take forever. The whole time, she wished that she'd never met him, because he'd made her believe that he was an honorable man. A man who might be the one. A man who might come to love, protect, and cherish her. But there was no chance of any sort of relationship, not when he was a duke.

She thought of that day in the park when she'd told him they couldn't become acquaintances because of their class differences. He'd purposely withheld the information about his title that day as well. That only made her wonder how many women had fallen under his spell.

Now she felt like a fool. She'd known by the cut of his clothing that he was no ordinary businessman, but she'd fallen for his charms far too easily. Never again. He'd concealed important facts about himself and waited far too long to reveal he held one of the highest titles in the kingdom. She despised him for his duplicity, and she most certainly never wanted to see him again.

The carriage rolled to a halt at long last. Granfield handed his dog to the young groom. Then he aided Grandmama on the steps.

When he assisted Lucy, she tried to avoid direct eye contact with him, but he regarded her with narrowed eyes. He evidently wanted her to know that he was angry.

"Excuse me, Your Grace," she said curtly.

"I thought you were different," he said under his breath, "but I was wrong."

She huffed. "Do *not* pretend you do not know what stands between us. You live in an entirely different world than I do, but you chose to seek me out even when I protested that the class differences between us made any acquaintance impossible."

"You're no different than all the others who judge me only by my title."

"What?" she said.

"You're blinded by the title like everyone else, and you don't even bother to look beneath the surface."

He turned and strode back to his carriage. She took her grandmother's arm and led her upstairs. When they reached the landing, Lucy heard the clopping of the horse's hooves. She refused to look back, but his words troubled her long after he'd left.

Chapter Six

Lucy had not slept well last night after visiting the park. She'd kept thinking about the duke and everything that had transpired yesterday. All last night, she'd veered from feeling he'd duped them to wondering if she'd judged him too harshly. She'd awakened with a dull ache in her temples.

When she'd cleaned the last set at the Albany, she was relieved. She bought a mutton pie for dinner and hurried home. All she wanted was a cup of tea, a hot meal, and sleep. She climbed the stairs and knocked on the door. The familiar sound of Grandmama's stick and the lifting of the latch made her sigh with relief. It had been a long day.

"There you are at last," Grandmama said. "Mrs. Green is here. We've been waiting on pins and needles for you."

"Why?"

"Come and see," Mrs. Green said.

Lucy walked into the small room and blinked. There was a beautiful vase of red roses on the table. "Oh my goodness. They're beautiful."

"The petals are so soft," Grandmama said. "A man delivered them earlier today. There is a letter as well."

"All day I wished I knew how to read," Mrs. Green said. "We had to wait for you to arrive home."

"Oh, I'm sorry you had to wait," Lucy said, "but I fear the letter and the roses were misdirected."

"Do open the letter," Grandmama said. "We are anxious to discover who sent it."

Lucy set the pie on the table and broke the seal on the letter. She glanced down the page and saw the signature. "It is from Granfield," she said.

"I knew it," Grandmama said.

"Please read it to us," Mrs. Green said.

She sighed. All day she'd thought of him with mixed emotions. All day she'd felt alternately guilty and then angry. Mostly she'd felt conflicted and unsure of herself. She feared that she'd judged him harshly because he was so far out of her reach.

"Lucy," Grandmama said. "If you prefer not to share the letter, we will understand."

"I would end up telling you about it anyway, and it would be cruel of me to make you both wait any longer. I'll read aloud:

" *'Dear Miss Longmore,*

After much reflection and little sleep last night, I have concluded that my conduct yesterday was neither gentlemanly nor fair to you and your grandmother. Yesterday, I allowed my pride to keep me from admitting the truth. Deep down I knew it was wrong to mislead you for even an hour. When I casually mentioned my title, you were understandably shocked. Had I told you

*from the beginning and explained the overwhelming
changes that have occurred since my uncle's death,
you might have understood. No doubt you would find
my presence abhorrent were I to call on you. If by
some chance you are willing to allow me to deliver a
sincere apology, I would greatly appreciate the opportunity. I will send a servant in the morning to ascertain
your answer.*

> *Yours, etc.
> Granfield*

P.S. I hope you enjoy the roses.' "

Lucy carefully folded the letter.

"Will you allow him to apologize?" Grandmama said.

"I don't know," Lucy said. She'd been so disappointed, and the wound was still fresh.

"Perhaps I should leave you both to your discussion," Mrs. Green said.

"No, Mrs. Green. I think I could use more than one objective opinion," Lucy said.

"Well, I don't know that I'm much help," Mrs. Green said. "I'm so impressed with the roses I'd probably advise you to forgive and forget everything. But I know it's not that simple."

"Lucy, you will need to make a decision tonight. His servant will call in the morning for your answer while you're teaching dance to Mrs. Vernon's girls," Grandmama said.

"What should I do, Grandmama?" Lucy asked.

"Listen to your own heart, dearest."

Lucy sighed. "If I had slept with a clear conscience last night, I could easily reject his apology, but my conscience was not clear at all."

"I'd better go home and leave you to your discussion," Mrs. Green said again. "I will call on you tomorrow, Mrs. Longmore."

"Thank you, Mrs. Green," Grandmama said.

Lucy walked with Mrs. Green to the door.

"Good luck, dear," Mrs. Green said.

After she left, Lucy closed the door and secured the latch. "I'll pump water for our tea."

"Thank you, dear," Grandmama said.

Lucy filled the kettle and set it on the hob. Then she put the teapot on the table along with the plates and cutlery. She sliced the pie, though she had little appetite.

"Tell me exactly what is on your mind," Grandmama said.

"I keep remembering what he said last evening."

"What did he say?"

"He said, 'I thought you were different, but I was wrong. You're no different than all the others who judge me only by my title.'"

"Then it is solely because he is an aristocrat?" Grandmama said.

"Yes. No. I don't know. I've never been so confused. He should have told us immediately, but truthfully, I would have been shocked regardless of when he told us. That's the part I'm having trouble reconciling."

"Lucy, he was amiable, considerate, and charming. Yes, he made a mistake, but he took responsibility. Surely you will allow him the relief of an apology. I truly believe his heart is in the right place."

"Yet something still troubles me," she said.

"What is it, dear?"

"That day at the park, I let myself believe that he might be the one and that tender feelings might develop. I knew I was spinning castles in the clouds. Then he revealed he was a duke, and I realized he was completely and utterly unobtainable for a girl like me."

"You should not say that," Grandmama said. "You are a remarkable young woman."

"Grandmama, you know what I mean."

Grandmama sighed. "What will your answer be?"

"Tell the servant I will receive him, if for no other reason than to discover why he misled us."

Mrs. Norcliffe had spent the following week calling upon her friends and asking for recommendations for an accomplished dance master. Unfortunately, she'd heard numerous tales of drunkards, opium eaters, flirts, and in some cases thieves. She'd begun to think there wasn't a decent dance master in all of London.

She called on young Mrs. Vernon, who had two sweet daughters. The girls were applying themselves to their embroidery.

"Thank you for receiving me," Mrs. Norcliffe said. "I must say it is good to see your daughters working so industriously on their embroidery."

"They are still learning," Mrs. Vernon said. "Anne, Marie, you may be excused."

"Yes, Mama," they said in unison.

Mrs. Norcliffe noticed the elder girl took her sister's hand. "It appears your girls are well behaved and on their way to being accomplished young ladies."

"Thank you," Mrs. Vernon said. "May I offer you a dish of tea?"

"No thank you," Mrs. Norcliffe said.

"I was sorry to miss your at-home last week," Mrs. Vernon said. "The girls had colds, so I stayed home with them."

"It was probably just as well. On Lady Blenborough's endorsement, I hired a dance master who frankly was inebriated and possibly under the effects of opium. He kept drinking from an apothecary bottle and was none too steady on his feet. Obviously, his instruction is out of the question. So I have been asking all of my friends for a recommendation."

"Oh, dear God," Mrs. Vernon said. "Was it Mr. Buckley?"

"Yes, it was. Do you know the man?"

"Unfortunately, yes. I hired him, not knowing his bad character. He did not bestir himself to lift a finger. His assistant did all of the instructing. Then he insisted upon speaking to me as if we were equals. He bragged about his connections to families I've never heard of before. The worst part came when he leaned closer to me. He reeked of spirits. I dismissed him immediately without pay."

"What about the assistant?" Mrs. Norcliffe said. "Is he capable?"

"Miss Longmore is very talented. She is wonderful with my girls. I must say she is patient and encourages them when they falter. I'm very pleased with her instruction."

Mrs. Norcliffe arched her brows. "The dance instructor is a woman?"

"Yes, I know it is unusual, but I am impressed with her. It's too bad you weren't here earlier. You might have met her. At any rate, my girls adore her. It is also a relief that she is pleasant and speaks in an educated manner. I suspect her family has fallen on hard times, and she is teaching dance in order to help them."

Mrs. Norcliffe set her hand over her heart. "Mrs. Vernon, do you suppose Miss Longmore would consent to instruct adults in my drawing room?"

"I imagine she would welcome the opportunity, if she is available."

"Do you have a means of contacting her? I would very much like to have her instruct in my drawing room on Tuesday next."

"I will send a servant round to her lodgings. I must warn you, I've already recommended her to several of my friends. I'm unsure about her availability, but I will inquire for you."

"Thank you," Mrs. Norcliffe said. "I am obliged."

Mrs. Norcliffe's spirits had risen substantially after calling on Mrs. Vernon. She was relieved that her nieces would have at least one practice session prior to the opening of Almack's in a sennight. She would ask the other patronesses to help her spread the word to ensure her drawing room was a great squeeze during the practice session.

Mrs. Norcliffe was more than a little concerned about the gossip over that drunken dance master. She knew it must have been bandied about in every drawing room in London. It was crucial for her to succeed with the new dance master. Of course, there was the unusual fact that the dance master was a woman, but Mrs. Vernon was trustworthy and without guile—unlike many others.

Mrs. Norcliffe knew she carried enough influence to sway the opinions of other ladies of the ton. Over the years, she'd befriended all of the right ladies and gentlemen and made sure her drawing room was the most popular in all of London. If she sanctioned a female dance master, others would think it fashionable.

The next evening

Lucy was anxious that everything should be spotless and neat.

She set out the teapot along with the cups, saucers, and spoons on the square table in the room that served as a parlor and dining room. She'd filled a kettle with water to set on the hob. The fire would provide light and warmth when the sun set.

A floorboard squeaked as she walked to the window. The light was just beginning to fade. Then she turned to Grandmama. "Do you think he has changed his mind?"

"No, I do not," Grandmama said. "You are entirely too restless. Come help me darn the stockings."

"Grandmama, I will not darn stockings in his presence."

"For pity's sake," Grandmama said. "You can put it in the sewing basket when he arrives."

She sat on the sofa and immediately popped up. "I'll add water to the roses."

Grandmama released a long sigh. "You are suffering from vexation."

"I can't just sit and do nothing." Lucy added a bit of water to the roses, smoothed the cover over the table, and set the vase in the center. Then she walked to the window again.

"The shadows are longer now," Lucy said.

"You must be at the window again. Do you intend to advertise how eager you are for his presence?" Grandmama said.

"I'm only eager to have done with him," she said. "Oh dear, his carriage arrived. My nerves are on edge."

"He is the one obliged to apologize. You need only accept it."

Footsteps clipped outside their lodgings. A knock sounded.

Lucy pinched her cheeks, moved the bolt, and opened the door.

He stood there with his hat in his hand.

"Please, come in," Lucy said. Why was she a bundle of nerves? He was the one at fault.

He bowed. "Thank you for receiving me."

Lucy took his hat and set it on the rosewood chest.

Grandmama rose. "Your Grace, will you join us for tea?"

"You are kind, but I do not wish to disturb you overly long."

"Please, be seated," Grandmama said.

He pulled out a chair for Grandmama and then for Lucy.

"I'll put the kettle on the hob," Lucy said.

His footsteps clipped on the wooden floor behind her. "The fire is burning a bit low," he said. "May I offer my assistance?"

"Certainly," she said, stepping back.

He took the poker and raked the coals. "It shouldn't take long for the water to boil now."

They returned to the table, and once again, he pulled out the chair for her.

When the kettle shrieked, Lucy retrieved it and poured water in the teapot. While they waited for the tea to steep, she said, "Why did you wait so long to tell us about your title?"

"I realized if I revealed my identity right away, you would probably be shocked. I was caught between confessing immediately or waiting until afterward. I chose afterward because I wanted you to know me for who I am rather than the ducal trappings."

"You are uncomfortable with the title?" Grandmama said in a dubious tone.

"I am proud of all that the title stands for, both the present and the future. Havenwood means a great deal to me, perhaps even more so now that my uncle is gone. But since inheriting, I've been besieged by sycophants and greedy matchmaking mamas. I can't walk into my club without a group of insincere toadeaters surrounding me. A year ago, none of these people acknowledged my existence.

"I never set out to deceive you, but I did a very poor job of enlightening you about my title. I made a grievous mistake. In hindsight, I ought to have told you immediately. If I had told you my feelings about the changes in my life as I've just described them, I could have avoided disgracing myself in your eyes. I beg your forgiveness, though I do not deserve it."

Lucy sighed. "You are not alone in making a mistake. I asked myself if I would have judged you as harshly if you had been part of the gentry rather than a duke. I realized that I was too severe because you are an aristocrat and that isn't fair to you. After much soul-searching, I realized I would have been shocked to learn you are a duke, regardless of when you had told us. You were very kind to my grandmother and me that day. I'm sorry for cutting up at you."

"You had every right to be angry," he said.

"Shall we take our tea to the sofa where the light is better?" Lucy said.

After they sat on the sofa, he raked the coals and joined them afterward.

"How are your mother and cousins?" Mrs. Longmore asked.

"They are all quite well. I recently dined with them on the occasion of my thirty-first birthday."

"I hope you had a nice celebration," Lucy said.

"Indeed, I received a gift from my mother. A silver saver for my manservant to bring my mail to me."

Lucy noticed mischief lurking in his eyes. "I suspect there is more to this story."

"You would be correct," Granfield said. "As you might

have guessed, I lack all toplofty ducal traits, much to my mother's distress. However, I did not wish to disappoint her, so I thanked her profusely for the saver. About this time, I noticed that my faithful companion Bandit was slobbering over his bones on the new carpet. Since he had damaged one carpet already, I decided Bandit needed a receptacle for his bones. I cast my eye about and what did I see?"

Lucy laughed. "The silver saver?"

"You are correct," he said.

"You gave it to your dog?" Mrs. Longmore said in an astounded voice.

"Oh yes. My valet Barlow, who is typically quite stoic, actually winced. For him this is akin to an attack of the vapors."

Grandmama's lips twitched. "I marked you as a charmer and now I must add rogue as well."

"I rather hoped to elicit a chuckle from Barlow," he said, "but thus far, I have failed in my endeavors to make the man laugh. Never fear. I am quite determined to elicit a chuckle from him."

"You are awful," Lucy said, smiling.

"You will not be surprised to learn I was especially mischievous as a boy. My friend Colin and I spent every summer at Havenwood. We bathed in mud, tried to ride Uncle Hugh's pigs, and stole biscuits from the kitchen. My uncle Hugh taught us to fish and ride, but when we were naughty, he made us muck out the pigpens. There are reasons I don't eat bacon."

Lucy's shoulders shook with laughter. She set her dish of tea aside. "Did you meet your friend Colin at school?"

"Yes, at Eton when I was eight years old. We're practically brothers. I recently learned he will be a father soon. It's hard to believe."

Grandmama sat up with a start. "Oh my, I beg your pardon. I must have dozed off."

Granfield rose. "I do beg your pardon," he said. "I did not mean to overstay my welcome. If you wish, I will bank the fire for you."

"Thank you," Grandmama said. "You need not rush. If you will excuse me, I will retire now. Lucy, be sure to secure the bolt when Granfield departs."

"I will, Grandmama."

He took off his coat and went to tend the fire. His wide shoulders needed no padding. When he rose and dusted his hands, she noted his superior height once again. In his waistcoat and shirtsleeves, she could discern the way his waist tapered.

He joined her on the sofa and laid his arm across the top of it. "Tired?" he asked.

"No." She was too aware of him. In the shadowy room, she could not see his bright blue eyes, but the soft sound of his breathing mingled with hers. The tension between them crackled all around her. A long moment suspended. Her senses were heightened, and her breasts felt heavier for some odd reason. She discerned the scent of wintergreen soap and something else—something masculine and irresistible. Something unique to him.

He leaned closer, and she could feel the whisper of his breath on her lips. "From the first moment we met, I could not get you out of my head."

His words made her feel giddy, but she held back, because she was still a little wary. "I am undoubtedly the first woman to threaten you with a knife."

He grinned. "Indeed you are. Now that you are unarmed, perhaps we could be friends."

"We will shake on it," she said, offering her hand.

He took her hand and turned her wrist, palm up. He looked up at her beneath his dark lashes, and then he kissed the tender underside of her wrist. When he touched his tongue to the pulse point, her breath shuddered out of her. She thought she might melt from the heat in his seductive gaze.

"I'd better go," he said. There was a knowing look in his eyes, as if he was aware of exactly how he'd affected her.

When she inhaled on a shaky breath, he helped her to rise. She walked with him to the door as if she were enveloped in a fog.

He halted and gazed into her eyes. Then he drew her in his arms and kissed her gently on the lips. His mouth moved over hers and his hand slipped down the curve of her spine. Heat and longing surged inside her. He wrapped his arms around her, and she could feel the hard, unyielding muscles of his arms, chest, and thighs as he pressed her against him.

"Forgive me in advance," he said.

"For what?" she whispered.

He kissed her gently once more, and then he drew his tongue along the seam of her mouth. Her lips parted and then his tongue was in her mouth, tasting her while his hands slid down her spine and to her bottom. He pulled her flush against him, and she could feel his hard body. She was breathing faster and everything inside of her was on fire for him. God help her, she wanted his hands all over her.

He broke the kiss, and she was aware that his breathing had quickened as well.

When he released her, he said, "Good night, sweet Lucy."

Her limbs trembled a little as he strode out into the night, leaving her to wonder if he knew it was her first kiss.

Chapter Seven

Wednesday afternoon, one week later

$\mathcal{H}$arry spent much of the day in dull meetings with his solicitor. When he arrived home, he intended to deal with more paperwork, but he discovered four missives from his mother.

He opened the first one and sighed.

Dearest son,

As you are undoubtedly aware Almack's opens for the season tonight. Bring your new carriage at precisely nine o'clock. I expect you to be sober and do not dally.

> *Yours etc.*
> *Mrs. Norcliffe*

He snorted. "That's unlikely," he muttered, and opened the next one.

Harry, I await your answer. Please be prompt in your reply.

> *Yours, etc.*
> *Mrs. Norcliffe*

Mrs. Norcliffe was well known for her imperious demands, but he'd long ago learned it was best to ignore her when she got a bee in her bonnet. Harry set it aside and broke the seal on the last one.

Harry, I am not amused! Send your answer now!

> *Yours, etc.*
> *Mrs. Norcliffe*

No one, including his meddling mother, ordered him about.

Harry took out a sheet of paper and dipped his pen in the inkwell.

Dear Mama,

I regret that I am unable to escort you to Almack's this evening, as I have a previous engagement. Do enjoy the festivities. May I recommend the watered down lemonade, stale bread, and dry cake?

> *Your disobedient son*
> *Granfield*

Harry sanded the missive and sealed it with wax. Then he rang the bell. Barlow covered a yawn and trudged into the parlor.

"Barlow, please deliver this missive to Mrs. Norcliffe's town house in Grosvenor Square."

"Yes, Your Grace. Shall I wait for a reply?"

"Certainly not. It will only result in additional trips to my mother's abode."

"Yes, Your Grace."

Harry decided his mother needed a lesson in patience. "Barlow, do take the scenic route to Grosvenor Square. Be sure to admire the budding leaves and wildflowers."

Barlow, to his credit, did not blink an eye. "Yes, Your Grace."

"After you deliver the message, you may take an impromptu holiday. You will have earned it from all the exercise today."

"Thank you, Your Grace. I shall take advantage of your offer."

Harry considered taking Bandit to the park in hopes of seeing Lucy, but he really needed to attend to his correspondence. He supposed he'd better hire a secretary soon, as he'd begun to fall behind on the paperwork. That meant he'd have to interview candidates, and when would he find time for that?

Bandit's nails clicked on the marble. He trotted over to Harry with a bone in his mouth and dropped it on the floor. Harry grinned. "For me? Why thank you, Bandit, but I find bones don't agree with my digestion."

Bandit lay down on the cool marble and chewed his bone.

A rap sounded at the door. Harry had half a mind to ignore it, as he was certain his mother had sent another blasted missive. With a gusty sigh, he strode to the door and opened it. "Bell, come in."

His friend hung his hat and greatcoat on the pegs in the foyer.

"Have a seat," Harry said.

Bell stretched out his legs and surveyed the parlor. "You've spruced the place up."

"Maid service, mostly for the copious dog hair. Speaking of service, I'm in the market for a secretary. Know of anyone?"

"I'll ask my secretary for a recommendation."

"Brandy?" Harry said.

"Hell, yes. Have you got a cheroot?"

He opened a silver case and offered one to his friend. They lit them from the lantern on his desk.

Bell inhaled and blew out a smoke ring. "It's been too long since I've had one."

"Why?" Harry said.

Bell looked chagrinned. "Laura threatened to kick me out of bed if I ever came in stinking of smoke again."

Harry guffawed. "Tell her I blew smoke on you."

"She won't believe it."

Harry flicked an ash in a tray. "I suspect you're here for a reason."

Bell nodded. "According to Laura, something is in the wind. Apparently there has been quite a bit of speculation about the opening of Almack's tonight. The patronesses have planned something unusual."

Harry sipped his brandy. "What can that have to do with me? It's not as if I'm planning to attend."

Bell inhaled and blew out a smoke ring. "You might wish to reconsider."

"Why?"

"This may come as a shock, but your mother is one of the patronesses now."

Harry scowled. "Surely not."

"Sorry, old boy. Laura confirmed it. I thought you ought to know."

"No wonder my mother kept sending me messages to escort her tonight. I intended to ignore her."

"Old boy, you might want to be on hand. Something is definitely afoot."

Wednesday, early evening

Lucy returned home to eat a quick dinner with Grandmama before reporting for her duties at Almack's.

"I hope you will have a chance to watch the dancers," Grandmama said.

"I'm not counting on it," Lucy said. The wages were low, but she figured every coin she saved would go toward her dance studio fund.

"Speaking of dancing, that servant came again today," Grandmama said.

Lucy frowned. "Which one?"

"The one who works for Mrs. Norcliffe. She's quite demanding and insists upon you instructing dance at her home in Grosvenor Square next week on Tuesday at ten o'clock. I told her servant he would have to return on the morrow for your answer."

Lucy sighed. "Tell him I will instruct for Mrs. Norcliffe next week."

"Dearest, you're teaching dance to Mrs. Vernon's girls and the Chaffin twins as well this week. Every day you are cleaning at the Albany. I worry you will fall ill."

"I'm perfectly fine, Grandmama. I must take advantage of as many opportunities as possible during the spring season. When the ton retreats later in the year, requests for my dancing instruction will diminish. It's important that I work as hard as possible now to ensure we have plenty of money saved." She finished her tea. "Now I must hurry," she said, donning her cloak. "I can't be late my first night at Almack's."

"Good luck," Grandmama said. "Please be careful while walking home."

"I will," she said.

Harry stared grudgingly out the window while his cousins spoke quietly. He'd always detested the highbrow patronesses and their schemes.

"This is a smart carriage, Harry," Mrs. Norcliffe said. "Perfect for a duke."

He wished she wouldn't make such a to-do about his title. All he cared about were his wonderful memories of summers he and Colin had spent with Uncle Hugh. His uncle had taught him and Colin how to care for the horses and the pigs. He would never forget those summers he'd spent fishing, riding, and practicing archery. Damn, he'd give anything for one more summer with Uncle Hugh.

Mina's voice interrupted his reverie. "Thank you for taking us up in your new carriage."

"You're welcome." He was fond of his cousins. They were sweet girls who tolerated his mother's overbearing ways far better than he did.

Helena and Amelia looked at each other and then at Harry.

"You do know you're the catch of the season, do you not?" Amelia said.

Harry scowled. "What?"

Mina laughed. "I told you he had no idea, Amelia."

"Well, it is to be expected, now that he has inherited the

dukedom," Mrs. Norcliffe said. "I will assist you in finding a bride, Harry."

He narrowed his eyes. "When I'm ready, I'll find my own bride."

"I knew you would say that," Mrs. Norcliffe said. "You'll end up like your bachelor uncle, God rest his soul, if I do not insist."

"First of all, I'm proud to follow in Uncle Hugh's footsteps. Second, do not make demands."

Mrs. Norcliffe raised her quizzing glass to her eye. "Marriage is your responsibility, and do not take that tone with me."

"Enough," Harry said tersely.

His cousins grew silent. The only sound for several minutes was the clop of the horses' hooves and the jangle of the harness.

"Well," Mrs. Norcliffe said. "I'm only trying to help."

"I neither want nor need it." He'd spoken harshly, but he knew from experience it was the only way to rein in his mother.

The carriage moved forward a few feet and stopped. Harry frowned. While he'd expected to wait in a long queue, the carriages ahead didn't seem to be moving. He looked out the window and was stunned to see a crowd of the lower orders gawking at the beau monde as they made their way to the building. "Something is wrong," Harry said. "I'm off to check out the situation."

"Harry, wait," Mrs. Norcliffe said.

"I'll return. Just stay seated," he said, climbing out.

His breath frosted as he strode along. To his amazement, dozens of street vendors were selling hot apples, cherries, and pies near the building. One man had set up numerous bottles on a barrel.

Harry saw Pembroke and hailed him. "What the devil is all this about?"

Pembroke shrugged. "There's quite a commotion. See that street vendor? He's filling flasks."

"You jest," Harry said. "The devil. Northcott is swigging it."

"It's probably rotgut gin," Pembroke said.

"Northcott will be sorry on the morrow."

"Most of us are the day after," Pembroke said. "I'm headed inside. And you?"

He shook his head. "No, I promised to collect my family after matters settled."

Pembroke shrugged. "You might as well fetch your family. I don't think this street party will end anytime soon."

Pembroke disappeared among the crème de la crème sweeping toward the entrance.

A few minutes later, Castelle trudged out of the building. "Bloody hell, I need a drink."

"Careful, I've heard it's rotgut gin," Harry said.

Castelle pulled out a flask. "I brought my own. Care for a little fortification?"

"No thanks. I'm surprised you're here," Harry said.

"My female relatives turned on the waterworks. It will be the last time," Castelle grumbled, and wandered away.

A ragged man struck up a tune on a fiddle. Several women and men started dancing in the street. Their boisterous laughter rang out.

Someone clapped Harry's shoulder. He turned to find Colin and his wife, Angeline. "I'm glad to see you both," Harry said. "The place has turned into a circus."

Colin frowned. "Look at the folks staring at us. I feel like one of the animals at the Royal Menagerie."

Angeline looked at her husband and said, "Go ahead, growl."

He whispered something in her ear, making her laugh.

"Have you seen Bellingham?" Harry asked.

"No, but he might have arrived already. It's impossible to tell in this crush."

"My mother and cousins are stuck in the carriage several blocks away," Harry said. "I've never seen anything like this before."

Angeline's mouth twitched. "If the rumors are correct, the patronesses planned something special tonight. Gossip is swirling in the scandal sheets."

Harry nodded. "So I heard from Bell earlier. I'd better go collect my family."

"We'll see you inside," Colin said, and escorted Angeline through the doors.

Like every other gentleman forced to attend Almack's tonight, Harry wore the required black knee breeches. He'd drunk two glasses of brandy earlier, but alas, he hadn't gotten even remotely foxed. The patronesses did not approve of liquor, but many of the gents were weaving up the steps, evidence they'd drowned their misery in advance.

Harry's nose and cheeks grew cold as he strode to his carriage. He assisted his cousins and offered his arm to his mother.

"There is so much excitement tonight," Mrs. Norcliffe said. "I daresay tonight will be talked about for ages."

Her words made him even more suspicious. He knew his mother was somehow involved, but even she couldn't stir up this crowd by herself. All of the patronesses must have been tangled up in this scheme.

"You are uncharacteristically silent," Mrs. Norcliffe said. "Are you not looking forward to this evening?"

"I have no words for my feelings." None that he would utter in her presence at any rate. Once he escorted his family members inside, he would head straight for the gaming room, and he would not poke his head out until the clock struck midnight.

After entering, Mrs. Norcliffe took her place on the dais with the other patronesses. The orchestra stood poised high above in a balcony. Almack's was an enormous place. The ballroom was supposedly one hundred feet long, and he believed it. There were gilt columns, mirrors, and even gas lighting. The number of guests swelled as Mr. Wilson, the master of ceremonies, stood by the doors to welcome everyone.

Harry meant to head straight to the gaming room, but Mina slid her hand through his arm. "Stay. Mama has a surprise."

The orchestra played a short introductory piece. Voices in the cavernous ballroom gradually hushed.

Lady Jersey stepped forward. "Please help us welcome our newest and most esteemed patroness, Mrs. Norcliffe."

Applause resounded. Harry noticed the bright flush on his mother's face. She was basking in her new role.

Mrs. Norcliffe clasped her hands and addressed the crowd. "Ladies and gentlemen, tonight we are introducing something new to Almack's."

The back of Harry's neck prickled. What did she have up her puffed sleeve?

"We have a new program," Mrs. Norcliffe said. "The patronesses and I welcome you to the first annual Almack's dancing competition."

Hundreds of guests gasped. One young lady burst into tears and had to be led to a chair where her mother passed a vinaigrette beneath her nose.

Bellingham and his petite wife joined Harry.

"Has your mother been nipping from the sherry bottle?" Bell asked.

Lady Bellingham frowned at her husband. "I'm sure there's a perfectly legitimate reason."

Harry groaned. "I should put a stop to it."

"No, you'll only make matters worse," Lady Bellingham said.

Harry shook his head. "How much worse could it get?"

Once again the orchestra played a short introductory tune, and the crowd hushed.

"Thank you," Mrs. Norcliffe said. "Now, our master of ceremonies, Mr. Wilson, will announce the dances. Gentlemen, as usual you will ask a lady to dance, but unlike the old rules, you will partner with that lady exclusively this evening."

Voices rang out. More than a few matrons were shaking their heads in apparent shock.

"Gentlemen, choose your partners well," Mrs. Norcliffe said, "for you will be competing with other couples. Each week, the gentlemen will choose either the same partner or a new one. The patronesses will judge and score the dancers on a scale of one to ten. Those who exhibit elegance and grace will earn the privilege of competing again next week. At the end of eight weeks, we will tally all scores."

Harry thought Bellingham might have been right about his mother and the sherry.

Lady Castlereagh stepped forward and held up her hand. When the din of voices gradually lowered, she said, "All of the patronesses will judge the couples on their dancing skills. Each week, the winning couples will advance to the next level. Be sure to step lightly, gentlemen and ladies. When the competition ends, we will award the prize...five hundred pounds to the best dancing couple."

The crowd erupted and voices rang with excitement. Harry turned to Lady Bellingham. "Do you know what prompted this turn of events?"

"Attendance at Almack's dropped dramatically last year," Lady Bellingham said. "Or rather the attendance of gentlemen. When was the last time you attended?"

He frowned. "More than three years."

Lady Bellingham leaned closer. "I heard the patronesses were growing desperate. It seems our gentlemen prefer the clubs to Almack's."

Bell looked astounded. "So they came up with an incentive to ensure the gents attend?"

She nodded. "That is my understanding."

Old Lord Houghton, who was at least eighty, slowly walked forward, leaning heavily on his cane. "Do I get the girl afterward?" he said in a strained voice.

Harry fisted his hand against his mouth, but his shoulders were shaking with laughter.

"Oh dear," Lady Bellingham said.

Lady Cowper rose. "Lord Houghton, you cannot dance with a cane."

He lifted the cane above his head and shuffled his feet. "Does that count?"

Houghton's young heir rescued him and led him over to a chair.

"Mr. Wilson," Mrs. Norcliffe said. "Will you announce the first dance?"

"It is the quadrille," he said. "Gentlemen, find your partners."

Bell grinned at Harry. "Well, what are you waiting for?"

"Good point. I'm off to the gaming room."

"Too late," Lady Bellingham said. "Your mother is bearing down on you as we speak."

"Good luck," Bell said, grinning as he walked off with his wife.

Mrs. Norcliffe brought over a plump matron and a very

young lady. "Harry, you remember my particular friend, Mrs. Osterham."

He bowed. "Yes, of course," he lied.

Mrs. Norcliffe smiled. "I wish to introduce you to Mrs. Osterham's eldest daughter, Miss Hortense Osterham."

He would have to ask the young miss to dance, and that meant dancing with her all evening. Harry swore he would never set foot in Almack's again. "It is a pleasure to meet you, Miss Osterham. May I have the honor of this first, er, all the dances?"

"Yes, y-you do m-me a great honor," she said.

The poor girl couldn't be much above seventeen. He offered his arm and realized her hand was shaking. Harry drew her aside. "Miss Osterham, I cannot help noticing that you're trembling. I don't bite, you know."

He'd been certain she would laugh, but she bent her head. "It is m-my f-first ball."

Damn and double damn. He was thirty-one, far too old for the girl. "If you focus on the dance steps, all will be fine." He wasn't certain that it would, but he'd no idea what else he could do to help her.

"Th-thank you," she muttered.

As he led her toward the dance floor, he searched his brain, trying to find some way out of having to spend the entire evening dancing exclusively with Hortense. It appeared more than a few men had found themselves caught in the same net. Harry feared his mother and Mrs. Osterham meant to pressure him to court the girl. First it would be the dance. Next his mother would suggest he take her for a drive, and from there, the two mamas would hint at marriage.

A wheezing sound made him stop. Hortense was gulping in air very fast. Fearing she would swoon, he took her to a chair. Fortunately, her mother rushed to the girl's rescue and applied her fan.

"My lord," Mrs. Osterham said. "I'm sure Hortense will recover shortly."

All of the color had drained from Hortense's face. Poor girl. "I'm s-sorry," she said.

Harry bent down. "You mustn't worry. It's all a bit overwhelming."

Hortense hung her head. "Forgive me, Mama."

Mrs. Osterham looked at him. "Oh dear, I think she only needs a moment."

Harry bit back his anger for the girl's sake and took Mrs. Osterham aside. "I believe your daughter is embarrassed. I'm sure it would be a kindness to take her home before others remark upon her discomfort." He shouldn't have had to make the suggestion to the foolish woman.

Mrs. Osterham fanned her daughter. "She does look pale. My sweet girl, of course I will take you home to rest."

"That seems the best course of action," Harry said.

Mrs. Osterham plucked at his sleeve. "You are very welcome to call upon my daughter, Your Grace."

"How kind of you," he said noncommittally. "My best wishes to you and your daughter."

He bowed and strode off, relieved to have escaped dancing all night with the poor girl.

How could his mother even think of pairing him with her? He was nearly twice her age.

Now that he'd resolved the dancing issue, Harry strode into the gaming room where gentlemen were getting up a game of vingt-et-un. The Earl of Hawkfield and the Duke of Shelbourne joined them.

Hawk shuffled the cards. "Shelbourne, I've not seen this much gossip in the scandal sheets since your bridal courtship."

Shelbourne laughed. "I must admit I never thought anything would top it, but the patronesses have succeeded in stirring up more trouble in the scandal sheets than my wife."

One hour later, Bellingham and Colin entered. "Harry, we came to see if you're up for billiards."

"I am." Harry bowed out of the card game and joined his friends in the billiard's room.

"We yawned one too many times. Our wives chased us off," Colin said.

"Thank the devil," Bell said. "I couldn't make myself watch the dancers any longer."

Bellingham sighted the ball. "Blue one, right rear pocket." When he took the shot, the white ball ricocheted and fell into the left pocket.

"Bloody hell," Bell said. "I'm rusty."

Harry sighted the red ball. "Right rear pocket." He eased the stick over his hand, hit the red ball, and sent it spinning into the right rear pocket.

"Whoa," Colin said. "You've been practicing."

Harry grinned. "A single man can spend long nights in the club at the billiard's table."

"True," Bell said, "but you can't take a cue stick to bed."

Harry handed the stick to Bell. "This from the man who swore he would never wed."

Bell grinned. "I'm glad I did. You are the last bachelor among us. Don't feel any pressure from us."

"I've no intention of remaining a bachelor for life. It's just too soon after losing my uncle. A mistress would suit me for now. I just have to find one who has a brain and doesn't drench herself in perfume."

"Oh Lord," Colin said. "There's a story there."

"Good luck with a mistress," Bell said. "My last one turned the town house into a pagoda museum, and set the sheets on fire in the street, and the fire brigade had to come put it out."

Harry and Colin guffawed.

"Whose turn is it?" Bell said.

"Yours," Colin said.

Harry propped his cue stick while Bell lined up the balls. After sighting them, Bellingham took his shot and every single one fell into pockets.

"Some things never change," Colin said. "How the devil do you do that?"

Bell shrugged. "It's all about the right amount of force."

"That's helpful," Colin muttered.

"You're up, Colin," Bell said.

Harry cleared his throat. "I'm off to get something to drink, however tepid it may be."

His friends laughed as he quit the gaming room and headed to the refreshments. He walked past the tables, examining the food. The plain cake and buttered sandwiches looked unappetizing. He meant to get a cup of tea, but an elderly lady advised him not to drink it, as it had grown cold. With a sigh, Harry turned to the other table, and his heart kicked hard.

Lucy stood behind the table dressed in an apron. A cap covered all but one wisp of her red hair. She handed a glass of lemonade to a matron. When the lady walked away, Lucy lifted up on her toes. Evidently, she was watching the dancers.

He strolled over to her table. "Lucy?"

Her green eyes widened. "What are you doing here?" she said under her breath. A blush stole over her cheeks. "Sorry, that was foolish."

"No, it wasn't. I escorted my mother and cousins...I didn't expect to see you here."

She wouldn't be here if she didn't need the coin, but she couldn't be earning more than a pittance.

"You are working?" he said. *Brilliant, you just sounded like a complete idiot.*

"Yes, isn't it obvious?"

He smiled. "Well, yes. You are well?"

"I am," she said. "And you?"

"A few minutes ago, I would have said tolerably well, but then I saw you and brightened considerably."

"Flirting again, Your Grace?"

"Who me?" he said, putting his hand to his heart.

She looked over her shoulder and returned her gaze to him. "You had better go."

He looked behind her.

"What are you about?" she said.

He grinned. "One of your curls escaped the cap."

She attempted to tuck it in.

"Don't," he said. "It's rather fetching."

"Please go. I cannot afford trouble."

"No one is paying attention to us. May I have a glass of lemonade?"

"Of course." She poured and handed the glass to him.

He took a sip and puckered his mouth. "It's terrible, but I should have expected it. Almack's is well known for its lackluster refreshments."

"One would think the ton would serve decent food and drink."

"Believe me, no one comes here for the refreshments," he said.

"Except *you*?" she said in a teasing tone.

He laughed. "I saw you watching the dancers. I wish you could dance with me."

"I'm working." She glanced over her shoulder again.

"You had better leave before someone notices you're talking to me."

He glanced out at the crowd. "No one is paying the least bit of attention. Everyone is focused on the dancers."

"Why aren't *you* dancing?" she said.

"I would if you were free."

"If you wish to flirt, I advise you to choose a lady of leisure. I must work."

"I wish I could dance the rest of the night with you. I can't, so I won't dance at all."

She shook her head. "I'm not the reason you're avoiding dancing," she said. "I know the patronesses changed the rules."

"Yes, and I narrowly escaped dancing all night with a young lady out in her first season. I felt sorry for her. She couldn't be a day over seventeen, making her much too young for the likes of me."

Her eyes narrowed. "Aren't you expected to dance?"

"I don't care about expectations."

She met his gaze straight on. "I wager your family does. I know courtships take place primarily on the dance floor."

"When I decide to court a lady, I will choose the time and place. I make my own decisions, and I answer to no one," he said.

She arched her brows. "Perhaps a higher power?"

He smiled. "Or a lower one."

Her mouth twitched in a slight smile. "Does that make you a devilish duke?"

His shoulders shook with mirth. "Clever."

A rotund maid walked out. "Lucy, give the gentleman a glass of lemonade and be done with it."

Lucy winced and poured a glass. "Yes, Mrs. Thompson. I'm sorry."

"It's not me you owe an apology." Mrs. Thompson regarded him. "She's new, but that's no excuse."

He'd made trouble for Lucy, and he'd better undo the damage. "Mrs. Thompson, I beg your pardon." Harry gave her his best flirtatious smile. "The lady did try to discourage me. I take all the blame. Do forgive me."

Mrs. Thompson's eyes grew as round as carriage wheels and her face turned pink. "Imagine me forgivin' you. Carry on, Miss Longmore," she said, and walked off.

Afterward, Lucy leaned toward him. "Please go now. I can't risk losing my job."

The devil. He shouldn't have teased Lucy. Her words worried him, because she couldn't be earning much. That only made him wonder how she was managing.

He wandered past the other tables, stopping occasionally to watch her. She and her grandmother lived in a rough neighborhood. That fact only increased his curiosity and his concern. Most likely, she held more than one job, because she couldn't possibly survive on whatever pittance she earned serving lemonade.

When she caught him eyeing her, she averted her gaze. A lady approached, and Lucy served her a glass of lemonade. Afterward, Lucy looked out at the crowd as if determined to avoid him.

Once again, he was struck by the contradiction of her. He told himself to walk away and forget her, but he couldn't. She was a riddle, one that he itched to solve, but that was not all. In truth, that one kiss had only made him want more. He wanted to pull her up to her toes and kiss her senseless. He wanted to hold her in his arms. He wanted her to surrender everything to him, but he mustn't rush her. That one kiss had assured him she was an innocent.

The orchestra ended the tune with a flourish. The master

of ceremonies called for silence. The guests moved closer en mass toward the dais where the patronesses sat.

Three ladies inside the refreshment room hurried out to join the throng. Harry consulted his watch. It was half past eleven. He turned around. Lucy was alone.

When he strode toward her, she eyed him warily. He set the half-finished glass of lemonade on the table and leaned closer to her.

"I want to see you again. Meet me at Green Park tomorrow."

"Why?"

"Because I want to know more about you."

She shook her head. "I do not think it is a good idea."

"Who will know but us?" he said.

She narrowed her eyes. "What if one of your friends saw me with you? I can well imagine what they would think of me."

"They'll be at Rotten Row during the fashionable hour. No need to worry."

A roar went up within the ballroom, followed by thunderous clapping. Harry turned around and saw his eldest cousin Mina and Lord Everleigh standing on the dais. "I had better go."

"Yes, go, and please do not jeopardize my job again."

He grinned. "I will see you tomorrow."

"You're awfully confident, but you are bound for disappointment."

He looked at her over his shoulder, winked, and walked into the ballroom.

Lucy released her breath as she wiped up the condensation from his glass of lemonade. When he'd first approached, her face had grown hot. She didn't care that he'd seen her serving. He'd been to her home after all, and serving lemonade was honest work. But she'd been uneasy with his flirtation while she was working. It was just her luck that Mrs. Thompson, the head maid, would see him with her. Lucy ought to have known he would attend Almack's. Only the crème de la crème received vouchers, and he most certainly was one of them.

When Mrs. Thompson approached, Lucy's muscles stiffened. Would the head maid chastise her for unseemly conduct? Or worse, sack her?

"Do you know who that gent was?" Mrs. Thompson asked with her ham of a hand on her hip.

"No." God forgive her for the lie, but it would hurt no one, and she would have a difficult time explaining how she knew him.

"I heard one of the society ladies talkin' 'bout him. He's the Duke of Granfield," Mrs. Thompson said.

She pretended ignorance. "Oh?"

Mrs. Thompson snorted. "Oh," she says. "He's the bleedin' Duke of Granfield, the one what inherited his uncle's fortune. He's the catch of the season or so one of the hoity-toity ladies said. If you don't believe me, have a look at those ladies circlin' him like vultures."

Ladies dressed in silk and satin thronged him. Their well-bred laughter drifted to Lucy.

She recalled his words the night he'd kissed her. *From the first moment we met, I could not get you out of my head.*

He'd spoken as if she were special to him, but the women surrounding him told an entirely different story.

Something hot rushed up her throat. She'd known they could never be anything more than temporary acquaintances. But it was one thing to know in the abstract that he was considered the most eligible bachelor and quite another to watch the ladies flirt with him. From all appearances, he was enjoying their attention.

Lucy pressed her nails into her palms. Jealousy flared inside her chest. She hated that she cared. Of course it was foolish, but the emotions swirled red-hot inside of her. She could never compete with those ladies.

Why was she comparing herself unfavorably to them? She knew plenty about young ladies of the ton. She'd hooked, fitted, and pinned enough spoiled aristo girls to know many of them acted like petulant and sulky children. If that's what he wanted in a woman, he was welcome to them.

She told herself her jealousy had been nothing more than a momentary lapse in judgment. Now she was doubly glad she'd refused to meet him in the park again. But the night he'd kissed her, she'd thought there was something between them. She'd felt the tension and her own yearning. Now she was confused and unsure what to make of his interest in her. He'd been so determined that first time they met in the park, but now watching him with the society ladies, she doubted him and herself.

"Best be wary, my girl," Mrs. Thompson said. "He looked at you with those blue eyes as if he was undressin' you. Toffs like him use a girl and leave her after they gets what they want. Nobody hires a gel what has a bun in the oven."

"That will never happen."

"See that you remember it," Mrs. Thompson said, and returned to the kitchen.

Lucy made herself watch him so that she wouldn't forget that she could never be anyone to him other than a passing flirtation. The trouble was she'd let him into her life, and she couldn't forget his kiss. Now she was torn between wanting nothing to do with him and wanting him to call on her again. If she was smart, she would shove him out of her thoughts forever. She'd known no good could come from an acquaintance with him, but she couldn't help wanting to be with him, even though she feared he would hurt her again.

"The dancing competition was splendid," Mrs. Norcliffe said as Harry's carriage rolled along the streets of Mayfair. "Mina, you and Lord Everleigh were the darlings of the night. I'm delighted *you* were chosen to advance in the competition."

"Lord Everleigh is a wonderful dance partner," Mina said. "Of course, Miss Fothergill and Mr. Castelle acquitted themselves very well tonight."

"You are entirely too modest, Mina," Mrs. Norcliffe said.

Mina sighed. "I do wish Amelia and Helena would have danced."

"You are the brave one, Mina," Amelia said. "Helena and I purposely faded into the background."

"I could not bear for others to study me while I dance," Helena said.

"I would have been terrified," Amelia said, "but, Mina, you looked happy."

"I suppose one's partner makes a difference," Mina said, lowering her lashes.

Harry had seen Mina's bright eyes and flushed face when the dancing ended. Clearly Mina liked Everleigh. Harry made a note to meet the man at White's for a drink. He meant to take Everleigh's measure before allowing him to court Mina, although most courting actually took place on the dance floor—or so he'd been told.

"Harry, we missed seeing you nearly the entire ball," Mrs. Norcliffe said. "I heard you were in the gaming room with your friends."

One thing he could always count on. His mother knew everything about everybody, including him. Mrs. Norcliffe and her haughty friends were known for gossiping, something he found more than a little disagreeable.

"I was disappointed that Miss Osterham grew ill," his mother continued, "but next week, she will be recovered, and you will dance with her."

"No, I will not," he said. "I must be nearly twice her age. If I wish to dance, I will choose my own partner." His mother was determined that he would participate in this ridiculous dancing competition, but she would not get her way.

Tonight, he'd been perilously close to being trapped into dancing with Miss Osterham all evening. No doubt the other patronesses would have agreed with his mother that he and Miss Osterham should advance in the competition next Wednesday. Then his mother would have said that Miss Osterham expected him to dance with her every week.

He most definitely would not set foot inside Almack's again.

"Harry, you did not dance at all," Mrs. Norcliffe said in an irritated tone. "The other patronesses took exception to your disappearance in the game rooms."

"According to their rules, I would have been required to dance the entire evening with the same partner. I did not wish to do so. Furthermore, I have no wish to be a part of the competition."

"Harry, you are the most eligible bachelor this season," Mrs. Norcliffe said.

"Mama, you may spread the word that I'm the most *ineligible* bachelor this season."

"You are a never-ending cause of my vexation, Harry."

"Sorry to disappoint you."

She huffed. "You enjoy it."

One year ago, no one would have ever considered him

marriage material. He'd always had pockets to let and possessed neither title nor fortune, both requisite necessities to winning the heart of the latest diamond of the first water. His cousins had once explained to him that meant a great beauty, but he'd no idea what first water was all about. It sounded ridiculous to him.

He intended to wed when the time was right. Lately, there had been too much upheaval in his life. He needed time to adjust to the numerous changes in his circumstances first.

He thought about his preferences for a wife. Naturally he wished for a woman who would shed all inhibitions in bed, but a virginal bride would likely be skittish. He was confident he could coax a shy bride. All the same, he would prefer someone who was clever and not easily conquered.

Such as a petite, strong-willed redhead who gave him no quarter.

He remained curious about her. How in the world was she earning enough money to support herself and her grandmother? And why would she take a lowly position serving at Almack's when she was clearly educated. He knew she'd not been in London very long and probably had few connections.

He could help her if she would allow it. Hopefully she would meet him at the park tomorrow. Since the first night he'd met her, he'd not been able to shove her out of his thoughts. That had never happened to him before. He'd teased and bedded more than a few women. Always he'd tired of them, usually rather quickly, and walked away with no regrets.

No woman had ever captivated him the way Lucy had done. He didn't know why he couldn't forget her, the way he'd forgotten so many others. Perhaps it was the combination of her saucy retorts mingled with her vulnerability. She *was* vulnerable, whether she admitted it or not. He wanted to protect her, but she was no hot-house flower like most of the women of the ton. Her bravery had stunned him the first night he'd met her when she'd flashed her wicked blade.

He had to admit he wanted her in his arms. He couldn't make himself stop wanting her, but instinct told him she wasn't the sort of woman who would take a man into her bed.

She was an original, nothing like the women he'd met in the ton. She was clever, determined, and independent in ways that no lady of the ton would ever dare. He liked that she was unique, and nothing like the vain ladies who expected compliments about their beauty. Lucy didn't simper and lower her eyes. She didn't hesitate to speak her mind.

She challenged him, made him laugh, and refused to give him any quarter. She'd insisted there could be nothing between them because of class distinctions, but he refused to let some arbitrary social rules stand in his way. When she was near him, he felt exhilarated and excited. For the first time in all the years he'd sought out women, he could not forget and walk away.

She was his first thought in the morning and his last thought at night.

There was only one answer. He would pursue her and before it was all over, he would make her his.

Chapter Eight

Harry's day had not gone well. He'd gotten a letter from the estate manager at Havenwood letting him know of several *inconvenient incidences*. The bridge needed repairs, four of the pigs had somehow escaped the pens, and the kitchen range had to be replaced. To top it all off, he'd gotten a headache in parliament over a nasty divorce petition. At the end of the day, he'd gone to Green Park only to find that Lucy had not gone there to meet him. Damn it all, he'd been disappointed.

The last thing he'd wanted was to go out this evening, but he'd agreed to meet Lord Everleigh at White's for a brandy. Harry was fairly certain the ginger-haired Everleigh held tender feelings for Mina, but he wanted to be sure. Harry was the only male figure in his cousin's lives. As such, he felt it was his responsibility to protect them and ensure their happiness to the degree possible.

Everleigh seemed a decent chap, although he was a bit tongue-tied at times. More important, Harry didn't want

Mina and Everleigh to feel obliged to dance the entire evening at Almack's week after week, unless both truly wanted to continue in the ridiculous competition. If they continued, others might think the pair was headed for the altar.

The situation was unusual to say the least. Everyone in the ton knew they had won the first night's competition, and Harry feared Everleigh and Mina might feel pressed to marry if they continued dancing together all season. The last thing he wanted was for the two of them to feel obligated to wed.

His fears were real ones. He knew of men and women who had felt obligated to marry for one reason or another. It had happened to Wellington of all people. Harry didn't want Mina or Everleigh to feel trapped by the weight of others' expectations. Tonight he meant to broach the topic of the dancing competition with Everleigh to prevent something similar happening to Mina.

After a brief discussion of today's events in parliament, Harry ordered two more brandies and raised his glass. "Cheers," he said.

"To you as well," Everleigh said.

"So, are you planning to attend Almack's next week?"

"Yes, I wouldn't miss it."

Harry set his glass aside. "In normal circumstances, a lady does not dance more than two dances with one gentleman." Harry leaned back in his chair. "However, the patronesses changed the rules for Almack's this particular season."

"Indeed, they surprised us all," Everleigh said.

"Are you planning to continue in the dancing competition?"

"Yes." He frowned and added, "With your permission, I wish to ask Miss Radburn to dance again, provided she is amenable."

Harry couldn't tell for certain if Everleigh truly wished to partner with Mina or if he felt obligated. The latter concerned him. He took a deep breath and said, "I imagine there are ways to bow out, if you or my cousin so desire," Harry said. "After all, it is highly unusual to dance with the same partner for an entire evening, much less week after week."

Everleigh stared into his brandy glass as if looking for a suitable response. "Well, I certainly would be most honored to dance with Miss Radburn every Wednesday night, provided she accepts my request—with your permission of course."

Harry sipped his brandy. "Let us metaphorically lay our cards faceup on the table, shall we?"

"Of course," Everleigh said. "What do you wish to know?"

Harry set his glass aside. "First, it cannot have escaped your notice that partnering my cousin several times this season will result in... shall we say *expectations*."

Everleigh frowned. "Well, I had hoped, er, I very much ."

Harry leaned forward. "The cards are faceup, Everleigh. Now is the time to be honest."

The tops of Everleigh's ears grew red as he looked at the table. "With your approval and that of Miss Radburn, I very much wish to continue as her dancing partner."

"Everleigh," Harry said, and waited for him to look him in the eyes.

When the man met his gaze, Harry sighed. "If you continue to dance exclusively with my cousin, everyone will likely expect you to propose to Mina for honor's sake. Are you prepared for that eventuality?"

"Of course," Everleigh said, a little too quickly.

Harry considered Everleigh's response. "Are you certain?

If that is not your wish, we will contrive a reason for you to bow out, such as a sudden illness of one of your relatives."

"I intend to continue," Everleigh said.

"Let me emphasize that I'm not trying to press you," Harry said. "You might as well know I won't let her wed unless I'm absolutely certain that the man adores her. Mina lost her parents when she was only ten years old. I'll not see her suffer again."

Everleigh inhaled. "When I asked about her family, she told me about the tragedy. I very much wish to continue in the dancing competition with her, provided it is still her wish."

"I suspect that it is."

After a long pause, Everleigh's expression grew anxious. "I fear I have given the wrong impression."

"I see." Mina would be terribly disappointed, but better that than enter into a marriage because one or the other felt obligated. Mina deserved someone who loved her dearly.

Everleigh drew in a sharp breath. "I wish . . . I mean I hope by the end of the dancing competition that Miss Radburn will do me a great honor." Everleigh's cheeks grew as red as his hair.

Harry's brows rose. "You're certain."

"Yes, I am," Everleigh said. "I couldn't bear it if she married another man."

Harry smiled. "Well, then, you are free to court her. Care for another round?" Harry asked. "The night is still early."

"No thanks," Everleigh said. "Another time, perhaps?"

"Yes, of course."

Harry sipped his brandy. Everleigh's certainty about marrying Mina made him think about his own life. He'd been a bachelor for thirteen long years. Back when he was eighteen, he and Colin had gotten into one scrape after another. They'd sneaked women and bottles into their rooms at Oxford and later at the Albany. While some of it was hilarious in retrospect, he didn't miss puking his guts out after a hard night's drinking and the inevitable morning after where he had the devil of a headache. Ye gods, had he really ever thought that was amusing?

He walked to the foyer, wrapped his scarf around his neck, and stepped outside of White's. His carriage waited for him a block away. He couldn't help remembering that first night he'd met Lucy on the street and her advice to him. Damn, she'd surprised and intrigued him that night, and she'd continued to do so every time they'd met since then.

When he climbed into his carriage, he picked up the cane and tapped it on the ceiling. He was all too aware of how much he thought about Lucy. It was like a madness of sorts. The women in his past had been jaded widows who lasted no longer than a night or two in his bed. Back then, he'd just been looking to slake his lust with a willing widow.

What he felt for Lucy was not simple lust. There was nothing simple about his feelings. He desired her, but he also felt protective of her. He worried about her safety, and yet he admired her courage. Then, there were the external obstacles that she insisted they could not cross. Those obstacles never gave him pause, but she was adamant that they could not overcome class barriers. He didn't believe it, but she did, and that was a problem, one he meant to overcome.

Harry envied Everleigh and wished matters with Lucy weren't so blasted complicated. But he vowed to pursue her. He would never give up and he would never let her go.

* * *

Friday morning

Lucy kissed her grandmother's cheek. "You are almost finished knitting the left mitten."

"Yes, I am close. Once this one is done, I'll start the other. When I finish one dozen, will you take them to the workhouse for me?"

"I will." She was amazed by and very proud of her grandmother. Because of her lack of sight, she'd taught herself to knit by touch.

Lucy walked to the peg to retrieve her cloak. She sighed, wishing she didn't have to leave her grandmother alone today.

"Are you tired, dear? You arrived home after midnight."

"I'm fine. The walk will leave me feeling energetic," Lucy said.

"I suppose the duke was among the crème de la crème at Almack's."

"Yes, I saw him there," Lucy said.

"You sound disappointed," Grandmama said.

"Not at all. It was as I expected. He was quite popular with the wealthy ladies. I'd better hurry. Tonight, I will tell you about last night's dance competition."

"I look forward to hearing about it," Grandmama said. "How very strange that the quality is holding a dance competition. I wonder what prompted such an odd turn of events."

"Perhaps they are bored with their too perfect lives and must invent new amusements."

Grandmama chuckled. "Undoubtedly, you are correct. And you are giving dance lessons to Mrs. Vernon's daughters?"

"Yes, I am. The girls will repeat last week's lesson to ensure they have the steps memorized, and then we will work on hops and jetés. Directly afterward, I'm teaching Mrs. Rohan's children. Then it's off to the Albany. Next week, I'll be teaching the Rylander children as well. I'm obliged to Mrs. Vernon for recommending me to her friends." But she needed far more clients if she were to support herself teaching dance. There would always be those who dropped the instruction or left the city for a holiday at Brighton. She had an opportunity now thanks to Mrs. Vernon, and she must seize additional ones.

"It does sound as if Mrs. Vernon is a sensible lady," Grandmama said.

"Today marks the third time I've taught her daughters. Mrs. Vernon seems to be a fair and caring mother—unlike Lady Blenborough."

"That poor child," Grandmama said. "How could Lady Blenborough be so cruel?"

"I don't know," Lucy said. "It broke my heart to see Prudence's misery."

Lucy pulled the hood of her cape up. "After the dance lesson, I will report to the Albany and then I will return home late this afternoon."

Grandmama frowned. "I wish you did not have to go into service."

"I don't mind. Really, a little cleaning never hurt anybody. Unlike those who work at the large country mansions, I'm able to leave after I finish for the day. Then I can spend the entire evening with you."

Grandmama rose and used her stick as she followed Lucy to the door.

"Latch the door after me," Lucy said, and hurried her step.

While the wind was a bit brisk, the sun was out, and

that made her journey to Grosvenor Square pleasanter. The chirping of starlings in the trees made her wish she could take Grandmama to the park today, but if she were frugal, perhaps they could take a hackney to the park in a fortnight.

She turned into the square and saw Buckley leaning on a walking stick by the gates. His presence irritated her, but she was determined to ignore him. She avoided eye contact as she walked past, but he limped beside her. "Is this how you planned to get rid of me? By causing my fall so you could steal my clients?"

"You fell because you were unsteady from drinking spirits."

"You spewed lies about me to Mrs. Vernon."

She scoffed. "You must have hit your head and knocked your brains about. I had nothing to do with your dismissal."

"If you mean to poach my clients, you had better watch your back. I'll make you pay."

She didn't take his bluster seriously. "Buckley, you reek of spirits now. You brought trouble upon yourself. I had nothing to do with it."

When he tried to grab her, Lucy scuttled out of his reach. "If you come near me again, I'll scream my head off."

Just then, a large footman opened the door. "Leave the lady be, sir, or I'll send the watch after you."

Buckley glared at her. "You haven't seen the last of me."

When the footman strode toward them, Buckley hobbled off.

In the aftermath, Lucy shuddered. She would have to resort to carrying her knife in her basket again. While Buckley had never been violent before, she thought it best to be prepared. If anything happened to her, there would be no one to take care of her grandmother.

"He didn't hurt you, did he, miss?" the footman asked.

"No, he did not. Thank you for your assistance," she said. "I'll go around to the servant's entrance."

"Mrs. Vernon bade me to tell you to come in through the foyer. She saw him by the gate and wanted me to escort you safely inside."

She winced. "He's liable to return again. Mrs. Vernon ought to know."

"I believe she is aware of that possibility."

"I'd best go up," she said.

After she reached the drawing room, Lucy curtsied. "Thank you, Mrs. Vernon."

"We will speak after the lesson," she said, sliding her gaze to her daughters.

"Very well." Lucy looked at the girls. "Shall we begin?"

The two girls stood before her.

"Today I will demonstrate the difference between a hop and a jeté. Are you familiar with them?"

"A little," the elder sister said, "but we have not practiced for many months."

"I fear I was a bit too indulgent during the winter months," Mrs. Vernon said.

"I understand," Lucy said. "Today's lesson should be fairly straightforward. With a hop, you land on the same foot. A jeté involves taking off and landing on the opposite foot. Watch me and then you will practice."

After the girls mastered the jeté, she clapped her hands. "Excellent. Your mother will be very proud of you. Since you did so well, we will work on the waltz traveling step. I'm sure you will both do very well. It is up, up, up, on the balls of your feet and down. That's four counts up and one count down. When you sink to your heels, you will perform a plié. Now follow me and remember not to worry about making mistakes. Practice makes perfect."

"You are always so nice to us," Marie said.

She'd learned from watching her mother's gentle teaching. "You are doing very well and encouragement is far more helpful than criticism," Lucy said. "Imagine your arms are as light as air. Think of the gracefulness of a butterfly's wings. Your wrists, elbows, and knees are pliant. When you perform the movements, you focus on the lightness of your steps. Now, my butterflies, we will practice the waltz traveling step once more with grace and lightness. Step up, up, up, on the balls of your feet and sink with lightness into a plié. Oh, that was wonderful, girls. I'm so proud of you," Lucy said.

As the lesson came to a close, Lucy curtsied. "You are to be commended, girls. You did very well today."

"You may be excused now," Mrs. Vernon said to her daughters.

After they left, Lucy regarded Mrs. Vernon with guilt. "I fear I've drawn Buckley back to your residence. He insists I'm responsible for his dismissal."

"He is a typical drunkard," Mrs. Vernon said. "They blame others for all their misfortunes."

Lucy's heart beat hard. Mrs. Vernon evidently had more than a little experience with it. Lucy's father had started drinking spirits after her mother died and blamed everybody but himself for his troubles. In truth, he'd complained endlessly of illness, but Lucy had known it was the effects of the strong spirits he drank much of the day.

"I'll ensure a footman is stationed near the gate next week," Mrs. Vernon said. "I won't allow that man near my property."

"I understand," Lucy said.

"You are an excellent teacher." She paused and said, "I would like to help you if you are amenable."

She didn't want to get her hopes up too high, but she crossed her fingers in the folds of her skirts.

"I told some of my friends that you are an accomplished dance instructor. Several of the ladies have a strong interest in watching your methods. I know you serve at Almack's and are aware of the dancing competition."

Lucy nodded. "Yes, I know about the competition."

"You might profit from demonstrating your teaching methods to some of the ladies of the ton. Are you interested?"

Her pulse leaped. "I welcome the opportunity. It is very kind of you."

"Very well." Mrs. Vernon sat at the corner desk, pulled out a sheet of paper, opened an inkwell, and paused. "Shall I write the address?"

Lucy regarded the paper. "Yes, please. I don't want to forget."

Mrs. Vernon looked up. "Were you educated at home or at school?"

"At home. My late mother taught me."

Mrs. Vernon nodded. "You are far too talented and refined to work for the likes of Buckley. I assume your family fell on hard times."

"Yes, madame."

Mrs. Vernon finished writing the address, sanded the ink, and handed the paper to Lucy. "The address is in Grosvenor Square. Do you know it?"

"Yes, I know the square."

"Excellent. Now here's a tip. Lady Jersey will be in attendance. She takes great pride in having introduced the quadrille to Almack's. If I were you, I would focus on that dance."

"Thank you for the advice," Lucy said. "It helps to be prepared."

Mrs. Vernon cleared her throat. "I do not wish to sound presumptuous, but if you are ever in need, I hope you will come to me."

Lucy curtsied. "You are kind, Mrs. Vernon. I appreciate your recommendations for my dance lessons."

She hesitated a moment. "In all confidence, my own family went through difficult times. I was able to make a good marriage and escape the difficulties. Our circumstances may not be the same, but I know the challenges a single woman faces."

Lucy nodded. "Thank you for sharing your story. I will keep it in strict confidence."

"My girls like you very much, and I would be disappointed if you did not prevail upon me in a time of need."

"I appreciate your offer very much," Lucy said. She'd struggled for the past six months and sometimes late at night she worried. Thus far, she'd managed, but it was a relief to know that there was help if she ever found herself in a bind.

One week later

Lucy tucked the paper with the address in her apron, donned her cloak, and kissed her grandmother on the cheek. "Wish me luck with the dance practice in Mrs. Norcliffe's drawing room today," she said. "I understand there will be ladies and gentlemen there."

"I know you'll do very well," Grandmama said. "You have the address?"

"Yes, it should be no trouble to find," Lucy said, "but I'm leaving early to be sure."

"Hopefully, you will add new clients."

"For now, I will concentrate on making sure everyone is able to follow the steps," Lucy said. "Now I must be off."

She set out at a brisk pace going west on Oxford Street, passing over Regent and Bond Streets until she reached the address in Grosvenor Square. Upon arrival, she went to the servant's entrance. The housekeeper bade her to follow a footman upstairs. When she gained the landing, Lucy heard numerous voices, both male and female. Her lungs constricted for a moment, but she knew it was imperative that she appear confident and capable. If the lessons went well today, she might gain more adult clients.

After the footman opened the drawing room doors, Lucy took a deep breath, walked inside, and curtsied. She rose to find more than a dozen ladies and three gentlemen staring at her, one of whom was a young buck.

Mrs. Vernon smiled at her and leaned toward another lady, who looked familiar. For a moment, Lucy had difficulty placing the unknown woman, and then she recalled the lady who had spoken at Almack's. It was Mrs. Norcliffe, the woman who had scowled at her near Madame Delanger's shop. Lucy's pulse quickened. Mrs. Norcliffe lifted her quizzing glass. "Miss Longmore, do join us," Mrs. Norcliffe said. "Mrs. Vernon recommended you."

Lucy curtsied again. "I am honored."

"You look familiar," Mrs. Norcliffe said. "Where have I seen you before?"

Another lady whispered to her.

Mrs. Norcliffe's lips parted. She regarded Lucy with narrowed eyes. "Ah, now I recollect. You served lemonade at Almack's."

"Yes, madame," she said. Her heart beat quickly. Mrs. Norcliffe seemed displeased. But why?

Mrs. Norcliffe sniffed. "So, Miss Longmore, are you a dance instructor or a servant?"

"Both, madame."

"I find it rather unusual for a female to teach dance," Mrs. Norcliffe said. "In my experience, all dance masters are gentlemen."

Lucy figured the woman was challenging her. "My mother taught dance in our village, and I assisted her. I also assisted a gentleman instructor in London until recently."

"How provincial," she said in a bored tone.

Lucy did not react to the insult. More than a few ladies had treated her with disdain when she'd worked at Madame Delanger's shop. Regardless of what transpired, she would remain calm.

"Mrs. Norcliffe," Mrs. Vernon said, "he is the one we both dismissed. It was clear to me that Miss Longmore was the superior instructor. My girls are doing very well under her tutelage."

"Your opinion counts for a great deal, Mrs. Vernon. I have high hopes Miss Longmore will prove herself a superior dance instructor."

Lucy's stomach clenched. Mrs. Norcliffe's tone insinuated the exact opposite, but she mustn't let fear overrule her. She was a skilled instructor, like her mother before her.

"We should concentrate on the quadrille," one lady said, "but of course I will bow to your superior opinion, Mrs. Norcliffe."

Lucy darted a grateful look at Mrs. Vernon.

"Lady Jersey, I do agree," Mrs. Norcliffe said. "We are fortunate that Lord Everleigh and his friend Mr. Castelle attended, but we need two more gentlemen to practice."

"Miss Radburn, may I have this dance?" a man asked.

"Thank you, Lord Everleigh," Miss Mina Radburn said.

Mr. Castelle bowed to another young lady. "Miss Helena Radburn, will you consent to dance with me?"

"Thank you, Mr. Castelle," the lady said.

A petite blond lady nudged the tall young buck next to her.

He stood. "Miss Amelia Radburn, will you do me the great honor?"

"It would be my pleasure, Lord Chesfield."

"We are still short a couple," Mina said.

"We only need one more gentleman," Lucy said. "Perhaps one of the ladies would not mind making up the numbers for practice purposes only?"

"Oh no, that is unacceptable," Lady Jersey said with a horrified expression.

Lucy curtsied, but inwardly she thought the woman entirely too finicky.

As the various conversations grew louder, matters quickly deteriorated. Lucy had no idea what they were discussing, but she felt ill at ease. Her hopes of gaining more clients began to dissipate like raindrops.

A maid arrived with a tea tray. Lucy stood with the couples, unsure what to do. The buzz of voices had grown louder, and Lucy's discomfort heightened. She wished someone would direct her.

Miss Mina Radburn approached. "May I offer you a cup of tea?"

"No thank you," Lucy said. She doubted Mrs. Norcliffe would approve of her partaking of refreshments.

The clock struck the hour. Two ladies departed. Not long after, another lady rose from her seat. Lucy's hopes dwindled, and her chest tightened. She tried once more. "Perhaps the ladies would reconsider dancing without a male partner for practice purposes only."

Mrs. Norcliffe gave her a withering look.

Her spirits plummeted. She'd hoped this opportunity would lead to more clients, but nothing had gone right from the moment she'd entered the drawing room. She would gain no clients or money today. Worse, she did not know if she should remain or leave. Mrs. Norcliffe would dismiss her, and no one would request Lucy's instruction after this day. She would have to find another job, because her earnings as a maid at the Albany were insufficient. Now she wished Mrs. Norcliffe would end the misery and dismiss her.

Footsteps clipped outside the drawing room doors. Mrs. Norcliffe rose and clasped her hands to her heart. "Harry, you arrived just in the nick of time."

Lucy's heart pounded. She turned her attention to the door and had to stifle a gasp. Dear God. It was Granfield. He was the last person she'd expected to see in this drawing room. What was he doing here? For a moment she couldn't think, and then she remembered. He had three female cousins. His mother had taken them in after they had lost their parents.

Lucy prayed he would not give her away. The last thing she needed was for Mrs. Norcliffe to realize she knew her son. There was no telling what his mother would conclude. Lucy regarded him with a warning look, but she'd no idea if he understood or not.

Harry felt as if he were having a strange dream, one where he'd stepped out on a stage dressed only in his drawers. What the devil was Lucy doing here?

Lucy stood there with a marble-like expression. That made him wonder what had happened prior to his arrival.

Mina hurried over to him. "Harry, I am so glad you got Aunt's missive."

He most certainly had gotten his mother's note and had come to tell her he had no intention of spending another Wednesday evening at Almack's. Unfortunately, that conversation would have to wait until his mother's numerous friends dispersed.

"Harry, your timing is perfect." Mina smiled at him. "We needed one more gentleman for our practice session."

He cleared his throat. "I've no wish to interfere."

"We were all in an uproar, but you arrived in the nick of time," Mina said.

He had no idea what Mina was talking about, but it did not sound promising. "I regret that I'm unable to stay."

"Nonsense," Mrs. Norcliffe said. "We were shy one gentleman, and fortune blessed us with your presence."

"Fortune has already blessed me," Harry said. "Really, I have an appointment." He didn't mention the appointment involved walking Bandit.

Mina took his arm and led him to Lucy. "May I present Miss Longmore? Miss Longmore, this is my cousin, the Duke of Granfield."

Lucy curtsied. "I am honored, Your Grace."

For a moment, he was stunned. His heart kicked hard.

"Harry has agreed to help us make up the numbers for the quadrille," Mina said.

He arched his brows. "I beg your pardon?"

"Do not worry, Harry," Mina said. "Miss Longmore will instruct us. Do cooperate for her sake."

He darted a look at Lucy. She curtsied and maintained a serene smile. What he didn't know was how she had come to be in his mother's drawing room. He dared not ask with so many people about, but apparently Lucy taught dance lessons. Had his mother hired her?

"Harry, Mrs. Vernon recommended Miss Longmore," Mrs. Norcliffe said. "I am anxious to see if Miss Longmore lives up to her reputation."

"Who will play for us?" Mina asked.

"I shall be glad to play," Mrs. Vernon said, approaching the pianoforte.

"Thank you, my dear," Mrs. Norcliffe said.

"Harry, you will partner with Miss Longmore," Mina said. "Do try to take her instruction seriously. I know how you like to make a jest of everything."

"I'm neither jesting nor dancing," Harry said.

"Harry, you must practice for the competition," Mrs. Norcliffe insisted. "I know you prefer the card room at Almack's, but you cannot hide there all evening again."

He put his fist on his hip. "I do not hide; I play cards and billiards."

"Do not be tiresome, Harry," Mina said. "Please be cooperative for Miss Longmore's sake. You will partner with her."

Mina's words struck him like a hammer. Lucy probably depended on the income from her dance instruction. He mustn't do anything to tip off others that they were acquainted, because it might create problems for Lucy, and that was the last thing he wanted.

Mina patted his shoulder. "We need your help, and it won't kill you to dance."

"It would be remiss of me to refuse," he said, keeping his gaze on Lucy.

"Shall we begin, Miss Longmore?" Mina asked.

Lucy broke eye contact with him and seemed a bit flustered. "Oh, yes, of course. If everyone will take your places, we will walk through the steps without music the first time. Afterward, we will practice with music, if that is acceptable."

"It is," Mrs. Norcliffe said. "You may begin."

Conversation in the drawing room dwindled as the guests craned their heads to watch the dance lesson.

Lucy regarded Harry. "Your Grace, as the head couple, we will pass each other with our right shoulders, making half a figure eight around the couples on the *outside*. Are you ready?"

He nodded and gazed into her eyes as he passed within inches of her. "We must talk," he whispered.

She shot him a warning look and immediately pasted on a smile. "Now, the opposite couple—that would be Miss Mina Norcliffe and Lord Everleigh—will pass one another in a half figure eight on the inside."

When Mina and Everleigh completed their movements, they halted.

"We will all join hands to form a star circle in one direction for an eight count," Lucy said.

Harry laid his hand over Lucy's, and his skin tingled. The devil. The mere touch of her hand made him breathe harder.

"Now, switch hands and circle in the opposite direction." Lucy met his gaze, and when her lips parted a little, Harry couldn't tear his eyes away from her. He set his hand over her much smaller one as they turned in the opposite direction in a star circle. He imagined her hands clasped behind his neck and then sliding ever so slowly down his naked chest, teasing him with her slender fingertips.

They clasped hands and turned in a circle. Without breaking the movements, she directed everyone to turn in the opposite direction.

"The head couple skips forward and turns to face in the opposite direction," Lucy said. He held her gaze as they skipped forward and turned to face in the other direction.

"Now the outside couples skip forward and turn to face the other direction."

Harry had to see her after the dancing ended. He wasn't sure what he would say. All he knew was that he had to talk to her. He was determined to win her. She'd played hard to get from the beginning, but it had only increased his desire for her.

Harry wanted her so badly that he couldn't take his eyes off her. When her lips parted slightly, his blood heated and sizzled through his veins. She averted her eyes and directed everyone to form a star circle to the right. He imagined giving her a long, hot kiss. He wanted to tangle his tongue with hers and hear her moan for him. Good God. His cock was stirring in the middle of his mother's crowded drawing room.

"The top and bottom couples move around the side couples on the *outside* in a half figure eight," Lucy said, "while the head couples skip forward and turn about."

When he turned about with Lucy, he met her gaze. "We must talk," he said.

She narrowed her eyes and continued giving direction. "Inside couples turn in a half figure eight with the left shoulder around the side couples on the *inside*."

As he passed her, he whispered, "I must see you afterward."

Her lips parted as they passed each other. He wanted more than anything to take her somewhere private. If they were alone, he would pull her into his arms. He would kiss her senseless and let his hands smooth down the curve of her spine. Then he would plant kisses along her jaw and follow to her slim neck.

After the dancers completed the movements, Lucy said, "Excellent. Now, is everyone clear about the steps? If you have a question, please ask."

"I think we've mastered it," Mina said. "Harry, you're doing well."

He was aroused and hot all over.

Two elderly ladies raised quizzing glasses to their eyes and peered at him. Damned tight trousers hid nothing.

"Let us walk through the steps once more," Lucy said, "and then we will try it with music."

On the second walk-through, Lord Chesfield turned in the wrong direction, but he laughed at his faux pas. "Sorry," he said. "I'll try to do better next time."

The third time, everything went smoothly.

"Now let us try with music. Will you play, Mrs. Vernon?" Lucy asked.

"Yes, when you are ready."

Lucy curtsied. "Then let us begin."

Harry's gaze kept returning to Lucy. As they danced past each other, he found himself mesmerized. She performed the steps lightly and with a natural grace. When he clasped hands with her, he dared to whisper, "Look at me."

She met his gaze and averted her eyes. "Careful," she murmured.

He despised the pretense between them, but it was necessary. He certainly couldn't reveal in his mother's crowded drawing room that they were acquainted. It might cause problems for Lucy, and she likely depended on her dance lessons for income.

When the dance ended, there was a smattering of applause. Harry put his hands behind his back while the guests slowly departed.

The two elderly ladies smiled as they approached him. "You were our favorite."

"Thank you."

"Oh, it was *our* pleasure," one of them said.

The devil.

"Harry, you surprised me," Mina said. "You've always claimed you have two left feet when it comes to dancing."

"Now you're found out, Harry," Amelia said. "You won't be able to hide in the game rooms this Wednesday night."

Since he had no intention of attending Almack's, he didn't refute his cousins.

"Miss Longmore, you made the dancing seem so effortless," Mina said. "Usually I feel apprehensive on the dance floor."

"Nonsense, Mina, you are always poised," Mrs. Norcliffe said.

Harry could not fault his mother for championing his cousins. His mother had her flaws, but she'd always treated the girls with affection.

Mrs. Norcliffe turned to Mrs. Vernon. "I do thank you for the recommendation. The instruction certainly helps one recollect the beauty of the quadrille. Hopefully tonight my Mina will advance in the competition."

"Aunt, I only wish to enjoy the dancing. I care nothing for prizes," Mina said.

"Care nothing?" Mrs. Norcliffe said, her voice pitching higher. "It is important that you do your best. I'm counting on you. It is crucial that you make a favorable impression. Hundreds of others will be watching."

"The very idea makes my legs turn to jelly," Helena said, "but, Mina, you are not bashful."

"I try not to think about others watching me," Mina said. "Otherwise, I'd be terrified of turning in the wrong direction and would most certainly make a mistake because I was apprehensive." She turned to Lucy. "Miss Longmore, how long have you been dancing?"

"My mother claimed I danced as soon as I learned to walk, but of course she was exaggerating."

"There is a great difference between country assemblies and Almack's," Mrs. Norcliffe said with a sniff.

Harry frowned at his mother's condescension. She'd clearly retained Lucy to direct the dancing. Why the devil did she have to treat her in this haughty manner?

"Indeed," Lady Jersey said. "Only those who have influential family, elegance, and a certain *je ne sais quoi* may pass through the hallowed doors of Almack's."

Mina's lips twitched as she exchanged an amused look with Harry.

He didn't give a damn about Almack's. He needed to see Lucy after this foolish practice ended. He had to speak to her, let her know he couldn't stop thinking about her.

Lucy curtsied to Mrs. Norcliffe. "Madame, I will be glad to return next week if you wish."

"No, you are dismissed," Mrs. Norcliffe said in a curt manner. "The butler will see to your compensation."

Harry ground his teeth at his mother's abrupt dismissal and scowled at her. Naturally she only lifted her brows. He took a step toward Lucy, instinctively wanting to defend her, but he checked the impulse, because he dared not make a scene in front of all these people.

Lucy curtsied, squared her shoulders, and walked out of the drawing room with her head held high.

He wanted to follow her, but he knew it would make matters worse. When they were at the park, he never felt the differences in their social stations, but his mother's brusque tone made it seem as thick as the London fog.

Lucy's face burned like a hot coal.

She was more than a little shaken as she stepped outside Mrs. Norcliffe's drawing room. Why had the woman hired her if she did not have confidence in her capabilities? Lucy knew she had taught the lesson flawlessly. It was one she'd taught dozens of times in the past. She knew the country dances well, and Mrs. Vernon had recommended her. She thought back to everything that had transpired, but she'd done nothing to deserve the curt dismissal. The only thing that stood out in retrospect was that Mrs. Norcliffe had recognized her because she served lemonade at Almack's. But why would that displease her?

She'd wanted the nobles to notice her so that she could gain new clients, but she'd been mortified by Mrs. Norcliffe's rude dismissal in front of Harry.

She was no stranger to aristos treating her in an offensive manner. She'd endured rude comments from spoiled little rich girls numerous times when she'd worked for Madame Delanger. She'd mentally dismissed them because they were strangers, and she didn't care what they thought of her—if they thought of her at all. She'd felt superior to the haughty, demanding customers.

But it had been an entirely different matter when Mrs. Norcliffe had humiliated her in front of Harry in an overflowing drawing room.

Damn his mother for treating Lucy with disdain.

After all the guests left, Mrs. Norcliffe put the sheet music aside and settled in her favorite chair. "Girls, you may be excused. I wish to have a private discussion with Harry."

He regarded his mother coldly. "There will be no discussion, and I will not escort you to Almack's. You can find your own way there."

"Harry, why are you doing this?" Mrs. Norcliffe said in a shocked tone.

"You know damn well. I will not allow you to abuse an employee or a servant."

"Mind your tongue. Of course you will escort us," Mrs. Norcliffe said. "If you do not, you will insult your cousins and me. Others will remark upon your absence and think that you have no respect for your family."

"I'm not escorting you tonight or any other night. That's the end of it."

"You are the head of the family, Harry. What you do reflects upon me and your cousins, especially now that you are a duke. You must think of your consequence."

His nostrils flared. "I don't give a rat's arse what anyone thinks. The dukedom is mine. Havenwood means far more to me than a ballroom full of haughty, pretentious sycophants who suddenly want to make my acquaintance. A year ago, those same people rebuffed me because I had neither property nor money. I will have nothing to do with insincere toadeaters. Enjoy your evening at Almack's. I won't be there."

Mrs. Norcliffe rapped her fan on the arm of her chair. "I saw you ogling Miss Longmore at Almack's and again in my drawing room."

Now he knew the reason for her curt response to Lucy, but that only strengthened his resolve. His mother and her fellow patronesses could go hang for all he cared.

As he strode down the stairs, she followed. "Harry, I will not tolerate this willfulness."

He ignored her as his boot heels clipped on the marble floor. Gibson watched him, wide-eyed, as he approached the foyer.

"Harry, come back here," Mrs. Norcliffe called out. "I have not finished."

Harry strode out to his carriage. Fury made his temples ache. How dare his mother treat Lucy in such a wretched manner? He wouldn't stand for her insults.

Right now, he needed to find Lucy and let her know he would never let anyone speak to her in that abusive manner again.

Since they had met at Green Park twice before, he hoped to encounter her there. He wanted Lucy to know that he respected her and that he would not allow his mother to mistreat her again. But first, he'd better see about Bandit. It was Barlow's half day off, and the puppy must be wild to go outside.

The moment Harry put his key in the door, Bandit started barking. He walked inside, bent down, and ruffled the collie's fur. "Shall we go for a walk?"

The puppy barked again. Harry attached the leash, and Bandit kept jumping on his legs. He strode along Piccadilly until he reached the park. Bandit nosed through the grass as they walked along. He'd hoped to see her waiting on the bench, but she wasn't there. Perhaps she had another dance lesson to teach. Or maybe she had errands. More likely, she'd purposely avoided him.

While Bandit explored the grass and pissed on a number of trees, Harry scuffed his boots in the damp grass. He hated that his mother had treated Lucy like a lowly servant. His mother was well known for her haughty behavior, but he'd be damned before he let her discredit Lucy ever again.

That same morning

After she collected the purse, Lucy fled the town house and didn't slow her steps until she reached the bench where she'd met Harry in Green Park previously. Then she inhaled on a shuddering breath. She couldn't face Harry now. Especially not now. She hurried out of the park, because she couldn't bear for him to know how much his mother's disdain had hurt her.

He likely hadn't gone to the park, hoping to meet her, but she didn't want to know if he'd done so or not. From the moment she'd met him, she'd known that he was privileged.

He was a duke, a man of power and prestige. A man whose servants catered to his every need. A man who lived in an exotic world of marble floors, lush Axminster carpets, and gold-plated mirrors.

His mother's words had said it plainly enough. *"There is a great difference between country assemblies and Almack's."*

She shouldn't care what Mrs. Norcliffe thought of her. Even though she tried to calm herself, the turmoil churned within her. All she'd wanted was to find new clients and earn money so that she could open her own dance studio one day. She'd wanted nothing to do with him, but he'd persisted and managed to charm his way into her life.

Today he'd witnessed her humiliation.

Her head ached. She needed guidance from her friends. Mary and Evelyn had always given her sound advice in the past. Lucy knew she must use caution. Madame Delanger would frown upon her presence, but she only meant to make plans with her friends to meet later. The shop bell jingled as Lucy opened the door, and Evelyn hurried to the entrance. "Lucy, I didn't expect to see you."

"I'll not disturb you long," she said. "I wish to meet you and Mary tonight after the shop closes, but perhaps I should greet Madame Delanger first."

"Madame is abed," Evelyn said.

"Is she ill?"

Evelyn shook her head. "Come with me to the sewing room. We can talk there."

Lucy perched on a chair. "What is this about?"

Evelyn finished pinning lace on a gown. "I arrived early to finish this gown and heard this awful moaning upstairs. I thought Madame was ill. So I ran up the steps. Then I heard the bed ropes squeaking and Madame crying out *Mon Dieu* over and over again."

Lucy covered her laugh. "Oh, my stars."

"When I heard footsteps, I peeked out and saw the man. His hair was standing up like a rooster."

Lucy's shoulders shook with laughter.

The shop bell rang. Evelyn walked out into the main room, and a moment later, Mary followed Evelyn into the sewing room. "Lucy, you are a sight for sore eyes. I'm so happy to see you."

"I've missed you both," Lucy said.

"Where is Ida? I don't want her to report you for fraternizing."

"She disappeared a week ago," Evelyn said.

Lucy's eyes widened. "So it is only you and Mary?"

Evelyn nodded. "I suspect Madame would take you back in a heartbeat. No matter how many hours we sew, two of us cannot keep up with the demand. Would you consider coming back?"

Lucy shook her head. "My list of dance clients is growing. I quit working for Buckley."

"Good for you," Mary said.

She told her friends how she'd managed to get more opportunities to teach after one lady recommended her to others. "I was positive my luck had changed, but something went horribly wrong today."

"Lucy, what happened?" Mary asked.

She told them what had occurred in Mrs. Norcliffe's drawing room.

"She's one of the patronesses at Almack's. For some reason, she scowled at me from the moment I arrived. I could not remain in that house after the horrible way she treated me in front of everyone, including her son."

Mary frowned. "Lucy, I'm surprised at your reaction. You're no stranger to how the quality belittles us."

"Yes, but there were others present," Evelyn said. "I think it would be very hard to maintain one's composure when a roomful of people witness your embarrassment."

"That's true," Mary said. "Lucy, don't let one bad experience deter you from your dancing instruction. It is your dream."

Lucy nodded. "Yes, that is the most important thing." She smoothed her hands over her apron. "I haven't told you everything."

Her friends gave her a questioning look.

"I met a man."

"Tell us about him," Evelyn said. "How did you meet him?"

"You'll never believe it." When she finished telling the story of how she'd met Sir Galahad—Harry—her friends were astounded.

"Mercy," Mary said. "Lucy, you might have been hurt."

"Oh no, he is a gentleman. Well, actually, he is the Duke of Granfield."

Her friends burst out laughing.

"Very funny, Lucy," Mary said, wiping tears of hilarity from her eyes."

Evelyn chortled. "The Duke of Granfield—ha!"

When Lucy bit her lip, Evelyn regarded her with a quizzical expression. "You're jesting, aren't you?"

She shook her head slowly.

"Oh dear God," Mary said. "He's an honest to God duke?"

"Yes."

After she told her friends the entire story, they gaped at her.

Mary sank to her chair. "Pinch me."

"What?" Lucy said.

"Pinch me, because this cannot be real," Mary said. "This sort of thing doesn't happen to girls like us."

Evelyn inhaled. "Lucy, you could be a duchess."

"Oh no," she said. "He lives in a very different world. His mother's furniture is gold-plated, and there are rich carpets on the floor. He owns a very stylish carriage."

"You've been in his carriage?" Mary said.

She told them the story of meeting him in the park. "Nothing will ever come of it. If I'd had any illusions, his mother's rude behavior put a halt to any silly dreams. I just missed you both and wanted to talk to you about everything that has happened."

"Lucy, did he kiss you?" Evelyn said.

She blushed. "Yes, once. I liked it."

"What is he like?" Mary asked.

"He's charming and agreeable. He was very kind to Grandmama."

"Is this man real?" Evelyn said. "Where can I find my own duke?"

Lucy laughed. "Oh, he's real enough, but he has faults."

She told them how he'd waited to reveal his true identity.

"But he apologized," Evelyn said. "That's the important thing."

"It's best not to believe everything a man says," Mary said, keeping her eyes on her stitching. "I learned that the hard way."

"Are you still courting Billy?" Lucy asked.

Mary's mouth thinned. "No. I saw Billy kissing another girl in the tavern. He claimed it was my fault."

"How can he blame you? That makes no sense," Lucy said.

Mary pinned another row of lace. "He said it was because I wouldn't let him...in my bed."

"Good for you," Lucy said, and didn't notice Evelyn's warning look until it was too late.

Mary reached up and brushed a tear from her cheek.

"Oh, Mary. What happened?" Lucy said.

Mary's lower lip trembled. "He s-said if I l-loved him I would let him. So I gave in. I haven't seen him for a sennight."

Lucy gave Mary her handkerchief. It was on the tip of her tongue to tell Mary she deserved better, but she kept that to herself. Mary needed a friend to listen. "I know you loved him."

Mary blotted her tears. "I knew there were other girls, but then he would show up and tell me I was *his* girl. He made me feel special. Turns out it was the ale talking." She sniffed. "You probably think I'm stupid."

"No," Lucy said. "I think you have a big heart and one day soon you will meet a man who appreciates and loves you."

Mary sniffed again. "I'll have to tell him there was someone before him."

"If he loves you, he will understand," Lucy said.

"What if h-he doesn't?"

Lucy took her hands. "Then he doesn't deserve you."

Mary released a shaky breath. "Enough about me. It will only make me sad to continue to talk about this. So the duke took you and your grandmother up in his carriage? Oh my goodness."

Lucy nodded. "I don't see how a courtship could ever develop."

"What makes you think so?" Evelyn said. "He invited your grandmother to an outing."

"He sounds wonderful," Mary said.   •

Lucy sighed. "I took a serving job at Almack's. Of course

he was there and tried to flirt with me while I was working. Then I saw him flirting with the aristocratic ladies in their finery. They are of his world and I am not. So that must be the end of our brief acquaintance."

"I think you're pushing him away because you're afraid of being crossed in love," Evelyn said. "Give him a chance. The worst that can happen is you discover he is not the man for you."

"I already know that," Lucy said. "He will never marry beneath him, and I am far below him."

"Why not enjoy a romantic interlude for now?" Evelyn said. "Most working girls would give anything to be in your slippers for an afternoon."

She considered Evelyn's advice. "I'll think about it."

Mary looked up from her sewing. "Lucy, he isn't pressing you for intimacies, is he?"

"Oh no," she said. "His mother may be rude, but he is gentlemanly." Lucy paused. "I didn't tell you earlier, but the reason I was so embarrassed today is because she embarrassed me in front of Granfield."

"Ignore his mother's insults," Mary said. "Your duke sounds like a keeper."

"He's not mine, Mary. He never will be."

Evelyn frowned. "This may sound crass, but regardless of how Mrs. Norcliffe treated you, can you afford to turn down an opportunity to teach dance in her drawing room?"

"She was not impressed with me. I'm sure I'll never be invited there again."

"You don't know that," Mary said.

Footsteps thudded from above. "I had better go before Madame finds me here," Lucy said. "Will you meet me at the park on Sunday?"

Mary sighed. "Madame promised six gowns would be

ready by next Wednesday morning. We can't take the time just now."

"We will meet soon," Evelyn said. "It's the start of the season. You know it's busiest at this time of year."

Lucy couldn't quite hide her disappointment. "I understand."

"Do not worry," Mary said. "When the initial rush of the season slows, we'll make plans to meet."

Lucy suspected it would be weeks before Madame allowed her friends a day off.

Chapter Nine

Wednesday morning

*H*arry glanced in the mirror after Barlow finished shaving him. "Thank you, Barlow. When I was a boy, my fondest wish was to be a pirate. I yearned to have a dastardly black beard. If only piratical looks were en vogue, I would not have to submit to the razor every morning."

"Yes, Your Grace," Barlow said.

Harry had tried everything, but he'd concluded that Barlow lacked all sense of humor. Nevertheless, he did a fine job of shaving, dog walking, and taking care of Harry's clothing. He was also quite rigid about ensuring every item was placed precisely in the same spot every day—unlike his master, who tended to forget where he left things. Harry suspected that Barlow secretly thought him eccentric at best and slovenly at worst.

A knock sounded at the door. Barlow answered and delivered a missive to Harry. His valet winced upon seeing Bandit chewing his bone on the silver salver that his mother had given him. Harry had rather hoped that Barlow would find it amusing, but his valet looked pained at the crunching sounds that Bandit blissfully made while dining.

Harry broke the seal and was surprised to see Mina's signature. He was not, however, surprised at his mother's latest scheme. Over the years, Mrs. Norcliffe had used numerous ploys in order to get her way. She was not above cajoling, inveigling, flattering, and fabricating. To-day, however, she'd invented an entirely new stratagem, one that was doomed to fail. This being Wednesday, Harry quickly deduced the reason for his mother's sudden afflic-tion. He briefly considered summoning the family physi-cian, but he would not waste the man's time. With a resigned sigh, he called for his carriage and traveled the short distance to Grosvenor Square.

Harry trudged up the stairs of his mother's elegant town house, where he found her ensconced among numerous pil-lows. Naturally his cousins were keeping vigil as Mrs. Norcliffe staged her indisposition. Harry took one look at his mother and said, "Mama, I must congratulate you. For one so ill, you are certainly turned out well. Not a hair out of place."

Mrs. Norcliffe briefly narrowed her eyes, and then as if remembering her "ailment," she pulled an embroidered hand-kerchief from the voluminous sleeve of her dressing gown and dabbed it at her dry eyes. "My nerves are pinching."

Ah, his mother's favorite malady.

"At least my darling nieces demonstrate their love and care. I do not know what I have done to deserve such an un-feeling son."

"Of course you know. I believe we discussed your ill-mannered treatment of Miss Longmore previously. You then demanded that I escort you and my cousins to Almack's. I refused. However, the point is moot. You have succumbed to an attack of pinching nerves and will be unable to attend the festivities at Almack's tonight."

Mina tapped Harry's shoulder. "May I speak to you privately?"

With a sigh, he followed her out of his mother's boudoir and downstairs to the drawing room.

Mina sat beside him. "Harry, I have not seen her so miserable in a very long time."

"I know my mother. She has her good qualities, but we both know she is manipulative. I daresay she asked you to speak to me."

"Yes, she did. The dancing competition means a great deal to her. I know it's a little ridiculous—"

"A little?" he said, arching his brows.

"It makes her happy to be one of the patronesses."

"Mina, I despise Almack's and all of the pretentious people involved with it. You know as well as I do that the patronesses arbitrarily approve or disapprove vouchers. Their vanity knows no bounds. I attended the first night and have done my duty."

"I think you should make an exception. If you do not, Aunt will stay abed, because she does not want others to know you refused to accompany her. I will leave the decision to you, but I hope you reconsider."

"She has no one to blame but herself. I'm not inclined to escort her when she spoke in a brusque manner to Miss Longmore. It is abusive, Mina, and I'll not tolerate it."

"Disagreements happen in all families, but they should never become public for the sake of all the family members.

If you refuse to escort Aunt, others will notice and remark upon it," Mina said.

"You believe I should ignore her ill-mannered address to Miss Longmore."

"I spoke to Aunt after you left that day. I said that her curt response to Miss Longmore was unwarranted. I also mentioned that others found it awkward and embarrassing. She knows it was wrong and that it reflected poorly on her."

"Did she admit she was wrong?"

Mina sighed. "She expressed concern that Miss Longmore was using her wiles on you."

"I've heard enough. If I escort her, I will be sending the message that her behavior is acceptable. It is not. She did this to herself, and she will simply have to live with the consequences."

"Very well," Mina said. "Will you inform Lord Everleigh that I'm unable to participate in the dancing competition any longer? I'm not allowed to correspond with him because of the proprieties."

"The devil," he said. "Sorry." How could he deny sweet Mina?

"Harry, you must follow your own conscience."

"You and Everleigh are well and truly entrenched in the dance competition. I do not want to ruin it for you."

"I know it's frivolous, but I enjoy being able to dance exclusively with Everleigh. We are able to talk freely during the dance. There, I've all but admitted my tender feelings for him."

"I will provide the escort tonight. I don't want to disappoint you and Everleigh."

Mina kissed his cheek. "Thank you, Harry."

* * *

Almack's, that evening

Harry looked out the carriage window. After speaking to Mina, he'd chastised his mother at length for her ill-mannered behavior in the drawing room and made it clear that he'd only relented for Mina's sake. He had thought Mrs. Norcliffe would be chastened and demonstrate remorse. Instead, she'd called for her maid, a pot of chocolate, and a rose in a vase.

As the carriage drew closer to Almack's, Harry realized the crowd was twice as large this week. "Every Tom, Jane, and Frank in London turned out to gawk at us," he said. "We must appear like so many peacocks strutting in our feathers and diamond stick pins."

His cousins laughed, but Mrs. Norcliffe inhaled audibly. "Harry, your irreverence is not appreciated."

"I suppose that depends on one's sense of humor—or lack thereof."

"You are disrespectful of long-standing tradition," Mrs. Norcliffe said.

"The dancing competition has not been in existence long enough to qualify," he said.

"Harry, let me be clear. Either you dance tonight or I will not speak to you for a fortnight," Mrs. Norcliffe said.

He was tempted to ask her if that was a promise, but thought better of it. Her demand, however, gave him an excellent idea. "As it happens, I do plan to dance tonight, and I know the lady I wish to ask."

"This is wonderful news," Mrs. Norcliffe said, clasping her hands. "I do hope this is not one of your horrid jests."

"You may rest your fears," he said. "I would be surprised if you did not approve of my choice of partner."

"Who is she?" Mrs. Norcliffe said.

"Patience," Harry said.

She snapped her fan closed, letting him know she was unhappy.

"Aunt, be patient," Mina said. "Harry will dance tonight and make you proud."

When the carriage rolled to a halt, Harry helped his mother and cousins step out. Everywhere he looked, there were costermongers selling their wares. The scent of roasted chestnuts wafted in the air. One seller hawked sweet cherries. Another offered hot eels. The area around Almack's resembled a fair once again. Someone was playing a flute and two women were stepping merrily to the tune. Undoubtedly these folks would have far better refreshments than the pitiful fare inside Almack's.

Naturally a number of the lower orders were selling rotgut gin again. Harry had fortified himself with an excellent brandy at home. If all went well tonight, he would send his female relatives home in the carriage while he spent the rest of the evening at White's.

He offered his arm to his mother and they slowly made their way through the dense crowd queuing up to enter Almack's.

"It will be a grand squeeze tonight," Mrs. Norcliffe said with glee.

His mother was definitely puffed up tonight.

Harry couldn't resist needling her. "I do hope your nerves aren't pinching."

"I am perfectly recovered," she said. "Now, Harry, I know your propensity for mischief, but you will choose an acceptable young lady as your dance partner. For my sake, please do not select Miss Forsythe. She's on the shelf. You do not wish to dance with a lady others ignore."

He bit back a grin. "I'm fairly certain no one ever ignores this lady."

"Well, you must tell me her name," she said.

"You will discover that soon enough. Allow me to escort you to the chairs for the patronesses."

Once he'd settled his mother, Harry spied Everleigh. He'd already found Mina. As usual, Helena and Amelia had managed to escape to the wallflower row. He looked around and spotted Charles Osgood. He was an amiable fellow known to be a favorite of the ladies for his good humor.

Harry greeted him. "Osgood, I haven't seen you in an age. Do you know my cousins?"

"I've not had the pleasure of making their acquaintance," he said. "Unfortunately, your mother appears too busy at present to do the honors. Ah, but there is Mrs. Amy Darcett. She was always one of my favorite ladies. Let me appeal to her for an introduction."

A few minutes later, a tall redhead wearing a striking jade gown appeared with Osgood. "I am honored to help with the introductions, Mr. Osgood," Mrs. Darcett said.

"First, may I introduce you to my friend, the Duke of Granfield?"

Harry bowed. "Ma'am, I believe we have a mutual acquaintance in Bellingham."

She smiled. "Indeed we do. Now, I understand there are two young ladies in need of partners."

Harry nodded. "Yes, my cousins Miss Amelia Radburn and Miss Helena Radburn. Amelia met Lord Chesfield previously."

"Well, then I shall introduce Mr. Osgood to Miss Helena Radburn," Mrs. Darcett said.

"I'm obliged," Harry said.

A short time later, the orchestra struck up an introductory piece.

The roar of voices in the cavernous building gradually lowered.

Harry looked over his shoulder to the refreshment area. Lucy was nowhere in sight. He pressed through the crowd until he was near the patronesses.

Lady Jersey stepped forward. "Tonight's dancing competition involves the quadrille. Gentlemen, choose your partners with great care. We shall begin momentarily."

Harry walked to his mother. "May I have this dance?"

"What?" she said under her breath.

He projected his voice intentionally so that others would hear him. "I realize you must judge the competition, but I hope you will not object to one dance with me."

"How sweet. One cannot fault such a dutiful son," Mrs. Drummond-Burrell said.

Other ladies were smiling fondly at him. Everyone but his mother.

Harry offered his arm and escorted his mother toward the dance floor. Thunderous applause sounded.

"You did this on purpose," Mrs. Norcliffe said under her breath, all the while maintaining her smile.

"Of course. I thought it would please you."

"I wasn't born yesterday," she said. "You devised a means of avoiding dancing with an eligible young lady of good birth."

"So I did. For the entire evening. I shall bear it as best I can."

"We will have a discussion tonight," she said. "I'll not stand for your tricks."

His smile faded. "Let me be clear. If not for Mina, I would not have escorted you here."

Lucy set up the pitcher of lemonade and glasses in the refreshment area. She'd missed seeing the first set of couples, but in between serving lemonade, she caught glimpses of the dancing. The second set of couples was dancing the quadrille as well. Mina had partnered with Lord Everleigh again. When they finished their set, they strolled toward her.

Lucy stiffened. She'd never minded teaching the children of the nobility to dance, she'd never minded serving lemonade, and she'd always ignored any callous comments. But she'd never felt inferior until Mrs. Norcliffe had humiliated her in front of Harry.

She had learned the art of making her expression as neutral as possible and employed it now. "May I serve you lemonade?"

"Yes, that would be nice," Lord Everleigh, said. "Dancing makes me thirsty."

Mina sipped her lemonade. "Thank you for the excellent dance instruction." She paused and her face flushed. She looked as if she meant to say something else, but she bit her lip and set her glass aside. "Thank you, Miss Longmore. I am not as thirsty as I thought."

Lucy suspected that Mina was embarrassed by Mrs. Norcliffe's brusque manners at the dance practice. Lucy liked Mina and hated the awkwardness. "I hope you and Lord Everleigh win the dance competition."

Mina smiled. "Thank you, Miss Longmore. That is very kind of you."

Lord Everleigh set his glass on the table and offered his arm to Mina. "Let us find Harry."

"He's probably hiding in the game room," Mina said. "He's avoiding all of the matchmaking mamas."

Everleigh scoffed. "He's also avoiding the dance floor."

"But we will not," Mina said, smiling.

Lucy noted the way Mina and Everleigh gazed into each other's eyes and thought it must be heavenly to be in love.

The next set began and Lucy lifted on her toes to watch.

Mina and Everleigh danced as if they'd danced together all of their lives. They never took their eyes off of each other. Lucy sighed, wishing that she could take part in the dancing tonight, but of course that wasn't possible. No one seemed interested in the lemonade, and that gave Lucy an opportunity to watch the dancers closely. She didn't recognize any of the other dancers.

A rotund gentleman turned in the wrong direction and stepped on Everleigh's shoes. Lucy covered her mouth upon seeing the obvious pain on Everleigh's face. "Oh no," Lucy said under her breath. Concern was written all over Mina's face, but Everleigh managed to keep dancing, although he winced now and then.

When the set ended, Everleigh bowed to Mina. The crowd came to their feet and cheered the couple. Obviously they were a favorite among the guests.

Lucy sighed. Two days ago, she'd learned Granfield's Christian name. Now she knew he was in attendance and hoped he would stay away. She would not care a jot what these nobles thought of her if not for him. In truth, most of them took their glasses of lemonade and ignored her. She might as well be part of the wall for all of their notice, and she preferred it that way. But she'd come to the ton's attention while teaching dance. She'd borne the brunt of rude comments when she'd worked as a seamstress. She'd never taken it personally. But when Mrs. Norcliffe had demeaned her in front of Harry, it had humiliated her.

Harry bided his time by playing a few hands of whist in the gaming room. He wished to speak to Lucy, but he didn't want to be too obvious, because she was working. The last thing he wanted was to create trouble for her with the head maid again.

He couldn't imagine that Lucy earned enough to make this job worthwhile, but obviously her choices were limited. Harry knew he could help her if she would allow it. His new secretary would start work next week and could draft the necessary letter of character, and his solicitor could inquire into respectable positions for a young lady in need of employment. A better job would allow her and her grandmother to move into a safer neighborhood, too. Just thinking of her walking along those dark streets made him wild to protect her, something he knew she would resist.

When Harry emerged from the card room, he looked at her. She saw him and turned away. It was a clear signal not to disturb her. Fair enough, but after he sent his mother and cousins home, he meant to wait for Lucy.

The music ended, and the guests surged closer to the chairs where the patronesses conferred below the balcony. He checked his watch. It was almost midnight. Obviously the patronesses were attempting to judge the dancers and narrow the field of candidates.

Someone clapped him on the shoulder. "Oh, Bellingham, I didn't know you were here."

"We arrived late. Stephen insisted upon a bedtime story. One story led to another, and then he kicked up a fuss when nurse tried to put him to bed." Bell looked chagrined. "Well, enough domesticity. Laura told me you were dancing to a lady dance master's tune in your mother's drawing room recently."

"I made an untimely appearance. My cousin Mina roped me into dancing."

Bell laughed. "I've no love for Almack's either, but Laura insisted upon watching the competition tonight."

"Shall we meet at White's tomorrow night?" Bell said.

Harry nodded. "Absolutely."

"I'll send round a note to Colin," Bell said. "I'll see you tomorrow night."

After the orchestra played the last note, the crowd surged forward. The cacophony of voices grew louder, echoing in the enormous building. Harry found an empty chair on the deserted wallflower row and stretched out his legs. Then he looked back at the refreshment tables. Three young bucks had surrounded Lucy. One of them touched her hand lingeringly when she gave him a glass of lemonade.

Harry's blood boiled. He fisted his hands and strode through the crowd. When he reached Lucy's station, he stared daggers at the trio. Damn it. She was his. "Leave her in peace," he gritted out.

The three disappeared quickly.

Lucy regarded him with narrowed eyes. "I do not need you to rescue me."

"They were bedeviling you. I won't stand for it."

She arched her brows. "Are you jealous?"

"Certainly not. I wished to protect you."

Her lips twitched. "From what? The lemonade?"

"You do not know what those men were thinking."

"You read minds, Your Grace?"

He folded his arms over his chest. "They swarmed you."

She regarded him with a knowing expression. "I'm not the one who got stung."

Damn and blast, he was not jealous.

"I want to talk to you," he said. "Will you meet me at Green Park tomorrow?"

She hesitated, giving him hope. "I shouldn't. I feel as if I'm standing too near a rushing river and am in danger of falling in."

He figured her use of the word *falling* was no accident. "You are in no danger from me."

There was a stark expression in her green eyes. "Yes, I agree," she said. "You are not a threat to me, but I am."

He was stunned by her confession and wanted to question her, but the roar of the crowd startled him. Harry took several steps forward and craned his neck in time to see Everleigh turning Mina in circles. The applause was deafening. The pair appeared to be a favorite with the crowd again tonight.

When he turned back, Lucy had vanished, though the lemonade pitcher and glasses remained on the table. He wanted to hunt for her, but he mustn't ignore Mina. Damn it all to hell. He didn't like having to choose between them, but Lucy had disappeared, giving him no choice.

As he walked away, he vowed to find her when the festivities concluded tonight. He managed to press through the crowd and kissed Mina on the cheek. "I take it you won tonight's competition," he said, raising his voice.

"Thanks to Lord Everleigh," she said.

Everleigh regarded Mina with tenderness. "No competition compares to Miss Radburn."

Mrs. Norcliffe finally broke ranks with the other patronesses and joined them. "Oh, what an exciting evening. I'm so proud of all my girls," she said as Helena and Amelia joined them.

"Aunt, I thought it very sweet of Harry to dance with you," Mina said.

"Well, he did impress the other patronesses," Mrs. Norcliffe said.

"My life is made brighter now," Harry drawled.

Mrs. Norcliffe tried to swat him with her fan, but he stepped out of harm's way. "Shall we head to the carriage?" he said, leading the way.

When they left the building, a fine mist dampened the air. Harry turned to Everleigh. "I have other business this night. Will you escort my mother and my cousins in your carriage?"

"Certainly," Everleigh said. "Is all well with you?"

He nodded. "Let me break the news to my mother."

Predictably, Mrs. Norcliffe complained. "Harry, it is your duty to escort us."

He leaned closer to his mother. "I wanted Everleigh to spend a bit more time with Mina. I'm fairly certain he's on the verge of proposing. Best to take advantage of the situation."

"Very well, but we will discuss your own single state tomorrow morning, Harry."

He ignored her statement. "Here is Everleigh's carriage now."

After Everleigh and the ladies boarded, Harry waved them off. The mist turned into rain. When he returned to the building, he was walking against the departing crowd, but eventually the room emptied of all the guests. Harry heard voices in the back of the building and strode there.

Mrs. Thompson called out, "Jane, bring those cakes here and don't be eatin' any of 'em on the way."

Jane gawked at Harry.

Mrs. Thompson turned around. "Your Grace."

"Where is Lucy?" He intended to take her home in his carriage to keep her off the streets.

Mrs. Thompson sighed. "She's gone."

"When did she leave?"

She sighed. "Your Grace, I mean no disrespect, but I don't make it a habit of givin' out information about the servin' girls."

"I understand, but I need to know how long ago she left."

"Your Grace, I could tell ye somethin' if you've a mind to listen."

He folded his arms over his chest. "Very well, I will listen."

Mrs. Thompson frowned. "I know from experience what it's like for girls like Lucy. They work dawn to dusk and sometimes longer. Lucy is bound to have more than one job. I know she didn't leave here until after midnight," Mrs. Thompson said.

His chest filled with guilt. Lucy was probably exhausted after a long day working. He scuffed his shoe on the floor. "I didn't want her to walk home in the dark."

Mrs. Thompson sighed. "Your Grace, I know your heart's in the right place, but she's probably been doin' that long afore you come along. You're not the first nob I seen fall for a pretty maid. I've been in service for thirty-odd years. I never seen it turn out well for the girl."

Ah, hell. "Thank you for being honest." Harry strode through the now empty rooms and collected his greatcoat, hat, and gloves from a servant.

Mr. Wilson, the master of ceremonies, opened the door. "Good evening, Your Grace."

Harry nodded and strode out into the mist. Many of the lower orders were still celebrating near the building. When his carriage pulled up next to the curb, Harry was tempted to give the driver Lucy's address, but he thought of Mrs. Thompson's words and gave his driver directions to the Albany instead.

He would prove Mrs. Thompson wrong.

Chapter Ten

The Albany, the next afternoon

Lucy paused on the step and took a deep breath. One of the maids had failed to report for duty today. When Mrs. Finkle offered to double her wages if she would take on more sets, Lucy had accepted immediately. Now she was a bit weary and must face the one residence she abhorred— G1. With a deep breath, she knocked. When no one responded, she unlocked the door and walked inside. "Maid service," she called out.

Satisfied that no one was at home, she set out to clean the parlor. Once again, she encountered untidy stacks of papers on the desk and on the carpet of all places. There was pet fur on the lumpy sofa as usual. Lucy wondered why a man who could afford to live at the Albany did not replace the shabby furnishings. Ah, well, the gentleman's unappealing décor was none of her concern.

After dusting and cleaning out the cold ashes in the fireplace, Lucy opened the double doors to the bedchamber. She folded back the counterpane. When she pulled the sheets off the bed, the book she'd seen the last time fell to the floor. Gritting her teeth, she picked it up. While she swore not to look, curiosity got the better of her. She gasped at the bawdy engraving. A woman was brazenly holding up her flimsy skirts and exposing her nude body to a crowd of men. With a grimace, Lucy snapped it closed and set the book on the night table.

She put clean sheets on the bed and dragged the bag of laundry out into the parlor. The scrape of a key in the lock startled her. Her heart knocked against her chest. It was the first time a gentleman resident had returned home while she was cleaning. She clasped the laundry bag and reminded herself that she was a mere servant. The gentleman would pay her little heed.

As the door opened, she lowered her gaze as befit a servant. "Miss Longmore, what are you doing here?"

She gasped at the distinctive sound of the duke's voice, stumbled over the bag of laundry, and fell against him with a squeak.

He caught her and laughed. "I believe it is my lucky day."

Her pulse raced. When she looked up, she found him smiling. She was all too aware of his big hands upon her and the faint scent of wintergreen soap she'd discerned before. He was so much taller that the top of her head barely reached his chin. She found herself staring at his deep-set blue eyes once again. When his gaze lowered imperceptibly, she realized he was looking at her mouth. Dear God, she was clinging to him. Had she lost her mind?

She continued to clutch him and told herself it was because her knees were weak.

They were not.

She forced herself to release him. "I beg your pardon."

"At the risk of injuring your feminine sensibilities, I give you permission to fall into my arms whenever you wish."

Her face grew warm. "How clumsy of me."

"Could you possibly contrive to fall into my arms once more?"

God help her. She was tempted.

"Truly your stumble was the best thing that happened to me today."

He startled a laugh out of her. "You must have had a bad day."

"Actually a boring day. Did Barlow let you in?" he asked as he set his key on a tray and removed his hat, gloves, and greatcoat.

"Barlow?" she said.

"My manservant. You did not see him?"

"No, I have a key. My instructions are to call out. If no one answers the door, I enter to clean."

"I don't understand," he said.

Her expression turned wary. "I work here—at the Albany, I mean. I did not know you live here." Belatedly she realized she was twisting her hands. When he noticed, she made herself clasp her hands hard.

He frowned. "Barlow must be walking Bandit."

She curtsied. "Pardon me. I must go, Your Grace."

"Will you call me Harry when it is just us?"

"I'll think about it." Then self-preservation kicked in. "Your servant will return with Bandit soon. One word from him, and I could lose my job just like that," she said, snapping her fingers.

"Barlow would say nothing, and we've done nothing wrong."

"I mean no disrespect to your manservant, but I can't risk gossip. I could lose my position."

"Right. Can't have that, can we?"

"Please excuse me. I must deliver the sheets to the housekeeper."

An arrested expression crossed his face.

Her face flamed as she recalled the book of engravings that had fallen from the sheets.

"You were the one who set the book in the middle of the bed," he said.

Oh, this was horribly embarrassing. She'd done nothing wrong, but of course he knew she'd looked. Her blush had given her away.

"You're shocked," he said.

"On the contrary, I'm appalled," she said, squaring her shoulders.

His mouth twitched once, and it was enough to set her temper off. "You ought to be ashamed. Those engravings are indecent."

"I beg your pardon, Miss Longmore. You played quite a joke on me when you placed the book in the middle of the bed."

She sniffed. "I meant to shame you."

He inclined his head. "I deserve your censure."

She might have believed him if she hadn't seen mischief lurking in his eyes. When she reached for the laundry bag, he intervened. "Allow me."

She shook her head. "I'm working. You must treat me as if I'm invisible."

"No one else is here, and it is ingrained in me to assist a lady."

"I'm a servant. You mustn't ever forget."

"It is quite obvious you are educated and a gentleman's daughter. You could do so much better."

His words stunned her. For a moment, she couldn't believe he'd said it, but there was no doubt he'd insinuated she hadn't tried hard enough to find a better job. "How dare you claim to know my situation? If I could do better, do you think for one moment I would be cleaning your rooms?"

He sighed. "I did not intend to insult you. Quite the opposite."

"Your meaning was clear enough to me. Evidently, you believe I haven't tried hard enough to find a 'better' job."

"Now you're twisting my words."

"I heard what you said. How dare you presume to know what steps I've taken to find better employment? What would you know about work? No doubt you hire people to do everything for you."

He fisted his hands on his hips. "That's correct, Miss Longmore. I simply put up my feet and do nothing all the day long."

The clock on the mantel chimed.

"I've got to take the laundry downstairs to the head maid." She hefted the bag. "Excuse me."

"Meet me at the park," he said. "I intend to finish this argument."

"I don't need your condescension."

His blue eyes narrowed. "I don't need yours either."

"We'll have this out, and then we will part ways—forever." Then she slammed the door behind her.

When Lucy reached the bottom of the stairs, she hurried to Mrs. Finkle's office. The head housekeeper handed over her wages and studied her. "You're lookin' a bit frayed around the edges. Is somethin' the matter?"

She must collect her wits. "No, I'm perfectly well. Will there be anything else?"

"That will be all," Mrs. Finkle said. "You don't seem yourself at all. Your face is flushed."

"I'm fine, really. It's the curse of being a redhead. A little exertion and it shows on my face." She didn't want Mrs. Finkle to think she was ill and unable to work.

"Are you sure?" Mrs. Finkle said.

"Yes, really, I'm well." She silently damned Granfield for stirring up her temper. Lucy bobbed a curtsy and hurried out the door. For a moment, she debated whether or not to meet His Haughtiness, but she had a score to settle with him.

Harry fisted his hands and strode back and forth by the bench where they'd met before. She'd lit into him like a cinder and made it sound as if he were insulting her, when he'd meant the exact opposite. If she'd just given him half a chance, he would have explained, but no, she'd flayed him with her sharp tongue.

He kept pacing and thought about everything he'd said. Damn it all to hell, he'd said the wrong thing, when all he'd meant was that she was obviously clever and educated and deserved a better position.

But that wasn't what he'd said.

You could do so much better.

If I could do better, do you think for one moment I would be cleaning your rooms?

Hell, he hadn't meant it that way.

That was no excuse. He'd seen where she lived, and now he was furious with himself. Stupid, stupid, stupid of him to speak to her in a patronizing manner.

He'd insulted her and hurt her pride.

He ran his hand through his hair. Bloody hell. One moment he'd been flirting with her and the next he'd acted like a prize ass. He'd spoken to her in a condescending manner as if he knew her situation when he didn't know the challenges she faced.

No wonder she'd cut up at him.

"Devil take it," he muttered.

A couple walked past and looked at him askance.

Wonderful. He'd been muttering to himself.

She probably wouldn't show.

Yes, she would. He hoped.

He'd been in the wrong, but he didn't want to admit it to Miss High and Mighty.

Damn, damn, damn. He'd have to eat humble pie. He'd rather eat dirt.

She'd cleaned his messy rooms and brushed all the dog hair off his cast-off sofa. He should tell her not to bother with the dog hair. Bandit would just shed again.

She'd also seen the erotic engravings. That made him smile a little. He wondered if she'd secretly been titillated by them. Of course not. She'd been *appalled*.

He heard footsteps and looked up.

Her face was the color of strawberries. Redheads supposedly had quick tempers. Her temper was probably popping and sizzling like the fireworks at Vauxhall.

He took off his hat. "Earlier, I spoke without thinking."

"You are a privileged aristocrat," she said, her voice rising. "You have very little idea of what my circumstances are, and yet, you proceeded to tell me that I could do so much better."

"I actually meant it as a compliment, but it came out all wrong. I know you're smart and talented. It's true I don't know all of your challenges, but I absolutely believe you are clever enough and capable enough to achieve whatever you want in life. That is what I should have said, and whether you believe it or not, that is my true opinion of you."

She lifted her chin. "I did not appreciate your condescension."

"When you fell into my arms, my brain turned to mush. I was thinking it was my lucky day. Instead I ruined the day."

"You wounded me." She blinked and swiped her hand across her face.

Ah, hell, he'd made her cry. He handed her his handkerchief. "What I said was stupid and unconscionable. Forgive me?"

"You must promise not to wound me again."

"I promise. Will you sit with me?" he asked.

When she nodded, he felt as if he could breathe again.

He reached over and clasped her hand when she sat beside him. Deep inside her chest it felt as if he'd left a bruise.

For a long while, he said nothing. "I know your circumstances are very different than mine," he said, "but it doesn't have to be that way here."

"You assume I will meet you here again," she said.

"I don't assume; I hope."

She folded his handkerchief into a small square and tried to hand it to him, but he waved it away. He'd left her a souvenir with his initials. "I'm not sure it is wise to meet again. I can't see where this could possibly lead."

"Can you not?" he said, searching her eyes.

She knew what would happen if she didn't break ties with him now. He would never mean to hurt her, but it was inevitable, because she could never be a part of his world. She had to break all ties with him today, but it was so hard because he'd become so dear to her.

"Lucy, please give me another chance," he said.

She bit her lip, because she wanted so badly to say yes,

but she knew if she didn't end it now, she would never be able to do it.

"I must go," she said, popping up from the bench.

He rose. "Will you meet me here tomorrow?"

Despite everything, she was torn between wanting to be with him and knowing that it would only create more pain for her. "I don't think it's a good idea."

"Don't do this to us," he said.

Her stomach trembled. He'd become special to her, and it scared her. She'd let him into her life and now she felt vulnerable. He hadn't meant to wound her today, but if she didn't end it now, she knew it would happen again and again. He wouldn't mean to hurt her, but it was inevitable, because she could never be a part of his world. If she did not end it now, she would awake one day, knowing that he'd married another because that was what was expected of him.

He took her by the shoulders. "What are you thinking?"

"I must go."

"No, not yet," he said.

"If someone we know saw us alone here, it could hurt my reputation. If that happened, I would lose most if not all of my dance clients. I can't risk it."

"No one comes here in the afternoon. Everyone is at Rotten Row at five o'clock. You're safe with me," he said.

My heart isn't safe at all. "That is where you should be."

"I'd rather be with you," he said.

"I need time to think, and I can't think properly when I'm with you."

"I'll wait on our bench tomorrow," he said.

You hurt me and it stings. "No, I won't be here."

"Lucy, I'm sorry for what I said earlier."

"I've allowed myself to get caught up in this whirlwind

with you. Everything has gone by so quickly, and I've not had a chance to think about what I'm doing. One minute, I'm ebullient, because I know I will see you, and the next my spirits are lowered, because I don't know when I'll see you next. I've thought of Green Park as our place, but we have made it a trysting place. I need time alone to consider all that has happened."

"How much time?" he said.

"I'm sorry, Harry. I don't know."

"You will leave me to wonder, not knowing if I'll ever see you again?"

"One week," she said. "If I'm not here at four o'clock, then you will know I won't return."

"I will not give up on us, and I will not lose you," he said, his voice full of determination.

It would be better for him if she disappeared from his life. There were too many obstacles standing in their way. They could only meet at her home or the park, because they had to conceal their affaire de coeur, and that alone should have warned her off from the beginning.

There was no hope for them. His family, friends, and political allies would never accept her. She would be an embarrassment to him. Too many had seen her serving lemonade, and they knew she was paid to teach dance lessons. The kindest thing she could do for him was to quietly disappear from his life. But even the thought of a permanent separation filled her with anguish.

God help her, it would be so hard to make this break, because even though she'd sworn to keep her head out of the clouds, she'd fallen in love with him.

She'd never meant to get involved with him that first time they had met at the park, but somehow he'd managed to charm her and challenge her. She'd thought she could keep her feelings in check, but like any other smitten girl, she'd allowed her budding feelings to grow and flourish. Now she must face the pain of separation. Part of her wanted to recant, to tell him that she'd made a mistake, but that mistake had led her to this place with him where they were living in a secret fantasy, one that no one in either of their worlds would ever accept.

One week later

Lucy had not felt so wretched since the day she'd pawned her mother's pearls.

After she took the last of the laundry to Mrs. Finkle, Lucy strode out of Vigo Street. She was heartsick and worried that Harry had found someone else in the interim. All week, she'd imagined him riding on Rotten Row with all the other nobles or calling on a lady. She'd been a fool to push him away, all because she'd gotten scared that he would hurt her again. The only person she'd hurt was herself.

The clopping of hooves drew her attention. A block away a carriage came to a halt. The door opened. Harry stood on the pavement. Then he motioned her to come to him. Lucy lifted her skirts and ran.

"Up you go," he said, lifting her into the carriage as if she weighed nothing.

When he followed her inside, he sat beside her and caught her up in his arms. "I missed you."

"I was miserable," she said. "I worried you would never want to see me again."

"No, Lucy. I will never give up on us, and I will not lose you."

He pulled the drapes closed on either side of the carriage "May I kiss you?"

She smiled. "I thought you would never ask."

Harry untied her cap and tossed it aside. He kissed her gently at first, and then with more intention. When he touched his tongue to her mouth, she parted her lips. He thrust his tongue inside her mouth. Soon she was swept away by his wet, hot, and bone-melting kisses. She loved being in his strong arms again. It felt like home to her.

"We're fogging up the windows," he said, laughing.

"Oh, dear Lord," she said. It was so good to hear his laughter and see his beautiful blue eyes.

He framed her face with his big hands, and then he stripped off his gloves. He trailed kisses from her lips to her jaw and down to her neckline. She inhaled on a ragged breath as he drew his tongue along the inner seam of her bodice. Her nipples tightened as he cupped her breasts, and it felt sinful, but she couldn't resist him. He kissed her again with more intention, and she dared to touch her tongue to his. He pulled her onto his lap, and she felt his hands tugging on her upper back. Then a shock of cool air hit her flesh. His breathing was faster as he lowered her puffed sleeves, trapping her arms and exposing her breasts. "Oh my God, you're beautiful."

She should stop him. She meant to tell him that they mustn't. She knew it was forbidden, but when he took her nipple in his mouth, a strange high-pitched sound came out of her throat. When he switched to her other breast, she squeezed her legs together and a spurt of pleasure sizzled through her.

"Oh yes, I love that you're so responsive to my touch."

After he broke the kiss, they were both breathing harder.

"What are you thinking?" he said, cupping her cheek.

Her face heated.

"Lucy?"

She took a deep breath and kissed him quickly, but he caught her in his arms again. "You're my captive now, and I will never let you go."

"I beg to differ, sir. This captive intends to escape the moment the carriage stops."

"Drat. Where are my manacles when I need them?"

She laughed. "You amuse me, Harry."

"I like the sound of my name on your lips." He angled his head and gave her another long, deep kiss. "I missed you," he said. "I feared I might never see you again."

She framed his face with her hands. "I swore to give you up, but I couldn't."

"I will never give up on us," he said. "Never."

"I was scared," she said.

"I know, but don't be afraid."

When the carriage halted, he helped her on the steps. They walked to their bench and sat next to each other.

"Being here reminds me of that first time we met in the park," she said. "I was determined to resist you, but you managed to charm me. When we met again, I let down my guard. Then I discovered that it wasn't mere wealth separating us."

"I knew you were a gentleman's daughter the first time I heard your voice."

Her eyes held a fierce expression. "My mother was born a lady, but my father was a younger son and owned no land. Even if he had, he would not have deserved the title of gentleman."

"What happened to your family?"

"My mother died, and Grandmama lost her sight." She took in a shaky breath. "I thought my father would take care of us." Her mouth thinned. "Instead, he turned to the bottle for comfort. When the money dried up, he started selling our possessions: crockery, shoe buckles, a clock, anything he could find. It was clear to me he would sell off everything we had. I hid my mother's pearls, because I couldn't bear for him to sell them. He was furious when he couldn't find them. I trembled the whole time he shouted and cursed. Two days later, he was drunk when he fell off his horse and broke his neck."

Harry reached over and squeezed her hand. She must have been terrified.

"There was very little money. I had no choice but to leave the only home I'd ever known. I had to find employment. So I hired a man to bring us and our possessions to London."

"I'm glad you have the pearls," he said.

She fisted her hands in her lap. "I lost my position as a seamstress, and the dance master I formerly worked for shorted my wages. I took the pearls to a pawnshop on Petticoat Lane. I had to pay the rent."

He winced. I'm sorry, sweet Lucy." He drew her into his arms. "I'm so sorry."

She lifted her chin. "I'm not. Those pearls kept a roof over our heads."

"Are there no other family members besides your grandmother?"

She hesitated. "None that I've met."

He frowned. "Who are they?"

She said nothing.

"Lucy, do you know who they are?"

She nodded. "My mother's maiden name was Forbes."

His eyes narrowed. Then it hit him. "As in the Earl of Wargrove?"

Her mouth thinned. "Yes."

He took her by the shoulders. "My God, your grandfather is an earl, and you are working as a servant?"

"He disowned my mother."

His eyes blazed. "Why?"

"She eloped with my father to Gretna Green when she was nineteen."

"Have you tried to contact Wargrove?"

"No," she said, her voice sharp. "After my mother died, I found a returned letter written in her hand. It was addressed to Wargrove. The seal was unbroken. He'd never bothered to read it." She turned her face away because the memory still held the power to wound her.

"After so many years, you may find matters have changed with your mother's family."

Loathing was written all over her face. "I want nothing to do with Wargrove or any of his kin," she said heatedly. "He was cruel to refuse my mother's letter."

Harry frowned. "How did your mother meet your father?"

"My father was Wargrove's secretary. I've no idea how they contrived to elope. Afterward, my parents moved to Westbury, but many in the village never accepted her."

"Why?" he asked.

"For the same reason you knew I was educated."

"Her cultured manner of speaking," he said.

"When I was younger, I did not understand. One day I overheard two women gossiping after church. I was twelve or thereabouts when Mrs. Rhodes said my mother put on airs. It wasn't true. Many in the village didn't like her because she wasn't one of them."

"Ignorant people," he said in a harsh tone.

Lucy could still picture her mother's determined smile when she confessed that she had been an earl's daughter and left it all behind to marry Lucy's papa. "I asked my mother about her family, but she only looked sad and said they lived far away.

"Matters changed as I got older. A new assembly hall was erected in town. My mother knew all the dances because a dance master had taught her. She offered to teach anyone wishing to learn. There were many who refused to acknowledge my mother, but the younger men and women were keen on learning the etiquette and steps. I helped teach the younger children."

"I wondered where you'd learned to dance."

"When we arrived in London, I found an advertisement for a dance assistant. Mr. Buckley made me do all the work and often shorted my wages, but it was a job I desperately needed. Then I found work as a seamstress and afterward a steady job at the Albany. I left the dance master weeks ago and am encouraged that I am gaining clients. You know the rest."

"If you will let me, I can help."

"I know you mean well," she said, "but I've proven myself more than capable of making my own way in the world. It wasn't a choice, but it has made me stronger."

He drew her into his arms again. "Let me be strong for you."

He didn't understand that she mustn't rely on anyone but herself. She'd learned that lesson well when her father had abdicated his parental duties for the bottle. "You are an aristocrat, and I am a maid. A furtive meeting in the park or your carriage is all we have."

"It is not impossible," he said.

"It is not advisable, either."

"Plenty of my mother's friends have observed your talent in dance instruction. They have also marked your refined speech and manners."

"They also know I receive compensation for my dance instruction. I know that is unacceptable to the ton. I'm not one of them, and I never will be."

"Your grandfather is an earl," he said.

She inhaled sharply. "If you believe that I would welcome Wargrove after he disowned my mother, you are wrong," she said, her voice trembling with ire. "Harry, you know this isn't just about us. It's also about your family. Your mother will wish to find husbands for your cousins. If you were to marry a woman beneath you, it might affect your cousins' chances of making a good marriage."

"I don't believe that for an instant. Frankly, I don't care if you're a chimney sweep's daughter. I care about *you*. I don't give a damn about society. I don't give a damn what my mother thinks, and I certainly do not give a damn about the patronesses at Almack's."

"Will you deny that Almack's means a great deal to Mrs. Norcliffe? Would she not suffer embarrassment?"

"I berated my mother for her rude treatment of you. She retained you to teach a dance lesson and made rude comments. Believe me, she deserved my condemnation," he said, his voice rising.

Quite likely his rebuke had resulted in the opposite effect he'd intended.

"If you had not known me, would you have rebuked your mother?"

"Yes, because it is in poor taste to abuse those in one's employ."

"The point is I will never be welcome in your world."

"I disagree. Your manners clearly proclaim you are a lady. I knew it the first time we met."

"Harry, if you are seeking a lady of high birth, you had better look elsewhere. Wargrove never recognized my mother's marriage."

"Lucy, I don't care about rank," he said in exasperation. "I care about you, and I will not give up on us."

"Your peers, your cousins, your friends, and, yes, the patronesses have all seen me serving at Almack's. I am a servant and a dance instructor. That is *all* I'll ever be to the ton."

"I'm a duke, and that makes a world of difference."

A bitter laugh escaped her. "Your mother would never accept me. If we were foolish enough to get engaged, it would set off a scandal, one that would have negative consequences for your family. My mother suffered for having married beneath her station. I don't want you to be hurt."

"You worry for nothing. My influence counts for a great deal."

"Yes, but you must also consider your cousins. If you were to court a woman beneath you, especially a servant, it might well dampen their marriage prospects. Their beaux would question how it would affect their families. I can't do that to you and your family, Harry. I can't—"

"There have been plenty of ordinary people, like Brummel, who moved among society without a problem."

"They are men, and they are the exceptions."

"*We* can be the exceptions," he said. "I know we can do this."

"Your family, your friends, and society all expect you to marry a wealthy lady of noble birth," she said, her voice rising. "No one will ever question her pedigree. You are your mother's only son, and you have inherited a grand title and property. You need a wife who knows the intricacies of the ton. That would be someone who understands and is accepted in your world."

"Lucy, I'm a duke. I can and, if necessary, I will defy the ton."

"At what cost, Harry? If you were foolish enough to marry someone beneath you, it would affect every aspect of your life, including your political career and your acquaintances. Your friends would be uncomfortable, and so would you when the invitations stopped coming because you married a maid. No one in the ton would accept such a marriage. I won't be the instrument of unhappiness for your family. I can't do that to you."

"From the first words I heard you utter, I knew you were not what you appeared to be," he said. "Your grandfather is an earl," he said. "That changes everything, Lucy."

She reared back. "Do you think that I will go to them and beg to be acknowledged?" she said her voice rising. "I won't do it, Harry. I might have considered corresponding with them before I saw the returned letter, but I won't do it now."

"To me you are a lady, regardless of whether you recognize Wargrove or not, and, Lucy, I think you should make contact."

"Why?" she said. "So that it will pave the way for me to miraculously become a lady of the ton?"

"No, I think you should try to contact them because they are your family. You owe it to yourself to discover the truth about them."

"I need no more proof than that unanswered letter Wargrove returned," she said, her voice shaking with anger. "I will not contact my mother's family. It is clear to me none of them cared about her."

"What if there are extenuating circumstances? All of the trouble started before you were even born. I think you should investigate," he said. "It's quite possible there are things you know nothing about. It has been many years, after all. Will you think about it?" Harry said.

"I doubt they would welcome me."

"I suspect you would be surprised at their reaction," he said.

Her heart hammered in her chest. "I don't know if I can," she said. "He hurt my mother. What kind of man would disown his own daughter?"

"There is only one way you can find out," Harry said. "I hope for your sake you will consider it."

"What good could come from it?" she said, her voice pitching higher. "I doubt they even know of my existence."

"They are your family. It would be a shame if your family never had a chance to meet you, because they had no idea how to locate you."

"I will think about it, but I doubt I will change my mind." She sighed. "The light is starting to fade. I should leave soon to avoid walking in the dark."

"I'll take you up in my carriage." He leaned down until his breath whispered over her lips. The scent of his skin filled her senses. It was elemental, like the smell of rain, but unique to him. He drew her closer, and she held her breath, certain he meant to kiss her.

The sound of footsteps on the grass startled her.

He tightened his hold on her. "It's only a servant walking a dog."

She put her hand to her pounding heart. "I worry someone we know will see us and think I'm your mistress."

He took out his watch. "They'll all be at Rotten Row."

"I had better go," she said.

"My carriage is here. It makes sense for me to take you home. I insist."

"You insist?"

"Yes," he said, tickling her waist to distract her.

"Don't," she said with a squeak.

"You had better agree or I'll tickle you again."

"Stop, stop. I surrender."

"I like the sound of that," he said, his voice rumbling. Then he stood, pulled her flush against him, and gave her another lush, deep kiss. Her skin heated, and everything inside of her melted. She laid her head against his chest and breathed in his scent. "If I were a better person, I would give you up for your sake and the sake of your family. But I can't," she said.

"I would never allow it," he said, holding her tightly in his arms. "I won't give you up, not ever."

He kissed her again, and this time she rose on her toes, and his hands slid to her bottom. He pulled her flush against him, and she could feel the hard ridge of his erection. His breathing was faster and a little ragged. They were both breathing hard when he broke the kiss. She set her palm on his chest and felt the beating of his heart.

"I will make you mine," he whispered.

He offered his arm. When she took it, she knew he'd managed to charm her into doing his bidding once again. Despite all the obstacles between them, she couldn't seem to squelch the hope beating in her heart. The hope that he was powerful enough and determined enough to flout society. She desperately wanted to believe that somehow he was strong enough to overcome all of the obstacles so they could be together. Because even though she'd tried to resist him, even though she knew it was impossible, she loved him, and she wasn't ready to give him up yet. Just a little while longer and then she would end it. She must love him enough to do what was right for him and his family.

* * *

That night

Harry set out a sheet of paper, dipped his pen in the inkwell, and paused. What the bloody hell was he thinking? If he went against Lucy's wishes and contacted Wargrove, she would never forgive him, and she would be justified. It wasn't his decision to make.

He'd known it was wrong before he trimmed his pen, but he'd been worried about Lucy and her grandmother since he'd learned they lived in one of the worst neighborhoods in London. Just thinking of her walking in the dark made him wild with fear. He also worried about Mrs. Longmore. Lucy had told him their neighbor Mrs. Green looked in on Lucy's grandmother during the day, but that only reminded him that Lucy would be all alone if God forbid something happened to her grandmother.

That, however, did not give him the right to intervene on Lucy's behalf with Wargrove. In truth, she had good cause to be wary of the man. She knew very little about him, and what she did know was not positive. Yes, there was the possibility that matters might have changed after all these years, but it was equally possible that Wargrove would refuse to acknowledge his granddaughter. After all, the man had not even deigned to open a letter from Lucy's mother.

Harry had to consider the emotional impact on Lucy as well. What would happen if Lucy met Wargrove and he refused to recognize her as a family member? She would be devastated. Her father had failed her and God help him so had he. The last thing she needed was another man to disappoint her. If she would agree to marry him, he'd get a special license tomorrow, but she had misgivings and fears that it would hurt his family. He didn't believe it, but she did. Regardless, the worst thing he could do was to take matters into his hands without consulting her.

What he needed to do was persuade Lucy that they could be together. He must prove to her that he could scale that invisible class wall without hurting anyone in either of their families. He had no illusions about her resistance, but he'd sworn to make her his. He mustn't let doubts deter him.

Chapter Eleven

Two days later, Mrs. Norcliffe's drawing room

$\mathcal{L}$ucy arrived early for the dance lesson and prayed that Mrs. Norcliffe would not insult her again, but she'd prepared herself. If Mrs. Norcliffe dealt her an insult, she would simply ignore it.

When Mrs. Norcliffe had sent a letter requesting her dance instruction again, Lucy had read it twice, because she could hardly believe it, but even though she didn't care for Mrs. Norcliffe, she wouldn't turn down the opportunity. There was always a crowd in her drawing room, which meant earning money and possibly gaining new clients. It also meant she would be able to dance with Harry. Of course, they must be circumspect, but she looked forward to dancing with him again.

As she entered the foyer, the haughty butler looked down his long nose and installed her in the anteroom, where she sat primly on a sofa. The high bookshelves tempted her to explore the leather volumes, but she thought better of prying in Mrs. Norcliffe's home.

Footsteps clicked on the marble floor. Lucy rose and curtsied when Mina walked inside. "There you are," Mina said. "Gibson said you arrived early."

"I didn't mean to disturb anyone; I just didn't want to be late," Lucy said.

"Punctuality is a good trait," Mina said, "although I fear I'm late more often than not."

Mina led her upstairs to the drawing room and invited her to join her on a red mahogany settee.

"Ah, there is Anna with the tea tray," Mina said. "I'll pour."

When Mina offered her a cup, Lucy drank a small amount, but her cup rattled a little on the saucer, so she set it aside. The last thing she needed was to spill something on her dress.

"Tell me about yourself," Mina said. "Have you always lived in London?"

"No, I lived most of my life in Westbury, in the county of Wiltshire."

"Havenwood is in Wiltshire," Mina said. "That's Harry's property. Does the rest of your family live in London?"

"No, my grandmother and I live here."

Mina regarded her with a saucy smile. "You need a husband, preferably one with at least ten thousand a year."

Lucy's brows rose. "Ten thousand?"

"You drive a hard bargain. Very well. Twenty thousand and your very own coach."

Lucy laughed. "Why not add a pot of gold?"

"Oh, I like how you think," Mina said, wiggling her brows. "I think love matches must be the happiest of all."

"Especially if they are accompanied by a pot of gold," Lucy said.

"I wouldn't turn down the gold or the love," Mina said.

Lucy had seen the way Everleigh looked at Mina while they danced. They looked like a couple in love.

When Mrs. Norcliffe entered with Harry, Lucy stiffened involuntarily. She rose and curtsied, but even though she'd prepared herself, she felt as if her stomach was tied in a knot. She hoped nothing would go awry today. She inhaled slowly and exhaled slowly and swore that no matter what Mrs. Norcliffe said today, she would not allow it to overset her. Of course, that would not prove easy, especially in front of so many in the drawing room, but she would endure what she must with her head held high.

When Harry made eye contact with her, she averted her gaze. They had to be careful when others were about, especially his mother.

"Ah, Miss Longmore, I see you are prompt. I do hope you're prepared for today's practice session," Mrs. Norcliffe said. "Lady Jersey suggested My Lord Byron's Maggot. Are you familiar with that dance?"

"Indeed I am," Lucy said. "I am more than happy to instruct any particular dance you require."

"Very good," Mrs. Norcliffe said.

Mrs. Norcliffe seemed far more genial today. Lucy hoped it was a good sign.

Mrs. Vernon set up her sheet music at the pianoforte and smiled at Lucy. Yesterday, Mrs. Vernon had sent Lucy a missive explaining that Princess Esterhazy had decreed the dance at Almack's this week would feature My Lord Byron's Maggot. It was a particularly fun dance, and Lucy looked forward to instructing it.

After everyone was seated, Lucy directed the dancers to

select partners. Lord Everleigh stood up with Mina, while Justin—Viscount Chesfield—partnered with Amelia and Lord Fitzhugh asked Helena to dance.

Mrs. Norcliffe brought a pale, plump young lady forward. "Harry, you remember Mrs. Osterham and her daughter Miss Hortense Osterham."

Harry bowed. "Yes, of course, I remember you both."

Mrs. Norcliffe smiled at Hortense. "I understand you enjoy dancing."

A blush seared Miss Osterham's face. "Yes," she mumbled.

"Well, then you must participate in the dance practice today," Mrs. Norcliffe said. "I'm sure Harry will be happy to partner with you."

Lucy sighed inwardly. She'd hoped to partner with Harry again, but it was not to be. All the same, Mrs. Norcliffe's obvious maneuver was so awkward that Lucy winced. Poor Hortense's ears grew bright red. Lucy couldn't help feeling sorry for the girl.

Harry regarded Hortense with a stoic expression. "Miss Osterham, if you are not previously engaged, I would consider it an honor to dance with you."

"Thank you," Hortense said in a barely audible voice.

Lucy wondered why Mrs. Norcliffe had put Harry on the spot. In Lucy's opinion, it had been an ill-bred thing to do. Then she remembered something Harry had told her at Almack's. *I narrowly escaped dancing all night with a young lady nearly half my age.*

Was Hortense the young lady he'd spoken of? If so, this wasn't the first time Mrs. Norcliffe had attempted to play matchmaker.

The thought made Lucy's chest tighten, but it was foolish of her to worry. Yet, she thought of that night at Almack's when she'd seen all of the aristo girls surrounding him. She'd been a little jealous, but she'd pushed it out of her mind.

It had been far easier to ignore a group of ladies vying for his attention than to watch Mrs. Norcliffe press Harry into dancing with a specific young lady. Lucy told herself it was foolish to worry. Harry's reserved expression indicated he wasn't pleased with his mother's arrangement. Lucy felt sure he was trying to conceal his feelings for the sake of Hortense.

When Lucy turned, she happened to notice Miss Osterham's fingers trembling. The girl clasped her hands as if trying to control her vexation. Lucy couldn't bear to watch Hortense's mortification any longer. The sooner the dancing started the better.

Lucy regarded Mrs. Norcliffe. "If you are ready, I will commence the dancing practice."

"Yes, please proceed," Mrs. Norcliffe said.

Lucy stood in front of the crowd and said, "Today we will practice a particularly fun dance called My Lord Byron's Maggot."

Lucy hoped it would prove to be the best distraction for Hortense. Knowing the young lady was nervous, she thought it best to encourage all of the dancers to focus on learning and having fun rather than attempting to perfect the dance. Lucy vowed to do her best to put the girl and all the other dancers at ease.

"Ladies and gentlemen," Lucy said. "Before we begin, I wish to remind everyone that this is a dance *practice*. I will direct the dancers, but remember that we all make mistakes. At the last practice session, Lord Chesfield turned in the wrong direction, and everyone laughed. The practice sessions are to prepare for the actual dancing, and no one should feel embarrassed if they make a wrong turn or forget the next movement.

"Now, if the dancers will take your positions, I will direct you. Lord Bryon's Maggot is an amusing dance, and I'm sure you will enjoy it. First, we will walk through the steps to familiarize everyone. Gentlemen, dance forward, circle your partner, and when you return, cast off one place down the line."

After the gentlemen completed those steps, Lucy said, "Clap your hands together, and then clap your partner's hands."

By now all the dancers were smiling as the ladies and gentlemen clapped each other's hands. Lucy was glad to see Hortense laughing as she clapped hands with Harry.

"Next is the fun part. Gentlemen, motion your partner to come hither with your hand."

"I like this part," Justin said, motioning Amelia.

"Obviously Justin is eager," Lucy said, making everyone laugh.

Justin grinned. "I have to prove myself after my faux pas at the last practice."

"You are all allowed to make mistakes," Lucy said. "Now, clasp hands with your partner, turn in a circle, and move down one place in the line. Excellent! You're all doing very well. Now the ladies motion their partners to come hither."

"Mina, you may motion me to come hither whenever you please," Lord Everleigh said.

"Ha!" Mina said, and motioned him with her fingers.

Everleigh skipped forward. "Whether thou motion, I will go."

Mina burst out laughing. "You have many good qualities, Everleigh, but you are no poet."

The ladies watching in the drawing room were smiling and laughing as well.

Lucy directed the dancers to walk through the steps once more, and then she turned to Mrs. Vernon. "Will you play for us now?"

"Indeed I will," Mrs. Vernon said.

Lucy was gratified that all of the dancers appeared to be enjoying themselves. At one point, Hortense seemed lost, but Harry saved her by turning her in the right direction. When the dance ended, Hortense was talking to the other dancers and seemed far more at ease.

Lucy curtsied and said, "I wish you all well at the Almack's dancing competition."

"Thank you, Miss Longmore," Justin said. "I enjoyed this dance better than any other."

Everyone else chimed in their approval of the dance as well. All agreed it was great fun.

Lucy was glad the practice session went well, especially for Hortense's sake. Now she must wait until Mrs. Norcliffe directed her. She hoped the woman would not embarrass her again, but this time she was prepared to ignore it. She was proud of her dancing skills and knew she'd helped Hortense in particular.

Mrs. Norcliffe linked arms with Hortense and escorted her over to Harry. Shortly thereafter, Mrs. Osterham joined them. They stood in a small circle talking while the guests trickled out of the drawing room.

Lucy stood near a pillar, waiting for Mrs. Norcliffe to dismiss her. She regarded Harry from the corner of her eye. He'd clasped his hands behind his back, but his expression was inscrutable.

All of the other guests had left. The cavernous drawing room was quiet, and she couldn't help overhearing Mrs.

Norcliffe and Mrs. Osterham conversing. She kept her gaze averted so that it wouldn't seem as if she were eavesdropping.

"Mrs. Norcliffe, you must attend us at Madame Delanger's shop tomorrow," Mrs. Osterham said. "I wish to order three new gowns for Hortense and want your approval before we make our decisions."

"Mama, I am unsure about the primrose fabric Madame Delanger recommended. I am having second thoughts," Hortense said.

"Well, my dear, I shall be more than happy to advise you tomorrow," Mrs. Norcliffe said.

Lucy tried to focus on something else, but the mention of Madame Delanger's shop only reminded her how much she missed seeing Evelyn and Mary on a daily basis. Her friends were working miserably long hours sewing every day. Not so long ago, she'd been terrified when Madame had sacked her, but it had turned out to be a blessing.

Once again, her thoughts were interrupted by the conversation taking place in the drawing room.

"Mama, perhaps we could go for ices at Gunther's afterward," Hortense said.

"What a lovely suggestion," Mrs. Norcliffe said. "Harry, you must join us."

"I regret that I must decline due to other commitments," he said, his tone a bit flat.

"We shall change his mind," Mrs. Osterham said, tittering.

"Indeed we shall," Mrs. Norcliffe said. "Harry, you do not want to disappoint Hortense."

Lucy suspected Harry did not appreciate their insistence when he'd already declined.

"Mrs. Osterham, you must dine with us on Friday

evening," Mrs. Norcliffe said. "I'm sure Harry would be delighted."

The discussion about the dinner party proved to be the point of honesty for Lucy. She was not entirely selfless where Hortense was concerned. In truth, envy twined around her heart and made her miserable. She tried to think of pleasant things like taking tea with her grandmother and reading a book from the circulating library. She focused on keeping a serene countenance when she felt anything but tranquil.

At long last, Mrs. Osterham and Hortense departed with many well wishes from Mrs. Norcliffe.

Out of the corner of her eye, Lucy saw Harry approach his mother. He spoke in a voice too low for Lucy to hear.

"Oh, dear me," Mrs. Norcliffe said. "Thank you for reminding me, Harry. Miss Longmore, I do apologize. I quite forgot you."

Lucy couldn't miss Mrs. Norcliffe's gloating expression or her insinuation that Lucy was forgettable.

"Please return next week," Mrs. Norcliffe said in a jovial tone. "You may collect your wages from the butler."

Lucy curtsied and walked toward the door.

Harry glanced at her, but Lucy averted her face and hurried out of the drawing room. She closed the drawing room door and hurried down the stairs. All along, she'd known that there was no place for her in Harry's world, but right now all she wanted was to leave as fast as possible.

She collected her wages from the butler. Then she fled the town house and walked along Piccadilly until she reached Green Park. Lucy sat on their bench, hoping Harry would come looking for her. He would make her laugh and forget all her cares. Perhaps he would even bring Bandit with him.

She waited patiently, but forty-five minutes later, he still had not arrived. He probably had urgent business or an appointment. She decided to wait a little longer, because she didn't want to miss him. When she heard footsteps, she rose, but it was only a servant walking a dog. Lucy checked the watch she kept pinned to her apron. An hour had passed. Harry wasn't coming.

Lucy considered herself strong because she'd had to make her own way in the world. She was proud of her courage and hard work. This morning, however, she felt a little blue. Lately she'd started fantasizing about a life with Harry. He was so determined that she'd begun to believe just a little in the impossible. While she cleaned at the Albany, she would imagine a small town house where she welcomed Harry when he returned from a day of working in parliament or with his advisors. She silently chided herself for spinning foolish dreams that would never come true.

She told herself to be grateful that she had a steady job at the Albany and had begun to build her dance clientele. Nothing else should matter. But today it mattered very much that she could never be more than the girl he met at the park.

"Harry, please close the doors. I must speak to you," Mrs. Norcliffe said after Lucy retreated.

With an exasperated sigh, he did her bidding. "Mama, what is this about?"

"Please be seated."

He took a chair near his mother and gave her a hard look. "Make it quick, please. I have important business today." He'd hoped to see Lucy at the park after the dance practice, but his mother and Mrs. Osterham had delayed him with all of their frivolous plans. He'd known from the beginning that his mother had meant to trap him with her matchmaking schemes.

"I will not detain you overly long," Mrs. Norcliffe said. "I wish to remind you that this Saturday is my annual Venetian breakfast. You will attend, of course."

He folded his arms over his chest. "I have no recollection of you telling me about your garden party."

Mrs. Norcliffe lifted her chin. "It is a Venetian breakfast. I hold it every year, as you're well aware."

He drummed his fingers on the arm of his chair. "You gave me insufficient notice. Unfortunately, I have other plans." He didn't, but he knew damn well she intended to force Hortense on him again.

"You will have to cancel your plans," Mrs. Norcliffe said.

"I won't be there. In the future, I recommend you notify me sooner," he said in a stern tone.

Mrs. Norcliffe shook her fan open. "Do not be tiresome, Harry."

He rose. "I'll not attend."

Mrs. Norcliffe smacked her fan on the sofa arm and broke one of the sticks. "You are in one of your perverse moods, but I will not allow you to vex me. I have spoken to Mrs. Osterham. She has agreed that you may squire Hortense to the goldfish bridge at the Venetian breakfast."

His mother was nothing if not predictable. "You concocted these plans without consulting me. Let me be clear. You will not manipulate me again, and I will not escort Miss Osterham at your party or anywhere else for that matter."

"Harry, if you do not escort Hortense, you will wound Mrs. Osterham and her daughter."

"I'm not the one who will be responsible for the wounds," he said. "You made the plans. Now you must explain to Mrs. Osterham that you made a mistake."

"Harry," she said in shocked tones. "You cannot refuse."

"I can and I will. Let this be a lesson to you. While we are on the topic of Miss Osterham, I wish to make it clear that I have no interest in courting the young lady. This is the second time you have coerced me into dancing with Hortense. It will be the last time. I am entirely too old for someone of her tender years."

"She is almost eighteen years old, a perfectly suitable age for marriage."

"Did you not mark Miss Osterham's discomfort in the drawing room? She was mortified. You went too far today."

"She is merely young. I will take her in hand after you are married," Mrs. Norcliffe said.

He stared at her. It was as if she hadn't listened to a word he'd uttered. "I am not marrying Hortense," he said. "I am not attracted to her. I'm sure one day she will make a wonderful wife for some other man, but it will not be me."

"Harry, she has all the right qualities. She has impeccable breeding, ten thousand, and is accomplished at watercolors and the pianoforte."

He laughed. "You are deluded if you believe I would choose a wife based on her watercolors. This may shock you, but when I wed, I want passion."

Mrs. Norcliffe made a face. "Harry, we do not speak of such prurient matters."

"Enough of this nonsense," he said. "You made a spectacle today in the drawing room and embarrassed Miss Osterham and me. I will not tolerate another one of your matchmaking schemes. If there is a next time, you will find yourself in embarrassing circumstances."

"How dare you speak to me in this horrid manner?" she said, her voice pitching higher.

"I dare because it is necessary. You are determined to get your way, but this time, it will not work. The manipulation, coercion, and schemes will stop. Frankly, I've worried you might become a bad influence on my cousins."

She stared at him with evident shock. "You make me sound like a terrible person."

"I know you have been good to my cousins, but I've worried about the gossip sessions in the drawing room, and I fear you have slighted others in the past. I know for certain you insulted Miss Longmore. I ought to have spoken to you long ago about my concerns. I'm doing so now. You have gone too far this time. I will not attend your event."

"Harry, you will humiliate me," she said, tearing up.

"You've done this to yourself."

"What of Mrs. Osterham and her daughter? They will be mortified. I daresay she will never speak to me again. Harry, please think of the consequences."

He remained unmoved by her tears. "You are the one who did not consider the consequences. You promised I would escort Miss Osterham without consulting me. I'm not attending."

Mrs. Norcliffe worried her hands. "Harry, you must attend. If you will not think of me, think of your cousins."

"Under the circumstances, you may wish to cancel the party," he said.

Mrs. Norcliffe narrowed her eyes. "I know what this is about. You mean to spend all of your time with Miss Longmore. I'm not ignorant of your infatuation with that dancer."

"Enjoy your party. I won't be there." He strode across the drawing room.

"Harry, stop, please," she said, sniffling.

He turned toward her.

"I do not appreciate your harsh tone of voice," she said.

"I do not appreciate your insult to Miss Longmore. She has done nothing to deserve your censure. You, on the other hand, most certainly deserve mine. Your manipulative behavior today went too far. Badly done, Mama, badly done."

"It is very clear you have conceived a partiality for that dancer. More than one person reported seeing you flirting with her at Almack's while she was serving lemonade."

"There must be a dearth of gossip if others are reporting that Miss Longmore serves refreshments at Almack's," he said in a bored tone. "I cannot imagine what your friends found objectionable in a glass of lemonade."

"Do not try to pretend innocence. I know you do not appreciate my advice, but I will give it to you anyway. You will have your dalliance with her, but do not allow her to sink her claws into you."

He rolled his eyes. "Rest your fears. I am safe from bodily harm."

Her nostrils flared. "Harry, I am not amused."

"Neither am I. You will treat Miss Longmore respectfully. She has done an admirable job of instructing the dance practices, despite your discourteous manners."

"You believe me to be unfeeling?" she said in shocked tones.

He folded his arms over his chest. "I call it as I see it."

"I suppose I have something to prove. Invite her to attend the party on Saturday."

"She will not attend," he said.

"She will come if you point out it is an opportunity for her to meet other ladies in need of her dance instruction. You would not deprive her of the opportunity, would you? Of course you might wish to attend as well."

"That works well for you, but the walk to the goldfish bridge will be a group activity. Miss Osterham is entirely too young for me, and I do not want to stir up false expectations."

Mrs. Norcliffe dabbed a handkerchief at her eyes.

There was nothing he despised more than foolish tears. "What is wrong?"

"You have not danced once with a suitable young lady at Almack's. When all of the other bachelors are singling out dance partners, you make yourself scarce in the game room. It is *not* to be borne."

"Ah, I see. This is about the dancing competition and your role as one of the patronesses."

"Your willful refusal to dance affects me, Harry. Do you not care that I am embarrassed?"

"I will not participate in that foolish dance competition under any circumstances. You had better adjust your mind to it. Now, I will see you on Saturday, but do not count on Miss Longmore's presence."

Thursday, early afternoon

Harry sighed after a visit to the tailor. He knew he needed more shirts, but in the end he decided to add to his wardrobe all at once so he wouldn't be forced to endure the tailor's measuring and pinning for another two years or more. By the time he finished, he'd purchased five new coats, four waistcoats, a pair of gloves, and new stockings.

Harry meant to board his carriage when he saw Lucy approaching. After he stashed his purchases in the carriage, he strode toward her and hailed her.

"Lucy, you're just the person I need to see."

A savory scent wafted from her basket.

"I'm bringing meat pasties to my friends at Madame Delanger's shop. I don't see them very often," she said.

He drank in the sight of her. Her cheeks were a little rosy from the cool breeze. "I'll not keep you long."

The shop bell rang as a young woman poked her head out. "Lucy, come in."

"Here, take the basket for our luncheon," Lucy said. "I'll only be a moment, Evelyn."

Evelyn regarded Harry with wide eyes.

Harry smiled. "Lucy, will you introduce me to your friend?"

"Your Grace, may I present Miss Evelyn Rogers?"

Harry doffed his hat. "I'm pleased to meet you, Miss Rogers."

Evelyn curtsied. "Oh my goodness. Lucy, I'll see you inside."

The shop bell rang again as the door closed.

Harry watched Miss Rogers disappear. "Is your friend always this excitable?"

"Only when dukes appear," Lucy said, laughing.

"I've no wish to interfere," Harry said.

The shop bell rang again, and an older woman appeared.

"Your Grace, may I present Madame Delanger?" Lucy said. "This is her dress shop."

He bowed, realizing the shop owner was the one who had dismissed Lucy. Harry was a bit surprised that Lucy would return here since the shop owner had sacked her, but she probably wanted to see her friends.

"I am honored, Your Grace," Madame Delanger said.

Harry had the oddest feeling the woman was calculating the cost of his clothing as he stood there.

"Your Grace, please come into my humble shop," Madame Delanger said.

Harry followed them inside and turned to Lucy. "I meant to stop by your lodgings and give you an invitation. My mother has invited you to her annual Venetian breakfast, which is actually in the afternoon, but never mind. I do hope you'll agree to attend."

She looked uncomfortable. "I do not think it will be possible."

"Of course you must go," Madame Delanger said. "I happen to have the perfect frock for you to wear to a Venetian breakfast."

He had not even thought about the apparel.

Madame snapped her fingers. "Mary, bring the white crepe gown with the blue ribbons."

Lucy inhaled. "Madame, I cannot. I know what these gowns cost."

"Of course you can," Madame said. "It is the least that I can do. If anyone asks where you purchased the gown, you may direct them to my shop."

Lucy's eyes lit up. "Oh, I couldn't."

Harry approached Lucy. "We must have something made up for your grandmother as well."

"I appreciate your generosity, but Grandmama doesn't like crowds. It's difficult with her affliction."

"But *you* must go," Madame Delanger said to Lucy.

She bit her lip. "It is an excellent opportunity for me to meet potential dance clients," she said.

Harry clutched his hand to his heart. "She wounds me."

Lucy shook her head. "He jests."

"Come back tomorrow, and we will make all the necessary alterations," Madame said.

Lucy knew the gown must be one that another lady had refused.

"Miss Longmore, may I be permitted to escort you home?" Harry asked. "I'll wait if that is acceptable to you."

"Yes, thank you."

After Lucy finished eating luncheon with her friends, Harry led her from the shop to his carriage. Her friends waved as he assisted her up the steps.

Lucy's excitement dwindled the moment the carriage rolled off.

He turned to her. "Is something wrong?"

"I cannot attend your mother's party. I'll have nothing to contribute to the conversations, if anyone even notices me."

"Of course you will," he said. "No doubt others will ask your opinion about the dance competition."

She had no doubt Mrs. Norcliffe disapproved of her and would not appreciate her presence. "Why did your mother invite me?"

"I lectured her on a number of matters, all having to do with her manipulative and unkind behavior to you and others. My mother feels she has to prove herself. So she proposed I invite you. When I said you wouldn't attend, she suggested you might have an interest in acquiring new dance clients at her party."

Lucy narrowed her eyes. "I know she disapproves of me. Why would she make such a suggestion?"

"To ensure I attended. Thank you for agreeing. I'm actually looking forward to it now."

"I fear this will prove to be a mistake. I know nothing about Venetian breakfasts or how to get on with the ton."

"I have every confidence in you," he said, his voice rumbling.

"Other single ladies will resent me," she said.

"Why? They have no reason."

She huffed. "Of course they do. I wager most of them have you in their sights. My presence will be unwelcome."

"I will be mortally jealous each time another man looks at you."

"They will pay no attention to me. I lack the requisite noble birth and fortune."

"Lucy, do you not know how beautiful you are?"

"Are you flattering me for a reason?" she said.

"Any man with eyes will take second and third looks at you."

"I doubt it," she said.

Harry cupped her cheek. "I think you are perfect."

She wasn't, but he made her feel special and wanted.

He untied her bonnet strings and grinned at her.

"What are you about?" she said, laughing.

He removed her bonnet and tossed it aside.

"Give me back my bonnet."

He gazed into her eyes. "Later," he said.

The wicked tone in his voice alerted her. "Harry?"

"Close the drape, Lucy."

She was breathing a bit faster. "Why?" she said.

"Because I want you," he said, his voice low and a little rough.

She reached for the drape and slowly closed it.

"Good girl," he said, closing the drape on his side.

He pulled her onto his lap. "Wrap your arms around my neck."

When she complied, he kissed her with a fierce hunger. He touched his tongue to her mouth, and when her lips parted, he kissed her deeply.

"I should resist you, but I can't," she said.

He was undone by her words. When he kissed her again, she clung to him. He loved the way she felt in his arms, all soft curves and sweet surrender. His blood ran hot, and the temptation to touch her gripped him hard, but he mustn't drive her away by moving too quickly. He wanted the perfect place and time to savor every moment. When the time was right, he meant to introduce her to erotic pleasure. He would be gentle as he touched and kissed every inch of her body.

His groin tightened as he kissed a path along her jaw and returned to her lips. This time she opened for him immediately, and when he tangled his tongue with hers, she made a little feminine sound in the back of her throat.

He lifted his mouth. Something inside his chest expanded. All he knew was that she'd somehow become essential to him. He looked into her eyes and knew that one day soon, he would make her his bride.

She tried to right the world that he had so easily turned upside down. Her heart thumped crazily. She was elated and terrified at the same time. Deep down, she knew she was taking risks, but she told herself she would never let matters go too far.

He took her hand and pressed it against his chest. She could feel his heart beating.

A slow smile spread across his face, and she could not resist him. He pulled her onto his lap. Then he kissed her openmouthed, and she parted her lips for him. This time she dared to touch her tongue to his. He cupped her face, and the scent of him was like a wicked potion, one that threatened to undermine every decent principle her mother and grandmother had taught her.

She broke the kiss and the sound of their combined breathing portended trouble if she ever lost her head with him. "We must stop."

When she tried to slip off his lap, he locked his arms around her. "Not yet, sweet Lucy. Please, not yet."

She could not deny him, because she loved the feel of his arms around her. All this time, she'd been the one to say it was impossible, but now she wished with all of her heart that it would somehow work out for them. For now, she would let the exuberant feelings carry the moment. She remembered Evelyn's advice to enjoy a romantic interlude with him. Somehow that sounded selfish as if she were using him, but she could never treat him so cavalierly.

He was witty, charming, and determined when he wanted something. There had likely been many women who had fallen under his spell, but she pushed away the idea of others who must have come before her.

Harry kissed her again and this time it was as if he were starving. When he tore his mouth away, she felt something hard beneath the thin layers of her skirt and chemise. She knew so little of men that it took her a moment to comprehend he was aroused. She ought to move, but then he would realize she knew his predicament.

He held her tightly. "I've shocked you."

Her face got hot. "A little." She recalled that erotic book of engravings. Obviously he was a man of lusty appetites.

"I will never press you for more than you're willing to give."

Lucy dared not allow more than his lascivious kisses. Already, she was alarmed by the heady combination of desire and tender feelings that had sprouted, despite her resistance. She'd tried to put up a wall, but he'd scaled it so easily. Now she felt confused one minute and euphoric the next.

"You know I'll never hurt you," he said.

Not intentionally.

All too soon, the carriage rolled to a halt. "We cannot stay long," she said. "I must report to the Albany."

"Let us tell your grandmother about the party on Saturday. We'll talk afterward in the carriage."

After they were seated at the table, Harry told Mrs. Longmore about his mother's invitation while Lucy made tea. When Lucy handed him a cup, he looked into her eyes.

How did he manage to make her feel breathless with his I'm-a-rogue look?

Mrs. Longmore sipped her tea. "Granfield, I appreciate the invitation, but crowds are difficult for me, especially when I have not made the acquaintance of others previously."

"I understand," he said.

"Thank you, Your Grace."

"Please, call me Harry."

"I will settle for Granfield," Mrs. Longmore said. "I don't want my granddaughter subjected to those who might mock her because she is an outsider."

"No one would dare in my presence. Believe me, there are plenty of people who are welcomed to ton functions who are not aristocrats. Not everyone is a blueblood. Lucy has made an impact already with her dancing instruction."

Mrs. Longmore leaned forward, felt the table with her hand, and set her cup aside. "What of your mother?" she said.

"My mother suggested that I invite Lucy," he said.

"Lucy, are you certain you wish to attend?" Mrs. Longmore said.

"Yes, I am. It is an opportunity to gain more clients for my dance lessons."

"You've done very well without attending a party," Grandmama said. "I'm a bit concerned you will be out of your depths with the ton." She paused and said, "Your Grace, I mean no disrespect to you."

"I completely understand," he said, "but Lucy has already met my cousins and several friends of my family. My cousins are impressed with Lucy's dancing skills."

"Grandmama, I admit that I was a little reluctant at first," Lucy said, "but Madame Delanger offered to alter a gown that another girl refused. The fabric is white crepe with a beautiful blue ribbon."

Grandmama frowned. "Madame Delanger sacked you. Why would she do such a thing?"

"It is an opportunity for her as well. If I wear the gown to the party, others may inquire about her shop."

"Humph. Madame Delanger is an opportunist," Grandmama said. "I wouldn't go out of my way to help her if I were you, but enough of her. I worry that the party will be awkward for you. The haut ton is a closed society, and I worry you will be isolated."

"I will not let that happen," Harry said. "Lucy has met my cousins, and I wish to introduce her to my closest friends." He smiled boyishly. "Actually, I want to show her off."

"Granfield, you remind me of my late husband," Grandmama said. "He was a charmer just like you. He always managed to coax me into doing his bidding." She paused. "However, that does not mean you are permitted to do so yourself."

He laughed. "I promise to be on my best behavior."

"Grandmama, you will notice he did not specify what constitutes his best behavior," Lucy said. "I would not be surprised if his best behavior does not meet your high standards."

Harry grinned. "Miss Longmore, you have found me out. I will have to invent new tricks."

"Grandmama, I wish you could see his smile," Lucy said. "I believe he could light up all the lanterns at Vauxhall with it."

Grandmama sighed. "Lucy, I know I'm overly protective of you. At twenty-five, you are a grown woman, and I must allow you to make your own decisions. So you will forgive me when I cling too much."

"Grandmama, if you disapprove, I won't attend."

"Of course you will attend." Grandmama smiled. "Every girl should have a chance to wear a pretty gown to a party.

Lucy hugged her and whispered, "I love you."

As the carriage rolled along, Harry noticed that Lucy kept looking out the window. "Do not worry. I'll have you at the Albany in plenty of time."

"I try to arrive early. It keeps me in Mrs. Finkle's good book."

He'd noticed that she was fretful where her jobs were concerned. Little wonder after she'd had to pawn her mother's pearls to pay the rent.

He put his arm around her shoulders and nuzzled her neck. She angled her head, giving him better access. He kissed his way to her jaw, and then he tenderly turned her face toward him. He licked the seam of her lips and she opened for him. God, he loved that she was so responsive to him.

Of course, he wanted more than kisses, but he must progress slowly. He'd imagined it more than once: unhooking her gown and slowly slipping the bodice down her slim waist. Then he would strip away the stays and chemise, revealing her plump breasts. He'd fantasized suckling her nipples while he caressed her slick, intimate folds. His groin tightened, thinking of the pleasures they could share.

When the carriage turned onto Piccadilly, she said, "You must let me out a block away from the Albany."

"Lucy, I'll let you out at the entrance to Vigo Street."

"No, you mustn't. If Mrs. Finkle saw me with you, I would lose my job."

"I doubt Mrs. Finkle is patrolling the yard."

"Harry, please do it for my sake. I can't risk being seen here with you."

He thought it ridiculous, but he knew she would feel more secure if he followed her wishes.

"Very well," he said. "My carriage will be here when you are done."

Later that afternoon

Harry waited a half block from Vigo Street. The minute she walked by, he would climb out and escort her to his carriage. She was taking this business a bit too far. Why not allow him to take her up in his carriage without all this fuss and bother?

She probably did not want to get accustomed to letting others help her. He understood she'd had to provide everything for herself and her grandmother after her parents died, but he felt it was foolish of her to refuse him.

He couldn't help worrying about her. She was extremely vulnerable, whether she admitted it or not. The idea of her walking at night in her poor neighborhood made him wild with fear. Her trusty blade would be of no use if someone surprised her. Hell, he'd met her because she'd encountered a thief.

The carriage door opened, startling him. Lucy stood there with her basket. "I knew you would insist upon playing the part of Sir Galahad again. If you were not a duke, I would recommend you take up treading the boards at Drury Lane, not that I've ever attended."

He smiled as he assisted her inside the carriage and knocked on the roof. When the carriage rolled away, he said, "Will you let me take you to the theater?"

"Certainly not. Your friends would assume I am your mistress."

When he gazed into her eyes, she drew in her breath. "Do not look at me that way."

He covered his eyes. "Tell me when it's safe."

She laughed and grabbed his hands. "You enjoy being ridiculous."

"Actually, I enjoy kissing you."

"We must be careful that we aren't seen together," she said.

"You worry too much."

"Harry, it is imperative that we take every precaution. No one we know will bat an eye if you are seen in a public place with me, but I would be ruined if that were to happen, because others would assume I am your mistress. I can't take risks."

"I promise we will be careful." He gave her a wet, lush kiss.

When the kiss ended, her breathing was ragged. "How am I to resist you?"

"Don't," he said. "You must know by now how much I care for you."

"I'm afraid," she said.

"Of me?" he said in an astounded voice.

"No, I'm afraid of myself."

"I don't understand," he said.

"You have the power to beguile me, and I fear I will succumb to desire." He made her yearn for more of his touch, more of his kisses, and she feared that in a weak moment she might allow matters to go too far.

"Lucy, I know you're a respectable woman, and I know what is forbidden. My desire for you is like a fire inside me I can't extinguish. But it is not just desire. I want to hold your hand, I want to hear you laugh, and I want to waltz with you." He cupped her face. "I want you."

"We cannot be careless. Even the slightest hint could ruin everything I've worked to attain."

"Give me sufficient credit, Lucy. I know what is at stake for you."

"And for you and your family as well," she said. "No one must ever suspect."

"Your friends know about us."

"Yes, but that's different. They don't know anyone in the ton."

"I dislike the subterfuge. I don't want to hide what is between us. I mean to court you properly as you deserve. This is just the beginning as far as I'm concerned. I'm not saying it will be easy, but I have influential friends. They will champion you."

She smiled at him. How could she not adore him when he'd vowed never to give up on the two of them? Their time together would draw to a close sooner than she wished. She'd tried to end it once and failed, because he'd become so very dear to her. Lucy swore her time with him would last for a little while longer, and then she would make a clean cut, because she loved him too much to hurt him. There was no doubt in her mind that if their affaire de coeur was ever discovered, it would create problems for Harry and his family.

"We're almost to your lodgings." He quickly kissed her on the lips. "I find myself reluctant to take you home."

She sniffed. "Well, at least you are being a gentleman."

He leaned over. "Would you like me to be a little less gentlemanly?"

"Absolutely not," she said, staring straight ahead.

He reached over and tickled her waist.

When she shrieked, he kissed her. At first, she resisted, but she wanted him, wanted his kisses, wanted to be his, and wanted to keep him in her heart as long as she could.

"Oh yes," he said, and kissed her again.

She parted her lips for him.

Their tongues tangled, and he slid his hands up beneath her breasts. Then his thumbs circled her nipples through the fabric of her bodice. The sensations excited her and made her want more. She was breathing faster and his touch made her want forbidden things.

"I fear you will think me a wanton," she said.

He held her tightly in his arms. "No, Lucy, quite the opposite. Every night in bed I think about you, and I find myself wishing you were with me. I will make you mine, sweet girl."

"I cannot allow this to happen again," she said. "There is too much at risk."

"You risk nothing," he said. "I would never wound you or risk your reputation. I swear to you," he said.

"It isn't you," she said. "Well, it is you."

"Whew. For a moment I feared I had a rival."

She'd never thought she would be susceptible to desire. It frightened her.

"What are you thinking about?" he asked.

"Consequences."

"Consequences can mean many things," he said.

He'd spoken carefully.

"I'm thinking of the imprudent sort. It frightens me."

"What do you fear?"

She shivered. "That I will succumb to these powerful feelings and let matters go too far. The consequences would be disastrous." She knew what happened to servants who were discovered to be with child. They lost their positions.

"Well, I'm heartbroken," he said. "I must set aside my wicked designs on you and settle for squiring you about at my mother's dull Venetian breakfast."

She laughed a little. "You are fortunate I'm willing to allow even that."

When the carriage rolled to a halt, she searched for the bonnet. He found it on the floor of the carriage and grimaced as she put it on.

"What is wrong?" she asked.

"It seems a shame to cover your beautiful red hair."

She pulled a face. "You like it?"

He laughed. "Very much."

"I must go now," she said.

"You will allow me to escort you, and I will not listen to any arguments. Save your breath."

"Yes, master," she said.

He laughed. "Oh, I like that."

"I might have known," she said, rolling her eyes.

When they reached her door, he lifted her hands and kissed them. "I will call for you at two o'clock on Saturday." Unable to help himself, he drew her into his arms again and kissed her deeply. He slid his hands to her bottom and drew her soft curves flush against him. A small feminine sound escaped her. When he tore his mouth away, they were both breathing faster. "Until Saturday," he said. When she disappeared inside her lodgings, he ran down the stairs and started toward his carriage. The distinctive clop of hooves on the street alerted him.

A yellow curricle approached. Harry cursed under his breath as he recognized Castelle, but he would give away nothing.

"Granfield, what brings you to this dilapidated neighborhood?"

He'd no intention of answering. "Smart curricle. Is it new?"

"Indeed, I acquired it only three days ago. I'm planning to race on Monday. You should come."

"I might."

Castelle regarded him with a crafty expression. "Visiting your mistress?"

Harry retrieved his watch. "You will pardon me. I have an appointment."

"More than one, eh? I envy you, Granfield."

Harry doffed his hat, climbed into his carriage, and knocked his cane on the ceiling. The carriage lurched into motion.

Harry's heart still hammered in his chest. It had never occurred to him that anyone he knew might travel in this neighborhood. While Castelle had irritated him, Harry had prevaricated. The important part was that the man had not seen Lucy. Of course, there was nothing wrong with him calling at her home, but Castelle had immediately assumed he was calling on a mistress. In the future, he would ensure there was no one he knew driving in her neighborhood before he assisted her out of the carriage.

Thank God Castelle had not seen her. It was unlikely that any of his other acquaintances would travel in this rough neighborhood. In truth, he wanted to move Lucy and her grandmother to a safer neighborhood, but he had no say.

He could have a say, though. It would take only a ring and a vow, but he knew Lucy's fears. If he pushed too soon, she would balk. Fortunately, his mother's party would prove to be the perfect venue to ease her into society. It would be the perfect way to introduce Lucy to his friends and their wives. Bellingham and Colin would lend their support no questions asked, and he knew their wives would take Lucy under their wings.

But the incident with Castelle still bothered Harry. He'd come very close to exposing her in a compromising position. The devil. The consequences would have been bad. He must be vigilant and ensure that she was protected at all times.

* * *

Buckley stood in the shadows beneath a dilapidated stairwell across the street from Lucy's lodgings. His right ankle still ached like the devil. He took out a bottle of laudanum and swigged from it as he watched the toff walk Lucy to her door. Buckley swiped his filthy glove over his mouth, and then his eyes nearly bugged out. The toff plastered her against him and stuck his tongue down her throat. She stood on her toes and clung to him.

The swell's fancy carriage and cut of his clothing marked him as a rich man. No doubt the little bitch was spreading her legs and reaping the rewards of fancy gowns and jewels.

She'd cost him his livelihood. All of his former clients had instructed their butlers to shut the door in his face when he begged for an audience. No doubt, Lucy had spread ruinous lies about him. She'd probably told Mrs. Vernon that he'd been drinking. So what if he had a nip of gin with his laudanum in the morning? He needed it for his bad ankle, thanks to that bitch Lucy.

How dare she cut him out of his living? He'd given her a chance. Nobody else had wanted her, but he'd taken her on as an assistant. What had she given him in return? Less than nothing. She'd robbed him of his reputation and his clients, but he'd make her pay soon enough. He'd catch her unaware one night when the toff wasn't around. He'd grab her and sell her for six pence to dozens of men every night.

Buckley pictured himself collecting coins as men stood in a queue waiting to defile her. Oh yes, she'd pay dearly for double-crossing him.

He would wait for the right opportunity, and then he would snatch her off the street.

* * *

When Harry's carriage stopped on Petticoat Lane, he got out and instructed the driver to keep a sharp lookout for criminals. The neighborhood was exceedingly wretched. Just the thought of Lucy venturing in this rough place made his gut twist.

As he walked toward the building, he thought about Lucy's heartbreak and desperation the day she'd taken her mother's pearls to this seedy place. He doubted the pearls would still be there, but he would make the effort on the slim chance they were.

He walked inside, and a rancid smell nearly made him gag. A hulking, hunchbacked man eyed him. "Can I help ye, Governor?"

"A redhead came here recently and pawned a pearl necklace. Do you still have the pearls?"

The man regarded him warily. "I'm not a fence, Governor."

"I didn't ask if the pearls were stolen. I asked if you have them."

"Lots of folks come and go. I can't be bothered rememberin' all of 'em."

Harry glared at him. "I daresay this establishment would not withstand a thorough search by the watch. Now answer my question."

"Aye, she come in one mornin'. I paid her, Governor."

After issuing a threat to alert the watch, Harry realized his mistake. The pawnbroker would tell Harry what he wanted to hear to keep the authorities at bay.

It was entirely possible the man was lying about the pearls, but Harry decided to take a chance. "Let me see them."

The pawnbroker pulled out a blue velvet pouch and deposited a necklace on the counter. Harry picked it up and ran his fingers over the smooth pearls. Damnation, he knew nothing about jewelry. For all he knew the necklace was paste.

"What's it gonna be, Governor? I ain't got all day."

Harry left it on the counter and strode across the grimy shop. He would buy her a new one, because he didn't believe for a second that it was Lucy's necklace. When he opened the door, the pawnbroker called out, "Wait, Governor."

Harry paused and looked over his shoulder. "Well?"

"There's somethin' you might have overlooked," the pawnbroker said.

Chapter Twelve

Friday, early evening

"Your Grace," Madame Delanger said, and curtsied as Harry entered the shop. "My seamstresses are almost finished fitting Miss Longmore."

"Excellent," he said. Lucy had requested the fitting after the regular shop hours to avoid seeing any former customers who might recognize her. She'd wanted to avoid any awkwardness.

"Your Grace, please make yourself comfortable on the chaise," Madame Delanger said.

"Thank you," he said, stretching out his legs.

Earlier, he'd persuaded Lucy to let him take her up in his carriage to the dress shop so they could transport the gown in his carriage. After leaving Lucy in Madame's care, he'd taken himself off to White's for a brandy and read the papers.

He retrieved his watch. Poor Lucy. If the experience was anything like his recent visit to the tailor, he pitied her. All that measuring, trimming, and pinning was sheer torture to him. Then again, maybe ladies liked it. Lord knew his cousins were always discussing fashion.

Madame Delanger regarded him with a shrewd expression. "Lucy is fortunate to be in your good graces."

He suspected Madame thought he'd made Lucy his mistress and meant to disabuse the woman of the idea. "On the contrary, I am the fortunate one," he said. "I look forward to introducing her to my family and friends."

Madame's brows lifted. "Indeed, she will be elevated to a great degree."

He regarded her with a bored expression. "Lucy needs no elevation."

"Indeed, Your Grace. I quite agree," Madame said. "Ah, here she comes now."

Harry set his hat aside and stood. Lucy blushed as she walked out in a white gown with short, puffed sleeves decorated with pretty blue ribbons. The same ribbons were on the bottom part of the gown. She wore a close-fitting bonnet with a wide blue sash.

"Turn around slowly," Madame said.

Lucy blushed as she complied. Harry saw the artistry behind the simple style, for a wide blue bow with a long sash at the back drew the eye immediately. When he met Lucy's gaze, he realized she was a little uncertain of herself.

"You are stunning," he said.

"You approve?" Lucy said.

"Definitely." He regarded Madame. "The gown is almost as beautiful as Miss Longmore."

"Yes, Your Grace," Madame Delanger said. "Now, Lucy, there are gloves, slippers, and a parasol to finish the ensemble, but now you must change clothes so that Evelyn can box up everything."

Mary accompanied Lucy to the screen. Several minutes later, Lucy emerged and Mary helped Evelyn box up the items.

"Lucy, I will come to your lodgings tomorrow to help you dress," Mary said. "You looked beautiful in the gown."

"Thank you, Mary," Lucy said. "Thank you, Madame and Evelyn."

Madame bowed. "It is my pleasure."

Once the boxes were stowed in the carriage, Harry helped Lucy inside and sat next to her. Afterward, he knocked his cane on the roof. "You're quiet," he said.

"I'm a bit nervous about tomorrow."

"You needn't be. I will be there, and so will Mina, Helena, and Amelia. They're anxious to see you again and have talked endlessly about the dance lessons. Apparently you managed to put everyone at ease, even with others watching."

"If only I could be at ease tomorrow. I fear I'll have nothing to contribute to the conversations."

"I disagree. My sisters assured me the Almack's competition is much talked about. Others will want your opinion."

"That reassures me."

She didn't look reassured at all. "I promise I won't hover over you tomorrow, but I'll not stray too far."

"Tell me again what to expect. Will there be many guests?"

"Yes, my mother's annual party is always a crush. There will be tents for the refreshments. The other patronesses will be there, of course. I'll introduce you to my friends and their wives."

"You are so kind to me, but I find myself wishing I'd never agreed."

He took her hand. "I'm thankful you did. You're the reason I look forward to it."

The way he looked at her took her breath away, and it was an exhilarating experience to have all of his attention centered upon her.

"Don't worry," he said. "You will relax once we are there."

She lowered her eyes. "I fear I'll inadvertently make a faux pas and embarrass you."

He wrapped his arms around her. "You won't, but I will make this promise. If for any reason you are uncomfortable, we will leave."

"No, I can't do that to you. I'm just anxious. I'm sure all will be fine tomorrow."

He kissed her lightly on the lips. "I know you're a bit nervous, but you will enjoy the party."

When the carriage rocked to a halt, Harry got out and looked around, but there were no other vehicles traveling on the street. Then he assisted Lucy on the carriage steps and escorted her upstairs to her home. He gave her a quick kiss. "Until tomorrow."

She waved at him, and a moment later he heard the bolt slide home.

Harry ran down the steps again and strode to his carriage. He heard a scrabbling sound as if someone were trying to gain their feet. It seemed to come from the lodgings across the street. He retrieved his knife from his inner pocket and strode beneath the stairwell to investigate, but he saw nothing there. He approached the carriage and queried his coachman. "Did you see any suspicious persons?"

"I saw a limpin' man walkin' under the stairwell across the way. That was all, Your Grace."

"I don't like this neighborhood," Harry said.

"Not the safest, Your Grace."

"I'm going to check the stairwell on the other side," he said.

Harry walked beneath the stairwell. Broken glass crunched beneath his boots. The neck of a broken bottle lay on the ground. Someone had spent time here. After his mother's party, Harry meant to discuss safer lodgings with Lucy. He would be honest with her about his fears for her safety and that of her grandmother.

Buckley's ankle throbbed from moving too fast. It was still swollen, but not broken. When he'd seen the toff with Lucy, he'd had to hide quickly in the shadows. He figured the coachman had seen him limping to the stairwell. When the nob walked inside with a blade in his hand, Buckley had started shaking and managed to scrabble out the other side. The nob was no fancy man; he was big and muscular. It had been a close call, but Buckley had seen the nob carrying boxes tonight. Obviously Lucy's nob was buying her gifts in recompense for serving him.

He removed an apothecary bottle and tipped it to his lips, but only the dregs of laudanum remained. Tonight he'd have to pick pockets, a dicey business. If caught, he'd swing from the Tyburn Tree.

He wouldn't be in this sorry state if not for Lucy. She'd betrayed him, taken away all his clients, and now she was probably spreading her legs for the rich nob. But her man had taken himself off in his elegant carriage, and Buckley meant to take advantage of the opportunity. When he got to the stairs, he winced because his ankle ached. He made it halfway up the steps and sat. He pulled out a rag he meant to use to gag her, not that anyone in this neighborhood would care about a squawking female. He took a deep breath and shouted, "Help!" Once he had her pity, he'd snatch her.

Sure enough, her door cracked open. Lucy scowled at him. "Go away."

"I'm hurt. Help me."

She hesitated.

"You owe me, Lucy. I gave you your start. You wouldn't turn away an injured man."

She shut the door. A bolt slid home.

"Bitch." He swore he'd rough her up badly when he caught her.

After Lucy bolted the door, she leaned her back against it. Her heart hammered, but she mustn't hide it.

Grandmama held her hand to her heart. "What was that?"

"Buckley. He fell and wanted my help. I suspect it was a trick."

Grandmama worried her hands. "What does he want?"

"He claimed he was injured, but it was likely nothing more than a sprained ankle. He probably wants to ask me to be his assistant again."

"Oh dear. I don't like this at all," Grandmama said.

"Eventually, he'll tire of the damp fog and go away." Unfortunately, she doubted it would be the last time. He must be desperate. She hated having to carry her blade in her basket, but she must be wary of Buckley. He might be injured, but he blamed her for his misfortune. Buckley might want retribution, but she was far cleverer than him. She wouldn't let him within a foot of her ever again. That meant she must be aware of her surroundings at all times. She'd learned her lesson the night the thief had tried to steal her basket, and she couldn't afford to be caught off guard ever again.

* * *

Late Saturday morning

Mary arrived midmorning to put Lucy's hair up and help her dress.

Lucy looked in the mirror. "Mary, you have a real talent for styling hair. You could be a lady's maid."

"I never thought of it," Mary said. "I guess I just followed in the same shoes as my mother and sisters. Do you think it would be easier than sewing?"

"I don't know for certain, but sometimes you have to take a leap of faith. It never hurts to inquire."

Mary inhaled. "I've never had any confidence."

Lucy rose. "I think we all have to look deep inside to find faith in ourselves. I suppose I should take my own advice. I'm a bit anxious," Lucy confided. That was a colossal understatement. She never, ever should have agreed to attend this party.

"Step into the gown," Mary said, and then she drew the bodice up. "You look beautiful. Like a princess."

"Hardly that," Lucy said. Who was she trying to fool? She would never fit into his world. "Mary, I can't go. I can't."

"Of course you will go," Mary said.

"You do not understand. They will look at me as if I'm unworthy to be in their presence." She paced her small bedchamber. "Why did I ever agree to attend? I will be completely out of place and embarrass Harry. I'll not be able to contribute to the conversations."

"Stay still." Mary tied the tapes of her gown. "Harry, is it? That sounds promising."

She'd let his Christian name slip. "Mary, I admit I have

tender feelings for him, but I know his family would never accept me. Frankly, I'm terrified about this party."

"You won't let your man down," Mary said. "He's ever so handsome, and I wager he'll be very proud to escort you to the Venetian breakfast."

"Is that not the silliest name for an afternoon party?" Lucy said.

Mary smiled. "Well, perhaps they'll have gondolas."

Lucy laughed. "Oh, what would I do without you and Evelyn?"

"You're our friend, Lucy, but today, you will be the most beautiful belle at the party."

"No, I'm quite sure I won't. I only hope that I can make it through this day without a mishap of some sort."

"I saw the way the duke looks at you," Mary said. "He's in a fair way to falling in love with you, if he hasn't already."

"I know he cares for me, but I have to be realistic. Our affaire de coeur will likely end quietly when he returns to his property in the summer. It's inevitable."

"You don't know that," Mary said.

"Mary, my jobs are here in London. When the season ends, he will return to Havenwood, his property in Wiltshire. I want to spend as much time with him as possible before that day arrives, but I must prepare myself for the day he leaves."

"Lucy, do you love him?"

Her eyes welled. "I tried not to fall in love with him, but I did."

Mary gave her a handkerchief. "Don't cry. It will spoil the party for you. For today, you are a lady attending a Venetian breakfast with a very handsome duke. Don't let anything spoil this special day for both of you."

"Thank you, Mary."

"What troubles you?" Mary said. "I can see it on your face."

"I think his mother means to put me in my place. Why else would she invite me?"

"Perhaps she wants one of her nieces to win the Almack's dancing competition."

"Undoubtedly that is true, but I do not think I'm wrong about Mrs. Norcliffe's intentions."

"Try to think positive," Mary said. "No matter what happens, you have a wonderful beau."

"Mary, he's not mine. He never will be."

"He is today," Mary said. She bit her lip and hesitated a moment.

"What is it?" Lucy said.

Mary set the soft shawl over Lucy's shoulders. "I would give anything to be in your slippers."

Lucy hugged her. "You will find someone who adores you."

"I hope your day is magical," Mary said. "Now I must go."

"Meet me and Grandmama at the park tomorrow."

"I have to sew, but next week for sure," Mary said. "I'll bring Evelyn."

"I'll hold you to that promise." Yet she knew the decision was all in Madame Delanger's hands.

Lucy walked with Mary to the door. "Thank you."

"You must describe it all to me when next I see you," Mary said.

"I will."

"Good-bye, Mrs. Longmore," Mary said.

After Lucy closed and bolted the door, Grandmama said, "Come sit with me."

Lucy joined her. "I wish you were coming with me today."

"We've already discussed that," Grandmama said. "Granfield will be here soon. There are a few things I wish to say before he arrives."

Lucy's stomach clenched. "Is something wrong?"

"No, but I worry about your relationship with him."

Lucy wet her dry lips. Had her grandmother guessed she'd allowed him liberties?

"Do not mistake me. He seems a good and caring man. You know I like him very well. I do not believe he would deliberately wound you, but I advise you not to lose your heart to him."

She was scared because it would hurt when they must part.

Grandmama sipped her tea. "I've thought about this a great deal since he confessed he was a duke. His family will expect him to marry among his own kind."

"I know," she said. "I have no illusions about a future with him." Sometimes she imagined the three of them living in a small house and a hearth blazing with a warm fire. She shook off the foolish image, but she felt a little hollow inside knowing the image was nothing more than a daydream.

Grandmama sighed. "I suppose I'm trying to prevent you from being crossed in love. I only wish to protect you."

"I know." Harry was never far from her thoughts. When he kissed her, she felt exhilarated and cherished, but she knew it would hurt terribly when he left London this summer.

Grandmama patted her hand. "You're a sensible young woman. I know you'll act in a responsible manner."

She had already acted irresponsibly, but she would never regret his wicked kisses and touches.

"Now I fear I've put a damper on your day," Grandmama said. "I never meant to do so. You must enjoy yourself today.

I hope you're wearing your mother's pearls," Grandmama said.

Lucy focused on keeping her tone light. "The gown is adornment enough for an afternoon party." She had never told her grandmother that she'd taken the pearl necklace to a pawnshop. Perhaps she ought to have confessed to Grandmama, but Lucy hadn't wanted to make her grandmother sad. Maybe it had been wrong of her, but how could it be wrong to avoid hurting someone needlessly. Nothing would have changed if she'd told Grandmama.

Footsteps sounded on the stairs outside.

"I believe Granfield is here," Grandmama said.

Lucy opened the door, and there he stood with a single red rose. "For you," he said.

She inhaled the fragrance. "It's beautiful."

He bowed over her hand. "So are you."

Grandmama rose. "Well, Granfield, I am entrusting my granddaughter to your safekeeping. You will take good care of her."

"Grandmama, there's nothing to worry about."

Harry's blue eyes lit up as he met Lucy's gaze. "I will look after her, Mrs. Longmore."

"Very well," Grandmama said as she took her cup to the cupboard.

After she disappeared, Harry drew out a dark blue velvet pouch and handed it to Lucy. Chill bumps erupted on her arms when she held the velvet pouch. She held her breath as she opened it. She gasped. "My mother's pearls," she whispered. Tears sprang in her eyes.

"I couldn't be sure they were the ones," he said under his breath.

"I know it by the silver heart on the chain." She trembled a little.

"Thank God for the chain. I almost walked out of the pawnshop, but the pawnbroker pointed out the silver heart. He said he remembered you because of it. I decided to take a chance."

Her chest shook. "It's my mother's. I can't believe you found them."

"I had to try," he said. "Please don't cry."

In that moment, she fell hopelessly and irrevocably in love with him. "Th-thank you."

He handed her his handkerchief, and she blotted her eyes.

"Grandmama doesn't know about the pearls," she whispered.

He bent down and kissed her cheek. "I understand." Then he put his handkerchief away.

"This is the best gift I've ever gotten," she said.

When he clasped the pearls around her neck, she touched them, still a little unable to believe he'd found them.

Grandmama's stick tapped on the floor. "Have a lovely afternoon at the party."

"Thank you, Mrs. Longmore," Harry said. When he offered his arm, Lucy took it. Something inside of her tumbled over, and she knew it was her heart.

When Lucy looked at the street, she frowned. "There's another carriage."

"Yes," he said. "I'm sending you with Bellingham and his wife, Laura—Lady Bellingham—in order to observe the proprieties. However, we will leave the party early today and use my carriage."

He escorted her to the other carriage. Lord Bellingham and his wife stepped outside while Harry made the introductions.

Lord Bellingham bowed. "Miss Longmore, will you join my lady and me?"

"Yes, thank you."

Bell winked at Harry. "We'll take good care of her, old boy."

Harry lifted his chin. "Thanks, Bell."

Harry arrived first, so he waited in the carriage until Bellingham arrived.

"There you are," Harry said when Bell assisted the ladies out of his carriage.

Harry offered his arm to Lucy and led the way to the house. He leaned down and said, "I will be the most envied man at the party today."

She knew differently, but the expression in his blue eyes took her breath away.

"You are exquisite," he said.

"A lovely gown and pretty bonnet makes all the difference."

"No gown or bonnet could ever eclipse your natural beauty."

"Well, if you think so. I suppose it would be foolish of me to disagree."

"I meant it," he said.

She thought it best to keep the banter light. "I am onto your charming ways."

"Are you, now? I had better think of new ways to entice you."

She looked at him from the corner of her eye. "I think charm runs in your blood."

"Perhaps I could charm you into a kiss later?" he whispered.

"Maybe, if you are on your very best behavior," she said.

"Oh, now you've set me a challenge."

As they stepped inside the foyer, Lucy figured her biggest

challenge today would be Harry's mother. Lucy suspected Mrs. Norcliffe intended to ensure Lucy got her come-uppance. It certainly wouldn't be the first time, but Lucy meant to be as cordial as possible, regardless of what his mother said.

There was a part of her that hoped Mrs. Norcliffe would ignore her, but another part of her wanted to impress his mother. It was a silly wish. She doubted Mrs. Norcliffe would even acknowledge her. After all, not long ago she'd claimed to have forgotten her.

No matter what happened, she must remain serene for Harry's sake. He had wanted her to attend the party with him, and she was honored. Years from now, she would re-member this beautiful gown, her mother's pearls, and the chivalrous man who had stolen her heart.

"We're headed to the garden," Bell said, and led Lady Bellingham outside.

Footsteps sounded on the stairs, and Harry stopped. "Mina, is everyone on the grounds?"

"There's quite a crowd already. Aunt is in raptures. Miss Longmore, I'm so glad you came. Your gown is gorgeous. Harry, I intend to steal her away from you. Later you can take her to see the goldfish."

"Mina, I brought her at my mother's request."

"I know. Now go find your friends. No doubt they're smoking cheroots and swigging from their flasks. Do not think I've no idea what goes on behind Aunt's back."

He winked. "But you would never turn informer."

"I'll not spoil what passes for male entertainment, but you will be sorry if Aunt smells liquor on your breath."

"I'll keep my distance from her," Harry said, laughing.

Lucy noted the merriment in his eyes and couldn't help smiling.

Mina took her arm. "I see you have your parasol. We'll be safe from the dreaded freckles. Now come with me. I'll introduce you to everyone."

As they stepped out into the gardens, the fragrance of roses perfumed the air. Harry had obviously purloined the rose he'd given her from his mother's garden. "It's lovely here."

"Aunt loves her roses. Did Harry tell you my Christian name is Melinda? I thought you would be interested, as most people are taken aback by my sobriquet."

"It is unusual," Lucy said.

"My mother's name was also Melinda, and it upset my sisters to hear it spoken. It was Harry's idea to call me Mina. My sisters and I were very young when our parents died in an accident. My aunt has treated us like her own daughters."

Lucy's eyes widened.

"I understand you live with your grandmother," Mina said.

"Yes, I'm fortunate to have her."

Mina studied her for a moment, giving Lucy the impression that the young woman was wise beyond her years. "So you have made your own way in the world teaching dance."

"I have more than one job, but dancing is essential to me. One day I hope to have my own studio."

"You are ambitious," Mina said.

"Yes, but I do what I must," Lucy said.

"Our sex is supposedly the weaker one," Mina said, "but our strengths lie in our ability to find ways around the limitations society sets for us."

"Well put," Lucy said. She had always thought women of means lived lives of comfort and ease, but Mina's words reminded her that all women had trials and tribulations.

When they entered the tent, Mina took her toward the

back. Lucy spotted Mrs. Norcliffe, who was speaking to several ladies. As they drew nearer, Lucy suspected Harry's mother had seen her, but Mrs. Norcliffe seemed determined to ignore her presence.

Three young ladies walking past regarded Lucy with disdainful expressions. For a moment, Lucy wondered if she'd done something wrong until Mina took her arm.

"Never mind those three. They're jealous of you."

"How can that be? They don't even know me."

"They were present the first time you instructed dance in Aunt's drawing room. They saw you dancing with Harry. All the single girls have him in their sights, but he gets exasperated with their affectations. He especially abhors the girls who lisp because it has become fashionable."

Lucy had never heard of anything so silly.

"Oh, there is Aunt," Mina said. "Shall we join her?"

"Your aunt is engaged at present. Perhaps we could walk about the grounds," Lucy said.

"But then Harry would be affronted. I know he wishes to show you the goldfish. Shall we get a cup of lemonade?"

Lucy nodded. She certainly did not wish to stand about waiting for Mrs. Norcliffe to take notice of her. They found chairs in an area away from the breeze and sipped the lemonade. A footman paused before them with tiny iced cakes, but Lucy refused. It would be just her luck to drop something on her skirts.

A few moments later, Helena and Amelia joined them.

"Your gown is pretty," Amelia said. "Wherever did you have it made up?"

"A shop on Bond Street," Lucy said.

"Oh, that must be Madame Delanger," Helena said. "We recently shopped there."

Lucy said nothing. The three sisters would be shocked if

they knew she'd sewn and swept floors at the shop a few weeks ago.

"Ah, here comes Aunt," Mina said.

When Mrs. Norcliffe arrived, she frowned at Mina. "I saw you earlier, but you disappeared."

"You were much engaged, Aunt. You remember Miss Longmore."

"Of course I do. I invited her." Mrs. Norcliffe turned her attention to Lucy. "You look rather fetching in that gown."

Lucy rose and curtsied. "Thank you."

"Aunt, she had her gown made up at that shop we discovered on Bond Street. The one you liked so well."

A footman brought a chair for Mrs. Norcliffe, but she waved it away. "Miss Longmore, will you walk with me?" she said.

"Yes, thank you." Lucy opened her parasol and walked beside her. Mrs. Norcliffe walked at a brisk pace and nodded at others along the way. The entire time Lucy wondered if Mrs. Norcliffe would reveal why she'd invited her to walk. Unsettled by the silence, Lucy said, "It is a beautiful day. I imagine you are happy the weather has cooperated."

"I always plan for contingencies. In the event of rain, I was prepared to hold the event indoors."

"Very wise," Lucy said. She reminded herself to take the time to think before she replied.

"Do you have family?" Mrs. Norcliffe asked.

"Only my grandmother."

Mrs. Norcliffe pursed her lips. "You have no other family?"

She would not mention the Earl of Wargrove. "It is only my grandmother and me."

Mrs. Norcliffe's brows drew together. "That cannot be an easy life for you."

"I make the best of my situation, and I count myself fortunate to have my grandmother."

"Since you teach dance, I presume you did not inherit a fortune."

She smiled a little. "No, I did not."

"Forgive me, but surely dance lessons do not pay handsomely."

She felt no compulsion to explain. "I am fortunate that I enjoy it."

"You are certainly well spoken and mannerly. Lady Jersey was impressed by your dancing skills."

"I shall take that as a compliment," Lucy said.

"Your grandmother did not accompany you."

"No, she was unable to attend." Lucy did not think it necessary to mention her grandmother's affliction.

Mrs. Norcliffe regarded her with a crafty expression. "I gather you are ambitious."

Not where your son is concerned if that is what you mean. "I'm more than happy to assist those who wish to polish their dancing skills."

Mrs. Norcliffe sniffed. "A pretty way of saying you intend to make a business of it."

Lucy met her gaze. "One day I hope to open my own dance studio." She half expected Mrs. Norcliffe to recoil in horror.

"I admire your honesty." Mrs. Norcliffe shook out her fan. "However did you meet my son?"

She certainly wouldn't admit she'd threatened him with a knife. "We met in the park. His dog got loose and decided to befriend me."

She arched her thin brows. "My son or the dog?"

Lucy covered a laugh. "I beg your pardon."

"You need not."

"I see where he gets his sense of humor." And his blue eyes.

"He is a scamp. Always has been," Mrs. Norcliffe said. "His uncle encouraged him in mischief, but he was a good role model for Harry after my husband died."

"It must have been difficult for you."

She sighed. "Not long afterward, my sister and her husband perished in a carriage accident. I had three young girls to look after. I had no time to indulge in melancholy, but I cherish them. They are like my own daughters. My son is fond of them as well."

Lucy was surprised to find Mrs. Norcliffe far more amiable than she'd expected. "I imagine the girls adore you," Lucy said.

"We get on well. Have you seen the rose garden?" Mrs. Norcliffe asked.

Lucy was momentarily thrown off guard by the change in topic. "Only briefly."

"I shall give you a tour."

"Thank you. I would be delighted." Her curiosity heightened. Once again she wondered why Mrs. Norcliffe had invited her to the Venetian breakfast. Lucy suspected she was taking her to a secluded place for a reason, but she had no idea what to expect. Undoubtedly Mrs. Norcliffe would reveal her reason soon enough. Given her previous dealings with Mrs. Norcliffe, Lucy meant to be on her guard.

When they entered the garden, Lucy saw numerous rose-bushes of all colors, including pink, white, and red.

Lucy gently touched the soft petal of one red rose.

"That particular variety is called the velvet rose," Mrs. Norcliffe said.

"The fragrance is pleasing."

"Do you aim to please, Miss Longmore?"

Lucy's heart hammered as she sought an answer, but of course, she chose the safe response. "I hope to please when I teach dance."

An ironic smile played on Mrs. Norcliffe's lips. "A careful answer."

"I'm a careful person." *Liar. If you were careful, you would never have struck up an acquaintance with her son or kissed him.*

Mrs. Norcliffe broke off a stemmed rose. "Since you like scents, I believe you will find this one most unusual."

Lucy brought the rose to her face. "It smells of cinnamon," she said in wonder.

"You will not be surprised that it is called the early cinnamon."

"I imagine you spend many hours in your garden."

"Not as many as I would prefer. When the season is in full swing, it is quite hectic." She walked along the bushes and halted once more. "This one is known as the virgin rose."

Lucy's face grew warm, and of course she felt foolish.

Mrs. Norcliffe looked amused. "It is so named because there are no thorns."

"How convenient," Lucy said. That was quite possibly the most inane comment she'd ever made.

Thus far, Mrs. Norcliffe had been agreeable, but Lucy knew that something was in the wind. Clearly Mrs. Norcliffe had a reason for spiriting her away from the other guests. Most likely she'd done so because she didn't want anyone else, perhaps her son, to hear her words.

Mrs. Norcliffe led her to a wooden bench. "You will likely find my question intrusive, but may I ask how a dance instructor affords a gown from a premier modiste on Bond Street?"

Lucy suspected Mrs. Norcliffe thought her son had purchased the gown. "At one time, I worked at Madame Delanger's shop. This was an abandoned gown that her assistants made over for me."

Mrs. Norcliffe's brows lifted. "How generous of your former employer."

Lucy smiled a little. "I believe she hoped others would inquire about her shop."

"A shrewd tactic and a boon for you as well." She paused and added, "Your pearls look well with your gown."

Clearly his mother wanted to know how she'd afforded them. "They belonged to my late mother." Obviously she would not reveal that Harry had redeemed them from the pawnbroker.

"Since you worked for Madame Delanger, I assume you are talented with a needle," Mrs. Norcliffe said.

Like all girls, she'd learned to stitch, mend, and embroider. "I have an average proficiency with needlework, but dancing is my passion."

"Perhaps pretty gowns are as well."

She might as well be honest; after all, she was fooling no one, least of all Mrs. Norcliffe. "I've never owned such a fine gown, nor do I expect to do so again."

"It suits you very well," Mrs. Norcliffe said.

"I doubt I shall have another occasion to wear it."

"Are you pessimistic by nature?" Mrs. Norcliffe asked.

"I'm practical." If she found herself short of money, and it had happened more than once, she would likely have to sell the gown. But she could not let thoughts of what might happen distract her.

"Miss Longmore, your manners are refined. Your father must have been a gentleman."

"He owned no property." Of course, she didn't speak of her father's horrid drinking.

"Your mother must have influenced you, then. What of her family?" Mrs. Norcliffe said.

She had no intention of mentioning the Earl of Wargrove. "My mother was estranged from her family before I was born."

"Estranged?" Mrs. Norcliffe said.

"My mother eloped," she said.

"Oh dear," Mrs. Norcliffe said. "Too many girls think it romantic, until they discover they've no dowry. Well, your lack of family is unfortunate," she said. "Nevertheless, you are to be commended for looking after your grandmother. Now, I wish you to give dance instructions on Tuesday morning in my drawing room. May I count on you?"

Lucy's heart leaped. "I welcome the opportunity."

"I'm determined to see Mina and Everleigh win the dancing competition if at all possible. I have it on the best of authority that Mr. Fitzhugh and Miss Fothergill have been practicing daily. The lady in question is delightful, but Fitzhugh is a known libertine. I am appalled that Lord and Lady Tatten-Brown would allow their daughter near the man."

Lucy remained silent, though she was somewhat amused by Mrs. Norcliffe's opinions. "Are there any particular dances you have in mind?"

"Indeed," she said. "The Allemande will be among the first of the dances. I assume you are familiar with it."

"Yes, I know it well."

"You appear to be a clever girl." Mrs. Norcliffe toyed with the virgin rose. "As you may have guessed, I brought you to the garden so that we may speak privately."

Even though she'd known this moment was coming, Lucy's heart drummed.

"You are on friendly terms with my son."

Her mouth went dry. "We have not been acquainted long."

"I see. There is a young lady whom I intended for my son. I believe you remember Miss Hortense Osterham."

Lucy struggled to keep her expression neutral, but the news pummeled her. "Yes, of course."

Mrs. Norcliffe watched her closely. "Unfortunately, my hopes in that direction have not borne fruit. I was naturally disappointed. Miss Osterham's breeding and accomplishments are excellent. My son, however, has ideas of his own."

Lucy felt as if she'd dodged trampling hooves and her heart was still beating too fast. She should not have let down her guard in front of his wily mother.

Mrs. Norcliffe watched her with a hard smile. "My son is considered London's most eligible bachelor. I have every expectation that he will marry well—perhaps before the end of the season."

Lucy didn't want to think about the season ending, though it would come whether she was ready or not, but she didn't want to ruin the day with worries about tomorrow or the end of the season. A year from now, she wanted to remember this as a happy day she'd spent with him.

However, Mrs. Norcliffe clearly meant to make sure that Lucy wouldn't stand in the way of her plans for Harry and meant to warn her off. But why? There was no way Mrs. Norcliffe could know there had been anything romantic between her and Harry, but she did not need proof. Harry's mother could ruin her easily with a few words if she chose. Lucy's stomach clenched at the thought. She must be on her guard at all times around Mrs. Norcliffe—especially today.

The swish of skirts diverted Mrs. Norcliffe. Lucy concentrated on regaining her composure. Her heart felt as if it were in her throat, but she mustn't let Mrs. Norcliffe intimidate her. She would not give her the satisfaction.

"Aunt, there you are," Mina said. "I thought you might have given Miss Longmore a tour of the rose garden."

Lucy wondered if Mina had come to the garden in order to intervene. While she would never know for certain, Lucy had learned to trust her instincts, and it seemed probable.

"I had better return to the other guests," Mrs. Norcliffe said. "Miss Longmore, I will speak to you after the dance lesson on Tuesday."

Lucy rose and curtsied.

Mina took her arm. "Do come along with me. I've only spent a few moments with you. I suppose my aunt asked you to instruct us in our practice session on Tuesday."

"Yes, she did." Ruthlessly, she shoved her concerns aside. There was no point in worrying over what might happen. She'd been invited to instruct the dancing in Mrs. Norcliffe's drawing room next Tuesday, and that at least appeared to be a positive sign. Given her previous experiences, she knew better than to depend upon it.

"I hope my aunt was not too inquisitive," Mina said. "She prides herself on knowing everything about everyone."

Lucy hardly knew how to respond to Mina's statement. She let silence be her answer.

Mina glanced at her. "Oh dear, I hope Aunt did not pry."

"I answered to her satisfaction...and mine."

Mina smiled. "I rather thought you would be up to her challenge. Most people are not. "Oh, look. Harry, Everleigh, Charles Osgood, and Lord Chesfield are standing just outside the tent," Mina said. "Let us join them."

The wind blew their skirts as they crossed the lawn. When they reached the gentlemen, Harry smiled. "I wondered where Mina had taken you. Off to see the rose garden, I suspect."

"Your mother showed it to me. It's beautiful," Lucy said.

"We were planning to walk to the bridge to see the goldfish," Harry said.

Mina waved for her sisters to join them. Then she introduced Miss Hortense Osterham to Mr. Osgood.

Mr. Osgood's eyes lit up. "Miss Osterham, may I escort you to see the goldfish?"

"Yes, I would be delighted," Hortense said. She set her hand on his arm.

"May I escort you, Miss Longmore?" Harry asked.

"Yes, of course," she said, taking his arm.

Harry led the way across the lawn. They all crowded on the small wooden bridge and watched the goldfish wiggling their tails. Harry glanced at Hortense and joined her on the other side of the bridge. "I fear I may have inadvertently caused you vexation the last time we met."

She winced. "I beg your pardon, Your Grace. You have been a perfect gentleman. Our mothers, however, have been...determined."

"Yes, they undoubtedly have the best of intentions, but it can sometimes prove awkward," he said.

"I'm glad we have an...understanding," Hortense said.

"Indeed, Miss Osterham. I understand completely."

Harry joined Lucy shortly afterward.

"I expected the fish to be gold," Lucy said, "but some are orange."

Harry stepped beside Lucy. "My mother is proud of her pond."

"What do they eat?" Miss Osterham asked.

"Roast beef," Mr. Osgood said, making Miss Osterham blush and everyone else laugh.

"Feel free to wander the grounds as you wish," Harry said. "There is shade beneath the tents and benches beneath some of the trees."

Everleigh rubbed his hands together. "Granfield, I daresay our ladies will agree to accompany us."

Mina shook her head. "We will not live in your pockets. You will appreciate us all the more when we make you wait."

Everleigh fisted his hand on his hip. "What say you, Granfield? Have we just been given the boot?"

Harry winked at Lucy. "I think they wish to play hard to get. Have no fear, we will catch them."

"Lucy, I wish to introduce you to some ladies who are interested in your dance instruction," Mina said. "In particular, you must meet Lady Ravenshire. She's quite droll. You will like her and Lady Bellingham very much."

One hour later

Harry sat lounging in a chair under the tent with his friends. They were drinking lemonade since his mother refused to serve spirits.

"A year ago, we would have wandered far from the tent to smoke Bell's cheroots," Harry said, crossing his booted feet. "Do you have any, Bell?"

Bellingham let out a disgusted sigh. "No. Laura said they make me stink."

Harry sighed. "My dog stinks. Barlow refused to wash him."

Colin's shoulders shook with laughter. "Who the devil is Barlow?"

"My manservant. I suppose I'll have to bathe him."

Bellingham arched his brows. "Your manservant?"

Harry nearly spewed lemonade. An elderly lady passing by regarded him with a comical look of horror and hurried off.

"Oh Lord," Colin said, wiping tears of hilarity from his face.

Everleigh frowned. "I say, Ravenshire, are you weeping?"

That comment set off raucous laughter.

Bellingham stood. "The ladies are approaching, gentlemen. Pretend you're civilized."

Of course they guffawed.

Angeline shook her head. "Dare I ask what the four of you find so hilarious?"

Colin tugged on her wrist. "Wife, I doubt you would find it amusing."

"Oh, I find you endlessly amusing, husband."

He winked. "Be sweet to me, and I'll let you tear down the walls again."

"Ha-ha."

Lucy took a chair next to Lady Bellingham. Harry was glad she looked at ease.

"Miss Longmore, are you new to London?" Lady Ravenshire asked.

"Relatively new," Lucy said.

Harry noticed Lucy was adept at answering questions without giving away much information. He found it rather curious and wondered if she did it purposely to keep her life private.

"I found the city bewildering when I first came to London," Lady Bellingham said. "I'd lived a quiet and sheltered country existence."

"I enjoy the shopping," Lady Ravenshire said. "I have my eye on a new carpet."

"Oh Lord," Colin said. "First the carpet and next it will be paint. Wife, I beg you to stop making over our homes. You may decorate our friends' houses. They will likely turn you out when you knock out a wall or make them dig for buried treasure in the attic."

Everyone laughed.

Colin frowned. "Angeline, you look a bit weary. Let me take you home to rest."

"I am a little tired," she said, placing her hand on her rounded stomach.

Lady Bellingham walked up behind her husband and kissed his cheek.

"Checking for the stench of cheroots, my dear?" Bellingham said.

"Who, me?"

"I do miss them, you know."

"But you would miss me more," Lady Bellingham said.

"You drive a hard bargain, wife."

Her eyes lit up. "I know how to get my way."

"Everleigh and Harry should take notes," Bellingham said.

"Hah," Lady Bellingham said. "You would be far better off if you took instruction from your friends' wives."

"But I want them to suffer, my love," Bellingham said.

Harry rolled his eyes. "Everleigh, you see before you two men who are completely smitten and domesticated. We, on the other hand, are free as birds to do whatever we wish."

"I smell a wager," Bellingham said. "Do look for it in the betting book at White's on Monday."

Harry shrugged. "If you're willing to part with your purse, I'm more than willing to relieve you of it."

A few minutes later, Charles Osgood and Miss Osterham arrived looking more than a little windblown. "We ventured to the green house and lost track of time," Osgood said.

Lucy noticed the young lady's cheeks were rosy. It was a good thing they had returned before anyone else noticed their absence.

Mrs. Norcliffe appeared. "I daresay you all look as if you're enjoying yourselves."

"Indeed, it has been a fine party," Ravenshire said, "but we must depart. Angeline needs her rest."

"Thank you for a lovely afternoon, Mrs. Norcliffe," Lady Bellingham said.

When a crowd of ladies surrounded Mrs. Norcliffe, Harry took Lucy aside. "Let us leave before the mass exodus."

"Yes, thank you." She didn't want others to mark that she was traveling alone with him.

"Did you enjoy the party?" he asked as they strode through the house.

"Yes, I especially like your cousin Mina."

"Everyone adores her," Harry said. "In case I forgot to say it, you were the prettiest lady there today."

"You are sweet, Harry."

His smile lit up like a dozen candles. "No, I'm hopeful."

She knew what he meant. Thoughts of his mother's words in the garden dampened her spirits for a moment. Somehow in the midst of all their meetings in the park and his carriage, she'd managed to push his ducal status to the back of her thoughts. To her, he was Harry, charming, determined, and always optimistic Harry. But today his mother's words had reminded her that he was not just any man. He had duties in parliament and duties to his family as well. Everyone in the ton expected him to marry well. He was responsible for his lineage and his future sons and daughters.

For now, she would hold him in her arms and in her heart until the season drew closer to an end. The very thought made her chest tighten as if she couldn't breathe. She would have to be the one to end it, but she must be patient and wait for the right opportunity. When the time was right, and she would know it, she would inform him that he must find a woman who belonged in his world. Someone who had dozens of elegant gowns and an enormous marriage portion. Someone who didn't serve lemonade and clean gentlemen's rooms. Someone he wouldn't regret marrying for the rest of his life.

But not yet. She wasn't ready. She probably would never be ready. For now, she would take advantage of every moment until the season and their affaire de coeur ended.

Chapter Thirteen

The sun had started to set when Harry handed Lucy up into his carriage. No one observed that she was traveling alone with him. Once they were seated, he knocked his cane and the vehicle rocked into motion. He shut the drapes and turned to Lucy. "All day, I've thought about only one thing."

Her lips parted. "What is it?" she asked.

"You."

She inhaled on a shuddered breath. "Harry, you always make me feel special, even though I'm not."

He put his finger over her lips. "Hush. You are an exceptional woman."

She was only a maid and a dance instructor, but when he looked into her eyes, she believed him. "You are so dear to me," she confessed.

"Lucy, I was a lonely, dispirited man until I met you. Now you are the center of my world." He kissed her gently. "My God, what did I ever do to deserve you?"

She smiled and pushed back a lock of his dark hair. "You rescued me."

He cupped her face and kissed her gently on the lips. "Will you forgive me in advance for my confession?"

"Very well," she said.

"Sometimes I think I'm going mad with wanting you," he said.

She placed her hand over his heart. "You are never far from my thoughts."

He traced his finger over her lips, and her mouth parted involuntarily. There was a languorous expression in his blue eyes. His breathing was fast and a little rough. "I want you, Lucy. God forgive me, but every night when I go to bed I wish you were there with me. I can't help wanting you, needing you, craving you."

She cupped his face. "You are my first thought in the morning and my last at night."

His breathing sounded labored. "I want your kisses, and devil take me, I want to touch you."

A virtuous lady would deny him, but she could not when there was so little time left for them. This short season would be all that they would ever have. "I want you, too, Harry."

His lashes lowered, and she realized he was looking at her mouth. When she wet her lips, he caught her in his arms and pulled her onto his lap. "Now, Lucy. I can't wait any longer. I want to kiss you now."

He thrust his tongue in her mouth in a rhythm mimicking what he really wanted—to slide inside her wet, intimate heat and pleasure her until they both collapsed from exhaustion.

She opened her eyes and traced her finger over his mouth. He took her finger into his mouth and sucked.

She inhaled on an audible ragged breath.

He'd surprised her. "So sweet," he said, cupping her petal-soft cheek. She would be shocked if she knew how often he thought about baring her body and kissing every inch of her skin.

"You make me want things no lady should want."

"Your words make me desire you all the more," he said.

A pink blush stained her cheeks. "When you kiss me, I feel as if I've drunk too much wine."

"You've no idea how much you mean to me," he said. He was breathing harder now. "I want you so badly."

"So do I," she whispered.

"Oh God." He kissed her again, and she opened for him, but this kiss was no sweet, soft touching of lips. He plundered her mouth again and again. All the while, his big hands were sliding along her spine. She was vaguely aware of his fingers fumbling at the back of her gown, and a moment later, she felt the shock of cool air on her skin.

Harry broke the kiss. "Let me look. Let me touch."

She knew she ought to stop him, but she didn't want it to end. In truth, she wanted his hot hands on her skin. As he bared her breasts, he cupped them, and she was lost in his touch. He swirled his tongue around her nipple and suckled her. A bolt of sheer ecstasy coursed through her veins. When he ministered to her other nipple, she whimpered and squeezed her thighs together, eliciting more pleasure. God help her, she was panting and wanting more, much more. She was aware of dampness between her thighs, but she was beyond caring.

He lifted her skirts and petticoat, baring her thighs. "Straddle my lap and hold on to my shoulders."

She tried to stay his hand, but he whispered, "Let me pleasure you."

When he touched her intimate folds, she inhaled on a shattered breath. His fingers were sliding and parting. He rubbed a sensitive place, and she could not help arching into it. She'd touched herself before, but never like this.

He captured her nipple and sucked while he teased the sensitive bud again. Her feminine folds were slick and she was arching into his touch. "Yes, sweet Lucy. Let yourself go." Then he suckled her other nipple, and she shattered apart with a high-pitched sound in the back of her throat. Then she collapsed against his shoulder.

Gradually, she realized that he was still breathing hard. When she looked at his lap, she could see the bulge and knew he was aroused. She looked into his eyes. "I don't know how to...reciprocate."

He took out a handkerchief and sucked in his breath when she worked the buttons loose on his trousers. When she slipped the last one free, he sprang out. Her eyes grew rounder. "Oh, my goodness. You're huge."

"Why, thank you," he said. Then he took her hand and wrapped it around him. "You don't have to do this."

She met his gaze. "I want to give you pleasure, Harry."

He set his hand over hers and showed her how to slide up and down his hot shaft and touch the sensitive tip. When she kissed the tip and swirled her tongue around him, he groaned. His thoughts scattered as she continued. It had been a long time since he'd been with a woman. He was within moments of exploding. "The handkerchief," he said, his voice a little hoarse. His head fell back and he spent his seed, knowing he was soaking the scrap of linen.

He held her tightly and kissed her softly. She laid her head against his shoulder and set her hand over his heart. "I can feel you beating for me," she said.

He kissed her forehead. "So sweet," he whispered. He cupped her face. "You're so soft."

He was still breathing hard when he met her gaze. "I hope you have no regrets."

Her lips twitched. "Well, I don't know. I might ask for a repeat performance."

He laughed. "The carriage is slowing. We'd better make ourselves decent."

He finished hooking her gown and then buttoned his trousers just as the carriage rocked to a halt.

Harry opened the carriage door and frowned.

A matron ran toward them. "Help!" she shouted.

"Lucy, do you know her?"

"That's our neighbor Mrs. Green," Lucy said. Her heart pounded. "I fear something is wrong."

Harry jumped out and helped Lucy down.

She felt as if her heart had fallen to her feet.

Mrs. Green was out of breath when she reached them. "Oh, th-thank the Lord you're here."

"Is Grandmama ill?" Lucy said.

"No, it's a nasty bruise from a fall, but she's frightened half to death. A man tricked her into opening the door."

Lucy gasped.

"Where is she?" Harry said.

"In my rooms," Mrs. Green said.

"Take us to her," Lucy said.

Harry's heart pounded as they followed Mrs. Green up the steps.

When they reached Mrs. Green's rooms, Lucy ran to her grandmother. "Grandmama, are you hurt?"

"N-not too badly."

Lucy saw the nasty bruise on her grandmother's arm. "Who did this to you?"

"I've no idea."

Mrs. Green shook her head. "I don't know what the world is coming to when a villain hurts an elderly blind lady."

Harry meant to hunt the fiend down. "Mrs. Longmore, did he threaten you?"

"H-he said Lucy was hurt," Grandmama said. "I opened the d-door, and he shoved me. He demanded to know Lucy's whereabouts."

Lucy fisted her hands. She wished she could punch the blackguard in the face. "He is an evil man to hurt you, Grandmama."

Harry's jaw hardened. "Do you know this man?"

Lucy nodded. "It had to be Buckley."

"Who the hell is he?" Harry said. "I beg your pardon."

"The dance master I assisted until Mrs. Vernon turned him away for drunkenness. He believes I'm responsible for the loss of his clients, but he's deluded."

"I'll kill him," Harry said.

"Hush," Lucy said. "I must check our lodgings. He may have stolen items. I know he's injured and possibly desperate."

"You are not going there," he said. "I will check. He might have returned."

"I'm coming with you," Lucy said.

"Mrs. Green, will you look after Mrs. Longmore while I accompany Lucy?" Harry said.

"Yes, of course," Mrs. Green said.

Harry knelt before Mrs. Longmore and took her hand. "Do not worry. I'll take you and Lucy to a safe place tonight."

"Thank you, Your Grace."

"Mrs. Green will stay with you until we return."

* * *

When Harry escorted Lucy up the stairs, he felt her hand tremble on his arm. "No matter what, I will see that you and your grandmother are safe."

"Thank you," she said. Her stomach felt as if it were tied up in knots.

When they walked inside, Lucy had to steady herself against a chair. Buckley obviously had ransacked drawers. One of them had splintered apart on the stone floor. There was broken crockery everywhere. The wall mirror had shattered on the floor. The mantel clock lay broken in pieces near the hearth. When Lucy picked up her grandmother's cane, she started shaking.

Harry took the cane and set it aside. Then he pulled Lucy into his arms. "I will take you and your grandmother to a hotel tonight for your safety. Gather enough clothing for a few nights. Tomorrow, I'll send servants to clean."

She felt as if she were walking against a strong wind.

"Focus on your grandmother," he said. "She's had a nasty shock and needs you. Let the servants take care of things; you take care of your grandmother." When she looked as if she meant to argue, he added, "Your grandmother will feel more reassured if you are by her side."

"You're right, of course. I just could not think properly. There's so much to be done. I don't even know where to start."

"You and your grandmother are suffering from vexation. I'll stay in the hotel as well in case you need me."

"What about Bandit?" she said. "Someone must care for him."

He smiled a little. "I'll send a message to Barlow. He'll look after Bandit."

"I fear Buckley will return."

"We'll discuss what must be done tomorrow. Now go pack the valises for yourself and your grandmother."

She reached beneath the bed and pulled out the two small valises.

When she opened the cupboard in her room to retrieve her clothing, she saw the empty wooden box. Her eyes filled with tears. She covered her mouth.

Harry strode inside her room. "Lucy, what is wrong?"

"It w-wasn't enough for him to destroy our meager b-belongings. He took all of m-my money."

He held her against him. "Lucy, I know it seems bad, but I will help you. You are not alone."

"I worked so hard."

"I know, sweet girl. I know. You will come about. I promise, and I will be there every step of the way."

Buckley chuckled to himself as he strode along Covent Garden. He'd roughed up the old lady and best of all, he'd found money in one of the cupboards. He strode inside the apothecary's shop and slapped Lucy's coins on the counter.

"What about the girls?" the apothecary said.

"I need my tonic first."

The apothecary snorted and pushed a bottle across the counter. "I've put out the word there will be whores. You better bring 'em. I want my share of the takings. No hags."

Buckley guzzled his laudanum. "I'll bring the whores, don't you worry." He would snatch a couple of 'em tonight.

"Where's the redhead you promised?"

"I'll bring her next time." He'd missed his opportunity today, but he'd get another. Too bad he'd missed his opportunity to nab Lucy, but he'd catch her off guard soon enough. He'd make the bitch pay for stealing his clients.

Buckley swigged from his bottle again and limped out the door. He stood in a dirty old alley waiting for his prey in the dark. A woman wearing an apron stepped on the cobbled pavement. He tripped her with his foot. When she stumbled, he covered her mouth and dragged her deeper into the alley where no one dared try to rescue a screaming wench.

Lucy held her grandmother's hand as the carriage rolled along the streets of London. "All will be well, Grandmama. We will stay in a fashionable hotel."

"I'll see that supper is ordered in a private dining room," Harry said. "I'll make sure our rooms are adjacent in case you have need of me."

"You are v-very kind," Mrs. Longmore said.

"I assure you I will hire people to hunt this man and bring him to justice. Meanwhile, you are both under my protection and safe from harm."

"You do not have to stay," Lucy said. "I'm sure we'll manage."

"I would not rest easy," he said.

When he escorted them inside, Lucy drew in a sharp breath. There was a huge, tiered crystal chandelier full of lighted candles hanging in the foyer. Their shoes clipped on the marble floor and the mahogany tables attested to expensive furnishings. "This is too luxurious," she said under her breath. "We can make do in a small inn."

He shook his head. "Take your grandmother to the settee while I procure rooms."

"Do you think they will have any available?" she asked.

He smiled a little. "I imagine they will." The staff always reserved the best rooms for prestigious guests. Being a duke had its advantages.

A few minutes later, a porter appeared and took their

spare belongings up the stairs. Lucy was embarrassed that their valises were worn and frayed. She would have felt far more comfortable in a modest inn.

Lucy held her grandmother's hand as they waited for Harry to make the arrangements. Later she would inquire about the expense of the room. She had no idea how she would repay him, but she must find a way.

When Harry was done, he walked over to Lucy and her grandmother. "I sent a message to Barlow. We're all set now. The rooms are on the first floor. It will be very private."

They walked up the stairs slowly to accommodate Mrs. Longmore's affliction. When they reached the corridor, a maid stood at the door. Lucy walked inside and regarded the room wide-eyed. The four-poster bed had crimson hangings and numerous pillows for comfort. There were beautiful night tables with gold fixtures and a dressing table as well.

The maid turned down the covers on the bed. At first, Lucy felt like an imposter. She thought of all the linen sheets she'd changed at the Albany, but the maid lit half a dozen beeswax candles that smelled heavenly and reflected in the mirror above the dressing table.

Lucy led her grandmother to a chair, wrapped a shawl around her shoulders, and set her feet on a stool. "Do try to relax."

The maid filled the pitcher and curtsied. "Madam, there's a cake of rose soap by the pitcher and bowl." Then the maid laid a folded blanket across the bottom of the bed. "I'll bring a hot brick after dinner tonight. Will there be anything else, madam?"

She didn't tell the maid her correct address was "miss." "No, thank you." She was horribly embarrassed because she had no coins for the maid.

After the maid left, Lucy knelt beside her grandmother. "Are you unwell?"

"No, just a little shaken." Grandmama clasped Lucy's hand. "I'm so sorry. I should not have opened the door to that man."

"You are not to blame," Lucy said, smoothing her grandmother's gray hair from her temple. "He is a horrible person."

A knock sounded. When Lucy opened the door, a different maid entered with a tea tray. "Compliments of the establishment." While the maid set the tray on a small table, Lucy caught sight of her mussed hair and wrinkled gown in the mirror. She straightened the bodice, but the curls that Mary had carefully arranged were limp. She lowered her eyes, because she was mortified that the maid had seen her bedraggled appearance.

"Will there be anything else, madam?"

"No, thank you," Lucy said.

After the maid bobbed a curtsy and quit the room, Lucy saw Harry standing outside the door. She motioned him inside. Heat suffused her face. "I had no coins for the maids," she said under her breath.

He leaned down. "Don't worry. I left vails for the staff at the desk and instructed them to bring dinner in one hour."

"Oh, that is wise." She felt gauche, because she'd never stayed in a country inn, much less a refined hotel like this one.

He stood with his hands behind his back. "It would not take above half an hour to summon a doctor for your grandmother."

"No," Mrs. Longmore said. "It is only a bruise."

Lucy winced at the purple and green bruise on her grandmother's arm.

"I think tea is in order." Lucy poured and handed the dish to her grandmother. "It's plenty warm," she said.

"If you have need of me, my room is just beyond the dining parlor," Harry said, opening the connecting door.

"We could have made do with a lesser establishment," Lucy said.

He grinned. "Yes, but the food is better here."

She clapped her hand over her mouth. "How do you manage to make me laugh in the face of disaster?"

"It is not disaster," he said. "I promise all will be well. There are a few advantages to being a duke," he said, grinning.

Her brows arched. "Oh, what are they?"

"People tend to do my every bidding."

Of course it was a disaster. Her home was wrecked and she was penniless, but he had made sure they would be in a safe place tonight. "Thank you," she said.

He took her hands and kissed them. "I understand you're worried, but we'll discuss options tomorrow." He spoke under his breath, "Darling Lucy, you've nothing to fear. I will be by your side the whole time.

"You are safe now, and so is your grandmother. We will both ensure she is comfortable. If there is anything you need, please tell me." He cupped her cheek. "I would do anything for you, Lucy. Anything. I promise from this moment on that you will never want for anything or ever be scared again. Now, have a cup of tea with your grandmother, and I'll see you when the meal arrives."

She stood on her tiptoes and kissed his cheek. "What would I do without you?"

He framed her face. "Darling girl, I'll never abandon you."

* * *

They dined on succulent roast beef and Yorkshire pudding, but Lucy worried about Grandmama. She drank another cup of tea, but she had little appetite.

"Mrs. Longmore, you look done up," Harry said.

"I confess I'm weary."

Lucy rose. "Let me take you to the room so you can rest."

When Grandmama did not protest, Lucy knew she was at the end of her endurance.

Lucy closed the door and helped her grandmother into a nightgown. The maid brought the promised hot brick. Then Lucy tucked Grandmama into bed and sat on the edge of the mattress. "I will stay until you fall asleep."

Grandmama clasped her hand. "Enjoy the wine and dessert. The bed is soft, and I'm so very tired. I wish to sleep, dear. Go on now."

"I'm right next door if you need me." Her eyes misted as she thought of that horrible Buckley hurting and frightening her grandmother. Lucy dashed her fingers beneath her eyes and kissed her grandmother's cheek. Soon Grandmama's breathing grew slow and steady. Lucy thought it best to leave her in peace.

When she returned to the dining parlor, she found Harry in his shirtsleeves pouring wine. The connecting door to his room was open. His coat and cravat were draped over a chair in front of a desk.

A knock sounded. When he opened the door, the maid entered with a tray and started stacking the dishes.

"Leave the cheesecake and wine," Harry said.

The maid bobbed a curtsy and left.

He patted the chair next to him. "Sit with me."

Lucy took a chair and ate a bite of cheesecake. She closed

her eyes as the sinfully rich lemon custard melted in her mouth. When she opened her eyes, she found Harry watching her with a seductive expression.

"Like that, do you?" he said, his voice rumbling.

Was she imagining something suggestive in his words?

He poured a glass of wine and inhaled the fragrance.

"Is that claret?" Lucy asked.

"No, port. Would you like to try it?"

She sipped it and shuddered.

He laughed. "It's an acquired taste."

"I prefer cheesecake."

He looked at her from beneath his lashes. "Would you like more claret?"

"A little," she said, indicating a small amount with her fingers.

When she sipped, she caught him looking at her mouth. "What is it?"

"Your lips are red from the wine."

"So are yours," she said. "Would you like more cheesecake?"

"No, you're sweet enough."

"Flirting again?"

"Never," he said in an exaggerated manner.

Her smile faded. She toyed with her spoon, wondering how she would ever be able to leave her grandmother alone again, but she had no choice. She had to work.

He clasped his hands behind his head. "You're probably exhausted."

She was overwhelmed and felt as if she were moving through a thick fog. "I won't be able to sleep. I keep thinking of how scared Grandmama must have been, and I wasn't there to help her."

"It's not your fault, Lucy."

She stood abruptly, turned her back, and covered her mouth, but a wounded sound escaped her.

His chair scraped the floor. He set his hands on her shoulders.

She turned in his arms and wept.

"You've had a bad shock, but you're safe now."

Oh God, she was so scared.

"Please don't cry, Lucy." He tightened his arms around her. "I will never let anyone hurt you again."

To her mortification, she started trembling.

"You need rest," he said.

"I don't think I can sleep."

He lifted her in his arms. "Shhh."

He wanted to tell her that he loved her and wanted to marry her, but the time was all wrong. When he did propose, he wanted it to be as romantic as possible, for her sake. She deserved a fairy-tale proposal and wedding.

He took her to his bedchamber. When he set her feet on the carpet by the bed, she inhaled on a shuddering breath. He rummaged in the pocket of his coat hanging over the chair and found a handkerchief. Then he blotted her face.

"Harry, I don't know what we would have done if not for you. He m-might have come b-back and h-hurt Grandmama again." Tears sprang in her eyes again. "Thank you for taking care of us."

He held her tightly. "Lucy, the worst is over. You're both safe now. I will protect you and your grandmother."

"I d-don't know what we will d-do," she said.

"Shhhh. We'll figure all of that out later."

He wanted to tell her what was in his heart, but now was not the right time. She was overset and frightened half to death, poor girl.

"You're vexed and need rest." He frowned. "I could ring for a maid, but I fear it would wake your grandmother. If you will allow it, I'll untie the tapes of your gown and unlace your stays so that you'll be comfortable while you sleep."

She nodded.

When her neckline gaped, he helped her step out of the gown and petticoat. Then he laid them over a chair in the corner.

She stood with her head bowed as he loosened the laces of her stays and drew them off. There was a fire, but chill bumps erupted on her skin, and her nipples showed through the thin fabric of her shift.

He drew in a long, slow breath. Then he helped her up in the bed. He sat beside her and kissed her tenderly, but she parted her lips for him. When he swept his tongue inside, she clutched him hard as if she were afraid he would leave her. Eventually, he broke the kiss, and both of them were panting.

One of her hairpins fell on the counterpane.

"I will let you sleep now."

"No, don't leave me. Please don't leave me."

He held her hard against him. God in heaven, what would have happened if he'd not been there? He swore to protect and love her no matter what happened. He would never let her suffer again.

"Take your hair down," he said.

She took out the pins, one by one, until the braid wrapped around her topknot slipped down her back. Then she shook out her hair. It fell to her waist. He was mesmerized watching her, but the hour was growing late. "I'll take you to the other room."

"Stay with me for a little while, Harry."

"I will. Lay back and rest." When she complied, he set his hands on either side of the pillow and kissed her gently on the lips. She wrapped her arms around his neck. "Don't leave me."

"I won't leave you," he said. When he kissed her again, she opened her mouth for him, and he could not resist the invitation. As he tasted her, he imagined what it would be like to make love to her without any constraints, but he would not take advantage of her vulnerable state. She'd been through too much this day.

He kissed her cheek. "Lucy, you need sleep. I'll take you to your grandmother."

"Don't leave me."

"I'll stay for a little while longer. He pulled his boots and stockings off. Then he caressed her soft cheek.

"Harry, I'm so grateful. If not for you, I don't know what we would have done."

"Shhhh. All that matters is that you and your grandmother are safe."

" 'Thank you' seems inadequate."

"Darling girl, all I want is to see you safe and happy. I promise from this night forward you will never be scared or feel threatened again. Close your eyes and try to sleep."

"I can't sleep. Please stay with me."

"I'll stay until you fall asleep."

"No, stay, please stay."

"You've had a terrible shock. I don't want to take advantage of you when you're in this vulnerable state."

"I need you," she said.

He kissed her gently on her cheek. "I need you, too, Lucy."

She stunned him when she knelt on the mattress and attempted to pull his shirt over his head. A huff of laughter escaped him as he took it off and tossed it over the chair. "Sorry, I don't have my banyan."

"I'm glad." Lucy set her palms on his chest and kissed the sparse dark hair in the center of his chest. Then she looked up at him as she slipped one button free on the falls of his trousers. "You are the only one and always will be," she whispered.

He hugged her hard, and his breathing grew ragged. "Lucy, you've had a difficult day. I can't let you do this."

"Please." She undid another button. His groin tightened. The tight trousers could not hide his growing erection. As her fingers swept over the nankeen fabric, he hissed in a breath. Slowly, one by one, she unbuttoned both sides of the falls.

"Lucy, you shouldn't." He wanted her too much.

She shoved his trousers to the floor. With another huff of laughter, he stepped out of them, kicked them up off the floor, and tossed them to the foot of the bed. "Now we really must stop."

"Kiss me," she said. When he did her bidding, she reached between them and untied the ribbon on his drawers. He inhaled sharply when she measured him through the linen fabric. He caught her hand and groaned. "My restraint is limited."

"I want to kiss you," she whispered, holding her arms out for him. When she touched her tongue to his mouth, he opened for her. She kissed him deeply, passionately, as if it were the last time they would ever kiss.

The straps of her chemise slipped down her shoulders, and he pushed it off her. He cupped her breasts, and she caught his hands and pressed them over her breasts.

He inhaled on a shuddered breath, and when he suckled her, she made a feminine sound.

He was as hot as a bonfire. "Lucy, lay back on the pillow."

When she complied, she reached for him. "Make love to me."

"No, you've had a shock, and I fear you will regret it."

"Harry, I need you tonight. You are everything to me. Everything."

"I don't want you to have regrets," he whispered.

"I will never regret you, Harry. Never."

In the end, it was the look in her eyes and the conviction in her voice that decided him. "If you have any doubts at any point, you must tell me."

"I have no doubts," she said. "I will never regret you."

He could not deny her. He shoved off his drawers and knelt between her thighs. Then he slid his hands to her bottom and tilted her upward. He angled his head and gave her a deep, wet kiss. He was on fire as he pressed her soft body against him. His cock grew rock hard, and he wanted her so badly, but he felt guilty and tore his mouth away. "Tell me to stop."

"Don't stop, please don't stop."

"Jesus." He lost the battle and molded his mouth to hers, tasting her sweet tongue and thinking this was somehow destined from the first night he'd rescued her on the misty streets of London.

He kissed a path down the center of her body. When he reached the soft folds, he felt her legs tremble a little. He touched her intimately and found her soaking wet already.

"Lucy, tell me to stop now."

"No, don't stop."

He used his fingers to stretch her. She was tight, and he wanted to use as much care as possible. He kissed her again, a long wet tangling of tongues. Then he hovered over her. "Are you certain?"

She nodded. "Yes."

He positioned himself and slowly pressed into her by inches. He felt her maidenhead give way and heard her gasp. "Sweet girl, I tried to be gentle."

She was breathing quickly. He felt the tension in her and kissed her lips gently. Eventually, she sighed. He gazed into her eyes as he withdrew part of the way and slowly entered her again. The tension in her body had eased. "I like this," she whispered.

He moved slowly and reached between them. When he found her sweet spot, he massaged her and kissed her at the same time. She arched up. Her nails scored his back as she moved in rhythm with him as if they'd been born to dance the most primitive steps for a man and woman.

His control slipped, and he moved faster. She wrapped her arms and legs around him. He strained inside her, withdrew, and spent his seed on the sheets. Afterward, he kissed her softly on the mouth. "I'll return."

She turned to watch him. He brought a damp cloth with him and pulled the sheets from her hands.

She grew alarmed. "Harry, what are you doing?"

"Hush, and lay back."

"Oh, dear God, no, you musn't."

"Shhh. You bled a little." He set the cloth aside and kissed her cheek. Then he curled up behind her, drew the covers over them, and cupped her breast. "Sleep," he said.

Tears slid down her face. He'd cherished her and made her feel loved and wanted. She had not thought it possible to love him more, but her feelings for him were so strong and made her ache for a lifetime with him. No matter what happened, she would never forget this night as long as she lived. The warmth of his body soothed her, and the strength of his arms made her feel secure. She imagined what it would be like to be his wife and share this close bond with him every single night. But her status stood like a portcullis between them. She'd become a servant in order to survive, and everyone who had observed her teach dance lessons and serve lemonade at Almack's knew it. Her only entrée to the ton was through the servant's door.

She waited until his even breathing indicated he was asleep before daring to whisper the words in her heart. "I love you," she whispered. Pain lanced her, because she mustn't ever let him know. He might feel an obligation to wed her, especially after tonight, and she knew it would only cause strife for him. His family, friends, and political allies would talk about his poor choice of wife and pity him for it. Everything that he took for granted in his life would splinter apart, the same way it had happened to her mother. She loved him too much to hurt him.

Soon she must break all ties with him. It would hurt; it already did. Even though she'd known all along that there was no future for them, she would always regret having to let him go. Tonight he was hers, and she would hold the memory close.

Harry awoke to find Lucy gone. A ray of sun speared through the cracked drapes.

He scratched his itchy beard and heard feminine voices on the other side of the door. When he checked his watch, he discovered it was still early. He'd have to wait for Barlow to arrive for valet duty. Harry caught sight of his scruffy beard in the mirror. Ye gods, he looked like a pirate.

He donned his wrinkled shirt and trousers. Then he rang the bell. When a maid appeared, he requested hot water for a bath in the dressing room. Bachelor that he was, his manners went begging temporarily. He changed his request to bring the hot water for the ladies first.

He sat at the desk. Yesterday's events had brought everything to a head. Lucy had managed somehow, but she and her grandmother had been extremely vulnerable for some time.

Obviously they could not return to their lodgings without putting themselves in harm's way. The neighborhood had always been unsafe, but now there was a villain who wanted revenge.

Harry wished he could knock down all the barriers today. He could get a special license and marry her quickly. Given last night's events, Lucy and her grandmother needed his protection. But Harry realized that rushing matters would lead to all sorts of complications. He needed time to overcome Lucy's objections and fears about his family's reaction. He also realized that rushing to the altar might lead to wagging tongues. The last thing he wanted was for others to whisper that she must have been with child, forcing them to wed. Harry didn't want even a hint of scandal attached to Lucy. If it were only the two of them, he wouldn't give a damn, but he knew Lucy was sensitive about the difference in their stations.

He scrubbed his hand through his hair, knowing it would not be simple, but he'd planned all along to make Lucy his bride and he would not let anything come between them.

Lucy finished helping her grandmother dress. "Are you better today?"

"I'll do," she said, "but we must return home and set things to rights."

Lucy shivered. "I don't think it's safe for us to return yet, and Granfield offered to hire servants to put things to rights."

"Dearest, I appreciate all he has done, but I don't want to take advantage of his generosity."

"He would not see it that way, Grandmama. I'm certain he would prefer we allow him to help. He has expressed concern about our neighborhood in the past. Given all the turmoil, I think we should accept. To be honest, I can't face returning there yet."

Grandmama sighed. "I share your reluctance. In this case, we will accept his offer." She carefully set her dish of tea aside. "Lucy, you came to bed very late. I daresay you have not slept more than two or three hours."

Lucy held her breath. Had Grandmama guessed she'd slept with Harry? "I'm sorry to have awakened you," Lucy said.

"You must have spent several hours alone with him," Grandmama said.

Lucy's stomach knotted up with guilt. "Yes, I couldn't sleep."

"The circumstances are unusual," Grandmama said, "but we must adhere to the proprieties for the sake of your reputation."

Lucy bit her lip, but her eyes welled anyway.

"Dearest, I know you're a virtuous girl, but gentlemen sometimes are too eager and overstep the bounds. I feel it necessary to caution you. Do you understand?"

"Harry would never do anything to hurt me. I know it for certain." She had chosen to make love to him. While she had no regrets, she didn't like the guilty feelings swirling inside her. Yet, if given the chance to do it all over again, she would change nothing.

"You know how dear you are to me," Grandmama said, "and I will remind you that it is forbidden to lie with a man outside of holy matrimony. If there were consequences, you would be ruined. I don't say these things to overset you. I love you and want only the best for you."

She felt awful because she knew Grandmama would be disappointed if she knew the truth, but what transpired between her and Harry was between them and no one else.

When a knock sounded, Lucy dried her damp eyes with a corner of the linen sheet. Then she went to the door and opened it. The maid curtsied. "May I help you dress, madam?"

Lucy started to correct the maid and then thought better of it. She owed the maid no explanations. "Please, come in." She was accustomed to managing her front lacing stays on her own, but it was lovely to have help. When the maid offered to dress her hair, Lucy hesitated. She'd foolishly left her hairpins in Harry's room. "Please help my grandmother first. I'll return shortly, Grandmama."

Lucy opened the door to the breakfast parlor, walked inside, and halted upon seeing a man leave. Then she saw Harry and her heart turned over. His dark hair was a bit damp, probably from a bath, and he'd obviously shaved. She could still feel where he'd joined with her body and involuntarily clenched her inner muscles.

"Do I look presentable?" he said.

For a moment she just stood there mute. Then she shook her head. "Rogue, you look very handsome, as you well know." She looked at the door. "Who was that man?"

"Barlow, my valet, messenger, and dog walker," he said.

"Oh, right. I remember now."

Rain pattered the windows. He looked outside. "Well, it's not too terribly bad." Then he reached inside his waistcoat. "Your hairpins."

She breathed a sigh of relief. "I didn't want my grandmother to know I'd left them in your room."

A wary expression crossed his face. "Does she know you slept in my bed?"

"No," she said. "She's aware that I came into the room late and reminded me to guard my reputation."

"Are you...well today?" he whispered.

Her face grew warm. "Yes."

He kissed her softly on the lips, and when he looked into her eyes, she wanted so badly to tell him what was in her heart, but she mustn't. After last night, he might feel an obligation to her, and she would not allow it. She would always remember their special night, but she'd known all along that there was no permanency for them.

A knock sounded at the door. "That would be breakfast," he said.

"I'd better go and let the maid dress my hair."

"I like it down," he said.

She put her finger to her lips, escaped into the bedroom again, and set the pins on the vanity table.

While the maid dressed Lucy's hair, Grandmama sipped tea. "I will ask Granfield when he anticipates the servants will complete cleaning our lodgings."

Lucy looked in the mirror, but of course her grandmother could not see her. "We'll discuss it after breakfast."

"Yes, of course," Grandmama said. "I hope it is not too much longer. Mrs. Green will worry."

The sound of the rain grew heavier.

After the maid left, someone tapped on the door to the dining parlor. When Lucy opened the door, Harry stood there smiling. Lucy caught her breath. Was it possible his eyes were even bluer today?

He gazed at her with a tender expression, and she thought she would melt on the spot.

"Is that you, Granfield?" Grandmama asked.

"Yes, Mrs. Longmore," he said. "Breakfast is served. Will you and Lucy join me?"

"Of course," Grandmama said.

Harry went to her grandmother. "May I escort you?"

"Thank you," Grandmama said.

When they walked into the adjoining room, Lucy was stunned to see an enormous spread laid out for them.

The maid poured tea for all of them. "Is everything to your liking, Your Grace?" the maid said.

"Yes, thank you." Harry seated her grandmother first, and then he walked around the table and pulled out a chair for Lucy. His hands lingered on her shoulders for a moment. Lucy's face heated. Of course Grandmama could not see him, but she could sense when something was afoot.

"Ordinarily, we would attend church," Grandmama said, "but it sounds as if the rain is coming down harder."

"It is," Harry said. "May I make up a plate for you, Mrs. Longmore? There are baked eggs, sausages, toast, preserves, and fresh strawberries."

"Yes, it smells delicious," Grandmama said.

Lucy was heartened that her grandmother's appetite had returned. "Well, I suppose it would be wrong to waste food."

He brought Grandmama a plate with a little of everything and made one up for Lucy.

"I hope you enjoy the strawberries, Mrs. Longmore," Harry said.

"Oh yes, they're very fresh and sweet," Mrs. Longmore said.

Harry met Lucy's gaze with a sensual expression. Then he picked up a strawberry and sucked on it. Lucy bit her lip, thinking of the way he'd suckled her nipples last night. Her lips parted. Oh, he was a rogue to do this when her grandmother sat across the table.

"Your Grace, I was surprised that you and Lucy stayed up until the wee hours," Grandmama said.

Lucy cringed. Why had she brought up the topic when they had already discussed it? Perhaps because her grandmother was still suspicious of their late-night rendezvous. Lucy hoped her grandmother wouldn't ask too many questions.

Harry looked at Lucy. "We lingered after wine and dessert."

Lucy shot him a warning look.

"Well, I suppose young people have more energy," Grandmama said, "but I'm sure you do not wish to deprive my granddaughter of her rest."

Lucy's face felt as if it were on fire. There was no doubt that Grandmama was issuing a warning to Harry.

"Mrs. Longmore, I had no intention of depriving Lucy of her rest, but she couldn't sleep. To be honest, I was still agitated after what happened yesterday too," he said.

"Well, I'm her grandmother, and I had to be sure that all was proper."

Harry reached for Lucy's hand under the table and squeezed it. "I understand," he said.

He hadn't blinked an eye while answering Grandmama's questions, while she had been a bundle of nerves throughout the exchange.

"Your Grace," Grandmama said. "I know the servants aren't working today. How long do you anticipate it will be before they finish cleaning our lodgings?"

Lucy released her pent-up breath, relieved at the change of subject.

"It will take several days at the very least," he said. "I'm sorry to report there is a lot of damage, but I will inquire regularly about the progress and keep you informed. Meanwhile, you will stay here until the work is completed."

Lucy assumed some of their possessions were beyond repair.

When they finished the meal, he set his serviette on the table.

Harry leaned forward as if meaning to speak, but a knock sounded.

"Enter," Harry said.

"Beggin' your pardon, Your Grace. May we clear the dishes?" one of the maids said.

"Yes, please," Harry said. Then he helped Grandmama to her feet.

"I wish I had my knitting basket," Grandmama said.

"Where did you keep it?" he asked.

"Next to the sofa in our lodgings," Lucy said.

"I'll stop by your lodgings to check on the progress thus far and bring the knitting basket to you, Mrs. Longmore."

"That is very gentlemanly of you," Grandmama said, "but are you certain you wish to go out in the rain?"

"It's no trouble at all," he said. "I imagine you'll feel better with something to occupy you."

"Grandmama, I'll take you to our room," Lucy said.

Harry rose. "Lucy, may I speak to you afterward?"

"Yes, I'll return shortly."

Lucy settled her grandmother in the chair and checked the bruise. It was still purple but starting to fade a bit. She detested Buckley even more than ever for hurting her grandmother. He was an evil, awful man.

She placed the shawl around her grandmother's shoulders and set the stool beneath her feet.

The door to the dining parlor closed, and the maids' voices receded.

"The maids are gone. I must speak to Granfield before he departs," Lucy said.

"Very well," Grandmama said, "but do not stay overly long."

Lucy sighed as she closed the door behind her and found Harry sitting on the chaise reading the paper. "Ah, there you are," he said, rising. "Will you sit with me?"

"Certainly," she said.

He kissed her lightly on the lips.

"Harry, we must be circumspect," she whispered.

"I know. Sorry I couldn't resist. Now, I have a proposal, and I want you to consider it."

"What is it?"

"I wish to set you up in a town house for the immediate future," he said.

"I'm certain my grandmother would not approve. We will return to our lodgings as soon as the servants have finished their work."

"I realize your grandmother may object, but I think it would be safer if I removed you and your grandmother to a different neighborhood for a short while. I fear Buckley will return, and I can't bear the thought of something bad happening to you both."

"Harry, the hotel was a necessity, but a town house is out of the question. If anyone were to discover that you had paid for our lodgings, they would surely think I had become your mistress."

"I'll inquire with my solicitor tomorrow about a safe and private neighborhood. No one will ever know but us."

"What will you do with the town house once we leave? That is a big commitment for temporary lodgings."

"Not really. I can lease the town house and make a profit. My advisors have urged me to make investments. It is only for a short term," he said. "Just until I'm sure that you and your grandmother are safe. Will you agree for me? Otherwise, I'll be sick with worry for both of you."

"I will consult with Grandmama, but you're right. I get

ill thinking of leaving my grandmother in our old lodgings, knowing that Buckley might return."

"Let me speak to Mrs. Longmore about it when I return." He kissed her cheek. "Now I'm off to inspect the work at your lodgings."

When Harry entered Lucy's lodgings, the scent of paint permeated the place. His mood grew grim when he saw one of the chairs had a broken leg. The far wall now sported a hole. He fisted his hands. The bastard had set out to destroy as much as he could.

There was still a great deal of work to be done to make it habitable. There was evidence of sanding on the far wall in preparation for painting. He scowled at a deep gouge in the small dining table. He would return in a few days to check on the progress again. Tomorrow, however, he meant to hire a Bow Street Runner to flush out Buckley. Harry wouldn't rest until Buckley was apprehended.

He found the knitting basket and carried it out to his carriage and directed his driver to take him to the Albany.

After the carriage rocked to a halt, Harry managed to dodge a puddle and strode up the pavement. When he put his key in the lock, Bandit went wild barking. He let himself inside and bent down to ruffle the dog's fur. "Hello, Bandit," he said, pushing the dog away when he attempted to lick his face. "Ugh, dog breath."

"Your Grace," Barlow said. "I took Bandit out not long ago."

"Thank you, Barlow," he said. "I appreciate you looking after him in my absence."

"It is my duty, Your Grace. I delivered the messages earlier."

"Excellent," Harry said.

Not long afterward, Bell and Colin arrived. "What's this

about, old boy?" Bellingham said. "Did you promise me a cheroot?"

Harry opened a silver case. "May I tempt you?"

"You needn't ask twice," Colin said, lighting one from a candle.

Bell lit one. "Ah, this is the life," he said, blowing out a smoke ring. "My wife will kick up a fuss when she smells the smoke on me, but I'll blame it on Harry."

"She won't believe you," Harry said.

"I'll seduce her to make her forget," Bell said.

"Does it work?" Harry asked.

Bell arched his thick brows. "After she makes a few weak protests, yes."

Meanwhile, fastidious Barlow opened a window. "Your Grace, with your permission, I will walk Bandit," he said in his usual monotone voice.

No doubt his valet wanted to escape the cheroot stench. "Thank you, Barlow. I'm sure Bandit will enjoy another walk. It is merely sprinkling outside now."

After Barlow left, Colin said, "Harry, my fondest memory is of you passed out on that lumpy sofa with an empty bottle dangling from your fingers."

"I'm just a sentimental fellow," Harry said.

His friends guffawed.

"Harry, you were stinking drunk the night I saved your sorry ass—and I literally mean you stunk," Bell said.

Colin snorted. "None of us smelled like roses that night we took baths in the Thames."

Bell sat in a cross-framed chair. "You didn't invite us here to recollect the good old days. What is on your mind?"

Harry inhaled and blew out another smoke ring. "I've been thinking."

"Let us know if your brain starts to hurt," Bell said.

"Ha!" Harry slouched on the lumpy sofa. "So what are the requirements for joining the old married men's club?"

Bell's shoulders shook with laughter. "Damn, Laura was right. You're smitten with the dancer."

"Have you proposed?" Colin asked.

Harry shook his head. "I want to think this through carefully." He clenched his jaw. "You know the haughty people in the ton. I don't want anyone to wound Lucy."

"I understand all too well," Colin said. "I was very worried about Angeline after Brentmoor spread lies about her. I knew that marrying her would help to some extent, but I had to get rid of that fiend to restore her reputation."

Bell stubbed out his cheroot and sipped his brandy. "Laura is a vicar's daughter, but she married Viscount Chesfield. However, Lady Atherton was her entrée into society." Bell set his glass aside. "The problem is, Miss Longmore needs someone to champion her if society is to accept her. I'm certain Laura would be happy to help."

"I know Angeline will as well," Colin said.

"I want to say to hell with what anyone thinks," Harry said, "but I have to think about Lucy's sensibilities. I don't want her subjected to some of the cruel matrons."

"You probably don't want to alienate your family either," Bell said.

He knew his cousins would welcome Lucy.

"It may be a bit rocky at first," Bell said, "but my advice is brazen it out, and make it clear that she is above all others in your regard."

"She is," Harry said. "Oddly, the ton will not be my biggest challenge."

Colin drained his glass. "You mean Mrs. Norcliffe, I presume."

Harry took a deep breath and released it. "No, I mean Lucy."

His friends stared at him.

Harry cleared his throat. "She thinks that marrying me would hurt my cousins and all of my family. It's foolish, but she believes it."

A slow smile spread across Bellingham's face. "Old boy, I'm certain you know how to persuade a lady to do your bidding."

Harry laughed. "Good point, my friend. Good point."

Chapter Fourteen

That same afternoon

Mrs. Longmore thanked Harry profusely for bringing her knitting basket. "I am very glad to have an occupation," she said.

Harry sat next to Mrs. Longmore and told her about his proposal for the town house.

Grandmama shook her head. "It's too much risk to Lucy's reputation."

His jaw tightened, and Lucy recognized his frustration. "No offense, Mrs. Longmore, but I believe my concerns for your safety and that of your granddaughter are more important. You're not going to like this, but I must insist you allow me to relocate you to a safe place until that villain is apprehended. I've already notified the authorities.

"Now, you can argue all you want, but I am determined. If something bad happened, I would never forgive myself. If you love your granddaughter, and I know you do, let me do this for both of you."

Grandmama was silent a moment. "You care very much for her," she said.

He looked at Lucy. "I thought it was obvious."

Lucy was certain her heart was twirling in her chest.

"How goes the progress at our lodgings?" Lucy asked.

"The cleaning is progressing, but there are a number of broken items that had to go in the dustbin. I am sorry," he said. "The walls need repairing and painting as well."

"We will prevail," Grandmama said, bringing out her knitting needles.

Lucy knew it would be an uphill battle, but she couldn't let herself worry about it tonight. She knew from experience that apprehension only made one anxious and unable to concentrate.

When a knock sounded at the door, Harry answered it. "Thank you," he said, breaking the seal on a letter. He stood still and read the contents. "Good news. My solicitor recommended a town house," Harry said. "I'll take you both there tomorrow morning if that's acceptable."

"Yes, that will be fine," Lucy said. "Afterward, I must report at the Albany."

His expression was a bit guarded.

"Is something the matter?" Lucy asked.

"Not at all. Hopefully you'll approve of the town house."

Lucy started to tell him that it wasn't her place to approve or disapprove, because it was only a temporary arrangement, but she realized he'd only wanted to please her.

Afterward, Harry read articles from the newspaper to them until the maids arrived with dinner. The dishes consisted of an aromatic stewed beefsteak, salmon, stewed sole, potato pudding, glazed carrots, and scallops. Lucy tasted a small portion of everything, but she knew she'd be miserable if she tried to eat more than a few bites during the courses. However, when the trifle was served, she polished it off quickly.

Harry winked. "You like sweets. I'll have to remember that."

"Oh dear," Grandmama said, putting her hand on her stomach. "I ate too much."

"Ladies, will you mind if I drink my port?"

"Not at all," Lucy said.

Grandmama yawned. "Oh, I should not have eaten so much."

Harry grinned. "You will notice I ate large portions of everything."

"You're a big man and have more room for food," Lucy said.

"And you are very petite. The top of your head doesn't quite touch my chin."

The maids returned to remove everything except Harry's port.

After they left, a soft snore alerted Lucy that Grandmama had fallen asleep on the chaise.

"I had better see her to bed," Lucy said.

"Will you join me afterward?" he asked.

She met his gaze, unsure if he meant sharing his bed. "I'll return," she said. Then she roused Grandmama.

"Oh, I must have fallen asleep," Grandmama said.

"Let me take you to the room," Lucy said.

She helped her grandmother undress and slid a night rail over her along with her nightcap. A knock sounded at the door. When Lucy opened it, a maid brought in a hot brick for the foot of the bed. Lucy meant to enjoy the luxury of having a maid pamper them.

Lucy tucked the blanket up to her grandmother's chin and kissed her cheek.

"Don't stay up too late," Grandmama said.

"Good night, Grandmama," Lucy said, and quietly closed the door behind her.

Harry stood and took her hands. "It makes me happy to have you with me."

She stood on tiptoe and kissed him. "You are so good to us."

He drew her down onto the chaise with him. Then he leaned down and kissed her softly. She had every intention of leaving it at a kiss, but he pulled her onto his lap, leaned over her, and kissed her as if he were starving. She couldn't help parting her lips for him. He plumped up her breasts with his big hands and teased her nipples through the fabric of her bodice. Rivers of pleasure flooded her veins. She'd fallen into his arms with nary a thought, but her grandmother's admonition yesterday made her feel guilty.

She caught his hands. "Harry, we must talk."

He frowned. "Is something wrong?"

"Yes, and no."

"What does that mean?"

"Yesterday my grandmother reminded me to be careful of my virtue. If I were to let you make love to me again, I would feel terrible."

"You're a grown woman. What is between us is private."

"But I will know," she said.

He sighed. "Lucy, I am serious when I tell you that I won't lose you and I will never give up on us. If you wish to wait, I will wait, but I want you to know that you mean everything to me. There are things that I want to say to you, but I need more time to prepare. I've been thinking about this for weeks now. There are some complications, but I have supporters whom I know will be on our side."

"I'm not sure I understand," she said.

"I need you to trust me for now," he said, "but this much I swear to you. I will never let you go. Not ever."

She wanted to believe that he could remove all the barriers, but she knew what stood between them would not open like a magical door. She dared not allow herself to believe in the impossible. When she started to speak, he put his finger over her lips. "I can and I will make you mine. Will you trust me?"

She cupped his face. "I trust you," she said. But she didn't trust herself, because she was weak where he was concerned. She wanted more time. In truth, she wanted the fairy tale, but this was real life, and she must do what was best for him.

"Will you give me a good night kiss?" he asked.

Lucy wrapped her arms around his neck and opened for his hot, wet kiss. She clung to him, wishing they could be together always, but this was only a respite.

They were both breathing faster when the kiss ended.

"This is hell," he said. "Yet, I should never have touched you in the first place."

"I needed you that night," she said, "and I will always cherish it."

He held her and kissed her forehead. His groin tightened, and he wanted to take her to his bed and use his hands and tongue to stir desire in her. When he kissed her again, he used his tongue to imitate lovemaking. A feminine sound came out of her throat, and he knew she was aroused, too. He was breathing harder as he broke the kiss. "I will abide by your wishes."

She looked into his eyes and knew this would very likely be the last time. Tomorrow she and Grandmama would approve the town house and reside there temporarily until repairs to their lodgings were completed.

"I want you, Harry. I don't care if it's wrong. I want you."

He stood and lifted her in his strong arms as if she were as light as a feather. When they reached his room, he nudged the door shut with his boot and carried her to the bed. He unwound his cravat, stripped off his coat, and pulled his shirt over his head. He sat on the edge of the bed and pulled his boots off. Then he stripped her of the gown, stays, and petticoat. "Lie back," he said, his voice low and gruff with desire.

She sat up and watched him shove off his trousers and drawers. Then she slid her finger down the length of his fully erect member. She swirled her finger around the bit of moisture on the head.

He inhaled deeply. "I love your soft touch." He'd lain with many women over the years, but it had been nothing more than pleasure. With Lucy, it was truly lovemaking.

She kissed him there.

"Oh God, do it again," he said.

She circled her finger around the head of his member. "You like that?" she asked.

"Yes." He grew bolder. "Use your tongue."

She knelt before him, widened her eyes, and then she licked the long length of him over and over and over again.

This time he sucked in air between his teeth. "Your turn," he said in a gruff voice. "Lie back."

When she did, he slid his hands beneath her bottom and tilted her up. Then he slowly licked the length of her folds.

When she gasped, he whispered, "Quiet." Then he slowly drew his tongue along her again, and she whimpered. Moments later he focused all of his attention on one spot. When she whimpered, he slid two fingers inside of her and discovered she was soaking wet. She reached for his cock, and he almost spent his seed. But she was guiding him to her, and she was arching up to him. He thrust inside of her with a groan and reached between them to rub her in that special place. She was arching up to him, but he rolled to his back, taking her with him. "Guide me inside you," he said.

She took him inside by slow increments. When she was fully seated, he pulled her forward. "I'm going to suck your nipples while you ride me."

He took her in his mouth while she moved atop him. She was open to him and every movement brought delicious friction. His mouth was hot as he suckled her, and she felt the pleasure building and building inside of her.

When her eyes closed, he said, "Look at me, Lucy."

She gazed into his blue eyes, wishing she could awake and see them every morning. Then her inner muscles contracted around him. She pressed harder against him. He rolled her to her back and thrust inside of her. "Tighten around me," he said. When she did, she had to bite her lip to keep from moaning with the ecstasy. He kept pumping faster and faster. Then suddenly he withdrew and spent himself on her stomach.

He was still breathing hard, his eyes a little glazed. "Don't move," he said.

He found a towel and applied it to her and then himself.

God, she ought to be embarrassed and cover herself, but she didn't have the strength.

He sat next to her. "I will never get enough of you. How are you?"

"I've become a wanton," she said, still breathing hard, "and I cannot resist you."

"No, you are a woman, a very desirable and beautiful woman." He kissed her cheek and her mouth. "You are my woman."

She held his dear face in her hands, wishing with all of her heart that he could be her man forever. He lay on his side and pulled her into the curve of his big body. He cupped her breast and nuzzled her neck. "I must leave you soon," she said. "I don't want Grandmama to know."

"Just a little longer," he said, "and then we'll both dress."

There was a part of her that still wanted to hold on to the hope that he could knock down all of the walls that separated them. She'd let herself hope even though she knew she was destined for heartache. She brushed it away like cobwebs from her thoughts. Her time with him would end soon enough. For now, she must soak up every moment. She would memorize his deep-set blue eyes and the smile that weakened her knees. For this moment, she would forget about the end of the season and parting from Harry. Tonight he was hers.

The next day

Harry escorted Lucy and her grandmother downstairs and into his carriage. "I think you'll like it very well," he said. "It's fully furnished and there are four servants."

Lucy's lips parted. "You hired servants?"

"Yes, you are busy with your dance instruction and at the Albany. This way, you may spend more time with your grandmother as well."

"We could have managed, Harry."

"I know, but I wanted you to be comfortable."

"Thank you." What was the point in arguing with him when it was only a temporary situation, and in all fairness he owned the town house, so it was his decision, not hers.

When they stepped outside, she noted that the town house shared an adjoining wall with the neighbor's home. There was a tall lamp in the yard that likely burned animal fat for light in the evening.

"It does seem to be a quiet neighborhood," Grandmama said.

"My solicitor said it's very private, so you will not be disturbed," Harry said. "Shall we enter?"

When he rang the bell, a butler answered. "This is Davis," Harry said.

Lucy looked about the small foyer. It was similar to the small house that she'd imagined living in with Harry.

Five other servants lined up in the hall. A woman wearing a kerchief and a long apron approached. "I'm Mrs. Clark, the housekeeper, and this is Dottie, the maid of all work."

A tall, slender woman curtsied to Lucy. "I'm Mrs. Cooper, your lady's maid."

Lucy curtsied. "Thank you for the introductions." She glanced at Harry from the corner of her eye. Why had he gone to so much expense for a temporary stay at the town house? Of course, she wouldn't question him in front of the servants.

"I'll give you a tour if you're ready, madam," the housekeeper said.

"Yes, thank you," Lucy said. She started to correct the housekeeper's address, and then it dawned on her that Mrs. Cooper might conclude she was not a respectable lady. At any rate, their stay would be of short duration, and Lucy did not feel she owed explanations to temporary servants.

Harry escorted Grandmama up the stairs and Lucy followed behind.

There was a small drawing room on the first floor. Lucy's heart quickened upon seeing an unusual connected seat. "I've never seen anything like it," she said.

"It's a conversation settee," Mrs. Clark said. "The previous tenants brought it here and left it behind when they left for the country."

"Grandmama, I wish you could see it," Lucy said. "It's aptly named."

"I'm glad you like it," Harry said.

"The bedchambers are up the next flight," Mrs. Clark said.

When they reached the corridor, Mrs. Clark opened a door. "This is a connecting door to the gentleman's chamber."

Lucy's face grew warm. She wondered if Mrs. Clark thought she and Harry were married.

"There is another bedchamber down the corridor for your grandmother's use."

Lucy took her grandmother there. "Thank you, Mrs. Clark. This looks like a very comfortable and inviting bedchamber. Grandmama, will you be comfortable here?" Lucy asked.

"Oh yes, I like the rocking chair. I can feel the warmth of the sun from the window."

"If you need anything, the bell rope is next to the rocker," Mrs. Clark said.

"Mrs. Clark, would you arrange for tea in the drawing room?" Lucy asked.

"Yes, madam."

"I must leave for the Albany soon," Lucy said. "Then we can retrieve our satchels afterward."

Harry's lips parted as if he meant to say something, and then it was as if he reconsidered. "Very well. We'll leave your grandmother with Mrs. Clark."

Lucy waited until the carriage was well under way before speaking. "Harry, I was stunned to discover a crew of servants. We will not be there long enough to justify it."

"Lucy, I think it will be at least a fortnight if not longer before the work is completed. Buckley did a lot of damage. I own this property and it's far more comfortable than a hotel. A fortnight will go by quickly," he said. "Hopefully by then your lodgings will be in tip-top order."

When he saw they were nearing Vigo Street, Harry tapped his cane on the roof.

"I'll wait here at five o'clock," he said.

He helped her out of the carriage and kissed her cheek. Harry watched her hurry down Vigo Street. He despised having to stop a block from the Albany, but he didn't want her to lose her position. Now that Lucy and her grandmother were safely settled, he would propose to Lucy. His mother would kick up a fuss, but she would have no choice but to accept his decision. He smiled as he gave his driver directions to Rundell & Bridge, the premier jeweler in London. He'd look over the bands and then bring Lucy the next day to try on a ring. His chest felt as if it were expanding, because soon he meant to make her his wife.

Five o'clock

Harry kept watch as he waited in his carriage. Lucy would arrive in another ten minutes at the latest. Having taken several carriage rides today, he felt a bit cramped. He opened the door and stepped out. A few minutes later, Lucy appeared and hurried toward him. He opened the carriage door and lifted her up inside. When he started to climb inside, he heard Everleigh's familiar voice.

"Quickly," he said under his breath. "Pull the drapes over the window." Then he shut the door and turned to greet Everleigh and his father, the Earl of Beauland. "How are you both on this fine day? You chose not to visit Rotten Row?"

"Not today," Beauland said in a terse tone.

"Harry, was that Miss Longmore?" Everleigh asked.

The devil. "Yes, I saw her walking and offered to take her up in my carriage. She was on her way to see her grandmother."

The Earl of Beauland arched his bushy gray brows. "Granfield, if you wish to conduct your amorous affairs at the Albany, have the decency to be discreet."

"I beg your pardon?" Harry said, not bothering to hide his outrage.

Everleigh's face grew ruddy. "Granfield, do forgive us. Father, you are mistaken. Miss Longmore is the young lady who instructs dance in Mrs. Norcliffe's drawing room."

"We will discuss this privately," Beauland said. "Good day, Granfield." He barely nodded to Harry and strode off with his son.

"Bloody hell," he muttered. To hell with Beauland. The man was worse than any stiff-rumped matron. But the truth hit him. He had made her his mistress, and worse, he'd exposed her to gossip. Damn it. It was his responsibility to protect her.

Harry strode back to the carriage and realized his heart was pumping fast. It was just bad luck to run into the pair. Why the devil weren't they at Rotten Row like everyone else?

It was an unfortunate encounter, but it was over. Although he knew it wasn't.

Harry climbed into the carriage and took Lucy's hand in his. God, he hadn't expected this to happen. He should have been more cautious.

"Harry," she said, "was that Everleigh on the pavement?"

"Yes, that was him."

"Who was the older gentleman?" she asked.

"Everleigh's father," he said. "I told them I was taking you to your grandmother. It is the truth."

"They saw me alone in the carriage with you," she said.

"Everleigh is a gentleman and will never mention it. There is nothing to be concerned about." But he wasn't happy that he'd accidentally exposed her to Beauland, of all people. There was nothing to be done about it other than keep a closer eye on their surroundings. He had to use caution, because the wrong set of circumstances and a heaping dollop of gossip could ruin her reputation. She was going to be his wife, and he must do everything in his power to protect her.

Tuesday morning, the town house

"You have a dance lesson this morning, do you not?" Grandmama said to Lucy as they finished breakfast.

"Yes, I agreed to instruct for Mrs. Norcliffe again."

"Oh, dear, I know you're not bowled over by that superior lady."

"Mrs. Norcliffe has no use for me beyond dance instruction, and frankly, I've no wish to do more than instruct and collect my wages."

"Is Granfield taking you up in his carriage?" Grandmama said.

"Yes, he is." Lucy had wanted to walk, but Harry had been adamant that she shouldn't walk alone on the streets as long as Buckley was still roaming free. The problem was that the authorities might never catch him. He was just one of hundreds of miscreants walking the cobbled streets.

When the bell rang, Lucy finished her cup of tea. "Grandmama, I must go instruct the dancers and report to the Albany afterward." She didn't tell her grandmother that he must let her out a block away so that no one would know that she had traveled alone with him.

Lucy met Harry in the foyer. "I'm ready," she said.

"I'm not sure I am. I don't think I've ever danced the Allemande."

"Today, you will learn it," she said.

He led her out of the town house and helped her up in his carriage. As it rolled along the streets, he leaned over and kissed her lightly on the lips. "I find myself missing the hotel—or rather being there with you."

"The hotel was like a fantasy world," she said. "But now we have temporary lodgings and soon my grandmother and I will be able to go home."

"I want to ensure that you're in no danger from Buckley before you attempt to return to your lodgings," he said.

"I will take precautions," she said. "Believe me. I do not want to run afoul of Buckley or any other criminal."

She could tell from the stubborn set of his chin that he wasn't happy with her answer.

"I will escort you in my carriage a block away from my mother's house," he said. "I'll make sure no one marks that we're alone."

"You cannot continue to escort me everywhere I go," she said. "You have other responsibilities."

"Will you please allow me to escort you until that rat Buckley is discovered and taken to gaol? If you'll not think of me, then think of your grandmother."

"Harry, of course I think of you. I don't like putting you to so much trouble."

"You are not trouble to me. Quite the opposite."

* * *

Harry let Lucy off half a block away from his mother's town house. He watched her hurry toward his mother's door. Everything inside of him rebelled at concealing their relationship. He hated the subterfuge and wanted to end it. What he really wanted was to get a special license and marry her immediately. But he'd already thought all of this through and knew that for her sake he must stay the course. If he married her suddenly, it would likely create gossip. He would propose soon and marry her in a quiet ceremony in a fortnight. Then he would take her and her grandmother home to Havenwood when the season ended.

He waited fifteen minutes, and then he strode to the door and rang the bell.

"Your Grace," Gibson said, bowing. "Mrs. Norcliffe awaits your presence."

"Thank you," Harry said.

He strode upstairs and into the crowded drawing room.

"There you are, Harry," Mrs. Norcliffe said. "I hope you are ready to dance."

"I will see that he does his part," Mina said, laughing.

Lucy stood at attention near his mother, presumably waiting for a signal from her to proceed.

"Miss Longmore," Mrs. Norcliffe said imperiously. "You will instruct the Allemande."

"Yes, Mrs. Norcliffe, I have instructed the Allemande many times before."

Mrs. Vernon smiled at Lucy and took her place at the pianoforte.

Mrs. Norcliffe frowned. "Everleigh is late. I wonder if we should send a missive?"

"Oh no," Mina said. "He probably lost track of time. I'll ring for a fresh pot of tea while we wait."

Harry clasped his hands behind his back and regarded Lucy with a slight shrug. He rather looked forward to dancing with her this morning. Just to tease her, he would find the right moment and wink at her.

When the tea tray arrived, Mina poured and handed round cups. Harry walked to the window. Below, he could see the gardener tending to the vegetables.

He sat with Justin and spoke about fencing for quite a while. Harry hadn't picked up a blade in some time, but Justin had continued his lessons with Angelo. When the clock chimed, Harry frowned. At least thirty minutes had elapsed.

He rose and approached Mina. "I wonder if we shouldn't send round a missive to Everleigh. It's not like him to be late, is it?"

"No, not at all. Do you suppose he is ill?" Mina said.

Harry shrugged. "I've no idea."

Mrs. Norcliffe joined them. "Harry, perhaps you ought to call on Everleigh."

"Very well." He meant to ask Mina to inform Lucy that he'd left to check on Everleigh, but Gibson entered the room and gave his mother a sealed letter.

By now, others were watching with avid curiosity. Mrs. Norcliffe covered her mouth. Then she took a deep breath, rose, and said, "'Ladies and gentlemen, I regret to inform you that an unexpected family matter has arisen. I ask your forgiveness, but I do hope you understand.'"

Harry saw Lucy's alarmed expression. She went to his mother and said something. To Harry's astonishment, his mother glared at her. What the devil?

After everyone departed, Harry said, "Mama, something is wrong."

"Yes, something is definitely wrong. Helena and Amelia, please leave us."

When the two sisters departed, Harry said, "Will you please tell me what is wrong?"

"Miss Longmore, you will leave this house and you are not welcome here again," Mrs. Norcliffe said.

"Aunt, you cannot mean to speak to Miss Longmore in this manner," Mina said. "It is cruel."

Mrs. Norcliffe's eyes blazed. "You think so? I have just received a letter from the Countess of Beauland. Everleigh will not call upon you again. Do you hear me? He will not call again because of that harlot," she said, pointing at Lucy.

Harry inhaled sharply. "You had better make a sincere apology to her this moment and you will address her respectfully," he said. "I will not allow you to insult her."

"She is not respectable, as you well know," Mrs. Norcliffe said. "She was seen walking out of the Albany, no doubt fresh from your bed and thence into your carriage."

"Miss Longmore works as a maid at the Albany," he said. God, he was furious and trying desperately to contain his anger. "Now make your apology."

"Beauland has decreed that he will not have any association with our family until you rid yourself of your mistress. Congratulations, Harry, you have managed to ruin all of Mina's hopes," Mrs. Norcliffe said.

"Beauland will not dictate to me or any other member of our family," Harry said, raising his voice.

"Aunt, you are rushing to judgment," Mina said. "Miss Longmore has done nothing wrong, and I'm sure Harry is equally innocent of any wrongdoing."

Lucy lifted her chin and closed the distance to Mrs. Norcliffe. "Madame, I will depart immediately and will not bring censure upon your family again."

"You might have thought of that sooner," Mrs. Norcliffe said in a curt manner. "Instead you brought shame upon my family."

"Enough," Harry said, slicing his hand through the air. "Mama, I will not allow you to treat Miss Longmore in this disgusting manner again. I'm leaving. You may wish to reconsider what you have said. If you wish to keep this family together, I highly advise you to apologize to Miss Longmore now."

"I will not," Mrs. Norcliffe said, her eyes filling with tears. "I knew from the moment I saw you ogling her that she meant to sink her claws into you."

"I beg your pardon for offending you, Mrs. Norcliffe. I will leave you now."

Harry shook his head. "If you do not apologize, I will never forgive you," he said. "Never."

When his mother clamped her lips shut, he strode out of the drawing room and down the stairs. He opened the door and caught up to Lucy on the pavement. "Stop," he said, taking her arm.

"No, please leave me be."

Tears tracked down her face.

"I love you," he said. "And I will not let you go."

A servant walked past with a dog. "Come with me to the carriage so that we can talk."

He offered his arm, and she took it. As he helped her inside the carriage, he realized she was shaking. He called out to the driver, "Just drive until I knock the roof."

When he sat beside Lucy, he wrapped her in his arms. The carriage rolled off and Lucy's face crumbled. "I...I knew this was a m-mistake from the b-beginning."

"I don't believe it was a mistake," he said. "I think we were destined to be together."

"How can you say that?" she cried. "I told you before that I will not be the instrument of unhappiness to your family, but I have done so."

"Lucy, do you love me?"

A wounded sound came out of her throat. "I l-love you, Harry, but we cannot be together."

"Yes, we can," he said. "I will make it happen."

"You cannot," she said. "Have you not realized the damage that I have caused to your family and to Everleigh's family? You know Mina and Everleigh are in love. Even if Beauland had not made his accusations, there still would have been trouble. No one in the ton will ever accept me. Never. I am a maid, Harry, and worse, I am your *mistress*. I've been in denial, but it's true."

"Lucy, I mean to marry you."

"I am a maid and as of today that is all I am. No one will ever hire me to instruct their children." Her eyes welled with tears. "My reputation is ruined, and I have come between you and your family. I swore I would never do that to you, but I have. We must part now."

"No, Lucy. I will not let you go."

"You must," she said. "For the sake of your cousins and your mother."

"I love you, and I will not live without you."

"Yes, you will, Harry. That is my parting gift to you. I will disappear from your life. It is the kindest thing that I can do for you. I will always carry you in my heart, but we have known from the start that this would never work. You will find a lady of your own class, and I know she will love you."

"I won't let you go," he said. "I won't."

When she looked at him, his eyes were red. "I'm so sorry. I love you too much to do this to you."

"Don't leave me, Lucy."

She shook her head. "You know as well as I do that nothing you say will change what happened today."

"I will take you to the Albany." He knocked his cane on the roof. When the carriage rolled to a halt, Harry gave the driver new instructions. A few minutes later, his carriage halted one block away from the Albany.

She threw her arms around him and kissed him. "Goodbye Harry."

"I'll wait here this afternoon."

Acute pain shot straight to her heart. She stepped out of the carriage and squared her shoulders the same way she'd done that night she'd lost her seamstress job. Then she turned on Vigo Street and strode to Mrs. Finkle's office.

Harry was furious as he gave the driver directions to Beauland's town house. When he rang the bell, a butler admitted him. Harry gave him his card.

"I will return shortly," the butler said, and installed him in the anteroom.

Not long afterward the butler returned. "I regret to inform you that his lordship is not at home."

He would not stand for this insult. "Tell his lordship I am here on a matter of honor."

The butler's eyes widened.

He raised his voice. "Tell his lordship that I insist upon meeting him about a matter of honor. Do it now!"

The butler hurried up the stairs.

A few minutes later, the butler stood aside as Beauland walked down the stairs. "What the devil do you want, Granfield?"

Harry stripped off his glove and slapped it in Beauland's face.

"Damn you, Granfield."

"Apologize," Harry said.

"I will not," Beauland shouted.

"Pistols," Harry said, raising his own voice. "Dawn, Wimbledon Common."

Everleigh ran down the stairs. "For God's sake, stop."

"Apologize or I swear I'll make you a dead man on the morrow," Harry said in a seething tone.

"Father, stand down," Everleigh shouted.

"I will not," Beauland said.

"You are in the wrong, Father," Everleigh said in a heated voice. "Now stand down!"

Lady Beauland stood at the landing and started to sway. A maid rushed forward and caught her.

"Enough, Father," Everleigh said. "You are in the wrong, and you know it. I told you yesterday that Miss Longmore is a lady who has suffered from undeserved misfortune. She teaches dance lessons to support her blind grandmother. Granfield was not lying yesterday, despite what you think. You have leapt to conclusions and created a terrible scene."

"How dare you speak to me in that tone of voice?" Beauland said.

"I dare because you are in the wrong," Everleigh said. "Now make your apology."

"I will not," Beauland said, scowling.

"Then I am no longer your eldest son."

"What?" Beauland said. "You can't do that."

"Yes, I can, and I will if you refuse to stand down," Everleigh said.

Beauland scowled. "You are my son. You will do my bidding."

"I promise I'll walk out of your house forever if you do not apologize now," Everleigh said.

Beauland's breathing was audible.

"I'm leaving," Everleigh said. "Give my love to my mother."

"Stop!" Beauland said.

Everleigh turned about and folded his arms over his chest. "Say the words or I will leave."

Beauland inhaled and exhaled through his nostrils. Then he muttered, "I apologize for my mistake."

"Accepted," Harry said.

"I will walk with you to your carriage," Everleigh said to Harry.

The sun was shining brightly as they stepped out in the cool breeze. "Sorry about the scene," Everleigh said. "My father is difficult."

"He reacts first and thinks later," Harry said.

Everleigh gave him a curious look. "I think you are aware of my father's strict adherence to the proprieties, but you are not aware that my younger brother left home."

"For a woman who wasn't considered suitable, I suppose."

Everleigh hesitated and said, "Not a woman."

"Ah, now I understand."

"Father cast him out five years ago."

Harry winced. Why were some people so damned cruel?

"He is my younger brother," Everleigh said.

"You are close?" Harry asked.

Everleigh nodded. "My father refuses to see him."

Harry knew it must have been hard on Everleigh and his brother. "Do you visit your brother?"

"Yes. My father doesn't know."

Harry noted the raw emotions on Everleigh's face.

"You will always be brothers. No one can take that away from you."

Everleigh took a deep breath. "Granfield, for whatever it is worth, I hope all works out for you and Miss Longmore."

"Thank you, Everleigh."

Harry had made a vow that he would never let Lucy go. He'd be damned if he gave up now.

Chapter Fifteen

Lucy felt numb all over as she walked along Vigo Street. In the distance she could see dark clouds that seemed to represent the many dark days ahead without Harry. She was still in shock over what had happened, but she knew it was disastrous. Before this week was over, she would likely lose every one of her dancing clients. She would have to find a new second job as soon as possible.

The clouds were growing darker and the wind was picking up. A few drops of rain landed on her as she walked through the yard. She was aware of men ogling her. It bothered her, but Lucy pretended to be oblivious to their stares and knocked on Mrs. Finkle's door.

"Come in," Mrs. Finkle called out.

When Lucy stepped inside, Mrs. Finkle handed her a stack of sheets. "Clean the usual rooms," she said, "and don't be rushin' to avoid the rain. Nobody ever drowned from a little wet."

Lucy curtsied. "Yes, Mrs. Finkle." She was weighted down as much from her gloomy thoughts as from the heavy sheets she balanced.

As she walked up the stairs, the spare keys clinked in her apron. She decided to clean Harry's room last as a fitting farewell to the forbidden man she loved. By the time she reached Harry's set, Lucy was weary and her back ached.

Lucy knocked on the door and called out, "Maid service." No one answered, so she unlocked the door.

When she walked inside, Bandit loped over to her and lolled his tongue. She petted him, and her eyes welled with tears. She felt so guilty about what had happened today. If she'd kept her distance from him, none of this would have ever happened. Now, because of her, two families were in turmoil.

Bandit followed her from room to room as she cleaned. Traces of evergreen soap lingered in Harry's bedchamber, and the scent filled her with pain. How would she live without him?

She made herself hurry, because for some reason, it hurt to strip the sheets from his bed. When she realized the book of erotic engravings was missing, she wondered if he'd put it away for her sake. She shook off the thought and went to work sweeping. She wanted to keep as numb as possible, but she was more dispirited than she'd ever been.

She managed to brush off the dog hair from the sofa, even though Bandit kept nosing her hand. She cleaned out the bowl and pitcher with vinegar and water. Then she cleaned out the ashes from the hearth.

By four o'clock her lower back ached even more, and she was bone tired as she hefted the last bag of sheets over her shoulder. Thunder rumbled much closer and the wind swirled faster as she carefully picked her way down the stairs. All she wanted was to deliver the laundry, collect her wages, and find Harry's carriage.

A few raindrops fell as Lucy stepped into the yard. Her shoes sunk a little in the damp gravel as she walked to Mrs. Finkle's office. A group of men stood there talking. One man turned and stared at her. It was Mr. Castelle.

He smiled and walked toward her. "Miss Longmore, what are you doing here?"

She lifted her chin. "I work here."

Castelle did a poor job of hiding his shock. "It will rain soon. You might wish to take cover."

"Thank you, Mr. Castelle."

An errand boy hurried past and gave her a quick look, but she didn't think much of it.

Lucy fidgeted. "Please, excuse me. I must go."

"Yes, of course," Castelle said. "May I help? Your bag looks heavy."

"No thank you." She curtsied and continued on her way.

She'd drawn attention from the other men momentarily, but they ignored her now. It was unlucky to have encountered Castelle, but she reminded herself that it no longer mattered. Today marked the end of her affaire de coeur with Harry. She would tell him this afternoon, when she met him a block away from the Albany.

Lucy rapped on Mrs. Finkle's door and hoped the woman would answer soon, because the bag was heavy. When the door opened, the errand boy from earlier regarded her with a guilty expression and ran out.

Lucy thought his behavior curious but dismissed him from her thoughts as she stepped inside. "The last sheets are in the bag, Mrs. Finkle."

Mrs. Finkle rose and walked around her desk. "Well, I

thought you had more brains than most of the girls that work here, but obviously not."

"What?" Lucy said, stunned by her words. Her heart drummed. "I don't understand."

"Do you think I don't keep an eye on the maids? I told you there was to be no fraternizing. You broke the rules."

"I did nothing wrong," Lucy said, clasping her shaking hands hard. "One of the gentlemen recognized me from another job, but I did not linger." Oh, dear God, she couldn't lose this job. "There has been a mistake," Lucy said. "Truly, I didn't fraternize with the gentleman."

"A likely tale. I don't want your excuses. You're not the first to think you can slip into a man's bed for a coin or two at the Albany. But you won't do it under my watch."

"I did no such thing," she said. "You're accusing me of something I haven't done. Mrs. Finkle, he greeted me in the yard, and I did not wish to be rude."

"Do you think I don't know about that carriage what waits down the street for you every afternoon?"

"I beg your pardon? What difference does it make if a friend gives me a ride in a carriage?"

"I know who your *friend* is. I told you the rules the day you applied here. Rules is rules, and that's the end of it for you, miss." She turned around and opened a wooden safe. "Your final wages. Let this be a lesson to you. There won't be no character letter neither."

Lucy started shaking. "Will you not reconsider? I only greeted him for a moment. I've taken on extra shifts when others didn't show, and I've always cleaned every room until it was spotless." She gripped her trembling hands hard. "Please, won't you reconsider?"

Mrs. Finkle shook her head. "I gave you a chance and you disobeyed the rules. That's the end of it. Be gone with you."

Lucy walked out and felt an icy chill inside her chest. The errand boy gave her a sly smile and ran off. Lucy wondered if Mrs. Finkle paid the boy to watch the maids. She would never know, and there was nothing to be done about it now. As she exited Vigo Street and stepped onto Piccadilly, she once again felt as if she were moving through a thick fog. Raindrops started falling faster. She tried to find an awning to stand under, but there weren't any nearby.

She stood in the cold as the rain fell harder. She was cold, wet, and miserable as she stood on the pavement waiting for Harry. A speeding curricle drove past, splashing mud on her hem, slippers, and stockings. Her shoulders slumped, and she wondered how she would ever overcome this latest setback. She still had the character letter from Mr. Wilson, thank God, but she would not be able to list the Albany as her last employment. Lucy knew her dance clients would abandon her in droves once the scandal got out.

She shivered. Her threadbare cloak was little protection from the cold. The wind kept blowing her hood back. The rain fell harder, but there was no shelter. When she took out her watch, she noted it was half past four o'clock. It wasn't like Harry to be late. Ordinarily she would laugh at her disheveled appearance after a bit of rain, but she was chilled to the bone.

A carriage hurtled along the street. Lucy stepped back to avoid more mud. When the carriage halted, the door flew open and Harry jumped down. "Lucy, I'm sorry. There was an accident in the street, and I was stuck. Oh my God, you're trembling and wet through."

She couldn't stop shivering as he helped her inside the carriage. Her head fell back against the squabs. "I'm s-so c-cold."

* * *

Harry pulled out a woolen rug from the compartment beneath the seat. He helped her out of the cloak, but she was shaking so badly it took forever. Once he had the cloak off, he covered her with the rug. "I know it only traps the dampness." Her eyes closed, and she didn't respond. He found his cane and knocked the roof. The carriage rolled off in the pouring rain.

He surveyed her face. She was far too pale, and it scared him.

When he smoothed a stray red hair from Lucy's forehead, he gasped at the feel of her hot face. She was burning up with a fever. He must summon a physician as soon as they arrived at the town house, but damn it all to hell the streets were crowded with vehicles because no one wanted to walk in the downpour.

"Lucy," he said. "Sweet girl, talk to me."

She kept shivering, despite the woolen rug, and seemed completely insensible. God in heaven, she was very ill. Rain beat on top of the carriage. "Lucy," he said. Her eyes fluttered momentarily and closed again. He pulled her onto his lap, thinking to warm her with his body heat, but she still shivered. He rocked her against him. "Stay with me, Lucy, I need you."

By the time the carriage finally arrived in the modest neighborhood, Harry was doubly shaken by Lucy's lethargy and white complexion. When the butler opened the door, Harry shouted for him to send for a doctor immediately. He lifted Lucy out of the carriage and strode up the pavement. Once inside, he carried her upstairs and bade the maid to stay with her. The housekeeper sent him out of the room so that she could remove Lucy's sodden clothing. When the maid opened the door a few minutes later, Harry walked inside and brought a chair beside the bed. The housekeeper had managed to get Lucy in a shift and claimed some knowledge of nursing. Not knowing what else he could do, Harry took her suggestion and bathed Lucy's burning forehead and red cheeks.

No one seemed to know of a doctor, so he penned a missive to his mother, begging her to send for a doctor. He was so rattled he almost forgot to include the address of the town house he'd leased. It would have proved a disastrous error, and he could not afford to lose a spare moment.

Harry sent a footman in the carriage with the message and bade the driver to hurry as fast as he could. Then he ran into the house and up the stairs. He sat in the chair by Lucy's bedside and took over bathing her forehead. She moaned, but she was otherwise listless. His heart pounded with fear. "Lucy, sweet girl, can you hear me?"

When she did not respond, his throat tightened. God, he was scared. She was in a very bad way.

The housekeeper brought Mrs. Longmore into the room. Lucy's grandmother inhaled sharply after touching Lucy's fiery forehead. Her cheeks were bright red and each time he bathed her forehead, she flinched as if any touch hurt her.

Mrs. Longmore clasped her hands and her lips moved as she whispered a prayer for her granddaughter.

Harry walked to the window, wishing the doctor would hurry. He was growing more fearful by the minute. Why had he not left earlier to pick up Lucy? He ought to have known the thunder portended a bad rainstorm. He held his fist to his mouth, knowing his tardiness was responsible for her illness.

He returned to the chair and took her limp hand in his. "Lucy," he whispered. When he touched her forehead again, she lay listless. He could hardly bear to see her in this awful state. His chest hurt. "Lucy, don't leave me."

She thrashed her head side to side. His mouth dried as fear raced through his veins. "I can't lose you," he said, bathing her forehead again. "You're strong, Lucy. You can conquer the fever." But she was in an insensible state and her complexion was ashen.

Once again, he walked to the window, but still no one had come. Now he worried that his mother was from home and had not gotten his message. At his request, the housekeeper sent a footman to inquire about any physician he could possibly find. He could not chance waiting for his mother.

Harry bathed Lucy's forehead again. "Lucy, you're strong. You can conquer the fever."

She thrashed a little and then her head fell back. He clenched his jaw, because he was growing more terrified by the minute. "Don't leave me, Lucy," he whispered. "I'm so sorry I was late." He tried chafing her wrists, but she shivered again.

Harry continued to bathe her forehead, though it did not seem to make any difference. Then he heard a noise outside and walked to the window. His mother stepped out of the carriage with a man who held a black bag. "My mother and the physician are here," he said.

"Thank God," Mrs. Longmore said.

He ran down the stairs to meet his mother. "Thank you for coming."

His mother reached up to touch his face. "Be calm," Mrs. Norcliffe said. "This is Dr. Rhodes. He treated one of Mrs. Vernon's girls for a fever. Miss Longmore will be in good hands."

"Your Grace, please take me up to the patient," Dr. Rhodes said.

"Yes, thank you," Harry said.

"We'll see her through this," Dr. Rhodes said. "I brought

some willow bark. We can infuse it in some weak tea. It is effective for bringing down a fever."

A trembling maid ran over to them and curtsied. "Begging your pardon, Your Grace, I'll make the tea if it pleases you."

"Thank you," Harry said. "What is your name again, miss?"

"Dottie, Your Grace."

"Make it weak tea, miss," Dr. Rhodes said.

She curtsied. "I will, sir."

"Thank you," Harry said, and hurried upstairs.

When they walked into the room, Harry introduced Mrs. Longmore to his mother.

"Your granddaughter mentioned you when she attended my recent party," Mrs. Norcliffe said. "Miss Longmore is quite a talented dancer."

"She means the world to me," Mrs. Longmore said.

Dr. Rhodes felt Lucy's pulse. "It's not what I'd like. Keep bathing her forehead."

Dottie came in with the tea tray and set it on a table.

"Add the willow bark," Dr. Rhodes said, "then let it grow tepid."

Twenty minutes later, Mrs. Norcliffe tried to get Lucy to sit up, but she only moaned and fell back on the bed.

"We have to spoon it into her," Dr. Rhodes said. "We must bring down the fever."

Mrs. Norcliffe gasped when Harry got in the bed with Lucy and pulled her upright on his lap. But his mother must have guessed his purpose, as she handed him the spoon. He managed to get some down her throat.

Mrs. Norcliffe took the spoon and fed her while he held Lucy. The maid returned with a fresh pot of tea and added more willow bark.

"This may sound strange," Dr. Rhodes said, "but I'd like to listen to her heart. Lay her down now. I have a journal in my bag; it's a trick I learned." He rolled it up, set it on Lucy's chest, and put his ear to the rolled journal.

Harry left the bed and paced. Her pale complexion scared him.

"Her heart is beating a bit too fast," Dr. Rhodes said, setting the journal aside.

Mrs. Longmore brushed back Lucy's hair and gasped after touching her forehead. "She is too hot," Mrs. Longmore said, her voice trembling.

Harry's jaw clenched. He couldn't lose her. He couldn't. "Lucy, please try." Her lack of response made his gut twist.

"Let's continue with the willow bark tea and encourage her to rouse herself," the doctor said.

Harry got in the bed with her again and held her while his mother spooned the tea.

"Lucy," he whispered. "Please don't leave me."

She shivered and sank against his chest.

He looked at the doctor. "Surely there is something else that can be done."

"I could bleed her, but my observations have led me to believe the patients often grow weaker. Let's keep on with the willow bark tea."

Guilt consumed him. He should have left earlier. Now he was terrified of losing her.

The housekeeper came inside. "The maids put together a cold collation downstairs," she said.

"Your Grace should eat something," Dr. Rhodes said.

He shook his head. "I won't leave her."

The doctor sighed. "Your Grace, it won't help her if you make yourself ill. I know you have no appetite, but do eat a little something."

Dottie brought in more tea and curtsied. "If it pleases Your Grace, I could bring in a tray for you and the doctor."

"An excellent suggestion," the doctor said. "When was the last time you ate, Your Grace?"

Harry ran his fingers through his thick hair. "I can't remember."

Dottie poured two cups of tea. Harry only now realized he was thirsty. After the maid brought a tray, he shared the cold meat, bread, and tea with the doctor.

When darkness fell and Lucy still had not awakened, he found himself bargaining with God. *I swear I'll give up anything if you'll let her live. I can't live without her. Please let her live.*

Mrs. Norcliffe set her hand on his shoulder. "Harry, get some rest. We'll watch over her."

He shook his head. "I can't leave her, but, Mama, you must be exhausted. Please go home to rest."

"I'll stay," she said. "I will not leave you, son."

"Thank you, Mama." To his horror, his chest started shaking. He wiped the heels of his hands over his eyes.

His mother put her hand on his shoulder. "She's a strong woman and she will recuperate, mark my word."

"Beggin' your pardon," Dottie said. "There are three more bedrooms if anyone wishes to rest."

"Mama," Harry said. "If you won't go home, at least get some rest here."

"I think Mrs. Longmore is in more need than I am."

"I can't leave her," Mrs. Longmore said.

Dr. Rhodes cleared his throat. "I believe it is going to be a long night. I suggest everyone find a bed. If there is any change, I'll notify you immediately."

"That seems a sensible suggestion," Mrs. Norcliffe said.

Dottie offered to escort Mrs. Longmore to a room.

"Harry, come get some rest," Mrs. Norcliffe said.

He shook his head. "I can't leave her."

"I'll stay with Your Grace," Dr. Rhodes said.

Harry dreamed it was raining, and his carriage was stuck in mud. A soft breath against his cheek tickled him. He awoke to find Lucy looking at him.

"Harry," she said, her voice scratchy. "I did not give you leave to get in bed with me."

He laughed and then his eyes misted as he held her tightly. "I love you," he whispered.

"Harry, my hair is damp."

"You are sweating after a rather dangerous fever," Dr. Rhodes said.

Lucy looked at Harry again. "Why is that man watching us in bed?"

Dr. Rhodes's shoulders shook with laughter. "I think our patient is mending very well this morning."

Harry caressed her face. "You were very ill, Lucy."

Dr. Rhodes packed his bag. "I left willow bark in case the fever returns, but I don't expect it will. I prescribe bed rest, weak willow bark tea, and toast."

"I'm hungry," Lucy said.

"That is a very good sign, young lady," Dr. Rhodes said. "I imagine all of your family will be delighted to hear you have an appetite."

"All my family?" she said, frowning.

Harry slid out of the bed, rummaged in his coat, and gave his card to the doctor.

"Here is my card," Dr. Rhodes said to Harry. "If you have the slightest concern, do not hesitate to send for me."

"Thank you, Dr. Rhodes," he said.

"It's still dark out," Lucy said after the doctor left.

He kissed her cheek. "Everyone else is still sleeping."

"Who is here?"

"Your grandmother and my mother."

"Your mother?" she said in a stunned voice.

"I sent her a message to bring a doctor. You scared me, Lucy."

"I'm sorry to worry you," she said, her voice a bit weak.

He pushed a damp lock off her forehead. "Promise me you will rest."

"I will; I'm weary."

"I don't want to leave you," he said. "Never again."

She swept an errant dark lock off his forehead. "You're sweet, Harry."

"Let me help you sit so you can drink more tea."

She drank it quickly. "I was so thirsty."

He swallowed hard. "No more standing in the rain. Promise me."

"I promise. My stockings were squishy."

He laughed a little and kissed her cheek. "My beautiful Lucy."

"Not so beautiful now."

"To me you are."

She was astounded to see strong emotion on his face. "Harry, what is wrong?"

His jaw clenched and his eyes were red. "I feared I would l-lose you."

"Lie with me," she whispered. "I'm so tired."

He curled his body against her back, kissed her cheek, and closed his eyes.

Someone shook him. Harry turned on his back and rubbed his eyes.

Lucy hovered over him. "Harry, I hear the servants. You

must get out of the bed. They'll think we're doing lustful things."

His chest shook with laughter.

"I know, but you're better now. The doctor prescribed rest, and I will ensure you obey."

She knitted her brows. "I remember now. Mrs. Finkle sacked me. A messenger boy reported seeing me talking to Castelle."

"You are not to worry about anything right now," he said. "Please rest. We were all very concerned about you last night."

She caressed his cheek. "Poor Harry. I'm sorry I made you worry."

"Just rest until you are all better. Promise me."

"I promise." She sighed. "Harry, you're still in bed with me."

"So I am," he said, and kissed her neck. "Let me stay so I won't worry."

Early afternoon

Lucy ate soup and bread on a tray. She'd wanted to eat downstairs at the table, but she was still weak. After the maid took the tray, Lucy's grandmother helped her walk a few paces, but her head felt oddly light, so she went back to bed.

A while later, another knock sounded. Harry opened the door and sat on the edge of the bed. "How is our patient?"

"My grandmother helped me get up earlier, but I felt a little shaky."

"Please stay abed."

"I will," she said. Another tap sounded. "Come in," Lucy said.

Mrs. Norcliffe stepped inside. "You look much better, but you're not ready to dance yet."

"No, now I remember. Something bad happened. Harry," Lucy said, clutching his arm. "Mina and Everleigh are—"

He put his finger over her lips. "All is settled now," he said. "They will dance at Almack's on Wednesday night."

"Oh, I'm glad," Lucy said, sinking back onto the pillow.

"Mina sent word that she was attempting to instruct the dancers in the Allemande," Mrs. Norcliffe said. "Apparently she lacks your facility for directing others. It became something of a farce, but according to my nieces, everyone thought it good fun. My nieces asked me to give their well wishes to you."

"That is very sweet of them," Lucy said. "Are Mina and Everleigh still the leading contenders?"

"As of now, yes," Mrs. Norcliffe said.

Lucy managed a smile. "I do hope they win."

"There are still two more dance competitions," Mrs. Norcliffe said.

Lucy inhaled. "I completely forgot. I'm supposed to serve tonight."

"Almack's will manage without you," Mrs. Norcliffe said. "You must rest. Harry, will you attend me in the parlor?"

"I will meet you there momentarily," he said.

After Mrs. Norcliffe left, Harry cupped Lucy's face. "You are not to worry over anything. I want you to concentrate on recovering."

"I will," she said.

"Good, I'll return a bit later."

He met his mother in the parlor. "You have something to say?"

"I assume you purchased this town house for her."

His jaw clenched. "It is an investment."

"Harry, it is clear to me that you have formed an attachment to Miss Longmore, but you cannot live in sin with her."

"I keep rooms at the Albany," he said. "As for this town house, yes, I purchased it for safety reasons." When he finished telling his mother what had transpired with Buckley, she put her hand to her throat. "Dear God. He is the horrid dance master who stole a silver candle snuffer. The footmen had to drag him out of the house."

"I could not stand aside and do nothing," he said.

"Son, I know you better than you think. You've been rescuing wounded animals since you were a boy. I always knew it was your way of dealing with your father's death. After your uncle passed, I saw that same haunted look on your face. I worry that your feelings for Miss Longmore are yet another rescue attempt."

"That's not true. I care about her. That is all you need to know."

Mrs. Norcliffe sighed. "She truly seems like a sweet girl, and she has been through an ordeal, but you cannot marry her."

His jaw clenched. "You have no say in the matter."

"Harry, do you have any idea what it would be like for her? I can attempt to champion her, but no one will ever really accept her as an equal in the ton. Everyone has seen her serving at Almack's. They know she earns money teaching dance lessons. This morning one of the footmen brought my letters. Several of them reported that Miss Longmore was seen working at the Albany. If you were to make a misalliance, you would both feel it every day of your lives."

"I don't give a damn what anyone thinks, including you, Mama."

"What about your cousins? It may well affect their chances of making good matches."

"No, it won't. I've set up generous marriage portions for all three of them. The ton may act as if they're too good to acknowledge money, but they certainly care about money and property when it comes to marriage settlements. You can't refute that."

"Exactly," Mrs. Norcliffe said, "and evidently, Miss Longmore doesn't have a penny to her name. That will tell against her as well. The only way you could ever make this work is if she came to the marriage with a stupendous marriage portion. Even then, others would likely snub her. I do not say this to malign her; it is simply the way of things.

"Help her find decent employment, call on her and her grandmother from time to time to ensure they want for nothing, but do not make the mistake of marrying beneath you, because she will be the one to suffer in a misalliance."

He'd sworn never to give her up, and he would not. "I refuse to believe it is impossible."

"Even if you do not come to your senses, she will. Miss Longmore doesn't strike me as a fool. My guess is she has tried more than once to discourage you."

"I won't give up, and I won't lose her," he said in a heated tone.

Mrs. Norcliffe rose. "You need to return to the Albany and let your valet shave and dress you properly."

He rolled his eyes. "That is the last thing I care about."

"You cannot stay here. It's improper. Now, I've given you my counsel, but you will do what you will, regardless of my opinions. I do ask that you think this through very carefully. When there is a misalliance, it is always the woman who faces the difficulties. I know you care about her, and perhaps the best thing you can do for her is to cut off all ties."

"Never," he said through gritted teeth. *Never.*

Mrs. Norcliffe sighed. "She will never be fully accepted,

and she will feel it each time she pays a call, each time she attends a ball, and each time she attends a dinner party. It will be subtle, but she will know that others are attending events to which she isn't invited. Then there is the matter of children. This will affect them as well. I do admire her, Harry. You may not believe me, but it is the truth. I know you have formed a tendre for her, but you cannot rely solely on your heart. Because you will do her no favors if you marry her."

"I will prove you wrong," he said, banging his fist on the arm of his chair. "Mark me. I will never let her go."

The Albany, later that afternoon

After Harry's carriage pulled into the yard, he stepped out and asked a groom to direct him to Mrs. Finkle's office. A towheaded boy ran past, but he had no quarrel with an underage messenger who needed the coin. Harry strode to the office and knocked.

"Hold yer horses. I'm comin'."

When she opened the door, her eyes bugged out. "Your Grace."

"May I come in, please?"

"Of course, but what can you be wantin' with me?"

"You dismissed a young woman from your employ without just cause."

Mrs. Finkle's eyes bugged out. "Your Grace, I can't be havin' the servant girls fraternizing with the gents. Some of 'em has the morals of stray cats," she said with a cackle.

"I assure you, Miss Longmore is a moral and blameless young woman."

Mrs. Finkle's lower lip trembled. "Beggin' your pardon, Your Grace, I didn't know she was a friend of yours."

"It shouldn't matter. I feel quite sure the maids are far too exhausted after a day cleaning rooms to dally with the gentlemen tenants."

"Your Grace, I can reinstate Miss Longmore."

"She deserves better, but you don't. We can do this one of two ways. You can write a glowing letter of character for Miss Longmore or you can refuse. If you do refuse, be advised that I will report you for cruel treatment of the maids."

Mrs. Finkle's face took on a greenish cast. "I'll write the character letter immediately, Your Grace."

Twenty minutes later, he stepped out of Mrs. Finkle's office, walked to his rooms, and sent Barlow with a message to the Bow Street Runner. Harry wanted a report and felt the runner wasn't making the hunt for Buckley a top priority.

An hour later, the Bow Street Runner, Mr. Robinson, sat in his parlor making excuses. "These fellows are like rats. There are a thousand places they can hide. I'll do my best, but I don't have much faith in finding him unless we catch him red-handed.

"A couple of big footmen would go a long ways for prevention," the man said.

"That is not a permanent solution, but I suppose you don't have much to go on."

"I'm sorry, Your Grace. If I knew more about him, it would help."

"I just remembered something. I saw a man limping in the street a few weeks ago outside the lady's lodgings. He was drinking from an apothecary bottle."

Mr. Robinson's brows rose. "It's probably laudanum. I've seen him. We nearly nabbed him for picking pockets, but he managed to slither away in the crowd. Aye, I'd like to get my hands on the snake."

"His name is Buckley. He broke into a lady's lodgings

and hurt her grandmother. Can you can lure Buckley with a trick of some sort?"

"If he's got the taste for laudanum, he'll be looking to make money to support his habit. I'll offer him a chance at fencing stolen jewels; they'll be paste, but I wager he'll not know the difference."

"When will it take place?"

"I can't say for sure, Your Grace. It all depends on whether he's cautious or if he lets greed overcome him. I know you want to be there, but it would be difficult to set up."

"If possible, I want to be there."

"Your Grace, I can't let you put yourself in harm's way. It won't do the lady any good at all if you were to get injured or worse."

"When you catch him, I want a few minutes alone with him."

Mr. Robinson nodded. "I'll be happy to arrange it, provided we can catch him."

Two weeks later

"I'm perfectly well, Grandmama," Lucy said, "and it is necessary for me to speak to Granfield today. Mrs. Finkle sent a letter stating that she'd made a mistake."

"Humph," Grandmama said. "I wager Granfield had a hand in it."

"Perhaps he did, but the important thing is that I still have my job at the Albany, and I've heard from Mrs. Vernon, who wished me well and requested dance lessons for her girls as soon as I'm recovered. She has a friend who would like me to teach her children as well. I had always thought to instruct adults, but I have found I prefer teaching children. They are always so happy when they are praised."

"I worry it will be too strenuous for you. You were very ill."

"I'm well now, Grandmama."

One week ago, the workers had completed the repairs on their old lodgings. While Harry had encouraged her to make use of the town house for as long as she wished, Lucy had declined his generous offer. She had, however, agreed to a paid guard at their old lodgings until Buckley was apprehended. Mr. Jones had fought in the Peninsular War, and that had made Lucy feel far safer.

On that day, she'd taken the first step toward ending her relationship with Harry. She loved him so very dearly, but she'd always known that there must be an ending. There was a part of her that still yearned for the fairy-tale proposal and wedding, but she knew that she could never be the duchess he needed.

"Lucy, are you certain about this step you plan to make?" Grandmama said. "I fear you will make Granfield very unhappy today."

"It will be hard," she said, her voice trembling a little, "but I know that this is the right thing to do."

"Do you love him?"

She blinked back tears. "Yes, but it is not enough. In a perfect world, that would be all that matters, but it will never work. I've known all along that there must be an end." But even as she said the words, it seemed as if she were chipping away pieces of her heart.

"He isn't one to take no for an answer," Grandmama said.

"I know, but he will soon see that this is the best thing for him and his family." She'd managed to stay calm as she'd spoken, but inside she felt hollow and dispirited. She knew it would take months before she could think of him without pain pulsing in her heart.

* * *

Harry rose as Lucy walked into the small parlor in their old lodgings. "Roses from my mother's garden," he said.

She inhaled the fragrance. "Your mother's cinnamon roses." Her heart was beating hard, and already misery enveloped her.

He shrugged. "I don't know the difference. To me, they're flowers."

She desperately wanted to give him one last kiss, but she didn't want to mislead him. "I'll get a vase."

When Lucy returned with the vase, her smile faltered. She felt awful about what she must do and feared she would weep before she could say the words. "I persuaded my grandmother to let us talk alone," she said.

He searched her eyes. "I have a feeling this isn't good news."

"We must talk," she said. Oh God, it hurt already.

"Should I grovel in advance?"

"Harry, no. Please sit with me."

"Something is troubling you."

"You have been the best friend I've ever had."

"We are more than friends, Lucy."

She inhaled on a shaky breath. "I appreciate all the help you have given to my grandmother and me."

"You do not have to thank me. I only want to see you safe and happy."

She wet her dry mouth and her eyes started to well.

"What is wrong?"

"We must end this, Harry."

He took her hand in his. "Don't do this, Lucy."

She took a deep breath and released it. "In a perfect world, we could forge a life together and never worry what others thought, but there is no such thing. Nothing I do will ever change my status among the ton, and it could affect you and your family if you make the wrong choice. I can't let that happen."

"I care nothing about status or the ton. You know that."

"It is a part of your identity, the same as the dukedom. You have responsibilities to your family, parliament, and Havenwood."

"I have a responsibility to *you*. Lucy, I love you, and I will not give up on us, and I will not let you go."

"Harry, no one will ever forget that I served lemonade at Almack's. No one will ever forget that I earned money for instructing dance, and most of all no one will forget that I cleaned gentlemen's rooms at the Albany."

"I don't care if they never forget. I care about you," he said.

"Suppose I agreed to marry you. What do you think would happen? Your friends would pity you for making a misalliance. They would talk behind your back because your wife once changed the sheets on gentlemen's beds at the Albany. What about children, Harry? Do you think the off-spring of the ton will not know that the mother of your children swept out the hearths at the Albany?"

"If you believe that I am so shallow I would care what others think, then you do not know me at all."

"I'm sorry to paint such a negative picture, but I am doing it for you."

"No, you are not," he said, his voice heated. "You are afraid of the challenge. It is like that first time I met you at the park. You were ready to run away until I called you a coward. And, Lucy, what you are doing right now is cow-ardly."

Her nostrils flared. "The cowardly thing to do would be to

drag you down in a marriage that is so far beneath you that others will gasp in shock."

"No, Lucy, the cowardly thing is to pretend that you're doing this for me and my family when the real reason is that you're terrified of facing the ton."

"I saw how others whispered about my mother—when they weren't ignoring her. I discovered that ignoring someone is an active act. I will not allow that to happen again."

Something was different in the way she'd spoken about how her mother was treated. He realized she'd spoken almost as if her mother were present, but it wasn't her mother at all. "Lucy, it wasn't only your mother who was ostracized."

She stood and walked to the hearth. "It isn't important."

"Who hurt you, Lucy?"

"It's useless to discuss something that happened long ago."

He strode over to her and took her in his arms. "Lucy, who hurt you?"

"It is ancient history. You know children can be cruel."

"They were cruel because you spoke differently," he said.

She lifted her chin. "They never forgot it. Is that what you want to hear? They wouldn't include me in games. Is that what you want to hear?" She put her fist to her heart. "I know what it is like to be an outsider, Harry. If we married, no one would ever accept me as your duchess. They would never say it to my face, but they would rip me to shreds for having the audacity to marry you."

"I don't care about them. I care about you." He drew in a ragged breath. "I will not let you go, Lucy."

"I will always hold you in my heart," she said.

"Then don't do this," he said. "I love you."

"I love you, too, Harry. I love you too much to hurt you."

"You're hurting me now," he said.

"I said this once before, and I will say it again. I will not be the instrument of unhappiness for you and your family. I will always cherish the memory of our season together, but now I must end what never should have started in the first place."

He took her by the shoulders. "I will never give up and I will not lose you. Do you understand?"

"Harry, I don't want to part in anger."

"What did you expect?" he said. "You tell me you love me, but you refuse me. I can give you everything—a home and children. I can give you a lifetime."

"You will find someone worthy of you."

"I already found her, but she won't have me, because I'm a bloody duke."

Her face crumpled. "I'm so sorry. I love you, but the greatest gift I can give you is to walk away."

"It's not over," he said. "I will not let you go."

When he stalked out of her lodgings, Lucy sat on the sofa and wept.

Chapter Sixteen

Harry felt numb all over as he climbed inside his carriage and knocked the cane on the roof.

She might as well have stabbed him in the heart that first night he'd run to her rescue. He ought to have known better. She'd told him over and over again that the differences in their classes made any relationship between them impossible.

He'd been so damn sure he could overcome her objections, and those of society. But that day when he'd handed her in the carriage when Everleigh and Beauland had appeared, he'd purposely hidden her from view, because he'd wanted to protect her.

That was the problem. She shouldn't have to be protected from view.

Bloody hell. He didn't want to lose her, but it wasn't just about him. She and her mother had suffered because of class differences. Lucy likely didn't want to expose herself to ridicule and cruelty. If he married her, others would be especially cruel because she would be a duchess. They would skewer her behind her back and snub her in a thousand little ways. Looking at it from her perspective, he realized he'd been selfish. It would take a miracle to sway opinions in the ton.

Lucy deserved to be treated with respect and dignity. He had to think of her first. She would find someone, a wealthy merchant perhaps, who would ensure she never lacked for any material possession. But it killed him to think of another man kissing her and making love to her. He put his head in his hands and wondered how the devil he could live without her. But there was one last thing he could do for her. He would make sure Buckley paid for what he'd done, and when it was over, he would tell Lucy she need never fear him again.

Harry met Colin and Bellingham at White's. He figured if he got stinking drunk he might not care that Lucy had decided to end things with him. When he drank yet another glass of brandy, his friends stared at him.

"If you intend to get corn, pickled, and salted, you're doing a fine job," Bell said.

Harry poured himself another drink. "Women," he muttered.

Bell and Colin stared at him.

"Does this have something to do with the dancer?" Colin asked.

"I need to get foxed," Harry said.

"This reminds me of when he almost drowned in the bloody Thames," Bell said.

Harry's eyes watered as he drained another glass. "You're not my savior."

"Somebody needs to save you from the bottle," Colin said. "Come along, old boy, you need to go home."

"Bandit will bark."

"Dogs do that," Bell said, slinging his arm around Harry.

"We'll have a hell of a time getting him up the stairs," Colin said. "He's bloody big."

Bell snorted. "I haven't forgotten the first time we had to shove him up to his rooms."

"Good times," Harry muttered.

Harry wasn't quite sure what he'd done with his hat, but his friends offered to buy him dozens of new ones if he'd stop looking in the gutter for his missing one. Harry squinted. "I'm foxed."

"How shocking," Bell said. "Hold him up, Colin. I'll send his driver home."

Harry didn't remember the carriage ride with his friends or how they got him up the stairs. He found himself slumped on the sofa with a cup of coffee. Meanwhile, Bandit lay at his feet munching on bones in the silver saver.

"You're going to have the devil of the head tomorrow," Colin said.

"I forgot to tell her something."

"Her?" Colin said. "You mean the dancer?"

"Lucy," he said. "She thinks she'll ruin my life. She already did."

"How did she ruin your life?" Bell asked.

"She won't have me."

"Did you propose?" Colin asked.

"I brought her flowers—cinnamon flowers."

Bell frowned. "He is making no sense."

"I forgot to tell her."

"What did you forget to tell her?" Bell asked.

He stood and swayed. The room was spinning. "I must go see her. I forgot to tell her."

Colin managed to get him to sit down again. "Old boy,

you're stinking drunk. You don't want her to see you like this."

"Can't help it. I love her." Harry lay on the old sofa and Bandit jumped up beside him.

"You need to sleep off the spirits, old boy," Bell said.

Barlow entered. "Ah, I see the problem."

"In the morning, make him plenty of tea and add a shot of brandy, but not too much," Bell advised.

"I will." Barlow puckered his mouth. "Let us hope he doesn't cast up his accounts."

"I'll pop in tomorrow to make sure he's still alive," Colin said.

Bell snorted. "He'll wish he wasn't on the morrow."

Harry finally felt human by early afternoon. True to his word, Colin had popped in earlier to make sure Harry was still marginally alive. Lord, he was getting entirely too old for this sort of nonsense, but the headache didn't compare to the rotten way he felt after losing Lucy. He wished there was something he could do to change her mind, but he didn't know what else he could do.

He was eating some soup and drinking more tea when there was a knock on the door. With a sigh, he opened it.

"A message from Mrs. Norcliffe," the footman said. "She asked me to give you her reply."

Harry wondered what she wanted now. He broke the seal and chill bumps erupted on his arms. "Tell my mother I will be there in thirty minutes or less."

Lucy opened the missive from Mrs. Norcliffe and frowned. Harry's mother had specified it was extremely important. No doubt it had to do with dancing at Almack's. Obviously, Harry had given his mother her address in her old lodgings.

But why would Mrs. Norcliffe send her an urgent message? After speaking to her grandmother, Lucy decided to go and took her grandmother with her. After all, Mrs. Norcliffe apparently had shown a great deal of concern for Lucy while she was ill.

Lucy and Grandmama walked to Grosvenor Square since the weather was sunny and relatively warm. The exercise would do her good. She thought about sitting at Green Park afterward, but it would remind her too much of Harry and then she'd tear up again. Heaven knew she'd become a watering pot ever since she'd told him they must part ways.

When she rang the bell, the butler showed them inside.

"You are wanted in the drawing room," the butler said.

Lucy heard voices upstairs. Was she expected to give dance instructions after all? When she reached the drawing room, there was a hush as she led her grandmama to a chair.

When she saw Harry, her eyes involuntarily welled up with tears. He strode over to her. "Lucy, are you well?"

When she met Harry's gaze, his expression was serious.

Her lower lip trembled. "I missed you, Harry," she whispered.

He took her hands. "Lucy, I've been miserable without you."

She looked into his eyes. "I love you with all of my heart, and I can't live without you," she said under her breath.

There was a suspicious sheen in his blue eyes. "You are the only woman I will ever love," he whispered.

"I was scared and pushed you away."

"Darling girl, you have nothing to fear."

Mrs. Norcliffe joined them and cleared her throat. "Miss Longmore, thank you for coming."

Lucy was bewildered. There were people in the room she didn't recognize.

An older gray-haired man sat watching her. His eyes were red and watery. He looked ill.

Mrs. Norcliffe gently took Lucy's arm and led her across the room. "Miss Longmore, allow me to introduce you to Lady Thornwell and Lady Montjoy. They brought their father to London to see a physician."

Lucy curtsied. "I'm pleased to meet you."

"I made my debut with Lady Thornwell and Lady Montjoy many years ago," Mrs. Norcliffe said. "When I learned they were in town, I invited them to call with their son Viscount Hartford and the Earl of Wargrove. That is when I learned they are seeking news of a family member."

Lucy shook her head slowly in denial at the mention of Wargrove.

Lady Thornwell took a deep breath. "We have been searching for news of our long-lost younger sister. She left all her family many years ago and eloped. Since that time, we've heard no news until we came to London this week."

Chill bumps erupted on Lucy's arms. There must be a mistake. It couldn't have been her mother.

Lady Montjoy dabbed a handkerchief at her eyes. "Our sister Anne ran away with our father's secretary. His name was ... Bertram Longmore."

Lucy gasped. Her legs felt like jelly. Then Harry was at her side. "Come sit. You look as if you're about to swoon."

After he led her to the sofa, Lucy tried to keep the tears at bay, but she couldn't. Harry handed her a handkerchief and put his arm around her.

"I d-don't know why I'm crying," Lucy said.

"It's perfectly natural," Mrs. Norcliffe said.

"Mrs. Norcliffe told us your mother passed away a few years ago," Lady Thornwell said.

Lucy nodded. "She sent a letter, but it was r-returned unopened."

The older gray-haired man winced.

Lady Montjoy was shaking. "Oh, d-dear God, she is Anne's d-daughter."

"We rarely venture to London," the younger man said. "We did not know she would be here."

Lucy regarded him with sorrow. "She never left Westbury."

"Miss Longmore, this is Viscount Hartford, your late mother's brother," Mrs. Norcliffe said. "He is your uncle."

"My father came to see a physician," Viscount Hartford said, "and we worried about him, so we all made the journey."

Lucy was overwhelmed. In one fell swoop, she'd acquired a large family, one that she wasn't certain about at all, given the events that had transpired with her mother.

Lady Thornwell and Lady Montjoy were dabbing handkerchiefs at their eyes.

"Sister, do not make yourself ill," Viscount Hartford said, handing Lady Montjoy a handkerchief.

The elderly gray-haired man leaned on a cane as he approached Lucy. His eyes swam with tears. Viscount Hartford helped support the older man as he knelt before Lucy on bended knee. "I am not worthy of your r-regard, but I b-beg your forgiveness."

Lucy regarded him with astonishment.

Harry leaned down and whispered, "This is your grandfather, the Earl of Wargrove."

Lucy gasped and covered her mouth.

The younger man helped Wargrove to his feet. "Grandfather, have a care."

Lucy could plainly see that Wargrove was in poor health, but when she thought of his cruelty, she had trouble reconciling this man with the one who had refused her mother's letter.

Harry leaned down. "He is in ill health and needs your forgiveness, Lucy."

"Yes, I see." It would not be easy to forgive him.

"Lucy?" Harry said. "You are not obligated," he whispered.

"I know, but I will speak to Wargrove," she said, and rose to sit near him. "My lord, I will not pretend that your refusal to read my mother's letter was not a crushing blow to her. Your actions kept you from reuniting with your own daughter."

"I allowed my pride and anger to overrule me, and I have regretted that decision every single day, because I will never be able to see Anne again," Wargrove said.

"She is gone, but I am not," Lucy said. "If you wish, I will tell you about her. Her life was not one of ease, but she was a wonderful mother to me."

"It is more than I deserve," Wargrove said.

"None of us are perfect," Grandmama said, speaking up. "We are all fallible. It is not the mistakes that matter. It is what you do afterward."

"An excellent point, Mrs. Longmore," Mrs. Norcliffe said.

Lucy learned that Viscount Hartford had left his wife in Hampshire with their children. Her aunts begged her to journey to Lansdale, Wargrove's property in the north of England, for Christmas. Lucy promised to consider the invitation, but she was guarded. She needed time to sort out her feelings about her mother's family before making any commitments.

"It is a great deal to take in all at once," Lucy said to her aunts, "but I believe my mother would wish for me to know my family."

"Perhaps a bit of air would help," Harry said.

"I will chaperone them," Lady Montjoy said.

Mina, Helena, and Amelia regarded Harry with merriment.

"Do observe the proprieties, Harry," Mina said.

"Minx," he said.

Lady Montjoy and Lady Thornwell regarded the younger set suspiciously.

"Ladies, may I interest you in a dish of tea?" Mrs. Norcliffe said. "The young people these days are quite casual in their endeavors. Of course, that is why I hold dancing competitions in my drawing room. I wish to ensure that the proprieties are observed."

Harry leaned toward Lucy. "Did my mother just utter a bouncer?"

"I believe she did," Lucy said, smiling.

"Miss Longmore, you are reunited with your family now," Mrs. Norcliffe said. "This is a joyous day for all of you."

Harry looked at Wargrove. "You should know you have a very brave granddaughter."

"Not so brave," she said under her breath.

"Why do you say that?" Harry asked.

"I was so scared of losing you that I tried to make it happen before you left me."

"My sweet Lucy," he whispered. "I told you that I would never give up on us and I would never let you go."

"I know," she whispered. Even though she was glad to meet her family members, she mostly wanted to spend time with Harry. She'd been so sad after they had parted, and she never wanted to feel that way again.

His smile could light up a thousand candles. "Did you miss me?"

"I missed you the moment you left. I can't bear being parted from you," she said under her breath. "I've done nothing but cry since the day I told you we must part. I love you, Harry," she whispered.

A strong emotion showed in his eyes. "I love you more than words can express," he said. "I feared I would lose you, and I knew I could not bear it. You are my heart, and my life. I cannot live without you."

"I thought it would be kinder to set you free, but I could not bear it," she said. "I love you too much to ever let you go again. Would you do me the honor of walking through the rose garden?"

"Yes, I would enjoy that," Lucy said.

"Perhaps we should all visit the garden," Amelia said.

Mina laughed. "I believe Harry was hoping for a little privacy."

"First, I wish to speak to Mrs. Longmore," Harry said. "Lucy, I'll return shortly."

Harry led Mrs. Longmore to the adjoining library.

"Well, Granfield," Mrs. Longmore said. "What have you to say?"

"This may be a bit unusual, but I wish to ask your permission for your granddaughter's hand in marriage."

Mrs. Longmore squeezed his hand. "I know you will be a good husband to her. Permission is granted."

He bent down and kissed her cheek. "Thank you. I do love your granddaughter, and I hope you will come and live with us. I know that would make Lucy happy."

Harry held Lucy's hand as they walked down the fragrant row of roses. "Let's sit on the bench," he said.

Lucy recalled that afternoon when Mrs. Norcliffe had

made her so uneasy. It seemed like ages ago, but that was in the past, and she must look forward.

"My feelings for you have only grown stronger, but it is important that you know I love you regardless of whether you are a maid, a dancer, or an earl's daughter. Those designations are merely outer trappings. It's who you are on the inside that I love desperately."

"I love you, Harry. I always will."

"There is a serious matter I must deal with."

She bent her head. "You mean Buckley?"

"Yes, he will pay for what he has done to your grandmother and you."

The backs of her hands prickled. "I fear you will be wounded."

"No, I have no intention of letting that happen. He will pay the price for his crimes."

"Please be careful. I couldn't bear it if something happened to you."

"I'll be careful. I promise." His blue eyes filled with a mischievous expression. "It's deserted here except for the two of us."

"Is it? I wonder why you mention it?"

"May I kiss you?"

"I thought you would never ask."

He angled his head and kissed her softly at first, but he was so happy she'd taken him back, and he couldn't help kissing her deeply. She touched her tongue to his and his blood ran hot. She slipped her hands underneath his waistcoat. "I love the scent of your linen shirt and most of all the hard muscles of your chest."

"I love your bright red hair and your green eyes, especially when your temper is up."

She frowned. "You like it when I'm cross?"

"Yes," he said, pulling her onto his lap.

"Is this behaving?" she said.

"According to my mother, I've always been a scamp."

"Rogue is more like it," she said.

He kissed her again and loved the way she clung to him as their tongues tangled. Eventually, he broke the kiss. "We had better stop before someone decides to check if I'm behaving."

"Please don't. I like it better when you misbehave," she said.

"We had better leave. I'm getting a little...excited."

She hugged him hard. "I love you, Harry."

He captured her hand and set it against his chest. "My heart will always beat just for you."

"Harry, I don't think we should tell our children that we met on the street. It sounds bad."

He laughed. "Lucy, we will tell them we met in the park if that makes you feel better."

"You, I don't want our children to know I threatened you with a knife."

"They probably wouldn't believe us," Harry said. Then he knelt before her in the grass. "I love you with all of my heart. Will you marry me?"

"Yes, I will marry you, Harry."

He rose and helped her to her feet. Then he gave her a long, hot, sweet kiss. "My darling Lucy, you have made me a very happy man."

Chapter Seventeen

Five days later

The two Bow Street Runners disguised themselves as customers inside the apothecary shop.

The runners had stepped up their investigation upon getting a lead that Buckley and the apothecary were luring young women with promises of employment that turned out to be forced prostitution. It was a sickening business. For Harry, it was especially horrifying, as he realized Buckley might have had similar plans for Lucy. The thought only strengthened his resolve to see that the bastard paid the price for his crimes.

Now Colin and Bellingham waited in a back room, ready to jerk the door open as soon as Buckley entered the premises.

Three terrified young women huddled there, Buckley's latest intended victims. The bastard had sworn to kill their family members if they didn't do his bidding. But he would not succeed tonight.

In the main room, the apothecary was so frightened he'd pissed himself. Harry held a knife to him. "One word of warning to Buckley, and I'll slit your throat. Do you understand?"

"Y-yes."

Harry crouched behind the counter, ready to spring when Buckley made his nightly appearance for a bottle of laudanum. The bell over the door rang and the apothecary shouted, "Raid!"

The apothecary kicked the knife out of Harry's hand. He planted his fist in the bastard's cheek. The man collapsed to the floor. Harry tied him up like a hog and left him to squirm.

Colin and Bellingham ran inside the main room as Harry tackled Buckley. When he punched the bastard's nose, Buckley screamed as blood gushed out. Harry trussed his hands and feet. "Guess where you're going? How do you feel about swinging from the Tyburn Tree?"

Naturally the coward begged and screamed for mercy. Harry kicked him in the ass as the watch arrived.

Meanwhile, the Bow Street Runners were recording the girl's addresses in order to return them to their families. The girls were scared, but fortunately they were rescued before the villains had had a chance to harm them.

They thought it all over when they heard feminine voices. A few minutes later, Harry discovered a trapdoor and pulled it open. The watch helped pull the women up out of the dark cellar. After a thorough investigation, the watch informed them that Buckley had snatched them off the street and dragged them to the apothecary's shop, intending to force them into prostitution.

When it was over, the Bow Street Runners shook their hands. "Good work, gentlemen."

Colin arched his brows. "We have a little experience with devils like Buckley."

Harry grinned. "Damn, we might have thrown them in the Thames."

"Where we first met," Bellingham said. "I was minding my own business when I heard the splash."

"We had to rescue your sorry ass, Harry," Colin said, laughing.

"A lightskirt stole my money," Harry said, "and the waterman threw me overboard."

"He did not," Colin said. "You tried to stand up, and you were so drunk you fell in."

"The stench was disgusting," Bellingham said. "You called me your savior. Lord what a caper."

Harry grinned. "Good times, my friends."

"So, Harry," Bellingham said, "when is the wedding?"

"Soon," he said. "Colin, will you be my best man?"

"I would be honored," he said.

Two weeks later

Harry blindfolded Lucy and took her inside the town house where Lucy had convalesced while she was ill. Unbeknownst to Lucy, Lady Ravenshire had renovated it as a wedding gift.

"Are you ready?" Harry asked.

"Yes, please take the blindfold off of me."

He untied it slowly. Lucy inhaled. "Oh my stars, it's beautiful. Oh, I love the Palladian windows." Harry escorted her to the dining room. "This one I'm unsure about—there are no walls."

"Oh, how clever. She used columns instead of walls. I wish I had her eye for design."

Harry scratched his head. "I'll be honest; I'm glad you don't. Colin told me Angeline has knocked out several walls in their home. I think it's a little odd."

Lucy laughed. "I suppose she literally hammers out her frustrations."

"Knowing Colin? Probably so."

"The bedrooms aren't terribly different," Harry said, "but I'm more than happy to take you on a tour of them."

She shook her finger. "I know what is on your mind, but we agreed to wait until after the wedding."

"Woe is me."

He walked up behind her and wrapped his arms around her. "I can't wait to take you to Havenwood."

"I'm anxious to see where you spent your boyhood summers."

"It's a good place for children—and pigs," Harry said.

She turned in his arms. "I love that you make me laugh, and I hope one day soon, we have a little boy who has eyes like you."

"And maybe a little girl with eyes like you," he said.

"I think Grandmama will like Havenwood. She prefers the country because it's peaceful."

"It's peaceful until one of the pigs escapes."

She laughed. "I cannot wait to see the infamous pigs."

"I cannot wait until our wedding."

"Are you sure? You have only ten days left as a bachelor."

"You remember Bell's stepson, Justin?"

"Yes, I remember."

"He's moving into my old rooms at the Albany. He wants to keep the lumpy sofa."

"Oh, that is the most awful piece of furniture I've ever seen."

He laughed. "Good for bachelors. He's planning to get a dog, so there will be plenty of pet hair, and don't mention this part to Lady Bellingham, but he's looking forward to smoking cheroots out of her presence."

"Phew," she said, waving her hand. "I don't blame her.

"I suppose Justin will inherit the naughty engravings as well," she said.

"I can take a hint. Besides, why would I take an engraving over my beautiful bride?"

"Good answer," she said, smiling. "Tomorrow, Lady Bellingham and I are being fitted for new gowns for Almack's on Wednesday night. I know you can't abide the place, but we'll attend for your mother's sake. Even Grandmama has decided to attend."

"Hmmm." He lifted her up to her toes and gave her a thoroughly wet, deep kiss. When his hands slid to her bottom, she sighed. He was hard against her stomach. "Ten days is a long time."

"I know," she said a little breathlessly. "Whose idea was that?"

"Yours," he said, looking at her hopefully.

"Harry?"

"Yes."

"Oh, good, I'm glad you agree," she said.

He sat on the sofa, and she knelt between his knees. She undid each button slowly, letting her fingers tease over the fabric.

"You're killing me," he said.

When his cock sprang out, she looked at him. "I don't know what to do."

"I do. Straddle me."

She eased him inside of her slowly. "Lean forward."

She gasped as he suckled her. "Oh," she said.

He arched up to her and circled his finger around her sweet spot. She squeezed him and cried out. It felt so damned good. He shut his eyes as the erotic sensations overtook him. When it ended, he kissed her gently on the lips.

"I'm so glad I rescued you on the street that night," she said.

"Wait, I'm Sir Galahad."

"You have no steed."

"I beg to differ."

She burst out laughing. Then she laid her head against his shoulder. "You've made me so happy."

"What do you want for a wedding present?" he asked. "Jewels?"

"Do you know what I really want?" she asked.

"Me?"

"How did you know?"

"Because I'm so irresistible."

"And humble, too."

The mantel clock chimed.

She gasped. "Oh no. We'll be late to your mother's dinner party. She might guess we were doing lustful things."

"My mother wields a great deal of power in her drawing room, but even she can't see us all the way from Grosvenor Square."

Wednesday night at Almack's

King Street was crowded with numerous shiny carriages in a very long queue.

A man stood on the pavement playing a fiddle while the lower orders danced in the street. Harry looked out the window. "Lucy, look at the dancers."

"Oh, they look as if they're having fun," she said.

"Humph," Mrs. Norcliffe said. "It's quite undignified."

"So are those gentlemen weaving up the steps," Lucy said in obvious disapproval.

"My love, they have to get foxed in advance, because the patronesses forbid any alcohol inside the premises. Did you think they could exist solely on lemonade?" Harry said.

"They should not drink to excess," Lucy said with a sniff.

"Thank you, Miss Longmore," Mrs. Norcliffe said. "One should not need to seek entertainment in a bottle."

"Apparently, the men are filling flasks," Lucy said.

"Oh, dear God," Mrs. Norcliffe said. "Old Lord Houghton is drinking from a flask. At his age. Scandalous."

"Goodness, the music is quite lively," Mrs. Longmore said.

"The men and women are dancing in the street, Grandmama," Lucy said.

"It definitely sounds as if everyone is enjoying themselves," Mrs. Longmore said, "although it sounds boisterous."

"It's far more sedate inside, I assure you," Harry said.

Finally their carriage pulled up to the steps. Harry helped everyone down the steps.

Everleigh's carriage was right behind them. Mina and Everleigh descended with his family a few minutes later.

Mrs. Norcliffe took Grandmama's arm. "Your gown is perfect for the occasion," she said.

"Lucy assured me I have flounces and several rows of lace. I'm looking forward to listening to the orchestra."

Lucy smiled. Evelyn and Mary had helped both Lucy and Grandmama dress for the evening.

Mina and Everleigh caught up with them. "It is very sweet of you to attend tonight, Harry. I know how much you detest the place," Mina said.

"I've promised to be on my best behavior," Harry said.

Helena snorted. "Lucy, you realize that means trouble."

"I'm not that bad," Harry said.

"Not anymore," Lucy said. "I've tamed him."

He growled.

"Granfield, you have been spending entirely too much time with Bandit," Mrs. Longmore said.

"Enough," Mrs. Norcliffe said. "You are all as bad as the lower orders. Have some decorum, please."

Colin and Angeline hailed them from the top steps.

"Tonight is the last night for Almack's this season," Colin said. "I'm delighted."

"Hush," Angeline said.

"Why do men grumble about Almack's?" Mrs. Longmore asked.

"Because we're beasts and prefer brandy, cheroots, and gaming," Justin said, catching up with them.

"No cheroots for you, young man," Lady Bellingham said. "Don't think you can get past me. The stench is awful."

"I do miss them," Bellingham said mournfully, "but I would miss you more, wife."

"See that you remember it," Lady Bellingham said with a sniff.

"Shall we go inside or do you prefer the street version?" Harry said.

"Off we go," Bellingham said.

"This is the largest crowd yet," Mrs. Norcliffe said. "I'm so pleased."

Lucy looked back at the refreshment tables. A new girl in an apron stood there with the pitcher of lemonade. Lucy looked up at Harry. "I didn't make much money, but I enjoyed watching the dancers. I'm especially anxious to watch tonight. I hope Mina and Everleigh win."

Lucy sat between Harry and Grandmama. "I don't know what the first dance is tonight," she said.

"Actually, I heard a rumor about it," Harry said.

"And you did not tell me?" Lucy said.

"I didn't want to spoil the surprise," he said.

Lucy was delighted when the Earl and Countess of Wargrove sat with her and Harry. She was happy to have found her grandparents. Her grandfather had made a terrible mistake, but Lucy had forgiven him and knew her mother would have approved.

Mrs. Norcliffe stood as the orchestra in the balcony above played a short introduction. Then Mrs. Norcliffe stepped forward. "Tonight, there will be a change in the dancing competition."

The crowd sounds grew louder and eventually grew quieter as Mrs. Norcliffe held up her hands.

"We will still have a competition dance tonight, but first, I wish to honor my son's fiancée, Miss Longmore."

To Lucy's shock, the clapping was thunderous. She set her hand over her heart. Mrs. Norcliffe could not have bestowed a more poignant honor.

"Now," Mrs. Norcliffe said, "I wish to introduce the Earl and Countess of Wargrove, who have recently united with their granddaughter, Miss Longmore."

The earl approached Lucy and handed her a single-stem rose. "From Mrs. Norcliffe's rose garden."

Lucy curtsied and then she hugged her grandfather. "Thank you."

"Now," Mrs. Norcliffe said, "it is my son's turn to honor Miss Longmore."

He bowed to Lucy. "May I have the honor of this dance?"

She smiled. "Yes, thank you."

The orchestra played a tune for a waltz. He held her close

and never took his eyes off of her as they twirled round and round. Truly, his smile could light up all of London.

"I love you," he said. "I will tell you that every single day. If I happen to forget, I'm sure you'll threaten to make me sleep with Bandit."

She laughed. When the dance ended, he kissed her hand and led her to a chair.

They watched the dancing competition. It seemed no one, even the gentlemen, wanted to miss the final competition.

"I hope Mina and Everleigh win," Lucy said.

"They've done well all season," he said. "Knowing Mina, she will be happy no matter what the outcome is."

There were multiple couples dancing the waltz. Lucy found herself anxious. "I will be disappointed if Mina and Everleigh don't win, but I will congratulate them regardless."

It seemed like forever before the patronesses tallied up all the scores and made their decisions. The orchestra in the balcony played a short introduction. Then Lady Jersey announced that Mina and Everleigh won with the highest score among all the couples. Thunderous applause sounded. When the clapping finally ended, Everleigh announced that he and Mina meant to donate the five hundred pounds to the foundling hospital.

"I have one more announcement," Everleigh said. "Miss Mina Radburn has consented to marry me."

Everyone stood to applaud the happy couple.

Two months later

As the carriage rolled along, Lucy released an exasperated sigh. "Harry, please remove the blindfold."

"Patience," he said. "You will see your surprise shortly."

"It is very disorienting," Lucy said.

"You are just trying to get me to tell you now," he said.

She laughed. "You would be right."

When he knocked his cane on the roof, the carriage slowed and rocked to a halt.

"Now will you remove the blindfold?" Lucy asked.

"Not yet," he said.

Harry handed her out of the carriage and held her hand. Their shoes clipped on the floor. "We are going upstairs, so step carefully," he said.

"Harry, I'm anxious."

"Don't be. We'll be there soon."

At long last he helped her up on a landing and removed the blindfold. Then he opened a door and led her inside.

She gasped when she saw the wooden floor and the floor-to-ceiling windows.

"I thought my beautiful dancer deserved her own dance studio."

She ran into his arms and hugged him hard. "I love you so much."

"Happy?" he said.

"I'm thrilled. I never dreamed I would be this happy," she said.

"No tears," he said. "Smile for me, Lucy."

"I do have something to tell you," she said.

His brows knit. "What is it?"

"I'm fairly certain you're going to be a father, Harry."

His skin tingled. Then he picked her up and whirled her round and round before letting her slide down his body. "I didn't think it possible to be happier, but I am."

"So am I, my wonderful husband."

He gave her a long and lingering kiss. "Someday, I hope we have a pretty little daughter with green eyes who dances as well as her mother."

"I think we were destined to be together," Lucy whispered.

"What shall we tell our children when they ask how we met?" he said.

"The truth," she said. "They will never believe it."

His chest shook with laughter.

"Was your uncle anything like you?"

"Who do you think I emulated when I was a boy?"

"The pigs?" she said.

He guffawed.

When their laughter subsided, Harry kissed her gently on the lips. "When I left Havenwood after Uncle Hugh's death, my spirits were low. I wondered how I would ever be able to return here again, because of all the memories of my uncle. I believe he would have liked you very much," he said.

Then he kissed her and said, "I love you, my beautiful dancer."

Andrew Carrington, Earl of Bellingham, welcomes the opportunity to help a beautiful widow with her rebellious stepson. But from the moment he sets foot in her drawing room, he gets far more than he bargained for . . .

Please see the next page
for an excerpt from

*What a Wicked
Earl Wants.*

Chapter One

Lady Atherton's ball, London 1819

Andrew Carrington, the Earl of Bellingham, was on the hunt for a new mistress.

He stepped inside the elegant foyer, having timed his late arrival to avoid the ubiquitous receiving line in the ball-room. As he relinquished his greatcoat, hat, and gloves to the butler, he thought about the type of mistress he wanted. Beauty was a must, but equally important was cleverness. He couldn't abide foolishness in a woman, no matter how comely her appearance. Naturally he avoided married women and virgins. The former could cost him his life, and the latter could cost him his bachelorhood.

He straightened the stickpin in his cravat and strode into the great hall. A statue of Augustus stood at the base of the stairwell. The stone founder of the Roman Empire helpfully pointed the way upstairs.

* * *

Bell walked up one side of the U-shaped staircase, with its ornate iron balustrade. A dull roar sounded from the ballroom as a handful of guests spilled out onto the landing, no doubt to escape the heat generated by one too many bodies packed inside.

He gained the landing and entered the ballroom. The orchestra struck up a lively tune, and the voices grew louder. He pressed through the crowd in search of his friends, but he'd taken only a few steps when a stout matron glanced at him, grabbed the arm of a pencil-thin young lady, presumably her daughter, and hurried toward him. Bell turned and strode off in the opposite direction.

Hell. Five minutes into the ball and he was dodging a matchmaking mama and her daughter. The temptation to quit the place gripped him, but as he broke through the worst of the crowd, he saw his friends Harry and Colin standing by the sideboard.

When Bell reached them, he tugged on his cravat and said, "I need a drink."

Harry Norcliffe, Viscount Evermore, handed Bell a brandy. "Narrow escape, old boy."

Colin Brockhurst, Earl of Ravenshire, laughed. "We saw Lady Coburn and her daughter chasing after you."

Bell scowled. "I don't know her."

"She is Sir Harold Coburn's wife," Harry said. "Her daughter is Miss Anne Coburn, first season."

Bell downed the brandy in two swallows. "Intelligence from your girl cousins, no doubt."

"My aunt's drawing room is famous for the best gossip," Harry said.

Bell frowned. "I've had enough already. I say we quit the ball and go to my town house to play billiards."

"Wait," Harry said. "Last night you said you were looking for a mistress."

Bell set his glass on the sideboard. "The only available woman I'm likely to find here is a bored married lady, and I don't poach in other men's territory."

"You're in luck," Harry said. "There's a new widow in town."

Colin snorted. "Right. More news from the drawing room."

Harry nodded. "Yes. She's rumored to be quite mysterious."

Colin poured himself a brandy. "Harry, how can you take them seriously? Your cousins bamboozle you on a regular basis."

"They said she is beautiful and young."

"More likely old and ugly," Bell muttered.

"Always the optimist," Colin said.

Bell shook his head. "I'm a realist."

Harry shrugged. "I've yet to meet her, but she could be right beneath our noses."

"On the floor, you mean?" Colin quipped.

Harry pulled a face. "It's a bloody expression. Must you be so literal?"

Bell rolled his eyes. He'd only met his friends recently, but already he knew they argued over anything ridiculous. "In other words, Harry has no idea what her name is or what she looks like. At this point, I think the odds of meeting her are nonexistent."

"Because she doesn't exist," Colin said.

"Ha." Harry downed the rest of his brandy and poured another glass. "Her name is Lady Chesfield, and she hails from Hampshire. She's new to town and a particular friend of Lady Atherton."

"A close friend of Lady Atherton?" Colin's dark eyes

gleamed in the candlelight. "I daresay Bell will be delighted...despite the thirty-year age difference."

Harry narrowed his eyes. "You're wrong. I wager you a tenner he'll make her his mistress in a fortnight or sooner."

"You don't have ten pounds," Colin said.

Harry shrugged. "I will when you lose the wager."

The orchestra struck up the opening bars of a country dance. Harry and Colin left to find their dance partners. Bell poured himself another brandy and turned to watch the crowd. A circle of guests disbanded, and then he saw his former mistress, Barbara. He set his glass aside and strolled over to her.

"Bellingham, you are as handsome as ever," she said.

He bowed over her hand. "How is married life?"

"You know it was for convenience," she said. A sly smile touched her lips. "I couldn't wait for you."

There was something in her expression that made him suspect she wasn't jesting. "You have security." It was no small thing for a woman.

"Security is dull," she said.

He examined the diamond-studded ruby ring on her finger. "You also gained a title and wealth."

"I made a bad bargain."

He released her hand and didn't bother to mention the obvious. Marriage was forever—until death do them part.

She lifted her frank gaze to him. "I'm doomed to unhappiness in marriage for a second time," she said.

It wasn't the first time she'd revealed her fatalistic outlook on life. Perhaps it had started when her first husband had died in the war. Yet, she'd taken advantage of her freedom as a widow and had more than a few protectors. She'd likely spent every penny of her pensions and accepted Norris's marriage proposal out of desperation.

"I loathe Norris," she said. "I try to pretend it's you, but there is no comparison. I stare at the canopy and—"

"No tales from the boudoir." He remembered how she'd always worn her feelings on her sleeve like a naïve girl.

She twirled a dark curl by her cheek. "I miss you."

It had been nothing more than a short-lived liaison. He'd made the terms clear, but when she'd said she loved him, he'd ended it immediately.

She closed the distance between them and walked her gloved fingers down the front of his waistcoat. "Perhaps we could meet later tonight—for old time's sake."

Bell caught her hand, lifted it for the requisite air kiss, and released her. "Norris would object."

"He doesn't have to know."

"Your husband is staring daggers as we speak."

"I don't care," she said.

"You will if you're not careful," he said. "Don't do something you'll regret."

"I regret letting you get away."

"There is nothing to regret." He gave her a cynical smile. "I never stay."

"I'd almost forgotten what a heartless bastard you are," she said with a brittle laugh.

"You've got the heartless part right," he said, "but I was born on the right side of the blanket." He paused and added, "In all seriousness, you are courting trouble the longer you speak to me."

"Let me come to you tonight," she said.

She was foolish to even consider such a risk, but she seemed determined to enact her own tragedy. "Sorry, I won't be the instrument of your downfall." He walked away, fearing that sooner or later Norris would catch her in an indiscretion. Some men overlooked it, but by law Norris could beat her and sue her lover in civil court. He hoped for her sake that she would be cautious.

Bell returned to the sideboard and thrust Barbara out of his thoughts. He poured two fingers of brandy and turned, only to find a petite blonde looking over her shoulder. She had a flawless, creamy complexion and a button nose. As she met his gaze, her eyes widened.

He expected her to look away, but she seemed almost mesmerized. Bell frowned, wondering if he'd met her before. No, he would have remembered the way her lips turned up slightly at the corners, even though she wasn't really smiling, at least not full on. Any moment now, she would remember herself and avert her eyes.

Her lips parted a bit as she continued to stare. Over the years, more than a few women had given him second glances as they walked past, but this one was ogling him in a rather blatant manner. A wicked grin tugged at his mouth. He decided to see what she would do when he inspected her.

Bell let his gaze slide ever so slowly from her eyes down past her long neck to her plump breasts. He continued in a leisurely fashion to her slim waist and slender hips. As he inspected her skirts, he figured she had slender legs to match her slender arms. Then he slowly reversed his gaze until he lingered over her breasts. Devil that he was, he imagined pale pink nipples. When he met her eyes, his heart beat a bit faster. He was in the middle of a ballroom and had made no effort to hide the fact that he was mentally undressing her. Obviously the blonde was issuing an invitation. Or was she? There was only one way to find out.

He winked at her.

A rosy flush spread over her face. She spun around, her airy overskirt floating a bit. Then she shook out her fan with a hand as diminutive as the rest of her and covered the lower half of her face. He half expected her to peek slyly above the ivory sticks, but instead she pressed through the crowd as if trying to escape. A moment later, Lady Atherton tapped the blonde on the shoulder, startling her.

Could she be the mysterious widow?

Lady Atherton led the blonde a few paces forward, and the two engaged in a tête-à-tête. The blonde woman shook her head vigorously, causing her sapphire earrings to bobble a bit. For some odd reason, he found it alluring.

Obviously she'd never intended to flirt, and somehow that left him feeling a bit deflated, which was ridiculous. He'd been more than a little intrigued, but he should keep his distance. Lady Atherton was a well-known high stickler and would have put a flea in his ear if she'd seen him visually stripping the clothes off the younger woman.

Harry returned and poured himself a brandy. "Did you meet the new widow yet?"

"No." They hadn't met, but she'd intrigued him, and he couldn't recall the last time a woman had done that.

Harry sighed. "I think my cousins are leading me on a merry chase."

"Probably," Bell said.

"I'm to dance the next set with Miss Martindale," Harry said. "I'd better find her."

As Bell made his way through the crowd, he noticed that Lady Atherton was strolling with the petite blonde again. In all likelihood, she was too respectable to be any man's mistress. For all he knew, she was some man's wife.

He'd had enough of the noise and decided to walk out to the gardens to smoke a cheroot. Though he wasn't familiar with the layout of the house, he managed to find his way to the door leading outside. There were lanterns in the trees, but he detected no one about. The wind was a bit chilly as it whipped the tails of his coat, but he welcomed the cold as he used one of the lanterns to light a cheroot. The wind riffled the leaves in the tall trees. He inhaled the smoke from the cheroot and enjoyed the relative silence.

He blew a smoke ring and wondered about the best way to secure a new mistress. The Cyprians were giving another entertainment next week. He would see if anyone caught his fancy there.

For some odd reason, he couldn't get his visual encounter with the blond lady out of his mind. She was obviously Lady Atherton's protégé, but that didn't mean she was a widow available for dalliance. Lord only knew where or how these rumors got started, but he thought a widow might suit him, provided she understood that marriage was not in the offing. It would be a tricky business, trying to figure out whether the widow was amenable to an intimate relationship or not. If he made a mistake, he would cause a grievous insult. His lips curved a bit. Since when had he ever missed an opportunity to persuade a lady to loosen her morals?

He ground out the cheroot and lit up another. The low rumble of masculine laughter made Bell frown. Patches of misty fog made it difficult to see, but three young men emerged on the other side of the path. They halted and passed something around. Bell wagered it was a flask.

When the trio disappeared from his sight, he shrugged. They were safe from thieves and pickpockets in the garden. How they would fare guzzling whatever liquor was in the flask was another matter altogether, but they likely would pay for it with the bottle ache on the morrow.

A few minutes later, he ground out his cheroot. He thought of returning to the house but decided to indulge in one more cheroot first. Periodically, Bell heard the low laughter of the three young bucks. At one point, he was absolutely certain that one of them was pissing in the garden. By now, Bell was weary of the entire ball and the foolish young men. He inhaled from his cheroot one last time and put it out.

Then the door to the back of the house creaked open and shut.

Bell wondered if a pair of lovers meant to sneak out for a few kisses or more when he heard a feminine voice call out.

"Justin?"

The three bucks suddenly grew silent. Bell couldn't decide if he ought to expose them or not. In the end, he kept quiet. They weren't his responsibility.

The unknown lady's slippers crunched on the gravel path. A misty fog settled near the ground, obscuring the objects in the garden.

"Justin? If you're out here, please let me know."

She was nearing Bell, but he wasn't sure if she could see him or not.

Then she stepped out of the shadowy mist, right before him. In the flash of a lantern, he recognized her as the blond lady. God, even in this dim light, she was stunning.

She gazed right at him and gasped.

"Wait," he said. "Allow me to assist you."

"No." She backed up. Then she lifted her skirts, whirled around, and took off running as if she'd seen Lucifer waiting to snatch her.

He started after her, but his footsteps slowed. She'd said the one word every man should respect. *No.*

The low rumble of masculine voices sounded again. Bell released a long sigh as he watched the trio creep back toward the house like thieves in the night. They paused about five feet from the door and passed the flask around. Good Lord, they were brazen.

Eventually they stumbled inside the mansion and made no attempt to hide their laughter.

Bell wiped the dampness off the shoulders of his coat and strolled back to the house. He might as well return home, since he'd struck out on finding a mistress. Tomorrow he would think of a new plan.

He strode through the corridor, noting someone had lit a candle branch. When he emerged, he heard a cacophony of voices coming from the dining room. He had no wish to make himself agreeable to anyone else this evening.

Bell strode toward the foyer but halted beside the stairwell upon hearing a feminine voice from the staircase. "Justin?"

He couldn't see her from this vantage point.

He heard an odd sound beneath the stairwell. Bell looked underneath in time to see a man pushing a flask beneath it with his heel. Then footsteps clipped on the marble floor. "I'm here," the man said, walking to the bottom of the staircase.

Bell noted he was the young man with a shock of wheat-colored hair.

"Where have you been?" a woman said in a stern tone. "I've looked everywhere for you."

"Oh, we just moved about the ballroom and the adjoining rooms," he said.

What an accomplished liar he was, Bell thought.

"Your face is flushed," the woman said as she descended. Now Bell could see her. She was the blond woman he'd seen in the garden.

"I hope you haven't been drinking with your friends again," she said.

"Always suspicious," the young man said.

"It's late, and I wish to return home," the blonde said.

A few minutes later, their voices receded.

Approaching footsteps alerted Bell. He turned as Lady Atherton regarded him with a knowing smile. "Are you in the habit of listening to others' conversations, Bellingham?" she asked.

"Not if I can help it. And you?"

"I'm just the hostess of this grand squeeze," she said.

"Who is she?" he asked.

Lady Atherton took a deep breath and slowly released it. "She's not for the likes of you, Bell."

He recalled the way the blonde had stared at him earlier with parted lips. "I didn't ask if she was for me. I asked for her name."

Lady Atherton shook her head. "Leave her be, Bellingham. She's a widow with a boy to rear. You want no part of her life."

"I'm afraid I am part of it, unwillingly," he said. The blonde must be the widow his friends had mentioned, but he said nothing of that to Lady Atherton. He reached beneath the stairwell and retrieved the flask. "You see, I believe she needs to know her son is lying through his teeth."

"Oh dear. She did say he was at a trying age."

"That, I believe, is an understatement."

Lady Atherton sighed and held out her hand. "Give the flask to me, and I'll see that it's returned."

This was an opportunity to find out if she had meant to issue him an invitation when she'd stared at him earlier. He told himself he only wanted to warn her about her son. He told himself she had every right to know. He told himself that the boy might find himself in serious straits if he didn't alert her. But ultimately, he knew he wouldn't be able to get her out of his head until he spoke to her. "He's taking advantage of her. Someone needs to put the fear of the devil in that boy."

Lady Atherton's eyes widened. "And you think you're the one to do it? Hah!"

"I'm an eyewitness." He paused and added, "I want her name."

"Only if you swear this is about the boy and nothing else," she said.

He felt victorious, but he hid it. "Her name and address, please."

Lady Atherton hesitated again. "Her name is Laura Davenport. That's Lady Chesfield to you," she said, her expression sharp. "Her address is number ten, Grosvenor Square. And, Bellingham, I meant what I said. She's a respectable widow and not for the likes of a rakehell like you."

Perhaps, but he meant to find out. "She's incredibly naïve where that boy is concerned."

Lady Atherton clasped her hands. "Well, I agree he ought to have more respect for his stepmother."

Bell bowed. "Thank you for an interesting evening." Then he strode out the door.

The next afternoon

After dismissing his secretary, Bell opened the desk drawer where he'd stowed the flask last night. After retrieving it, he thought about his plans to return the flask to Lady Chesfield and reconsidered. What the devil did he expect to gain? The last thing he wanted was to become involved in the lady's problems.

She was a stranger to him. They had not been introduced, and yet, he'd pried her name and address from Lady Atherton, who was very strict about the proprieties. He ought to have left well enough alone. Now he was obliged to return the blasted flask.

Out of curiosity, he opened the flask, expecting to find cheap gin, but one sniff proved the liquor was brandy. Bell sipped it and realized it was of top-notch quality. Most likely the young buck had purloined the brandy from a decanter at home.

The wayward young man wasn't his responsibility. He could send a footman to deliver the flask, but Lady Chesfield wouldn't know why he'd sent it. With a sigh, he drew out paper, pen, and ink, thinking he would describe what he'd seen last night. No, that was too much trouble. He would simply state in his message that he'd found her son's flask. Whatever transpired afterward was none of his affair.

Bell started to shut the drawer when he saw the small leather sketchbook inside that had belonged to his mother. His heart drummed in his ears. A new maid had recently found it in the attic. That day, he'd looked at one page and shoved it inside the desk drawer. Bell ought to have told the maid to return it to the attic the day the sketchbook was discovered. Then it would have been out of his sight and mind forever. He walked over to the bell, intending to ring for the housekeeper. He meant to ask her to return the sketchbook to the attic. But he hesitated, because he didn't want her to touch it.

After four years, he ought to have put the past behind him. Most of the time, he managed to shove it to the far corners of his brain, but the periodic nightmares served as a reminder of all that he'd loved and lost.

He returned to the desk, determined to shut the drawer. But something beckoned him. His ears thudded as he retrieved the sketchbook and opened it to a random page. A small boy sat on a sofa with a bundled infant. He gritted his teeth at the inscription near the bottom of the page. *Andrew, age two, holding Steven one month after birth.*

His heart thumped at the sketch of him and his younger brother.

Damn it all to hell. He'd known nothing good could come of resurrecting the memories. They were gone forever.

He'd been too late all those years ago.

Bell shut the sketchbook and shoved it back inside the cubbyhole in the desk. The past no longer existed. There was only the here and now.

Gritting his teeth, he strode over to the bell rope and pulled it. When Griffith, the butler, appeared, Bell made arrangements to have his carriage brought round. He would deliver the flask to Lady Chesfield and have done with the matter once and for all.

Fall in Love with Forever Romance

SOULBOUND
by **Kristen Callihan**

After centuries of searching, Adam finally found his soul mate, only to be rejected when she desires her freedom. But when Eliza discovers she's being hunted by someone far more dangerous, she turns to the one man who can keep her safe— even if he endangers her heart…

WHAT A DEVILISH DUKE DESIRES
by **Vicky Dreiling**

Fans of *New York Times* best-selling authors Julia Quinn, Sarah MacLean, and Madeline Hunter will love the third book in Vicky Dreiling's charming, sexy, and utterly irresistible Sinful Scoundrels trilogy about a high-born man who never wanted to inherit his uncle's title or settle down…until a beautiful, brilliant, delightfully tempting maid makes him rethink his position.

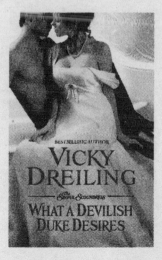

Fall in Love with Forever Romance

SECRET HARBOR
by Anna Sullivan

Fans of *New York Times* best-selling authors JoAnn Ross, Jill Shalvis, and Bella Andre will love the last book in Anna Sullivan's witty contemporary romance trilogy about a young woman who left her beloved home in Maine to become an actress in Hollywood. Now a star, and beset by scandal, she wants nothing more than to surround herself with old friends...until she meets an infuriating—and sexy—stranger.

MEET ME AT THE BEACH
by V. K. Sykes

Gorgeous Lily Doyle was the only thing Aiden Flynn missed after he escaped from Seashell Bay to play pro baseball. Now that he's back on the island, memories rush in about the night of passion they shared long ago, and everything else washes right out to sea—everything except the desire that still burns between them.

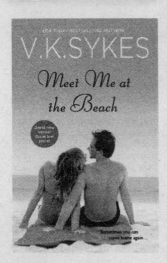

Fall in Love with Forever Romance

HOT
by Elizabeth Hoyt
writing as Julia Harper

For Turner Hastings, being held at gunpoint during a back robbery is an opportunity in disguise. After seeing her little heist on tape, FBI Special Agent John MacKinnon knows it's going to be an interesting case. But he doesn't expect to develop feelings for Turner, and when bullets start flying in her direction, John finds he'll do anything to save her.

FOR THE LOVE OF PETE
by Elizabeth Hoyt
writing as Julia Harper

Dodging bullets with a loopy redhead in the passenger seat is not how Special Agent Dante Torelli imagined his day going. But Zoey Addler is determined to get her baby niece back, and no one—not even a henpecked hit man, cooking-obsessed matrons, or a relentless killer—will stand in her way.

Fall in Love with Forever Romance

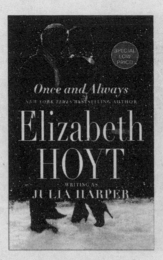

ONCE AND ALWAYS
by Elizabeth Hoyt writing as Julia Harper

The newest contemporary from *New York Times* bestselling author Elizabeth Hoyt writing as Julia Harper! Small-town cop Sam West certainly doesn't mind a routine traffic stop. But Maisa Bradley is like nothing he has ever seen, and she's about to take Sam on the ride of his life!

WAYS TO *UNEXPECTEDLY* MEET MR. RIGHT:

♡ *Go out with the sexy-sounding stranger your daughter secretly set you up with through a personal ad.*

♡ *RSVP yes to a wedding invitation—soon it might be your turn to say "I do!"*

♡ *Receive a marriage proposal by mail— from a man you've never met.....*

These are just a few of the unexpected ways that written communication leads to love in Silhouette Yours Truly.

Each month, look for two fast-paced, fun and flirtatious Yours Truly novels (with entertaining treats and sneak previews in the back pages) by some of your favorite authors—and some who are sure to become favorites.

YOURS TRULY™:
Love—when you least expect it!

Harlequin Romance ®

Delightful

Affectionate

Romantic

Emotional

Tender

Original

Daring

Riveting

Enchanting

Adventurous

Moving

Harlequin Romance—the
series that has it all!

HROM-G